# SCORCHED EARTH

# DAVID L. ROBBINS

## SCORCHED EARTH

BANTAM BOOKS

SCORCHED EARTH

A Bantam Book / April 2002

All rights reserved.
Copyright © 2002 by David L. Robbins.

*Book design by Lynn Newmark.*

0-553-80176-7

*Published simultaneously in the United States and Canada*

Bantam Books are published by Bantam Books, a division of Random House, Inc. Its trademark, consisting of the words "Bantam Books" and the portrayal of a rooster, is Registered in U.S. Patent and Trademark Office and in other countries. Marca Registrada. Bantam Books, 1540 Broadway, New York, New York 10036.

PRINTED IN THE UNITED STATES OF AMERICA
BVG   10   9   8   7   6   5   4   3   2   1

This book is dedicated to children, especially: Jamie Bacon; Avery and Clara Banks; Jane and Sarah Wilson Dykers; Christian Lowe; Daniel, Audrey, and William McMurtrie; Marcus, Adam, and Maya Pendleton; Meg and Jeremy Price; Patrick and Abby Poats; Chris Powell; Rebecca and West Redington; Connor Wingo; and Tommy, Annie, and Rosemary Barnett-Young.

Thanks to Irwyn Applebaum and Nita Taublib, who run a very classy house over at Bantam.

Thanks to Mike Shohl, my editor, who turned this mystery into a mystery.

Thanks also to Tracy Fisher and Owen Laster, my agents at William Morris. Without them, I'd have to be the bad guy all by myself.

These folks, plus many friends, put up with me and propel me along. You know who you are and you know what you do. If I've done my job along the way, you also know how much I appreciate you.

To all aspiring writers, I give this constant advice: Keep writing. Work hard. Get clever people around you, like those mentioned above, and listen to them.

*We only keep forever*
*that which we have lost.*

HENRIK IBSEN
*BRAND*

*The line separating good and evil*
*passes not through states,*
*nor between classes,*
*nor between parties either,*
*but right through the human heart.*

ALEKSANDR SOLZHENITSYN

# NORA CAROL

# ONE

1

The place where they lie making the child is beautiful.

They lie on a bed of ferns, which like a cushion of feathers tickles them. Only a few strides off the old dirt road, they are beneath a tall red oak, thick as a chimney, bearded with gray bark; the tree is a gentle old presence. The leaves of the oak bear the first blush of whistling autumn.

If they were to stand on that spot they could see the fields. South lie forty acres of beans, leafy and ripe for the harvest machinery resting now after church on this Sunday afternoon. High pines and turning sugar maples make this field a green leafy loch where every breeze riffles. North of the road, beyond barbed wire and honeysuckle, is a cleared pasture for the cows, which are out of sight behind hills that rise and roll down, suggesting by their smooth undulation the couple lying under the oak.

He is a black man, blacker than everything, blacker than the soil of the road, everything but the crows. His name is Elijah, named by his mother for the loudest of the Hebrew prophets, though he has not grown into a loud man. He is as silent as his skin, as the dark of a well.

Beneath him, wrapping him like roots seeking water, is his wife, Clare. Her green eyes are closed behind white, blue-veined lids. Waist-length blond hair spreads over the ferns and under her back. She kisses him and their tongues twine.

A band of starlings crisscrosses the field. The ebon birds strike something invisible in the center of the field and disperse, to clot again and circle some more, somewhat aimlessly. Clare and Elijah, tangled together, white and black, are absolutes, the presence and absence of all colors at once, sharing a smooth, perfect motion.

## 2

Clare and Elijah Waddell live in a shotgun shack two miles down Postal Delivery Route 310. Their small house stands five miles east of the town of Good Hope, the county seat for Pamunkey County. Local wags call these single-story, slant-roofed homes shotgun shacks because if you stood in the front doorway and fired a shotgun blast, you'd kill everyone through the whole house. Elijah and Clare bought the place last year, just after they married. For five months they sanded the heart-pine floors, put in new kitchen cabinets, and painted the clapboards. Clare wanted the exterior painted pink and got dusky rose, their compromise. The house came with ten acres; all of it except Clare and Elijah's vegetable garden is leased to a corn farmer who cultivates four hundred acres on both sides of the road down to the river. The house and yard and the dusty lane are walled in by rising corn from May through October, until the crop is harvested. Elijah and Clare enjoy the isolation. Coming home once from their jobs at the paper mill, Clare took Elijah's hand and stood beside their mailbox, the silks' tassels higher than their heads.

She said, "It's like being Hansel and Gretel coming up on the gingerbread house, isn't it?"

Elijah is ten years older than Clare; she is twenty-two, but they share the same wiry build and long frame. His is a face of circles, pliant, with wide nostrils, long earlobes, and arching brows over dark pupils. Clare's features are round too, but resemble the roundness of an infant's.

When it can be, theirs is a sweaty, dirty love. They groom their big summer garden and work on the house. They bring each other iced tea. They make love in the rope hammock at nightfall in full sight of the road, daring the path to bring them an intruder. In winter they chop and carry wood. Elijah has knocked down a wall to take the space from a closet and add it to a baby's room. Clare carries the detritus outside in a wheelbarrow, shoveling chips and scraps into the pickup to be hauled to the dump. They pull off their clothes to laugh at the dirty regions, hands, arms, necks, and faces, her whiteness showing the grit most, his grime blending into his skin. They make love that way too, with the dirt of home chores or the stink of the paper mill in their hair and clothes. Work seems to make them want each other, like thirst.

Clare and Elijah have a dog, a gray cocker named Herschel. It is Herschel who in this first year of their marriage shows Clare that her husband contains in him places she has not yet entered.

On a summer Saturday Herschel lies heaving on the back stoop of the house. His breath grates in his throat. His tongue lolls from his mouth onto the boards. The dog's neck is swollen terribly, as though bees have built a hive inside it. Elijah finds him on the stoop and shouts for Clare to bring the truck around. Herschel has been bitten by a snake.

Elijah lays Herschel on the seat, the dog's head in Clare's lap, his tongue on her bare thigh. He drives fast to the vet, who confirms Elijah's diagnosis and gives the dog antivenin. The vet tells them to leave Herschel overnight.

Returning to the house, Elijah walks away from the pickup to the backyard shed. Clare remains in the yard. Elijah emerges with his rubber fishing waders over his arm.

"There's another pair," he says. "Come if you want."

Clare watches him enter the house. In a minute he exits carrying his old side-by-side shotgun and a box of twelve-gauge shells. She runs to the shed for the other rubber coveralls.

Elijah slowly drives the quarter-mile to the end of the dirt road where he turns left up the farmer's tractor path. He stops the truck at the foot of the trees and looks at Clare. His face is blank as slate, as though all purpose has been drained from it to better fuel his will. He climbs out and Clare follows. The cornfield stops here, the rim of it barbered neat. The air tastes musky along the riverbank in the shade. These trees were left in place two centuries ago when the land was first put under the plow, to hold the bank together. The roots of the trees closest to the river stick out of the bank, exposed by times of high water. Elijah pulls on his waders, then breaks the shotgun, slips in shells, leaves the barrel open over his arm and clambers down the bank holding on to the roots. Where the roots meet the water, spreading like arteries, is where the copperheads make their nests.

Elijah moves into the water as though he were himself reptilian, without ripple or sound. Clare puts on the second pair of rubber bibs, they go on easily because they are too big. She eases herself into the water but still makes a small splash stepping in. Thirty yards ahead, Elijah does not turn. He snaps closed the shotgun and raises it. He lets go with one barrel, then another, the branches overhead shake with the report and where he has aimed smoke whorls on the water. Something thrashes. Elijah unsnaps and reloads. He fires again into a cascade of roots, leaving another specter of smoke as a marker.

He wades the river the length of the field, almost a half-mile, firing the shotgun into the water, against the bank, under roots. Green plastic shells and shredded bits of snakes and bark float past Clare on the slow current. She is surprised the water is not redder with blood. After most of an hour, when an empty cardboard shell box drifts past her, Elijah stops walking, the shotgun under his armpit. He does not turn to Clare but stands watching the current slide past his thighs. Clare clambers out of the river and walks back to the truck. She removes the overalls and sits in the cab. Elijah does not appear. She considers honking the horn but does not. She sits alone for another hour eyeing the yellow palisade of corn. I had no idea, she thinks, no idea how much my husband can love.

## 3

Crossing the Mattaponi River your eyes are not on the bridge or the car ahead of you but on the mill. This plant is the giant, smoking, multitiered centurion of the town. Employed here are thirteen hundred people from the five thousand residents of Good Hope and twelve thousand total in the county. A stench issues from the tallest structure, the new boiler, which always sports a cone of steam the entire town uses to gauge the direction of the wind. The smell is sulphurous, the by-products of wood fibers being separated from each other in order to turn logs into cardboard and bleached white top. "It's the smell of money," say the townsfolk, and just an egg stink to those driving through on their way to summer cottages elsewhere in the river country. Two red tugboats are tied at the massive pier, waiting to guide waterborne shipments of timber. Rail tracks cross the road leading into the wood yard. A sign welcomes you to the town. GOOD HOPE, the sign reads. A GOOD PLACE TO WORK, LIVE, AND PLAY.

In July the heat and river humidity bear down on the town, pasting the odor to the ground day and night regardless of breeze. Clare is thirty-six weeks pregnant, so she has transferred from her forklift in the warehouse stacking giant rolls of bleached paperboard. She is in the office handling paperwork, sidling up to desktops and cabinets as best she can. She worries about the smelly air her baby is getting through her umbilicus.

Inside the plant, the Number 3 machine is down. Number 3 is longer than a city block. While it is down, mechanics and maintenance workers swarm over it. Elijah climbs a ladder at the wet end where virgin craft pulp is dumped into the machine's maw. Brown paper mud splats onto a wire screen and is swept through the machine's heat and pressure and rollers, forging a three-ply paperboard at the dry end 150 yards away where men wait for it with blades and pneumatic lifts. Elijah climbs with his tools into the spot called Hell. The metal ladder he mounts is slick with the congealed scum of pulp fibers and steam. Brown dregs hang from the rungs. One lightbulb glows, silhouetting the bits floating on the steam. Elijah hunkers low to fit under the beams and pipes, also ugly with dangling pulp drool. He squats beside a massive shaft and unhinges the coupling to inspect the cogs. He spills kerosene over the bearings to degrease them, then adds fresh grease. In July in this spot in the mill, you cannot wipe the sweat from your brows fast enough. Elijah's drips fall on the bearings under his slippery, glimmering fingers.

When he is finished and has cleaned his tools in the shop, his foreman approaches.

"Elijah."

Elijah looks up. He says nothing.

"There's a meeting this afternoon at three o'clock at the chip-yard trailer. I want you to go to it."

"I'm on 'til four."

"That's all right. I need you to go."

"Why?"

Elijah pours kerosene over his hands to dig the grease from his nails with a rag.

"They're forming a Diversity Committee. This is the first meeting."

Elijah draws in his lips.

The foreman leans his backside against the counter. He lifts a hand to help conjure the point he wants to make.

"What, with you being married to Clare and all," he says, "I figured, well . . ."

The foreman brings his hand down on Elijah's damp back.

". . . you know, you might could shed some light, is all."

Elijah blinks at his hands and makes no answer. The foreman springs away from the counter. He says over his shoulder, "We all got to get along."

At three o'clock, Clare is one of the twenty-five at the meeting. Elijah enters the trailer. She drops her jaw comically at him in mock surprise. She draws from him a head shake. He does not sit beside her.

Men and women, black and white, two Asians and one Hispanic, from departments across the mill sit in four rows of folding chairs. Coffee and doughnuts are on a card table. Most of the people from the machine floor and the wood yard still wear their hard hats and safety glasses. The few office workers fidget in their seats, especially the heavy women from customer service and the suited men from management. Clare watches Elijah, who has knit his hands in his lap and lowered his head. He has removed his green hard hat and safety glasses and sits gathered to himself.

She thinks of the other plant-wide committees formed in her three years at the mill: excellence, international quality standards, cleanup, collective bargaining, safety. She'd seen them come and go and they never stuck and they never before invited her or Elijah. Now it's diversity and here the two of them are at the table.

Clare thinks of her mother Carol buried not too far away at the Victory Baptist Church. She wonders what her mother would think of this meeting. Her mother was a godly woman, Gran Epps has told her that many times. Her mother died of breast cancer eighteen years ago in North Carolina. Gran went down there and held her only child on the hospital bed, rocking her, singing a Jesus song. Gran Epps made arrangements with a funeral home in Winston-Salem for a long-distance hearse for her thirty-year-old daughter. She packed up her four-year-old grandchild and put her own child in a casket and ferried them both back to Good Hope, Gran's hometown, where Gran's husband, Granpa Charles Hutto Epps, is buried. If Clare's mother were here, she would feel what? What would a godly woman read into this diversity meeting? She wouldn't feel creepy, the way Clare does. More than likely she'd pity them, that they need to be organized and drilled just to get along with each other. But her mother is dead, and it's easy, Clare understands, to make the dead wise.

A man in a plaid short-sleeved shirt stands from his chair at the corner of the first row, revealing finally who will run this meeting. His name is Sipe, a crane operator in shipping and receiving. Sipe is tan and robust, his shirt sloshes over his belt line like a water balloon. He wears khakis and loafers. Today is his day off. He's come in just for this meeting.

"How're y'all?" Sipe asks. He raises his thick hand quickly and uncomfortably. Clare cannot figure if it is in greeting or to ward off responses.

"As I hope you all know, this is the first meeting of the plant's new Diversity Committee." He grins hastily and a comradeliness flashes across his face, implying, Yeah, yeah, I don't want to be here either.

"There's been a situation here at the mill that management has said needs addressing. Each of us has been nominated to be on this committee. From the looks of things, we got a pretty well-rounded representation."

Mother, Clare decides, would lean forward and touch Elijah on the shoulder lightly and whisper to him, Lift your head, sweetheart. They mean well.

Plaid-striped Sipe crosses his arms to ask everyone in the room to identify themselves, and they do. The first few shyly stand to say their names and departments, then others rise only halfway from their seats, holding the backs of their metal chairs and plopping down when finished. Elijah is the first one to stay seated, and the rest follow suit.

When this is done, Sipe tells the story of what happened at the mill to create in management's mind the need for a Diversity Committee. Two days ago, a woman wore a T-shirt to work that read: IT'S A BLACK THANG, YOU WOULDN'T UNDERSTAND. Yesterday, in response, one of the woman's co-workers walked in wearing a T-shirt on which he'd drawn with Magic Marker a burning cross, under the scrawled slogan: IT'S A WHITE THANG, YOU WOULDN'T UNDERSTAND.

One of the black women in the meeting volunteers, "We thought it was funny." Clare figures this is the woman who wore the original offending shirt.

Sipe nods. He says defensively, "We did. That's right. But a few others didn't. So," he clears his throat, "here we are."

The room settles for a moment on the stupidity of these two people, and there is the sense that it is a very stable and big platform, their stupidity. The blame is not that these two should have known better than to taunt each other that way, even as friends, but that they are responsible for the birth of another committee. One man in the last row mutters, "Sheez."

Sipe unfolds his arms. He holds up his hands. Clare sees they are callused.

"All right," Sipe says. "Okay, look. We been told to form this committee and that's what we're doing. Our goal is for us as a group to explore ways to coexist with each other as well as we can. We're going to talk about topics, put together a diversity newsletter and workshops, and after a couple months we'll take what we learn in here out to the mill at large and it'll be a big help. Because I'll tell you for one, I missed my guess at how big this thing is to some folks."

The woman who wore the Black Thang T-shirt says, "And people, it's not just black and white. It's men and women, too."

"That's right," says Sipe, and nods, refolding his meaty arms. "We need to find ways to be more sensitive to each other. And it's not just for the mill. It's the whole community." Clare thinks that this man has had his ass chewed out bad to be talking this way.

Then Sipe points at Elijah and says, "We all need to find ways to be more like Clare and Elijah here. More accepting. Like them."

Elijah's hard hat dangles from his fingers between his spread knees, his eyes turned to the floor. The hat spins a revolution in his hands. He catches it. He stands. The hard hat goes on his head.

Looking at no one, not even Clare, he softly says, "This is y'all's problem."

Knees and legs slide out of the way, allowing Elijah to exit his row. No one looks up to his face moving past them as though fearful his face is where he keeps the blow he would throw at them if he were to throw one, because it wasn't in his voice.

The trailer door opens with the break of a seal and Elijah closes it gently. When he is gone, again the room ponders on something and now it is Clare. But she has a baby in her belly soon to be born and so she is not disposed to carry the weight of their inquiry. She will not explain Elijah to them, he is her husband and the father of her child and they all, all of them in the world, are not.

Clare stands. She wishes she had her own hard hat to put on. To get to the door she has to pass only one set of legs in her row.

"Look," she says, walking, "you all know him. He's got a mind of his own."

Clare grips the trailer doorknob. Her back is to the committee. She turns fully to them. The globe of her coming child is included when she says before leaving, "I'm sorry, but we are not your damn role models."

4

Clare and Elijah do not like being made to feel they love each other despite something. They are not better people because they have married someone outside their own race. They are not tolerant because the other is of a different color.

They do not in this first year of their marriage discuss race, in the same manner they do not discuss gravity. That he is black and she is white is a subject for others, who once in a while try to hold the matter up to Clare and Elijah with curiosity, seeking feedback and impressions, postcards from someplace exotic and perhaps taboo they themselves will never go.

He is a black man only the first time she sees him. She is at the high school track, jogging. She finishes and walks past the basketball court to watch a game. Elijah's name is called a lot by the other players. "Nice take, Elijah." "Fuck, man! Put a stop on Waddell, will you!" When the game is done, he stays and shoots on his own. His bare chest and stomach glisten with the sweat which ripples like hot oil poured down cobblestones. He shoots, retrieves, shoots again. Often the ball flies through the hoop and comes back to him as if it is on a tether. She walks beneath the basket to catch the ball after his shots. He says nothing but takes her bounce passes and shoots again. He makes eight in a row, never looking at her, only the ball and the rusty rim. She knows he's trying to impress her. When he misses, she keeps the ball, as is protocol, and takes her own shots. She misses her first, but she is not yet warmed up so Elijah bounces her the ball. When she misses her third in a row, he keeps the ball and shoots again, making it. She knows he is telling her, You make it, you keep it. No special girl rules. Clare likes this, feeling equal, measured by the same standards that measure him. After he misses, she gets the ball and hits three in a row. The fourth rims out. It drops near Clare and she wants it, she is getting loose, but Elijah is quicker. He stabs a hand under hers and dribbles the ball away from her. He grins over his shoulder and Clare decides to guard him. He turns to shoot. She stays with him, she is almost as tall as he, she jumps and puts a hand in his face and he misses. She retrieves the basketball and looks at him. He stands hands on hips and smiles again. He nods and says only, "All right." She will remember this moment when Elijah's blackness became not something missing from what she has but a remarkable presence not bound or described by color. She opens her mouth in a moment of shame, fleeting but like a pinprick fast and sharp, for having ever felt whatever ugliness it was she has just said goodbye to. She stands with the ball pressed against her stomach, where Elijah's baby will be.

## 5

It is time for the baby.

Clare and Elijah stand in front of their bedroom mirror making love. Elijah is behind her, the child in front. She flattens her palms against the wall on both sides of the mirror to keep from rocking the baby too much. But she wants Elijah inside her badly, and with both the man and the child tucked up in her where she can warm and please and care for them, Clare is happy.

When they have finished they linger before the mirror. Her breasts are swollen almost twice their normal size but otherwise she has gained little girth about her shoulders and neck. Her skin and hair are infused and radiant. Elijah circles his open hands over her belly. There is something magical for Clare in this, like watching a black-robed sorcerer swirling his arms over a large white crystal ball. What is the future? she wonders: Tell me, Elijah. See it in my belly and tell me.

Clare lies on the bed in the waft of the air conditioner. He stretches beside her. She is on her back and, within minutes, a knob appears above her navel.

Elijah leans closer to inspect. He says, "It's a knee."

Clare does not lift her head from the pillow to look, she keeps her hands beside her. She lets Elijah have this alone.

The knob slowly disappears and is followed by other protrusions, each of which Elijah examines with his fingertips and identifies. An elbow. A shoulder.

The baby rolling over touches Clare with fingers and toes, with a heartbeat and a kick. The movement inside her is liquid, and she thinks she cannot express to Elijah what she feels, so powerful is it. She covers his hand on her stomach with both of hers and concentrates on the child.

Two hours later, near midnight, she rises to pee. In the bathroom, there is blood on the toilet paper and Clare knows her mucus plug has broken.

She does not wake Elijah. In the dark she sits in a chair beside their bed, listening to the labor of the air-conditioning window unit, thanking it. She is thankful for everything she senses around her. Elijah does not hear Clare's grunt with the first cramp. She glances at the red digits on the bedside clock, waiting for the next wave.

Near five in the morning Elijah stirs and knows she is not beside him. He sits upright to find her in the chair, sitting on a towel. He snaps on a light.

"How long you been up?"

"Since almost midnight."

Elijah bites his lower lip.

"Girl," he says. He stands, naked and beautiful. He runs his hand over her brow. "You want to do this alone," he says, joking, "I'll head over to the mill and put in some overtime."

At seven o'clock Elijah calls the plant to say they will not be in for their shifts. Her contractions are six minutes apart. He calls Gran Epps, then drives Clare to the hospital.

Her obstetrician, Dr. James, knows she does not want an epidural but she tells him No again when he asks. Elijah's left hand stays clutched in her right and they do not let each other go. Anything Clare needs her right hand for Elijah does for her.

In the hospital room she stays in labor for five hours. Just after noon, she is wheeled into delivery. She squeezes Elijah's hand, gritting her teeth. She will not close her eyes. She watches everything and thinks of her mother, wishes she were alive, thinks of Gran Epps waiting at home by the phone to hear that she has a great-grandchild, and the thankfulness that began in Clare's bedroom last night is eclipsed by a love so anchored in her it is a harrowing pain as it moves through her. She cries, she knows her face is pink and crushed together like a soda can. Elijah's hand wipes a tissue over her cheeks.

Clare's bulging middle is the center of a whirl of hands and faces. The lights are so bright she feels them in a warm lace against the insides of her thighs hoisted in the stirrups. Elijah whispers to her, "Yeah, baby," and, "Good, baby," mopping her brow, kissing the top of her head. The two nurses nod agreement with Elijah. "You're doin' great, honey."

Dr. James is a handsome man in his early forties, graying just at the temples. He has the gaunt face and rueful eyes of the avid runner. Clare winces and watches his eyes.

The obstetrician tracks Clare's contractions. He says, "Now push. Soft at first. There you go." He fiddles with his hands out of sight between her legs. She barely feels his fingers, so engorged are her nerves and muscles there. For several minutes the doctor asks her for soft pushes. Finally he says, "Okay, now give me one good hard push. Come on. There you go. Almost . . ." Clare bears down, squeezing her abdomen as hard as her pain will let her. She fixes her stare on the doctor's face. He sees the baby coming into the world, she wants to witness the arrival but cannot so she will watch the man who does see it.

Suddenly the creases like wings beside the doctor's eyes flinch and fold. He pauses and all action in the room ceases, even Clare's push. She senses the instant change. The air in the room has cracks running through it, like hot glass plunged into ice. The doctor softly shifts his voice, he speaks not to Clare but to his nurses. "Bring me a blanket," he says.

Dr. James firmly says to Clare, "Push again. Push." Elijah's grip tightens over Clare's. The doctor continues to pull and support the emerging baby. His paper face mask puffs, he has said something but to himself.

Elijah asks, "Doctor?"

Dr. James glances up at Elijah with the look of a man at the bottom of a long and tedious hill, who must run up it and is certain he cannot. Then he looks down.

Clare cannot see around her belly and the spread of the hospital gown to her child. Elijah stays strong in Clare's hand.

She pushes her hardest. If something is wrong, she will cure it by dint of will and effort. She and Elijah will bring their child into the world even if the doctor is worried, even if he has quit looking up at them.

The infant does issue into Dr. James's waiting hands. He takes a small suction device like a turkey baster and uses it to remove the mucus blockage from the baby's nostrils; Clare hears him discharge the thing twice into a napkin. He takes a clamp from a nurse, throttles the umbilical cord, and snips it with scissors. He reaches to the nurse for the blanket and swaddles the child. He does not rise to lay the newborn on Clare's stomach to be loved in its first seconds but turns away from Clare and Elijah, carrying the child. Clare's back is on fire with the pain of birthing. The blanket is pink and the doctor has wrapped her baby in it from head to foot, she cannot see her child.

Keeping his back to Clare and Elijah, the doctor hands the newborn to a nurse. While the woman cradles it, the other nurse helps Clare take her legs down from the stirrups. Clare watches the rear of the doctor's arms and shoulders doing his final work, sees him wipe the little body with sterile cloths that he tosses into a bin with a heavy arm. She hears her baby cough in the nurse's arms behind the obstetrician's white back. Elijah says again, "Doctor?" Clare keeps herself on the table, though she wants to get up and wrest her infant away from the doctor. The child has been in the world a minute now. Clare yearns to begin.

She cannot hear what the doctor says to the nurse. But the nurse does not want to do what he asks. She hesitates. Clare hears the nurse say, "No, doctor. Please."

Dr. James steps aside. The nurse comes closer to Clare and Elijah bearing the pink blanket. She hangs back from the bed. She does not lay the blanket across Clare's flattened and flabby waist. The nurse says, "It's a girl."

At last Clare lets go of Elijah's hand. Her palm is soaked. She reaches both arms for her daughter. The nurse withholds the child.

From the foot of the bed Dr. James speaks. He pulls down his blue mask. Clare sees the defeat in his face. He has not, he never could, run up the long hill.

"Clare. Elijah. Wait a minute."

Clare says, "Give me my baby."

The doctor says their names again, "Clare. Elijah." Clare drops her arms. Elijah's hand returns into hers.

The doctor says, "I need to tell you something first."

Clare waits for the man to continue. In those seconds she feels a wall erect itself inside her, stolid and fast, of love and loyalty for her baby. Dr. James batters the wall with his pauses and anguished eyes but the wall is holding.

He says, "There's a serious problem. With the baby's brain."

The child in the nurse's arms, as though to refute this terrible statement, squeaks inside the pink blanket.

Clare shakes her head. "No. I can hear her. She's fine. Give her to me."

No one moves. The child is held away from them. Elijah adds his voice, it is firm.

"Give us the child, doctor. She's ours."

The doctor stands his ground in silence, staring into Clare's eyes. He shifts his gaze to Elijah, then nods. The doctor says to them, "Prepare yourselves."

The nurse presents the wrapped infant to Clare's eager hands. With no hesitation, Clare lifts the blanket from her daughter's head. She hears the doctor say, "I'm sorry."

Above the baby's brows, there is nothing. The cap of her head, the bowl of skull where the brain should be, is not there. Instead the skull is flat, covered in warm, pink skin; the child is horribly incomplete. The wall inside Clare cannot take this, not this, she draws a breath as if bashed; Elijah's grip has moved to her shoulder, his hand tightens there. She cannot let out her breath. She closes her eyes; the child in her arms feels so right, so perfect, it is the right weight and it is breathing and needing her. Clare's breast aches with the desire to give to it. Inside her, under this assault—the worst of her life—somehow the wall holds. Clare releases a cry. She opens her eyes and knows she loves this child, just as she loves the pain which brought her daughter into the world, pain which did not stop and will not stop now that she is here. It is the softness of the top of her child's head, smooth and flat to Clare's lips, which breaks her heart and cements the wall forever. Clare sees that her daughter's hair, when dry, will be white and wispy as corn silk.

Elijah's hand comes to the baby's cheek. Clare hears him whisper, "Oh my Jesus." The baby gurgles, seeking the tip of Elijah's finger with her lips. Clare laughs with a gasp. Her tears splash over the baby's face.

The nurse says, "She'll feed. Go ahead, she'll suckle."

Clare looks to the doctor for confirmation. He gives it with a strained, tight mouth. Clare turns a smile up to Elijah. He nods to her. She sees him swallow. He stands so straight, she thinks, the glint of tears in his eyes. Turning her gown down, she gives the baby her nipple.

One nurse shuts off the hot lamps beside the bed, leaving only the soft glow of dimmed ceiling lights. The child sucks. There is no milk yet, not for another day or two. Elijah laughs quickly, almost a weep, and Clare's sense of loss flies up into him, like birds to his branches. He will hold the grief, she thinks. I must hold our child.

The doctor, standing back, speaks.

"It's called anencephaly. It's a failure of the neural tube to close soon after conception. The brain, it . . . never develops beyond the stem. Your baby can suckle, swallow, respond to stimuli, but that's going to be all. Don't misinterpret those reactions. You should know . . ."

Elijah leaves Clare's side for the first time in thirteen hours.

"Doctor, can we go in the hall?"

Outside the delivery room, away from Clare, Elijah asks him to continue the explanation. The doctor speaks carefully, reaching to take Elijah's arm while he speaks.

Anencephaly, Dr. James explains, is the most common major central-nervous-system malformation in the United States, striking one in every twelve hundred births. Anencephalic babies, if born alive at all, do not survive infancy. The absence of higher-level neural structures makes it impossible for these children to feel pain or demonstrate awareness.

"Your daughter," the doctor tells Elijah, "developed this problem within two or three weeks after conception. We might have caught it early with a sonogram, but you're a young, healthy couple with no histories of birth defects in your families. We never thought there was any need for one. And even if we had seen it coming there's nothing we could have done, Elijah, except give you the option to abort."

"What caused this? Was it me, something in me that isn't right?"

"No." The doctor talks eagerly. Now he can ease some pain. "No, Elijah. There's no way to know exactly what affected the fetus. It could be genetic, it could be infectious. It could have been environmental."

"What do you mean, maybe the mill?"

"No way to know," the doctor replies. "Don't lay blame. That's not going to be a healthy thing to do."

Dr. James removes his hand from Elijah's arm.

"Do you and Clare want more children?"

"Yeah. I guess. After this . . ."

"Okay. Make sure Clare gets plenty of folic acid before and during her next pregnancy. That's green leafy vegetables, peas, beans. It's a B vitamin. Make sure she gets a lot."

"All right."

The doctor lets a nurse walk past in the hall. The woman carries a tray of food and wiggly Jell-O, reminders of life going on elsewhere, away from this tragedy.

"Elijah." The doctor says his name quickly. "You need to know your daughter is not going to live long."

Elijah yanks in a breath. He nods.

Dr. James presses on. Something is chasing him. "I have to ask you this and I have to do it right now."

"All right."

"Your daughter is going to die. Maybe in minutes, maybe in a few weeks, but that's all, I promise you. Before she does, as painful as this is for you to hear, I have to remind you of other mothers and fathers crying today and tomorrow for their babies, also born with problems. But those others are problems that maybe we can cure. We can save some of those children, if you and Clare will consider donating your daughter's organs."

Elijah turns his face away, working his jaw. He brings both hands to his face; breath comes between his palms.

When he drops his hands, his cheeks glisten. His teeth are bared.

"How long can you wait?"

"The child has to be living. It's hard, Elijah. But it's hard on other parents too. That's all I can say."

Elijah turns. He puts his hand on the door, lowering his head as if he has to bull his way into the delivery room, as though the door weighs tons. He holds there for a moment.

Over his shoulder he says to the doctor, "You wait out here."

The door opens. Elijah stops. Clare's eyes meet his and her face is like hard rain, stinging and wet. Her cheeks are vivid crimson, her mouth seems puffed and crammed with words she cannot speak. Her sagging breast is exposed. The baby's lips are no longer at the dry fountain. She has returned the child into the pink swath of the blanket. The nurses weep, having retreated to the dim corners of the room.

Before Elijah can move to his wife, Dr. James catches his arm. In the doorway, Elijah turns to him. The doctor winces and the wings of the man's mourning eyes are spread. This tragedy is done and he can fly away now, perhaps to another tragedy. Gently, he wags his head. No. Too late. The doctor leaves. The nurses follow, slipping past Elijah. One turns in the hallway and whispers, "We'll stay right outside, y'all."

Clare does not reach for Elijah, she does not take her arms from about the child. Elijah sits on the foot of the bed.

"What's her name?" he asks.

Clare sniffles deeply once, then again.

"Just like we decided," she answers, hefting the motionless bundle against her bare skin. "Nora."

Elijah repeats, "Nora." He lays his hand on Clare's leg. "Yeah, baby."

"And if it's all right," she asks, "now that she's passed? I'd like her middle name to be Carol. After my mother."

Nora Carol. The naming for both of them is merciful, like the infant's blanket. It wraps them and muffles all flaws. It is the child's first resting place.

# TWO

T he spire towering above the Victory Baptist Church is narrow and sharp. At its apex is a copper cross, like a barb, as though on the off chance that if God ever were to descend to Earth, when He returned to Heaven this white clapboard building and its congregation might hook like a burr in His hide and be swept upward with Him.

The Victory Baptist resides on State Route 101, a winding lane that for miles seems like nothing more than a paved interruption of pine, elm, and underbrush. In the spring, wild pink and white dogwoods bloom in the woods around the grass churchyard and cemetery. The nearest neighbors are a quarter-mile away. East is the Finchers' rancher and collection of front-yard wind vanes and whirligigs. West is the parsonage, a small Cape Cod covered with gray siding, where this afternoon Pastor Thomas Derby sips a whiskey.

The chapel dates back to 1781, constructed out of ax-hewn heart-pine beams and pegs. It has always been painted white and the double front doors always bottle green. The sanctuary seats up to three hundred members uncomfortably in rigid high-back wooden pews. The pews are divided left and right by a worn mahogany rail. Until

1967 men and women sat separated by this rail during services; two
hundred years of pastors and churchgoers alike presumed on Sundays who was courting whom by which couples sat side by side with
the rail between them at the shoulders. The church is heated by an
oil-fired furnace installed in the 1930s. There is no air conditioning.
Fans made from glued popsicle sticks and stapled children's Christmas cards are jammed beside the hymnals on the backs of the pews.
In the river humidity of summer the fanning congregation resembles
from the pulpit a flock of multihued pigeons eternally taking flight.
Behind the pulpit is the iron tub of the baptistry. To the left stands
the organ. Above the pulpit hover the bleachers of the choir loft.
Over the sanctuary floor hangs the gallery, two rows of chairs where
until 1865 slaves sat attending their masters' church. In 1866, three
years after the Emancipation Proclamation, the membership of Victory Baptist built for the black folks in this part of the county a separate black Baptist church, Zebulon Baptist, three miles farther west
on State Route 101. In 1970, Victory Baptist raised enough money to
construct a second building on its own grounds, a one-story wood
frame structure also painted white, to house Sunday school classes
and offices. In 1990 this annex got a new shingle roof.

Mrs. Rosalind Epps was the driving force behind the fund-raising
effort for the new shingle roof. Mrs. Epps has not missed a day of
church in twenty-six years of Sundays. She lets others do the watching and the counting of her attendance. She heads several church
committees and will not relinquish her recipe for buttermilk biscuits.
Privately, she has said she is disappointed that first her daughter,
Carol—who chose to follow a carpenter down to North Carolina, a
man who soon left her to fend for herself—and then her granddaughter,
Clare, had both lapsed in their commitment to Victory Baptist where
their ancestors back 150 years have worshiped. Others, also privately,
say of Rosy Epps that the old woman just can't stand to think that
her authority will sooner or later be broken up and handed off to
other church families.

Sixty years ago, while a girl of eighteen, during her first year as a
secretary at the paper mill and attending night school at the community college, Rosalind met her husband, Charley. He was a crewman

on one of the tugs that docked river barges at the quay alongside the log yard. The two young folks sparked across the church center rail until they were married in 1942, eight months before Charley went off to fight the Japanese with the Marines. He died on Palau in 1944, never to see his only daughter in the flesh. His flag-draped coffin was shipped home to Good Hope and laid to rest in the little cemetery at Victory Baptist, which is reserved for the families of church members. Mrs. Epps, a church deacon since 1976, regularly admonishes the head of the custodial committee, Mr. Snead, to keep a little American flag on her husband's grave, since Charley died a serviceman. The flags regularly tatter in the weather or get stolen by kids from town.

Mrs. Epps was Pastor Thomas Derby's third-grade teacher. She had him again in sixth grade. Thomas Derby developed a crush on her in third grade and wrote her a poem. For twenty-five years she has sent him Christmas cards. Because of the number of times he has moved, Derby has his own page in her address book. Every time she scratched out in pencil another mailing address, she grew more attached to the boy. He never came near Good Hope after he graduated the high school. He mailed photos twice in two decades and called Mrs. Epps every few years to give her an update on his life.

He first heard his calling down in New Orleans. Then he was in Bible College in South Carolina. Soon after graduation, his first church, then another church and another chance. Then he was going to quit preaching and get a job, he met a woman, no, that didn't work out. Another church, he's preaching better than ever, he observes how you get a few years under your belt and the Lord releases a lot of demons on you but also a lot of wisdom; no, it got time to move on from there. He got a line on another church, they like him there, no, he's not there anymore, he's traveling. Then God won out again and called him back, another church. No.

Six months ago, when young Pastor Bailey and his wife, Anita, were called to a larger church upstate near Washington, D.C., Mrs. Epps said it was time to bring Thomas Derby home. She solicited his resumé from the Baptist Mission Board. Her motion was opposed in the first selection committee meeting, not in the second.

## 2

Thomas Derby swishes the ice cubes in his highball glass. The cubes click. They mutter the tumbling word, *demons*.

Under his long left forefinger a Bible lies open. The finger glides right and left over the page like a hawk above a hunting ground, searching lazily. A silver crucifix dangles from a length of chain to dab and dance on the pages of scripture, then to swing against his bare chest. The cross was a gift from Rosy Epps upon Derby's return to his hometown. She told him it had been hers since her own baptism seventy-eight years ago and because there was no one left in her family who was any longer close to the church, she wanted Derby to have it. Chiseled into the face of the cross are symbols depicting the twelve Apostles of the Lamb. On the rear, in letters so worn they are barely decipherable, is the name Rosalind Martha.

Derby's eyes track his finger on the page. His eyes are blue-green and inviting, like warm ocean water. He is blond and lithe with athletic limbs, and a big Adam's apple makes him appear tender and thoughtful. People—good churchgoing people—see Thomas Derby's beauty and attribute it to God.

To the right of the Bible, his other hand leaves the cold contour of an emptied glass to grip the neck of a bottle. He pours another shot over the ice, glancing away from the Bible only quickly. He sets the bottle down. His right hand scratches a day's stubble on his chin. He smells on his hand a salted musk blended with his own flesh. He looks up from the Bible to the green sofa in the living room and wonders: When they run him off from this church, will the next preacher smell sin on that sofa? Will the blue flagstone sidewalk out front tell of late-night arrivals and departures? Will this table talk of cold glasses, will the sink reek of liquor? Will the grass, will the trees, will the fields spout his demons?

Derby eases his back in the wooden chair and considers himself. His left hand spread on the Bible. Right hand telltale of iniquity. Cleft down the middle, he thinks. A battleground. What is so holy, so strategic or important about me that neither side will withdraw? Let me go, he thinks, tipping the chilled whiskey to his lips. Before he swallows he looks out the window to the parsonage's backyard into the bottom branches of a tall pine. In the heat, sap is cooking out of the tree to run down the trunk. Touch it and you're gummy for the rest of the day. He sniffs. You get used to the egg odor of the mill quickly in this town but on days like this the smell weds itself to the humidity so densely it flows through the window air conditioner and comes inside. He swallows the liquor, hoping his throat will close on its own, asking God's hand to choke him and stop him and declare Himself the winner. He dares God, but God has never helped Thomas Derby. God has only used him.

Derby thinks, Maybe I've got it backwards. Maybe God is the demon. Jealously He calls me back to Him time and again. He has given me His voice, His word in thunder, but will not make me a full storm. He has left me parched, sound and clouds only, without rain, without the only blessing a storm bears to people thirsting, for crops dying, for scorched earth. When the people see I am empty, with nothing to give them but noise, they release me to drift again, God's dark dry cloud over the land.

The telephone rings. Derby lifts the left hand from the Bible to answer.

"Hello."

"Pastor Derby?"

"Yes."

"This is Dottie Orange. Good morning."

"Good morning, Dottie. How are you?"

"Middlin', pastor. It's so hot."

"What can I do for you, Dottie?"

"Elmo and I wondered if you'd have Sunday supper with us. My daughter Marie Elizabeth is in town from Roanoke and we'd love you to meet her. We're trying to talk her into moving back down here. Roanoke is so far."

This is how it goes, Derby thinks. They listen to my voice. They see my face from their stiff wooden benches on Sunday mornings, from folding metal chairs at Bible study classes, across supper linens and old chipped china and steaming coffee cups, and I become what they want me to be. It's not necessary that I be good. I simply have to be standing above them.

"Yes, thank you. Tell Elmo I said thank you too."

"Good, pastor. We'll look forward to it. Pastor?"

"Yes, Dottie?"

"I do so enjoy your scriptures and homilies."

"That's kind of you, dear."

"If you don't mind my asking, what are we going to hear from you this Sunday?"

Dottie Orange will tell Lou Ann Fincher and Mrs. Wallin and Mr. Birdsong that the pastor has told her on Monday about next Sunday's sermon. Derby wonders, Did these nice people work all the other preachers like this, wheedling, jockeying for position? Were those other pastors, two centuries' worth of them, so blind and lucky in their fealty to God that they didn't see the demons at work in their own assemblies, the pride, covetousness, rivalry?

A softness caresses Derby. He does not know if it is the whiskey breeze in his blood or God's pity, but in another moment he cannot feel contempt for Dottie Orange and her angling and supper matchmaking. He closes the Bible. With his thumb he riffles the stacked pages like a deck of cards. They can't afford to hire anybody better than me, he thinks. All they can get out here is young pastors and their young wives, first church, wet behind the ears. They brought me back, looking for a bargain, a tarnished firebrand preacher, a blacksheep native son. They're reaching out to help me in their own way, figuring maybe I'll turn out all right for them because I grew up here. Rosy Epps stuck her neck out for me. Dottie Orange is sticking out her daughter's. I'll try. I have to. Because if you have cut down all the trees, where will you hide when the devil turns 'round on you?

Derby tells Dottie Orange, "I was thinking something from the Old Testament."

"My," she says, "go on, pastor."

"The story of Saul, David, and Jonathan."

"Yes, uh-huh."

"You know King Saul loved David."

"Yes he did."

"The boy was a boon to the king with his songs and gentle company. Saul's household loved David too, as did Saul's son Jonathan. But Saul grew spiteful and jealous in his old age. And though David's harp and voice could ease Saul's aching head, his heart grew hard against David."

Dottie Orange says, "Saul wanted to kill David." Dottie wants to show that she knows her Bible too. Her tone inquires, Aren't I one of your favorites, pastor? Yes, Dottie, he thinks, you are because you make yourself easy to handle, you are so conniving.

Into his voice Derby puts a minor peal of the thunder. She'll hear it over the phone.

"Jonathan turned against his father the king and warned David to run and save his life."

"Well, yes," she says, a little shaken, "of course he had to turn against Saul. Jonathan did the right thing. He had to save David."

"Did he?" asks Derby. "When a father is wicked, do we rebel against him as if he is no longer our father? When a father has banished from our house kindness and justice, do we then become our father's judge? Do we turn our faces away from whatever and whomever displeases us, offends our own notions of right and wrong? Would we do that to God if He offended us, tried to kill our pleasant and beloved friend? Because you know God does this. He takes away our loved ones. He exiles from us truth and light and expects us to continue in His house. At what point, then, do we defy Him? When does the son become the parent? When does the worshiper become the god?"

"But David was beloved of God." She spouts doctrine. "He had to be spared."

Derby softens his tone, like a man delivering bad news. "Dottie, if only the beloved are spared pain and death, then none of us are beloved."

On the phone Dottie Orange says nothing. Derby hears her breathe. In this silence Derby looks to the table, at the whiskey bottle and dewy glass. He would throw them away, sweep them off the table—but these are trees he must hide behind from Satan. From

God too. He cannot face either God or Devil because he cannot ever trust himself to know for certain which is before him.

"Pastor," Dottie says now, "that is . . . I have never heard that . . ." she hesitates, figuring the right word; she says, *"spin,"* and it is not the right word for her, it is too modern but there it is, ". . . put on that story of Saul and David." Derby knows she is shaking her head in her kitchen. "It is an interesting interpretation though."

"We'll see how it goes over on Sunday."

She chuckles, staying good-natured. "Well, I guess we will. Certainly the young folks will have something to talk about in Bible study." She sighs and Derby can sense her smile in resignation. He sees her tightening her apron about her waist; time to fix lunch for Elmo.

She says in parting, motherly, "You stay out of the heat now, pastor."

Derby laughs loudly. He does not care that Dottie does not know why.

3

Rosy Epps stoops to the graves of her husband and daughter to lay pink roses from her garden, one each. Charley's rose is set beside a tattered little American flag that hangs from a graying dowel. Mr. Snead, the custodian, obviously has not heard the sad news and so has not yet replaced the faded pennant, which he would have done out of respect for Rosy. To help her rise, Thomas Derby takes her hand. When Rosy is erect again, he holds her hand. She squeezes his fingers and with her free hand mops a kerchief across her brow.

"It's been a lifetime of trial, Charley," she says, a little winded, into the ground. "A lifetime of trial. And it's not over."

She blinks and brings the kerchief up again, now to sop a tear. She is thick and squat in a pale peach dress festooned with images of green beans, heads of lettuce, and corn on the cob. When she called Thomas Derby to tell him about the tragedy of her great-grandchild being born with no top to her head and dying in her mama's arms, she informed him also that she was just not going to wear black this afternoon, she couldn't bring herself to do it in this heat. Derby is in a navy poly/cotton suit; it breathes no better than a trash bag and he is hot. Today Rosy's silver crucifix hangs outside his shirt; when he touches it he can feel how it has warmed in the sun. Rosy's hair, frosty blue on cooler days, takes on in this humidity the warmer blue of a flame. Her skin swims with color today. That might be the crying, thinks Derby. He remembers she was beautiful when he was in third grade.

The graves of Charley Epps and his daughter, Carol, are in the sun. Mr. Omohundro sits in coveralls in the shade of the church portico with his shovel, watching. The whole cemetery is bright and hot. Despite the heat Derby likes the neat little cemetery, the community of weathered headstones from the eighteenth century lined up next to pristine, square-edged tablets from more recent years. Though some of those buried here died very old folks, their fresh markers with square shoulders and clear-eyed letters make them seem young again among the grizzled veterans of the graveyard. Several of Victory Baptist's former pastors are interred here, and the names of many of the church's current members are here too: Blinson, Dahl, Quantrill, Darlington, Pederson, Orange. Derby squints across the sun-blasted grass—he doesn't wear sunglasses to funerals—and thinks there's a roundness to the church and its cemetery together that appeals to him. The whole is like a heart. It opens and closes, opens and closes, brings in new blood through the front doors, taking and sharing life with the blood, then laying it to rest out the back door, to the cemetery, exhausted of life, but keeping everything in the circle, to come around again with the same names. The church and the cemetery and even the mill and Rosy Epps are what Thomas Derby is not. They are constant. He wants to stay at this church in his hometown of Good Hope. Derby wants a grave here and the occasional flower like Charley and Carol. He is forty-three years old and figures he might live that span one more time. Afterward he wants his grave to be manicured by Mr. Snead's descendants. Derby is tired of moving and failure.

"There's company coming, y'all," Rosy says to the ground. "Carol, it's your granddaughter. They named her Nora Carol, after you. That was sweet, I thought." Rosy pauses. "She died after about ten minutes, Carol. She didn't have much of a chance."

Rosy shakes her kerchief, one, two, at the graves, then three, at the small, deep hole dug that morning by Mr. Omohundro for Nora Carol Waddell. Two mounds of clay sit beside the fresh hole like rusty pyramids to mark the burial of a pharaoh's child.

Without looking at Derby, she says, "Three of 'em, Thomas. Three. Why am I the one still standing here?"

Thomas Derby does not answer because he does not know what God wants. He has stopped reconfiguring God daily out of the brick and mortar of the Bible and doctrine to ease his church's mind or his own. This, he knows, is his job but he has quit doing it. He is left with nothing but questions and guesses, no knowledge at all of God. Derby looks for Him now in the questions. He calls them out to God and man from the pulpit, asks in his soul, blows private, sonorous notes across the mouths of open whiskey bottles to help the bottles break the too much silence. He has grown comfortable with the asking and the profound absence of answers, the same way he is comfortable in the patience of the cemetery. But something awaits, something is inevitable, he knows. All things will come. Derby glances at the vacant hole in the ground for Nora Carol. The hole, too, is a question. Soon the answer will be laid in the dark cool bottom of it. That answer, like all the others that are right in front of Thomas Derby, will awhile longer mock him with its silence.

Rosy asks, "What is it God wants from me to outlive three of 'em?"

"I suppose," Derby replies, "when He decides to tell you, He'll bring you in, too."

Rosy blows out a breath. "She was just an infant. Only ten minutes old."

Derby gently pulls the old woman by the hand to face him and not the graves. "It seems sometimes God takes a liking to a person right off. Others . . ." He lifts Rosy's hand and fleshy arm in the air as though to show her off or to begin a dance with her. "It takes a while before He warms up to them."

Rosy raises her eyebrows and says, "Thomas Derby. You." She

smiles. They do not release their hands when the hearse pulls up in front of the church.

The hearse parks, a wedge of night on this sultry, shining day. Behind it is only one vehicle, a tan pickup truck with its lights on. Two men in black emerge from the hearse to slide a small, plain pine casket from the rear. Thomas Derby is struck by the dimensions, the large size of the hearse, the width of the black rear door swung wide, the girth of the suited men carrying the little coffin easily between them. Their steps chew on the gravel parking lot approaching the graveyard.

Elijah and Clare leave the pickup. Both are swathed in black. She wears a long dress and silk shawl, her blond head bare. Elijah, ebony from head to toe, even a black shirt and tie, seems a monolith of mourning. They walk slowly, as though they are the ones carrying the casket. Rosy Epps whispers, "Maybe I should've worn the black. I feel a bit silly." Derby says, "You're fine. You're here. It doesn't matter."

The two men from the hearse set the casket beside the grave and back away. One holds the ropes with which they will lower the casket. Derby thinks, It really is just a tiny pellet going into the earth's mouth, a little pine box with a little girl inside it. Why? What is sick in that mouth that this pill is needed to heal it? Isn't there more sickness up here on the ground, where maybe Nora Carol might have been a joy to help heal us? Is her spirit needed in Heaven so much more than her mama and daddy need her?

Thomas Derby does not know Clare and Elijah. In the four months he has been at Victory Baptist they have not attended his church. The burial request was made to him by Rosy Epps only that morning, for the child passed away late the previous afternoon. Derby called Mr. Snead straightaway but did not find the custodian in, so he took it on himself to phone Mr. Omohundro and make the arrangements for the grave, which was dug by lunch. Derby moves in front of Clare. She is as tall as he, she looks at him eye to eye. He holds his hands out to her. She gives him back only one, the other stays with her husband.

"To tell you how sorry I am," Derby says, "would be to ask you to

consider even for a moment my sorrow. I won't do that." He takes in
Elijah's eyes, thinking of the grave behind him, and finds Elijah's eyes
just as unspeaking. "I can only tell you there's a reason this happened. I don't know what that reason is and neither do you. But,
Clare, Elijah, do not close your hearts today when you close this
ground." Derby touches Clare's and Elijah's clasped hands. "Feel
*this,* how you hold each other. And I give you my word, you will feel
happiness again."

Derby turns from the couple. He walks past Rosy, brushing a finger against her elbow. At the foot of the grave, he folds his hands and
closes his eyes to lift his face to the sun.

"We are told in Luke 13 to travel the narrow way to God, that
many of us will knock at the narrow gate and be informed we cannot
come in if we have been workers of iniquity. Nora Carol, among all of
us, is virtuous. She ought to glide right on through the narrow gate.
And we are told also in Luke that there are last who will be first and
first who will be last. Nora Carol was born to us with a perfect soul,
and she is perfect still. She is first today. She is first forever."

Derby lowers his head and nods to the two men from the funeral
home. They attach the ropes and slowly lower the casket. When it is
at the bottom, Derby approaches Clare and Elijah. Standing in front
of Clare, he lifts the silver crucifix from around his neck. He holds it
up before Clare's hard face. Rosy's faded engraved name sways on
the back of the cross, the signs of the Apostles face Clare. Derby
talks to the girl through the loop of the silver chain.

"Clare, if you take nothing else away with you this morning,
please take God's grace. Please take this."

Derby raises the chain to set the cross around Clare's neck.
Before he can lower it, she lifts her hand to stop him.

Derby says, "It belonged to your grandma." Derby cuts his eyes
to Rosy, who nods. "We talked and she wants you to have it."

Derby sees in the girl's eyes the same touch of God he suffers.
Why has this happened to her? There is nothing, Derby wants to answer her, nothing but the question. Even when we scream and weep
at God, we accept His existence.

Rosy says, "Please take it, Clare."

The girl wraps her hand around the crucifix. She stuffs it and the chain into the pocket of her black dress.

Clare and Elijah walk hand in hand to Rosy. The girl kisses her grandmother once on the cheek, Rosy presses her hand on Elijah's arm. Without a word, Clare and Elijah turn and walk to the pickup. They seem almost to prop each other, like wounded soldiers. Rosy watches them go. When they have pulled out of the gravel lot, she sighs at Thomas Derby.

"Well," she says, and makes the smacking noise with her lips, "I suppose they're entitled to their privacy. Although . . ." She shakes her head and does not complete the thought out loud.

"You go ahead, Rosy. It's hotter'n blue blazes out here." Derby hopes she has not caught his inadvertent pun on her coif. "I'll stay awhile longer 'til they finish up."

Rosy sniffs. Some spectacle she'd hoped for has fallen flat. "All right, Thomas. Thank you." The old woman steps to the lip of the grave. "Goodbye, sweetheart," she says down to the little pine box. "I'll bring you a rose too after you get some grass on you." With a glance to Derby of relief and appreciation, she walks to her car.

When she is gone, Thomas Derby watches the funeral home employees coil their rope. To say something, one of them says to Derby, "Shame." The other points a finger at Derby with approval. "That was nice," he says. "Short. Nice."

Derby understands. It's hot for these large young men and their hearse is air-conditioned. They see a lot of burials. With the temperature so fierce today, they were probably glad it was just a baby they had to carry.

Derby points back, a little gunfight of callousness. "Thanks," he says sportily as they depart. "See you."

Derby stands beside the grave in the teeming green heat and watches Mr. Omohundro shovel the piles of clay over the coffin.

An old Buick wheels into the parking lot a little fast, spewing dust. Out of the car clambers Mr. Snead. The head of the church custodial committee walks quickly and with some agitation to Pastor Derby.

Mr. Snead is one of those men who keeps his story in his face, the way others store their histories in their palms or wallets. He is a runt, wrinkled, thin, and bald with jumpy eyes that seem always to be following someone walking behind you. His nervous energy gives the people he talks with the same jittery sensation they get in their hands from pushing a lawn mower all day. This is what Mr. Snead does at the church, cuts the grass, trims shrubs, checks signs of weathering in the clapboards, fixes the boiler. He took early retirement from the paper mill last year and the church has become his work. He is always on Derby's periphery; he is the gardener of the church and believes it cannot bloom without him.

"Pastor," he says just before reaching Derby. He nods at Mr. Omohundro.

"Mr. Snead," says Derby when the man has stopped beside him, standing a bit close for the heat and the noiseless day, only the shoveling and dropping dirt sharing the air with the humidity. "Afternoon."

"I passed a hearse going the other way," Mr. Snead says, pointing. The man uses no formalities with his pastor. Apparently Snead has never seen a need for formalities in his long dealings with paper, paint, and plants, and so he deals with people in like fashion.

Derby says, "I tried to call you this morning but couldn't reach you."

"Well," Mr. Snead says. He seems to want to complain but can't figure what to strike at. He fidgets.

Derby indicates the sweaty gravedigger. "I called Mr. Omohundro. Hope you don't mind but the family wanted the burial done today. There wasn't much time, so I went ahead."

"That's all right," says Mr. Snead, but it clearly is not. "What family? I didn't hear nothing about a death. I passed Rosy Epps on the road first. Was she here for the funeral?"

"Yes. It was her granddaughter's baby."

"Clare's child."

"Yes."

Mr. Snead follows the fall of a shovelful of clay. The little casket is mostly covered now, the thumps are muted, dirt on dirt. The man's eyes fix on a pine edge still showing through the clay. Derby does not like it when Mr. Snead's eyes are still.

"That Elijah Waddell's?"

"It was his daughter, yes. Nora Carol."

"Pastor."

Mr. Snead lifts his gaze out of the grave. Shoving his hands in his pockets, he does not look at Derby but winces. His eyes dart to the church, around the cemetery, to the sky. He is calculating some damage done, or that he must now do. "I'm not sure about this."

"Not sure about what, Mr. Snead?"

"You know," the custodian says, pointing at the church building, then waving his hand across the graves. "This is all over two hundred years old."

"And that means exactly what, Mr. Snead?"

"I suppose no one mentioned this to you." Mr. Snead is holding the pastor blameless with this, to make it easier for the pastor to agree. "But this graveyard here is separate."

"What do you mean, separate?"

"Well, segregated. But we can't call it that."

Something in Derby's look makes Mr. Snead back up. Derby hasn't said or done anything but the custodian has his palms up to deflect some expected retaliation from the pastor.

"Look," Mr. Snead says, jittery, "I know nowadays this probably don't sound good and all but it's been this way for more'n two hundred years. It's not my call and frankly, pastor, it ain't yours either. If a black person's going to be buried here, well, that'll take some doing. We just can't, you know. . . ."

"It's done. Mrs. Epps owns this plot and she can do with it what she likes."

"Well, not according to church rules, pastor. But you didn't know about that so I'm sure it'll be okay. Mr. Omohundro." Mr. Snead holds out a hand to stop the gravedigger from finishing his task. Mr. Omohundro leans on the shovel.

Derby turns calmly to Mr. Omohundro. "You're working for me today, Mr. Omohundro. You go on ahead. I'll take care of this." Mr.

Omohundro waits. No matter who called him this morning, he knows he'll work next for Mr. Snead, or not.

Mr. Snead shakes his head and spits. It is an awfully inappropriate thing to do, thinks Derby, repelled. "Mr. Snead," the pastor says without rancor—Derby has twenty years' experience modulating his voice—"please stop telling me how I didn't know about this. I know now and I'm standing by it. This child is going to stay where she is."

Mr. Snead takes another step back. "Pastor, if that's the case I got no choice but to call a deacons' meeting for tonight. We'll decide what to do there."

"I want to take it up with the whole church," Derby says. "On Sunday."

"No," Snead replies, now in full retreat. "This sort of thing's what the deacons are for. No need to get everybody's dander up. We'll take care of it and we'll do it quick." He looks at Mr. Omohundro and decides not to fight this battle now. "Go ahead, Mr. Omohundro. It won't make no nevermind if you finish up."

Mr. Omohundro resumes flinging the dirt. The sound of his spade is joined by Mr. Snead's hurrying steps in the gravel lot.

The custodian calls back to Derby. "Seven o'clock in the chapel, pastor."

"Mr. Snead, can we talk about this?" Derby shouts after him, disbelieving what is happening.

"Tonight."

Derby turns to the grave. He loosens his tie. He wants a drink. Mr. Snead drives away.

Thomas Derby watches the last pale edge of the casket disappear under the earth. The moment should be resolute and final under the clay. But it is not. It churns under the rumble of Mr. Snead's car up the road, it snags in the throat of the man's threat.

Derby leans over to Charles Epps's grave. He takes up the long-stemmed pink rose. "Excuse me, Charley," he says. "You don't mind." Suddenly Derby is weary. He stares into the baby's grave filling with the rusty clods flying from the point of Mr. Omohundro's shovel.

He drops the rose into Nora Carol's grave, thinking somehow this might add one more reason to leave the child alone.

## 4

By five minutes after seven all thirteen deacons of the Victory Baptist Church are seated in the pews. Their punctuality speaks of the unusual nature of the meeting. Derby sits alone in the rear of the sanctuary. The pastor has the right to speak at deacons' meetings but cannot vote. The deacons run the church; the pastor is in charge of their spirits. Derby watches the old cliques form by knots of seating and conversation. No one talks about the reason they have been called to the church. No one wants to express an opinion without the camouflage of the others. The three farmers are missing their supper. Dottie Orange and another woman still wear their aprons, they've come from serving at their own supper tables. Two of the mill workers had to get someone to cover for the ends of their shifts. Only one of the women, Jeannie Stallings, is young enough to have natural color left in her hair; she is a mill worker and gossips with the men about some new employee's mistakes. All are thick from hard work and country diets, only Mr. Snead and Jeannie are thin at the waist. Rosy Epps sits by herself.

Derby feels callow. These people belong here, every echo of their voices sounds right bouncing overhead in the choir loft and gallery. These are the faces and hands of the two hundred years of this congregation. These are the trunk and bark of the family tree, the church is the taproot, Derby is no more than a bird sitting on an ancient branch. He's been in the employ of these deacons for four months. They have been children together.

The front double doors are open like it was Sunday morning but this is not morning, it is early on an August evening. The deacons take up the Christmas-card fans and cool their faces. In the field across the road the first crickets sing through the open doors. Derby uncrosses his arms; he senses his body language might make him seem closed off and apprehensive. He links his hands and presses the tips of his forefingers together, making a steeple, waiting.

With no sign from anyone, oddly, all thirteen mouths fall silent at once. This adds to Derby's sense of dislocation and rawness. There was a signal and he did not catch it. The sanctuary is silent. The crickets add to an almost embarrassing quiet. Mr. Snead's pew creaks when he stands.

Mr. Snead holds out his hands, palms up. He now wears a striped long-sleeved shirt, his belt sports a big brass buckle. His hair is slicked down. Mr. Snead is the only deacon who has showered and prepped for the meeting.

"All right, y'all," he says, "what are we going to do about this?"

Right to the point, Derby thinks. Everyone here already knows what Mr. Snead thinks, he's worked them so much on the phone that he can stand and call it "this." The only peace Clare and Elijah will know begins and ends with the grave out back. Mr. Snead calls it "this."

No one speaks. Several clear their throats.

Mr. Snead turns his gaze to Rosy Epps, expecting her to make some opening remark. After all, it's her actions and her kin that are tonight's topic. Derby sees the profile of the pinched look Rosy sends back at Mr. Snead, which makes the man's eyes resume their darting way. "We got to make a decision," Mr. Snead says, "and I think we ought to make it tonight. Do y'all agree with me at least that before we leave here we'll have a decision?"

Heads nod, eyes dart. No one agrees out loud.

"All right." Mr. Snead continues. "Look." Derby sees that the man is reaching his cruising speed, that tone and insistence where folks will agree with Mr. Snead just to avoid disagreeing with him. "You all know what's been done out there in the cemetery."

Derby hears "what's been done" and cannot sit; this thing that's been done has names and a tale, an infant's lifeless lips and a mother's undrunk nipple and a father's emptied eyes. It is a calamity for them and to hurt them more is a mortal sin. Derby rattles his head. He does not want to wait to see where the deacons will go with their views. He stands, his pew announcing his rise. The deacons turn, all their pews complain.

Mr. Snead says, "Pastor, you'd like to say something?" The words sound clipped, as though the skinny man is trimming a troublesome hedge.

Derby will not address them from the rear. He knows he must stand before them. That is his, and only his, place. He is a new pastor to them. These people have done him a kindness and given him a place when it seemed he'd run out of places in his life. But what he has to say to them is the truth, and the truth is not new and hesitant, it does not hide and wait to see what others say. Derby bears it solemnly, erectly, to the front.

He does not begin right off when he reaches the head of the courting rail running down the center of the pews. He stands for a moment to establish who and what he is, as he does on Sundays when he grips the pulpit and glowers just for a moment, smiles a second or two, greets them and holds them with a nod. Derby looks to Mr. Snead. Derby will not begin until he, the pastor, is the only one standing. Mr. Snead sits in the mute church.

"I assume you all know about the tragedy that has befallen Rosy Epps's family. In case you don't, her great-grandchild, Nora Carol Waddell, was born yesterday afternoon with a terrible deformity. Nora Carol died shortly after coming into the world. She died in her mother's arms. Rosy graciously offered to lay the child next to her husband, Charley, and her daughter, Carol, out here in our cemetery. This afternoon, that was done. It was done quickly, without going through the normal channels because of the circumstances. That was my doing. I couldn't reach Mr. Snead, so I went ahead. It was my belief the family needed to begin healing as quickly as possible after a tragedy like that. You can all understand, I'm sure."

Derby pauses. None of the deacons looks at him. All heads are down as though in prayer but he knows they are not praying. They are biding their time; the followers wait for the handful of leaders, the leaders wait for their chance.

Derby extends one hand, shaking it at the deacons with his words. "You cannot take Nora Carol out of the ground. She's just a poor baby. Her parents have been through so much in the last two days, think about what they have to go through in the years ahead. Will you add to that? Would you want them to do this to you? Nora Carol has a right to her sleep. She's at rest next to her great-grandfather and her grandmother. She's laid beside her kin. She asks nothing of you that you do not ask of each other, to go to Judgment among your own people."

It is not Mr. Snead, as Derby thought it would be, who casts the first stone. It is Dottie Orange.

"Is she, pastor?"

Then comes Mr. Snead. "That's right. Is she?"

Heads lift now.

"That's the question, isn't it?" asks Jeannie Stallings. "Are we her own people?"

"She's Rosy Epps's great-granddaughter." Derby looks to Rosy. The older woman holds her mouth in a taut round pucker, wrinkles circling her lips.

"Everybody," says Mr. Street, who farms lima beans and feed corn on the acreage across the stream from Clare and Elijah's house, "let's just say it." He squirms left and right on his large rump. "Her father's black. All right?" Mr. Street sits back hard against the groaning pew; the farmer has planted a seed and is done.

"Yes," agrees Derby with exaggerated cool, "her father, Elijah Waddell, is a black man. And like I asked Mr. Snead this morning beside Nora Carol's grave, and like I ask the rest of you right now, what does that mean?"

Derby rakes the deacons with a look and doesn't wait for an answer.

"In Matthew, Jesus tells us that what we do to the least of his brothers and sisters, we do unto him. Nora Carol's blood is half black. Somehow that makes her unfit in your eyes to be buried at Victory Baptist. I tell you, if you dig that baby out of the ground and hand her back to her parents, if you reject her from the earth of your church, you reject Jesus and God. That child *is* among her own people because she is a Christian child."

Derby swallows. His eyes wince.

He persists, "Why do you hate Elijah this much? To rip a child from the grave because she's his? Why?"

Derby clamps his teeth and breathes heavily through his nostrils. This is to tell them he could go on but is breaking off so they can stop him, so they can agree, admit shame, and go home.

No one speaks. The deacons' heads are not bowed but rigid, all eyes on him. Standing above them, Derby feels an undertow.

One of the deacons, Derby does not see whom, says unhappily, "Oh, pastor, no."

Dottie Orange, cheerless, wags her head at Derby. Others do the same. "Pastor, no," she echoes. "Nobody here hates Elijah. Nobody here hates anybody."

Then the voices come, the ones who will decide tonight.

Mr. Hillenbrandt stands. He is one of the chubbiest and the wealthiest men in the church, he owns a farm machinery dealership. Derby likes him, he has the typical salesman's jocular nature. But by rising to speak Mr. Hillenbrandt challenges Derby, and Derby briefly wonders about the compliments and backslaps of the past four months.

"This is not about hatred, pastor. That's a cruel thing to imply." Mr. Hillenbrandt takes in the other deacons, gently forming his consensus. "I think most of us know Elijah and Clare, and all of us certainly know and admire Mrs. Epps. We wouldn't do anything to hurt them if we could avoid it. But can we avoid it? What you've said so far is all good and right and we all agree with Jesus. But there's procedures, pastor, and those procedures got short shrift today, from what I can tell. Those procedures exist for the same reason this church exists. To do honor. The church honors God and Jesus Christ. The cemetery honors those that have gone on before us. And just like there's a way we worship at this church, pastor, there's a way we bury our dead. Both are old ways, and both, I still think, are good ways."

Mr. Hillenbrandt pauses to collect more words. In the gap, Jeannie Stallings stands. She is so skinny her pew does not sound off. She has safety glasses tucked in her shirt pocket; her job at the mill, like Elijah's, is on the machines.

"That's right." Her voice is firm. She is the newest of the deacons, appointed since Derby has been at the church. She craves a larger role. "This is not about Elijah."

"It is," Derby replies.

"No, it's not, pastor. This is about two hundred years." Mr. Hillenbrandt sees he is not getting the floor back so he sits. Jeannie Stallings continues. "The fact that it's Elijah, the fact that it's such a sad thing that happened, just makes this harder. Pastor, you know I got two girls at home. If anything happened to them, I'd be broken up bad. And it would be a blessing to know my girls were buried right here near me. They'd be buried next to folks who been going to this church since after the Revolution, and the Civil War, and World War One and Two and whatever. And every one of those folks going back all that time had the opportunity to decide if black folks could be buried here with them and they said no. Not out of hatred. Not out of racism. But out of community. Out of who we are and who we've always been. Look out there, pastor. Those are our names on those gravestones. Those are our history and the history of this church, our people. They set the rules, not us, and I don't see how we ought to make a change just because something sad happened. Every one of those graves is something sad."

Jeannie Stallings sits. She has a keen sense of drama. She knows when she has hit a lick. The floor is open for another voice. Derby jumps in before someone else can build the momentum.

"Yes, I agree with you, Jeannie. Community is important. But remember, this is Mrs. Epps's flesh and blood. Her family has its share of headstones out there too. And, Mr. Hillenbrandt, you're right. The old ways are good." He spreads his palms, in the manner of a man welcoming a friend. "But I remind everyone here that compassion is an old way. Generosity is an old way. Kindness is an old way. And some others are old ways too." He brings his palms together in front of his chest, in the posture of a beseeching man, praying for enlightenment. "Racism is old. Ask the Jews. Ask Jesus. Closed minds are old, but Christians must go forth against closed minds." He draws himself up. "I ask you not to do this. It's very wrong. I plead with you."

Derby looks to Rosy Epps for support. Her eyes are straight ahead, her lips still pursed. She is unblinking, her face waxen.

He surveys the deacons. Many are sweating. Derby knows the ones who are fanning themselves will not speak, they are the sheep. The crickets outside sing loudly, impatiently, ringing down dusk. One other deacon besides the ones who have risen and Rosy keeps his hands in his lap. Mr. Quantrill. He farms the cornfields surrounding

Clare and Elijah's house. His family is the oldest of Victory Baptist. In 1788 his ancestor was its second pastor. He is a sober man in overalls who has confided to Derby that he has never liked Mr. Snead. He sings tenor in the choir.

Derby tilts his head. "Mr. Quantrill, please, sir?"

Mr. Quantrill does not stand, which Derby appreciates. But Mr. Quantrill shakes his head slowly, staring into his lap. His voice is honest.

"You know, pastor, I hate to say it. But you look outside these windows here and what do you see? You see a world we built with our fathers and their fathers and on before them and that world is getting smaller every day. Today we got quotas and affirmative action and set-asides. There's Black Miss America contests and over at the high school they got a Black History Week. You got black farmers' associations and black businessmen's associations and black congressional caucuses. And we don't say nothing about it. We go our way. We don't argue, we don't form organizations to oppose 'em, we even help 'em along when we can. Back a hundred and forty years ago, a bunch of folks out there in the graveyard started a black Baptist church up the road so's the blacks could have their own private place of worship and their own cemetery, so's they could do like us, worship and be buried among their own."

Mr. Quantrill lifts his eyes from his lap. He fixes his gaze on Thomas Derby. It is the gaze of a man who drives a tractor straight, who hammers a nail in two strokes, who rises early every morning. "So I got to ask you, pastor. How much smaller is our world going to get? Is it so small now that we can't even lay our heads down together with the folks we come up with? With our own kind? Do we have to throw open every door? Is that how it is? I like Elijah, by God I do, and I feel awful for what's happened to him. But that don't mean I want to be buried with him or his kin. That poor little baby ought to be laid to rest in a place surrounded by her own people, and that place isn't here, it's up the road. I don't believe it's a sin to want that for her, or to want the same for me or these good folks here with me tonight." Mr. Quantrill stops and studies what he's said. "I just don't."

The farmer's words are like a plow, they have riven a long, even row, deep enough for the other deacons to plant themselves inside. Many heads have popped up like sunflowers and turned to Mr. Quantrill, who does not revel in their support; he looks only to Rosy Epps, and because he is a fair man, says, "I want to hear what Rosy has to say."

The pews squeal with the deacons' turning now to Rosy. The old woman's eyes are fixed on something in the air before her, perhaps on that far horizon where the spirits of the dead dip below sight, perhaps she looks on a sepia memory of Charley or a scrap from daughter Carol's childhood, or that sweltering afternoon's little pine coffin. Without looking left or right, she works her jaw. Quietly she says, "Well." Rosy's faraway face sets Derby's mind to flight as well. He sees his old teacher's face turn pretty and young for him. He sees her the day he handed her a love poem in third grade and she read it, then rolled it up and bonked him over the head with it, saying loud enough for the whole class to hear, "Thomas Derby. You have some nerve flirting with a widow woman." He smiles and she smiles as she did that day, but no, it is not the kindness and fond eyes of his long memory he sees on her but sinking melancholy.

Firmly she says, "I think it's time for a vote." Derby realizes that Rosalind Epps is thinking not of the dead, not the cemetery where her kin lie, but of the very living, the squeaking pews around her where her community sits with their eyes all on her now in this church as they have been for decades.

Derby asks, "Rosy, would you like to say something first?"

"I've said it, Thomas."

She calls him Thomas, not pastor, in front of the other deacons. This way she tells him she is sorry.

Mr. Snead gets to his feet again. He walks to the front with quick steps. Derby wants to keep on talking, to stir the deacons' hearts one more time before they can set hard. But Mr. Snead is there before Derby can think what to say and so he must retire and move to his place in the rear.

"All right," Mr. Snead says, "somebody make a motion."

No one speaks.

Mr. Hillenbrandt grunts. "Oh, for God's sakes, Snead," the salesman says, "just take a vote."

"I'll do it." It is Mr. Quantrill. In a voice mild and sorrowful—it could be the voice of God and Derby cannot say in his soul that it is not God's graceful voice doing this terrible work—Mr. Quantrill says, "All in favor of exhuming the child buried in our cemetery today, raise your hand."

Mr. Quantrill lifts his hand while saying the words, like taking an oath. Other hands go up. Every deacon votes except Rosy. Lastly and slowly, her hand rises. With this she is again with her people, the thing the deacons have just denied Nora Carol.

To Derby the hands seem to stay up a long time. They are lifted as though the deacons have taken some stand, accepted some responsibility, but Derby thinks the deacons point elsewhere, to Heaven and their ancestors, upon whom they lay the blame. He sees in the raised hands the white headstones of the church graveyard, the steam from the Good Hope mill, the tan tufts of corn, yellow marsh grass, and cattails swaying by the Mattaponi River. This is Derby's home, and in these hands it has risen against him.

The hands come down. The pews wrench. The deacons rise and shuffle into the aisles, another silent signal Derby has not caught. The meeting is over. Mr. Snead says to the retreating folks, "I'll take care of it first thing." They all file out in somber fashion past Derby, a few say "Good night, pastor," the rest leave without a word. Rosy is gone, Dottie Orange's arm around her shoulders. Derby sits in the empty sanctuary listening to trucks and cars disperse out of the gravel lot. Once they have departed, the crickets are at their loudest. There are no lights on in the church. The pink half-light of the waning day flows in the open doors.

Derby sits until full dark drains the room. For a long while he sits with the music of crickets and the grinding of frogs in the ditches. Then he rises. He closes the double doors and does not lock them. Derby never locks the doors of his churches.

# THREE

1

It will be a dingy day. Early morning clouds clamp down the brewing humidity and mill stink. A heavy mist mires thigh-deep on the roads and in the fields, in the stands of pine planted by the paper company that owns the mill, on the weedy turf and watered green lawns, and in the old cemetery beside the Victory Baptist Church when Deputy Monroe Skelton drives past at 7:36 A.M. The ubiquitous gravedigger Mr. Omohundro is already at work with his shovel and a pile of dirt. The mist in the cemetery evokes hovering spooks without the strength to stand up straight, so they lie down and watch Mr. Omohundro dig.

Ten minutes later Monroe is at home. The house is a brick rancher on three acres, set off the road under a dense canopy of trees. The perpetual shade keeps his grass from growing fast, which is fine because he does not like nor often have the time to cut it. His wife will never cut the grass; that is their bargain. Rey Ann takes care of the inside, Monroe the outside. He enjoys this little advantage of the shade. Rey Ann tells him he thinks he's slick and finds chores for him anyway.

She is awake. On entering the house he smells her, she is fresh from a morning shower. He sees her in his mind first, yellow terry cloth robe, towel around her neck like a boxer, barefoot and hippy. Her eyes, almond-shaped and beautiful, black hair cropped shorter than his, high Indian cheekbones under brown skin smoothed and pampered by oils and gels touted in the black women's beauty magazines. Mother to his son, teacher to others' children, she is nearing the return date to school and so is practicing in these last few weeks, waking up early again. She will shout from the bedroom—and she does—"Money, sit down to the table. I'm running a little behind. I'll be right out."

Monroe does not sit. He wonders who died that Mr. Omohundro was digging for at the white Baptist church on Route 101. Monroe knows he likely wouldn't have heard. This is his week to work the 9 P.M. to 7 A.M. shift. It ends Friday, then three of the other eleven county deputies will take the shift. That time of night you know who's drinking, who's speeding, who beat up who, which asshole in one of the three holding cells in their little jail snores, but you don't hear much about old white folks passing on.

"Money, sit down," she calls. On his way to the breakfast nook Monroe passes the photo portrait of his son in army uniform, hung beside the picture of a trim Monroe in his own Ranger days at Fort Benning, Georgia, thirty years ago. Not so trim now, he thinks, running his hand over his belly which pulls taut his brown deputy's tunic. Monroe raises a gentle salute to his boy, a strong black lad, a drill sergeant hoping to be a lifer, who would have insisted on a snappier salute from an old soldier. Monroe looks at his hand when it drops from his brow. It's still a powerful mitt at the end of a strong arm. He pouts at the traitorous gray hairs on the back of his wrist joining those white tattletales at his temples and in his moustache. Getting on, he thinks. Fifty-two. And still a deputy kissing George Talley's butt.

"No, you are not!" Rey Ann shouted at him last time he said that out loud two years ago. "You do not kiss butt, Monroe Skelton. I am not married to a man who kisses anybody's butt except mine. You understand me?" That day, another early morning like this, she stomped over to the picture of the soldier Monroe Skelton and rammed her finger right into its face. "Who the hell is this?" Rey Ann shouted, with no invitation for an answer. "This is a man! This is a goddamn Ranger. This man don't kiss no butt. This man *kicks* butt. This man marches right up to George Talley and announces, yes, announces! that he is going to run for sheriff himself and George Talley better look out. That's what." Rey Ann danced and threw punches in the air. Other women love Elvis, she loves Muhammad Ali and big George Foreman. She lowered her head, bobbing and weaving, stepping in, shifting her hips, firing a left-right combination. "We got a message for George Talley," she said, and mimicked the boxing announcer on TV. "Get ready to ruuuummmm-bulllll . . ." Monroe stepped in front of his wife and playfully sparred with her, ". . . 'cause we are *comin'* upside yo' head," she chanted. He blocked more shots than he threw, until her housecoat slipped open and she had nothing on underneath. Monroe scooped her up. She was damp and smelling of lotions. He carried her to the bedroom.

Rey Ann comes out now just as Monroe envisioned her. She always looks like a middleweight in the mornings, robed and feisty. Monroe—groggy and spent from a night of driving and sitting, tired after two domestics and one shoplifting call, from hours of Mike Benson's sports talk and Rob Schultz's doughnuts at the jail—just wants to climb into bed. He figures that twenty-four years as a deputy ought to free him from the graveyard shift. George Talley is ten years younger. Let him pull a week of midnights once a month. Let the sheriff put up with these other younger deputies in the bowels of the night, eager to catch someone, bash some heads, be lawmen. But Talley runs for office and gets elected. Talley has all the good ol' boy connections in the county and keeps getting elected. So Talley sleeps when it's dark. Rey Ann goes to the kitchen.

"That's all right," Monroe says, his stomach feels acidy, "just some milk."

She opens the refrigerator. Bending behind the door, she says, "You leave the coffee and doughnuts alone, you'll have some appetite when you get home. I'll make you a couple eggs and toast."

Monroe will not contest her. "Who died?" he asks.

He slouches in the dining room chair. She is busy behind him with sounds of cabinets and drawers.

"I didn't hear about anybody dying. Why? What'd you see?"

"Omohundro. He's up at the Victory Baptist."

"This early already?"

"Yeah."

"Gonna be hot. Maybe he's beating the heat." Monroe hears a skillet slap the stove top. "That man," Rey Ann says, "when he dies he's gonna lay on the ground waiting for a week. Ain't gonna be nobody to dig a hole for him."

Monroe makes no reply. He is tired. His mind succumbs to an image of bodies piling up after the death of Omohundro. His eyes float to the photo of himself in army drab and he recalls that he has seen this, stacks of unburied bodies. He swallows and drums his fingers on the dining room table, it helps moor him in the place and time he is, not the war and thirty years ago. My son, he thinks, shifting his eyes to the picture of Grover. Please Lord let my son never see that.

"How come you didn't hear about somebody dying?" she asks. "You're the law."

"All I hear that time of night is the police radio and my stomach."

Rey Ann is quick with the eggs. She sets a plate in front of him, sunny-side up with two slices of rye toast. It is a simple moment and gesture, she in her canary-yellow robe, her nails painted red, the plate makes a metallic sound on the table, the eggs and bread are bland and usual. But Monroe tastes ashes in his mouth. He recoils as though she has served up something foul on the plate, and in his mind she has. This is the best Deputy Monroe Skelton can provide for himself and his wife: a yellow robe, a grassless lawn, 7:50 A.M., and indigestion.

He says, "I'm going to bed."


2


Monroe drives his white Pamunkey County cruiser to work. It is 8:32 P.M. Already a chin of moon juts from a violet sky.

For ten minutes he drives and measures how much land and water he sees and crosses. Hundreds of square miles. He imagines himself a king or owner of all this ground and tar whizzing past his bent elbow in the open car window. What would it be like to preside over all this? Monroe knows he could drive around these back roads for another hour, even get on the interstate for a piece, and never leave the domain of Sheriff Talley.

George Talley, he thinks. Son of a bitch is a winner.

Some of the twelve thousand residents of Pamunkey County have other names for Talley. They will tell you he is a bully, and he is, but then no one ever calls a loser a bully. They will say he is a shameless self-promoter and a trafficker in favors, and he is, because in a democracy those who seek shortcuts, who are easily impressed or cowed, they have votes too. You will hear he is tough on crime but fair, and he is, scrupulously so, for being on the side of the law is the root of his power. He is a devout Catholic and devoted member of St. Bede's Catholic Church on Main Street. This affiliation works to his political advantage; Good Hope and Pamunkey County, in the manner of many other American localities founded around manufacturing plants, is substantially Irish Catholic. So George Talley maintains his infrastructure even on Sundays. Monroe has seen him build bridges to the African-American community. Talley has hired several black deputies, three of whom, including Monroe, are still with the department. But Monroe thinks the efforts are insincere, just political beachheads. When a black is in trouble in Pamunkey County the sheriff often shakes his head and says things like, "What are we gonna do?" or tells Monroe or one of the other black deputies to "talk to him. He's one of yours." The man is exactly what his name says he is: a tally. He is that figure at the bottom line when all is added up and subtracted. When you are finished doing whatever it is you do in Pamunkey County, there is always George Talley.

At Pamunkey High School he was a sports star, football, basketball, and baseball, captain of all three teams. He was an altar boy at St. Bede's. A rumor spread about Talley that he'd slept with his history teacher, earning him for a time the nickname "Talleywacker." After graduation he spent three seasons in the St. Louis Cardinals' minor-league system as a right fielder until he took a swing at a hitting coach who'd been riding him too hard. The story went that the swing missed and the hitting coach spat, "No surprise, boy. My head must've been a curve ball." Talley was waived. He came back to Good Hope, a handsome hero with a hard luck tale. The mill workers understood a man taking a poke at a nettlesome supervisor. At age twenty-three Talley joined the sheriff's department as a deputy under Sam Ralston, a man who'd been sheriff quietly for ten years, serving with neither great distinction nor scandal. During his tenure Ralston put in place county initiatives to deter drunk driving, increase seat belt use, and delivered a series of law-enforcement lectures at the high school. Two years after joining the department Talley ran against Ralston and beat him. Quietly, Ralston left the county. The day Talley was named sheriff, Monroe was thirty-five years old and had been a deputy for six years, after eight years spent in the army, including two tours in Vietnam. Rey Ann wanted to hand Monroe his head when Talley won the election. "You're respected," she told him, "you're liked. Why didn't you run too?" Monroe had answered, "George Talley's known. Respected don't beat known."

That was a big year for George Talley. He was elected sheriff, got married to a local Catholic girl, and had a daughter. Six years later the wife divorced him, moved to Maryland, and remarried. The daughter spends summers in Good Hope with her father, not because she loves him but because she dislikes her stepfather so much, and Talley, with his official duties, does not have much time for her so she gets left alone a lot. This suits her. This is all common knowledge in Good Hope.

The girl, Amanda, is seventeen. Monroe sees her at the office once in a while or around town walking by herself. He thinks she is pretty, with George's angular face, lean body, and thick brown hair. But she is moony and self-absorbed, a little mousy. She lacks her father's flame. Monroe will give him that, the man comes right at you. Monroe keeps a picture of his own child, the drill sergeant, on his desk. Talley never inquires about Monroe's boy.

In eighteen years as sheriff, Talley has continued Ralston's programs. He's brought in computers, got the county signed up for some federal grant money, and improved regional cooperation with the surrounding three counties. He has exploited every bit of publicity there is in a rural county. He has kept himself slim and good-looking. At forty-two years old, Talley still has the arms of the young athlete, arms that swing and hurry at his sides like two powerful dogs keeping up with their master. Juxtaposed beside his black cartridge belt and brown pistol grip, pressed khaki uniform pants and brass key fob, his forearms boast sturdy spreading veins, bolts of blue lightning. A handshake with George Talley is a better memento than a bumper sticker.

Sundown cools the breeze in Monroe's open car window. Even so the air is thick as a horse's breath. He drives past the Victory Baptist and there again is Omohundro, again dodging the high midday heat. His shovel, always with him like the staff of a magician, tamps down bare dirt over the same grave Monroe saw him hollowing that morning. The gravedigger is filling in a grave. Odd, Monroe thinks, to be doing that with no one else around, no ceremony, this time of the evening.

In town, Monroe parks in the deputies' lot between the old brick courthouse and the sheriff's office. He pushes open the glass door and heads for his desk through the cuddle of air conditioning. Before he can settle in his chair, George Talley shouts from the hall, "Hey, the Money Man is in the house!" This is one of the ways Talley controls you. He hands out these little moments, so cheap and plentiful, like campaign buttons. And when you turn and nod, say, "Hey, George," you pin the button to your shirt.

Twenty minutes later Monroe is alone in the office. Deputy Benson has walked back to the holding cells, probably to talk baseball with the old fellow waiting for court in the morning for stealing at knife-point a six-pack of beer and a carton of cigarettes. The man was brought in ten minutes ago from the regional jail in Rappahannock County wearing an Atlanta Braves hat.

Monroe answers his phone.

"Sheriff's department. Deputy Skelton."

It's a young woman, Clare Waddell. Monroe knows her grandmother, Mrs. Epps. He has seen Clare around town, tall girl, long blond hair. It's dark out and she does not know where her husband Elijah is. Not since this morning, she says. Not since the burial. She sounds concerned.

"Was that burial for your family," Monroe asks, "this morning real early at the Victory Baptist?"

He hears her control tears. She draws in a jerky breath. She tells him that her daughter was buried at the Victory Baptist, not this morning but yesterday. This morning that was them digging her up. And tonight, that was Omohundro finishing the job, tamping the grave dirt down.

"Her name was Nora Carol," she says. "She's half black. My husband Elijah's black." Monroe replies, "Yes, ma'am." He's seen Elijah but does not know much about him, the man keeps mostly to himself.

She says, "That was enough for them to dig her up." Monroe senses how hard she fights to speak. Her voice catches like silk on thorns.

He says, "Yes, ma'am. I understand. Try and compose yourself and tell me what happened."

Clare works for a grip. Monroe waits for it to take hold. Digging up a black child out of their damn cemetery, he thinks. I'll be damned, these people. He picks up a pen and slides over a legal pad. He says, "All right, ma'am."

She tells him how her baby, Nora Carol, was born like she was, deformed, she says. Died in the hospital while she was holding her, ten minutes was all. "I'm very sorry to hear that, ma'am," Monroe says. How her grandmother Mrs. Rosalind Epps wanted the baby buried near her own husband and daughter at the Victory Baptist Church. "That was yesterday," Monroe says. He does this to keep Clare Waddell moving through the story. She will break down and weep if he lets her go too long without his voice to remind her she is not only thinking and feeling but speaking to someone. And last night, she says, they voted to dig Nora Carol up and make her and her husband bury the baby somewhere else this morning. Over to the black Zebulon Baptist Church. That wasn't right.

"No, ma'am. It doesn't seem so." Monroe pauses. He asks, "So this morning over at the Zebulon Church was when you last saw your husband?"

Yes, Clare says. You know the Victory Baptist folk didn't even clean the pine casket off when they called her and Elijah to come get it. It was still dirty with clay. Elijah was going to take off his own shirt and wipe it down but the preacher Thomas Derby went into the church and took a cloth from the altar and wrapped the little box in it so it was nice and white. Clare and Elijah carried Nora Carol to the Zebulon Baptist in their pickup truck around ten this morning. Pastor Derby followed in his car. Gran Epps wasn't there at all.

"How did your husband react? I guess he was pretty upset. I suppose you both are."

Yes, she says. They are upset.

Monroe hears anger infuse her tone. Along with the notes he scribbles on the pad, he makes a mental memo of this turn in her.

Some man name of Mr. Snead called this morning around eight-thirty. Told her the church had voted. Mr. Snead was sorry but Mrs. Epps and Pastor Derby had no authority to do what they did. The deacons have to vote on everybody who gets buried at the Victory Baptist. It's always been that way. Over two hundred years, he said, like that was the thing which let it all make sense. Snead had already called the preacher at the Zebulon Baptist for her and Elijah and made the arrangements, if that was all right.

"Fuckers," she says. "Sorry."

"That's okay."

Elijah didn't say maybe ten words all morning. Pastor Derby was real kind, stayed right with them all the way until Nora Carol was resting at the Zebulon Baptist. The black preacher there was a kind man, but he wanted to make a point with his prayer next to Nora Carol's grave, talking about prejudice and uncharity. Right while the preacher was speaking Elijah grabbed the shovel from the old grave-digger and started filling in the hole. Elijah gets this look, Clare says, and it's not at her or the machines at the mill or Nora Carol's grave or whatever's in front of him in the world. He has this place where he goes inside him, where it's all calm and smooth. Like a lake. When he's like that, when he's in there, he can do anything.

Monroe writes this down. "What do you mean, anything?"

She stops. Monroe supposes she hadn't intended to reveal this about her husband.

"Clare, tell me what you mean."

She's worried. That's all. Just worried. She hasn't seen him all day, not since after the Zebulon Church. He drove her home and walked off into the cornfield. He didn't go to the mill. Nobody's seen him.

Monroe says, "What was he wearing? Give me a description."

When she has done that, Monroe says, "He's probably just out walking off some steam. We'll find him for you. We'll bring him home. Don't worry."

"Deputy," she says, her anger dissipated. "I'm more than worried."

"Yes, ma'am."

"I'm angry."

"Yes, ma'am."

"And I'm scared."

### 3

Monroe drives at a crawl down Main Street. His headlights shove into the night. He thinks of those TV documentaries where explorers descend in tiny subs far under the ocean to shine their lights on huge wrecks. The walls and windows of Main Street's storefronts are dark and mute as dead, coral-encrusted bulwarks. The air is matted with humidity. The car's engine purrs smooth as a propeller. Tree branches overhead make his drive down Main Street a slow-motion tunnel, recalling the interior of a giant ship in a graveyard at an impossible depth.

It's quiet. It's always quiet, Monroe thinks, right up until it's not. Five thousand people live in the town, just twelve thousand spread over the whole county. That ought to be room for everyone, space enough to breathe and stretch out. Enough for one grieving and hurt man to wander around until he gets himself under control again. But there's only one way for people to live with each other and that is with trouble. Mayhem is the by-product of civilization, just like the rotten smell from the mill. It's the effluent of good intentions, loyalties, contracts, desires, and love. In Good Hope and Pamunkey, a small town and its rural county, like anywhere else, it's not quiet or safe for long. In the big fine houses and the workers' humble abodes, in the fields, by the river, and along the railroad tracks, Monroe has seen the bloody spillage of man's attempts to live among men, the beatings, thefts, murders, passion crimes, cold crimes, drunk crimes. He saw them in the army. He saw them in Southeast Asia. The quietest of us, the simplest of us, he thinks, is a keg. A fuse burns inside everyone. What is different in each man and woman is only the length of the fuse.

It is one-thirty in the morning. There has been no word or sign of Elijah Waddell. His wife calls the dispatcher every hour or so. Here is a woman who just lost her baby, she cradled it alive for only ten minutes. She buried the infant yesterday, only to have it gouged out of the ground this morning as though the child were nothing more than a tree stump. Humiliating. She says her husband loves her, says he's a good man, no problems there. Never been in trouble before. Monroe checked that out; no record of arrests. But this good man left her alone on this terrible day. Why? Sixteen hours now, with no contact. Monroe senses Elijah Waddell, lurking like some wounded animal, dangerous. She's right. He could do anything. Because what pain could he feel worse than what he feels right now?

If that was me? Monroe wonders. If that was my mixed-race child they scooped up out of their two-hundred-year-old white cemetery? What would I be feeling? Pissed. Very pissed. Monroe spits out the window onto Main Street. These damn people.

He reaches the end of Main Street's business sector. Some porch lights are on, plastic tricycles decorate a few front sidewalks. Two blocks from downtown the houses turn large and Victorian, the tree trunks fatten. Set back on a deep lawn, at the end of a boxwood-lined flagstone walk, is the gray stone St. Bede's Catholic Church. It is a keep, Gothic and foreboding. It only looks right on rainy days. This is where the plant managers and George Talley come to worship. The building is lit with floodlights; the town sleeps, while God and Monroe and Elijah Waddell are wide awake.

These are Monroe's thoughts when the night crackles. His radio screeches in the same moment he hears sirens on the edge of town. A fire, the dispatcher says. Big one out at the Victory Baptist Church. Get out there, Money.

## 4

Monroe can speed along the bends of Route 101 better than the fire trucks, he's ahead of them. Still a mile from the blaze, he sees the flicker behind the fields, above the trees. The dark fights hard against the flames, containing the reaching light to an amber bowl. The rest is black and starry and uncaring. The dark does not surrender easily out here in the country.

He skids to a stop in the church's lot. Victory Baptist is lost, he knows this instantly. The rear of the church is swarmed with flame, the roof is fallen at the back and is on fire across the spine. The wooden ribs of the walls are exposed as far forward as the portico, the centuries-old clapboards are already eaten, the pine beams underneath—thick as men—turn to etched charcoal. Four of the five stained-glass windows on the side facing Monroe have blown out. He looks up at the white spire and copper cross. They are as yet untouched, as if they fled forward from the flames and climbed high as they could to shout for rescue.

Monroe gets out of the cruiser. A blacksmith's blast of heat swipes him. His eyes feel dried by the gust, and he sees the thing he'd hoped most not to see at the Victory Baptist. He sees Elijah.

The man takes long, athletic strides along the side of the burning church. One arm is bent, his fist is up, pumping. Elijah is shirtless, glimmering with sweat from the heat, from the exertion of exulting. He sees Monroe approaching and stops.

Monroe walks nearer to the roar and heat. He feels singed this close, but Elijah stands in it without seeming to notice. The man is muscled like chiseled stone, dripping as though the Maker is still carving him.

Elijah drops his hand. Once it is at his side, he wobbles a bit.

Monroe sees how tired this man is. There is no expression or thought on Elijah's face. Sweat trickles from his chin and nose.

Monroe keeps his own face tilted away from the flames to keep the heat out of his eyes. He shouts, "Elijah Waddell?"

Elijah nods.

Monroe wants to move away from the fire to talk, but first he has to stand this hot ground with the man, no backing down. "You know your wife's been looking for you all day, son?"

Elijah nods again. His eyes are watery and red, while Monroe feels his cooking.

"You been drinking?"

Elijah returns his gaze to the racing flames. With his thumb and index finger he makes a "just a little" sign.

Monroe is going to arrest him. He's seen enough.

"Elijah, can we step over here for a moment, please?"

Monroe backs several paces out of the reach of the heat. Elijah does not react.

"Son?" Monroe unbuckles the leather safety strap over his sidearm.

Elijah stands rooted, staring into the flames. Monroe asks him again, "Son?"

Elijah does not move. Slowly Monroe reaches to the handcuff sheath at the back of his belt. Without jangling the cuffs, he eases up to Elijah, who stands frozen in the clutch of this furnace blazing only a dozen yards away. Monroe lifts one of the man's drenched hands and takes a solid grip, in case Elijah should awake from his fiery reverie and bolt.

"I'm gonna have to arrest you." Monroe cannot tell if Elijah even hears him.

He moves behind Elijah to shift the man's right hand for the cuffs. He snaps the metal link around the wrist rinsed in sweat. Elijah, with his hands chained now behind his back, turns his head to Monroe. The face is a miracle of stillness in the crunching of scored timbers, the boiling of air, sparks trying to become stars, and the sirens' howl of the fire department's arrival. Elijah's wet face and chest flash hot red bathed in the arching flames and the strobing beacons of the trucks. Monroe thinks Hell has marked this poor man.

Elijah's lips part. "Why?"

Even in the withering heat from the dying church, the word is wrapped in the reek of beer.

"For burning this church. That's arson."

Monroe wraps one fist around the chain connecting the handcuffs where he can control Elijah best if he struggles. With the other hand he turns Elijah by the arm away from the fire to walk to the parking lot and the cruiser. Under his grip, Monroe feels Elijah's arm tense, the muscles firm up like water running through a hose. Elijah is alert now.

He says, "I didn't do this."

Monroe tightens his hands on Elijah. He begins the Miranda warning. "You have the right to remain silent . . ." Elijah says again he didn't do it. Monroe completes the Miranda. Elijah walks with him to the car without resistance, listening, licking his lips. The heat fades on Monroe's neck. Yelling firemen rush past them toward the church, unfurling hoses. Monroe hears one of the firefighters say to no one, "Shit, forget it."

Monroe opens the rear door of the cruiser. He lowers Elijah's head to help him into the backseat and slams the door. Monroe climbs in the driver's seat. He calls the county dispatcher to advise her he has made an arrest at the Victory Baptist Church. He will be proceeding to the regional jail with the suspect in custody.

The regional lockup is twenty minutes away. It is a forty-cell facility shared by three adjoining counties, centrally located in Rappahannock County. Monroe pulls out of the Victory Baptist lot. The stink of embers and fire lingers in the car, rising from Monroe's uniform and Elijah's body. Monroe glances in the rearview mirror at the man behind the wire mesh that cages the backseat. He sees Elijah, dimly lit by the dashboard, has lowered his head. The head wags back and forth, Elijah is saying to himself, No, no, no, no. In twenty-four years of arresting people, it never fails to dismay Monroe to see in his mirror a human being inside that cage. They look like animals, always, either fractious and barking, afraid, or beaten down like this one.

Monroe gently says, "You don't have to talk to me. You can wait for a lawyer. You understand?"

"Yeah."

"But I'm gonna ask you. All right?"

"I don't care."

"Is it all right, son?"

"Yeah. What."

"You telling me you didn't do this?"

Without lifting his head, Elijah replies, "I didn't."

"Then what were you doing there if you didn't do nothing?"

"I was just there."

"Just there," Monroe repeats. "You should've been with your wife. She needs you."

Elijah makes no response. This time of the morning there are no other cars on the road. Monroe drives quickly. In the mirror he sees Elijah, with his hands cuffed behind him, rocking when the car takes a curve. Monroe slows down.

"How much you had to drink?"

"I don't know."

He says, "Clare told me what happened. I'm sorry about your baby."

Monroe watches Elijah close down. The shirtless man draws in a shaky breath, clenches his lips, and shuts his eyes tight. Inside this tight casing, Elijah cries. Monroe thinks of a house where the family slams the shutters, locks the doors, and does its best to keep its tumult private.

Monroe levels his eyes to the road while Elijah wrestles his grief. The cruiser moves onto a flat stretch of road. It is wide and treeless here, with hundred-acre fields on either side. The sky looms vast, full of summer bugs and moisture and pricks of light. Monroe's headlights shed little of the night speeding through it.

He's seen too many young black men's lives destroyed this way, by their own hands. He wonders, What's missing? He is sure it is discipline, the old ways, the ways of the fathers. But he knows also this may just be the Army Ranger in him, the habits and training, unable to let go of lessons long and hard learned, the lure of having a duty, the quest for loyalty to self and a purpose. He thinks of the wooden church, covered by now in useless steamy water. Monroe looks in the mirror and thinks how both of them, Elijah and the church, are tonight in needless ruins.

"Elijah. Talk to me."

The man lifts his head. He draws a few breaths to compose himself. His rheumy eyes gleam. He scrunches them to squeeze out the last of the tears.

"What were you doing there if you didn't burn it?"

Elijah does not hang his head again but holds it up. He finds Monroe's eyes in the rearview mirror.

"Watching."

"Just watching?"

"Yeah."

"Watching what?"

"To see if I would burn it."

Monroe mumbles, "Uh-huh." In the mirror he can tell Elijah is not being a smart-ass. There is no smirk or challenge with the comment. Elijah looks drained.

Monroe asks, "Did you?"

"No."

"You know who did?"

"No. But I saw him."

Now it is Monroe who smirks. "You saw him."

"Yeah."

"You saw the guy who burned the church."

"Yeah."

Monroe will bite. "All right, tell me. What'd he look like?"

"Hard to tell. It was dark and all."

"Figures," Monroe says. "Where were you when you saw him?"

"Across the street in the trees. Sitting on the ground drinking. He wouldn't of seen me."

"No. I reckon not."

"I could tell he had on a baseball cap and a . . . a bandanna or something around his mouth. He wore a long-sleeved shirt."

"What color?"

"I don't know. A dark shirt."

Monroe lets a mile of road whisk by without speaking. Then he says, "Some guy in a cap and a dark shirt comes out of nowhere and burns a white Baptist church. Not you."

"Not me."

"Uh-huh. But you were mad enough to do it."

In the mirror, Elijah nods slowly.

"Ever seen him before? Was he white or black?"

"I told you I don't know. Might have been wearing gloves, I don't know. He was all covered up. I didn't get much of a look."

"Tall or short?"

"I don't know . . . neither. Maybe my height."

Monroe knows he is listening to lies: made-up bullshit. Let Waddell tell it to his lawyer. The regional jail is five minutes away.

Elijah is not done. "He came out of the dark. Went behind the church. I don't think nothing of it. Couple of minutes later flames are shooting out and he takes off. I only see what he's wearing for a second, you know, when he's running under the light. He took off east through the graveyard. I was just sitting there."

"Yeah, you said."

"What'd you want me to do?"

Monroe doesn't want to hear any more. He is tired too. The heat from the fire has left him feeling dusty and itchy. Even so, because he is growing irritated, he replies with a sarcastic edge.

"You tell me. What did you do?"

Elijah makes no sound for several moments, until he emits a slurred chuckle.

"I thanked God Almighty is what I did. That place needed burning."

Without thinking, Monroe lets escape a rueful sigh. His sympathy for the young man in trouble in the backseat has leached out of him with the inebriated, evasive tale he's just been told and that little chortle. Monroe feels waste, loss. He says, "Okay. Shut up."

A black man has burned a white church in Pamunkey County, he thinks. George Talley gets elected again.

# Nat Deeds

# ONE

He thought he was finished with that town.

His phone rings. It's Judge Baron of the Pamunkey County General District Court.

"Morning, Nat."

"Judge, how are you?"

"I'm fine, fine. How's things working out for you up in Richmond?"

"They're good."

"I hear you're doing wills and trusts. You're a criminal trial lawyer, Nat. You don't mind my asking, what the hell are you doing with yourself doing wills and trusts?"

"Taking a break, judge. Just getting my head on straight."

"Uh-huh," the judge says, and waits. Judge Baron has a way of saying "uh-huh" that sounds like "ah-hah." Like he's caught you at something.

Nat fills in. "Judge, I'm guessing you didn't call me to ask how I am."

"I'm interested." Nat thinks he is not.

He asks, "What can I do for you?"

"Is your head on straight yet?"

Judge Baron does not mince words. Nat Deeds practiced in front of him as an assistant commonwealth's attorney in Pamunkey County for eight years. This is as much small talk as Nat has ever heard from the old man. The two of them never drank beers and they never broke bread.

The judge says, "I'm going to need it straight."

"It's straight enough for wills and trusts."

"That your way of saying no before I ask?"

Nat speaks plainly because that is the method you fall into with Judge Baron. That is how the judge drills right at the truth.

"Yes, sir. It is."

"Well, that's a shame, because I'm assigning you a case."

"Judge, I'm not on the court-appointed list. I've been out of Good Hope for eight months. I live in Richmond."

"You're still a legal resident of Pamunkey County until you've lived elsewhere for a year."

"Judge, that's not so."

"I got some case law on point, Nat. It's old and you could beat it if you tried. But that's the way I'm ruling. I put you back on the list. Now hear me out. I put up with you for eight years down here in the sticks. Don't go big-city attorney on me so fast. You owe me this much."

Nat lowers the phone from his ear. He looks around his little office. It's a mess. File drawers open. Papers on the floor. He does not yet have a secretary. He is trying to build a quiet civil practice here in Richmond, fifty miles from Good Hope. When he left the county he wanted also to leave behind crime scenes, scumbags, country cops, well-meaning juries, even the notions of innocence and guilt. But these last two, he thinks, innocence and guilt, oh, they are stalkers. They follow you into your sleep, they whisper their way into every memory.

"Go ahead, judge."

"Thank you. I got a fella down here, Elijah Waddell, accused of burning the Victory Baptist out on 101. He needs a court-appointed lawyer." The judge pauses for effect. "He's black, Nat. This is a black man accused of burning a white church."

Judge Baron reads a memo, sent to the Pamunkey prosecutor's office that morning from the sheriff's office. The U.S. Treasury and Justice Department have joined up to form a National Church Arson Task Force. They've compiled the numbers on church burnings over the last seven years. There's been an annual average nationwide of about three hundred suspicious fires on church properties. Of that total, forty-five percent have been black churches, a number disproportionately high to the black population in America. Thirty-three percent of those arrested for burning black churches are black. But for those accused of burning white churches, like the Victory Baptist, the numbers say ninety-five percent are white.

"And out of those five percent of blacks who burn white churches," the judge says, "I doubt very many of them were arrested standing right there next to the fire at two in the morning cheering the flames on. So."

Elijah Waddell's arrest, the judge correctly concludes, is news.

"Judge, I still don't see why you need me."

"Hang on a minute, there's more. Seems this man and his wife gave birth to a baby this week that died just after delivery. The child was buried at the Victory Baptist two days ago. The baby's mother was Rosy Epps's great-granddaughter."

Nat knows Mrs. Epps. The woman probably taught half the county in grade school, including him. He has memories of her, young and pretty, and as an elder widow, stately always. She's had bad luck in her family, over the years a lot of untimely deaths. Now this.

The judge says, "Rosy's granddaughter, Clare, married Elijah Waddell. Their baby was mixed race."

"What happened, judge?"

"Yesterday morning, twenty-four hours after laying the child to rest, the church deacons had her exhumed from their graveyard."

So, that's it, Nat thinks. The burning of Victory Baptist is more than news. It's vengeance, black and white.

"Look, if this case gets drawn out at all, you can see how I can't have some local defense attorney shopping at the grocery store, catching lunch at Redd's, and walking around town. These people'll wear him down to the nubs. This has got racial overtones all over it and dammit, I want to provide these people here as few reminders to get upset as I can give them. Also I want this poor bastard Waddell to get fair representation without a lot of pressure being brought on his lawyer. There's gonna be enough pressure around here as it is until the dust settles. You with me on this?"

"Judge, you know there's reasons I don't want to come back down there."

"Yes I do, yes I do. And I hesitated all of thirty seconds before calling you. But this is bigger than anybody's reasons, Nat. This is about a fair trial for a man. This is about keeping the lid on your hometown. And I've seen you work for eight years. You know criminal law and you know this county. This boy's not gonna get a better lawyer than you. And I need good lawyers on both sides of this case to help me keep the lid on. So do this for me."

"Who's prosecuting?"

"Fentress is doing this one himself." Nat visualizes his old boss, Ed Fentress, commonwealth's attorney, the best-dressed man in Pamunkey County. Ed wants to be a state senator someday soon. Jogs so he can wave, a one-man parade.

"You set bail yet?"

"This morning. Fifty thousand dollars."

"Does Waddell have any priors?"

"Nope. Squeaky clean. Married. Mechanic at the mill. Lived here about five years, up from Norfolk."

"Why so high? He doesn't sound like a flight risk."

"To be honest, it's either fifty thousand on Waddell for arson or a half-million on someone else for blowing his head off. See my point?"

"Yes, sir."

"All right. He's at the Rappahannock lockup. Go see your client, counselor. We're gonna do this today, I don't want it going over the weekend. Since you just heard about it I'll give you to the end of the day. Initial appearance in my court at four o'clock sharp. You and

Fentress can work out the date for the prelim hearing. But I'll want it done fast."

"Judge—"

"Nat. I don't want to hear it. Objection overruled."

Nat breathes into the phone.

The judge says, "Stop thinking just about yourself, Mr. Deeds."

The judge hangs up.

## 2

Early Friday afternoon, driving west over the Mattaponi River, Nat is snared in a line of cars heading to the weekend river houses. He thinks of Christmas.

There is nothing of Christmas about Good Hope right now. Heat waves shimmy above the water and wetlands. Trees beside the road have scrolled their leaves, parched from an August drought. The egg smell is not sweet like nog.

It was Christmas, eight months ago, when Nat last crossed this bridge, headed the other direction, out of town. Coming back to Good Hope, his chest has tightened over the past few highway miles. When he is across the bridge and idling at the first stoplight, waiting while a massive lumber truck inches backward into the mill's wood yard, he grows dizzy, besieged by something swirling, as though he'd held his breath too long. The light turns green but the big truck is still in the way. Nat hits his horn. When he can at last move through the light, the action of driving and the clot of weekend traffic and brake lights around him shoo away the cobwebs. He looks at the town and recalls the last time he saw it, under the big snow that stayed for Christmas week, when Good Hope was soft. In that week Nat quit the commonwealth's attorney's office, turning his caseload over to Fentress. He moved out of his house to stay with friends. He walked the river on Christmas morning, making snowballs and throwing them into the green current. When the snow on the town turned grimy, when the tires wept to drive through brown slush and the sun again showed Good Hope to Nat with clarity, he left for Richmond. He left his wife.

He does not feel at all triumphant or independent on his return. Driving through town, there is a sensation of sneaking. He is an exile. Nothing has changed about the place—though he expected no changes—and that gives him a puncture of disappointment, for so much in his life has changed and this diverges him from the town. Passing the great mill, the Little League field, streets whose names he knows in order and what other streets carve out of them, he cannot come up with a single pleasant memory. He bites his lip, realizing this tainted feeling for his hometown is unfair, but like a cheap string of Christmas lights, wired in sequence, once one bulb winks out every light behind it goes dark.

3

In his head it's last Christmas again. He's got the house warm. Outside it smells like impending snow, that wet and metallic tang present in southern winters that foretells precipitation. The morning smells like spray starch on cold linen. It's an aroma from Nat's deeper past, of the maids who worked for his mother when he was young here and his family lived just two blocks from the big wood-frame house he and Maeve own now on Main Street. He has scraped the creosote off the glass door of the woodstove so she can see the logs flaring when she comes in from her midnight shift in the Pamunkey General ER. It's a twenty-minute bus ride, her shift ends at seven A.M., so he runs the vacuum and straightens Christmas decorations on the mantel for another ten minutes before she will walk in.

In his head he calls this "pitching in." It is his participation in the home. Do some weekend chores, cook a meal or two a month, plant some tomatoes in the spring, enough to kid himself that Maeve considers him helpful and handy, the man around the house. But he knows Maeve tends the tomatoes and cooks most of the meals, she cleans the house and nurses forty hours a week. Nat Deeds understands evidence, the finding of truth, and judgment. This is his training and inclination. Maeve understands wounds and healing.

His hours as an assistant commonwealth's attorney for Pamunkey County are long. He believes his job is noble, that his services and skills are needed to keep the county and town safe. Nat is aware of sacrifice. He is a crime fighter, she a nurse; he thinks of them as an heroic couple. They live in the small town of his birth and that preserves something wonderful and American. He knows the price he pays and guesses at Maeve's: She is home alone some, she cooks and scrubs and nurses gunshot and stab wounds and broken legs and heart attacks, she lives beside him in this house near the street where his parents raised him, and he pitches in.

He stows the vacuum and stands at the cold storm door, expecting Maeve, expecting snow. Across town at the mill the steam plume from the big boiler slumps around the chimney in a white skirt; there is no wind over the mill, the air is sopping today. It is chilly enough for snow. It is Saturday. Nat thinks of the men of the mill who will go hunting today, and fishing on warmer Saturdays a few months hence, perhaps play softball and work on their cars in summer, go camping in fall. He admires that trait of men to have hobbies and collections, interests in sports teams, favorite golf courses. He has none of these, nothing beyond reading and occasional jogs. These seem pastimes, not real pursuits. Nat works. But he and Maeve will be together all day today. Nat wants to snuggle by the fire. Go shopping. He feels pent up and a little melancholy today as it nears Christmas.

She's ten minutes late. Her bus stops at the curb and she comes up the sidewalk in white shoes, baggy blue scrub pants under her winter coat. Her breath hangs about her face in a veil, there is no wind in their yard. Her hands jam in her pockets, she carries nothing. She is black Irish; cream skin, dark brow and mane—her jet hair is tied back in the nurse's bun—lips and cheeks that grow red with the oak leaves when the weather cools. This morning coming onto the porch she looks pale and worn. It must have been a long night at the emergency room. Nat will put her to bed and keep the house warm and quiet for her. Later, if she likes, he will say he is sorry for something, whatever she wants to bring up. Nat feels some unnamed need to give her gifts. Penance is a good gift, he thinks.

He holds the storm door open for her, remembering she is beauti-ful. Strange it should feel like that, he thinks, but it does feel like re-membering. Perhaps it's seeing her on a Saturday morning after spending the night at home without her, seeing her right now as he does only infrequently, from the viewpoint of someone waiting for her. This morning he is not already gone off to work or rushing past her to do so.

He asks, "How was it?"

She walks inside. She unbuttons her heavy coat but does not take it off, sliding her hands back into the pockets. She sits like that on the living room sofa and looks up at him.

"Nat."

"Maeve." He closes the front door. The light in the house is cut in half, there's so little coming in from outdoors through the low clouds. He turns on a lamp and sits near her on the sofa. She does not turn her body to him at all. She does not release the coat from around her-self, like she is holding closed some hole in her gut.

"Maeve, everything all right?"

She scoots away from him on the cushions. With a deep breath his wife pivots to face him.

"Nat."

"Sweetheart." This is said carefully, as though trying to coax her in from a ledge.

She says, "You know how I am about cold water."

"Y . . . yes." He is still careful.

"I hate it. So you know what I do when I want to get in and the water's really cold."

"You jump . . ."

Maeve is tense, she plows through him. "I jump in, yes. So, Nat." She takes a breath and plunges.

"I slept with someone."

In that instant he feels immobile; these few words are dumped over him like Maeve's freezing water and Nat cannot move. A crackle in the woodstove reaches his ears, which makes him mad, he shoves it away, that he should hear such a little nothing sound after what she's just said. It is his mind trying to flee out the back door, not attend, not believe. He yokes all his attention back on Maeve. Still he cannot move and does not want to. To move would be to begin the next second. She stares at him, waiting. He can come up with nothing to describe how this feels except—and it is silly, almost comic to think, but—like the desert in Nevada where they test nuclear weapons underground, an explosion, completely contained. The bedrock shock of the blast devastates his heart, it rumbles up to quake his breath, and his face, which melts. He senses everything fall, his eyes tumble from hers, his mouth opens, his head bends.

"Nat," she quietly says, "it's . . ."

"I know what it is," but he does not know. He cannot understand this any more than a jackrabbit in that desert near ground zero could understand.

There's more than just an event, an action, at work here, there are concepts, huge ones. He is not prepared for them, he hadn't thought this out in advance. He never saw this coming. He knew he was guilty of some unspecified charges the last few months, perhaps working too many hours, not participating enough in Christmas this year, maybe even inattention to romance. He was in the dog house over something but let it go, figuring they'd take care of it sooner or later, they've been married for eight years, they've always taken care of it. But this punishment? This? He is lost, overwhelmed, startled, to find his wife has slept with someone else. Staring stupidly at Maeve he does that trick of the dying, the flashing of life before your eyes. He was married, had a home and a career and a shared future; in a dresser drawer there were several photo albums of eight years of life together. He had pictures in his head never taken with any camera but shot anyway and committed to memory, of her with her legs spread, her mouth open, the married couple heaving and laughing. Right now, the only thing he can be sure that he has is words for her, and words, without being thought out, will be useless and probably regretted later. He cannot speak from his unvetted emotions, she would hear him pronounce nothing but the roar of the blast.

Standing, feeling the nuclear explosion in his legs—this image continues to distract him but it gives him a form, some template, and he badly needs something to follow—he is a mushroom cloud, rising.

Maeve looks victimized by his reaction. This makes Nat, who considers himself to be the actual victim, even grimmer.

"Nat, it's over with him. I broke it off. It was only one time."

Suddenly the nuclear bomb metaphor dissipates. He pulls together the flying fragments of himself and he is Nathaniel Deeds, lawyer, prosecutor. On his feet. His wife plea-bargains: First offense, light sentence, probation. He wants to cross-examine her, ferociously. Who? When? Where? Why, goddammit, why?

She sees his glare and relaxes her grip on her coat. It is an elegiac gesture, it seeks clemency, the coat opens and of course she wears a blue scrub top from the hospital. Nat considers himself a man of precision but at the moment he seems stuck in a groove of images—he supposes he is panicky—so she appears to wear a blue prison outfit. She is guilty, she is sentenced, she is gone.

But she is not gone, he thinks. I, the one standing, am gone. The innocent get to walk away, the guilty have to stay behind, that's the way it works. He turns to leave the living room, intending to go upstairs, pack a bag, and drift somewhere. His office.

"Nat," she says, "please."

Wait for a second, he thinks. Want it all to go away. Want to talk, to inspect the damage and find it survivable. Want to fathom and forgive. But he doesn't know what is programmed inside him to make him this angry, what is this righteousness, or vanity, rushing to his defense in the teeth of his wife's admission, walling him off from forgiving her, thwarting him? Inside Nat a mad dash starts to find a way around the wall before it grows too big, but in a moment it is and there's no path out to her. This makes him hard, confined, bad, worse than her. Some finger points at him now, guilt has switched sides. That is all the confusion he can stand.

He fades from the room without looking back. She says again, "Please."

She gets an answer over his shoulder. He manages only to ask something selfish and unoriginal.

"Why the hell did you have to tell me?"

## 4

The Pamunkey County Courthouse is a three-story Federal brick structure. The facade features two tall white Doric columns on either side of a semicircular arch, set high above the sidewalk atop wide granite steps. In the keystone of the arch is the date of construction, 1855. There is little color to the courthouse. Everything but the white window sashes and black doors is of stone or clay. It is a harsh-looking building, intended by its Christian builders to be—and it remains—a stolid lecture on the immutability of law and community to all who pass by. It resides on a small sward of grass and trees, flanked by two Confederate cannons that unsuccessfully protected the courthouse from the Yankee advance up the Virginia peninsula to Richmond. For six months the building was occupied by Northern troops, becoming a Yankee hospital. Everyone who knows this, which is everyone in Good Hope, sees phantom stretchers and amputees in the hallway each time they enter.

Connected to the courthouse by a covered sidewalk is the sheriff's office. This is a one-story municipal building constructed in the 1960s of that shiny brick that is almost pink. Nat, whose office used to be on the third floor of the courthouse, never liked walking into the sheriff's office. It is too modern, without history; it makes him think of walking to class on a high school campus. But late on this morning Nat hurries under the protection of the green corrugated metal sheeting which covers the sidewalk to the sheriff's office. It's so hot out he imagines his shadow might anneal to the ground.

Pushing open the door, Nat is greeted by almost a blockade of air conditioning. George Talley keeps it cold, a meat locker for his deputies. Talley looks up from a computer screen. His voice rises with his body.

"Son of a bitch! Look who's here. The man himself."

"George." Nat stops; Talley comes at him so fast, if Nat were to keep walking they might pass each other. Talley grips his hand and pumps it. Nat waits for the crunch and it comes. Talley likes to see eyebrows move when he shakes hands.

"Where you been? I hear all kinds of stories about you up in Richmond."

"None of them are true, George. Just trying to get a solo practice going."

Talley lets go of Nat's hand. The fingers actually feel mashed. "What's this I hear about you doing nothing but civil practice?" Talley points out a chair for Nat. "That's a waste of talent and you know it." Nat waves off the offer of the seat. This greeting from the sheriff seems overly boisterous, as though Talley is trying to turn Nat away by welcoming him so hard. Nat figures this is probably just the politician in the man, always working.

"Fentress says you're handling Elijah Waddell."

Nat nods. "Yeah. Baron dragged me into it."

"Good," the sheriff says. His head moves with the word, as though he means it. "Good."

Talley continues in his voice high with enthusiasm and bonhomie. Nat knows the man well, they both grew up in Good Hope. They've been on the same team for a lot of their lives. Talley was the star pitcher and left fielder in Little League, Nat played third base because he was gutty and would stare down any grounder, even the hot ones. In high school Talley was the record-scoring forward on the basketball squad to Nat's backup point guard. Once Talley peed on Nat's leg in the shower, another time he and Bill Coughlin stretched a towel between Nat's naked legs in the locker room and lifted, making Nat beg to be let down. Talley went from Pamunkey High to play pro baseball, while Nat went to college and law school. Talley came home and got elected to make arrests. Nat clerked for two years in D.C., stayed there to work for a big firm, then returned to prosecute Talley's arrests. Nat stretches his fingers and decides in his eight months gone he has not missed George Talley.

Talley's voice climbs down from its peak. It levels out and he drops his volume. "I'm sorry," he says, "about you and Maeve. I didn't hear what went wrong, but . . . I'm sorry."

"It's okay."

"You all right with it?" Talley belts him lightly on the shoulder. "Hell, you look all right."

"I manage."

"Divorce can be pretty tough. I know."

"We're separated, George."

"Right." Talley doesn't take it in, the look on Nat's face to change the subject. "You talking to Maeve at all?"

"Look." Nat hears the curtness in his own tone but can do nothing about it. "I'm here to see Monroe. He was Waddell's arresting officer."

"Yeah. Sure, Nat. Whatever you need." Talley nods quickly, cooperatively, as though he is dealing with a victim of a crash. "Glad to have you back."

I'm not back, Nat thinks. And we'll see if you're glad, George. I'm defending this time.

Talley turns to one of his deputies. "What time's Money coming in?"

"He's on nights 'til tomorrow."

"He's probably out at his house," says Talley to Nat.

"I'll drive out."

"I'll call and tell him you're coming. If he's not home, we'll get him on the beeper and have him meet you there. That okay?" Talley is very agreeable, his hands are up in jocular surrender.

"Thanks, George. I'll see you later."

"See you, now."

Nat pivots from Talley before the sheriff can initiate a goodbye handshake. In his car again Nat moves toward the outskirts. Traffic is pooled on the town's one thoroughfare, it's the end of lunchtime and the paper mill has a shift change. Moving at the slow rate of the river, floating like jetsam, Nat experiences a tidal pull from the town. He feels washed, bobbing on his memory as though his past is the river overrun its banks to course down this street. It washes him into every door, under oaks and elms. He feels this physically, a gush he must swim through, here in Good Hope, his home, which he has abandoned because he found he was not devoted enough to tread water and stay. And steeping everything, everything soaked in her presence here, is Maeve.

Outside town, driving faster under the trees on the country road to Monroe Skelton's house, Nat senses a receding, he has reached some high ground. His mind dries out from the cataract of memory downtown and his old eddies, the courthouse and sheriff's office, the shops and restaurants on Main, the avenues of disconnected friends, who do not know he is in town, and the streets of his parents' old home and his own home where she is or is not right now.

After a while Route 101 takes him past the Victory Baptist. Nat pulls over to look. The church is a sooty wreck. Nothing of it stands except the twin pillars of the portico, both blistered. The sanctuary has fallen to a charred heap and lies beneath the fire-ruptured remains of the roof. The stained-glass windows are melted or in shards, the steeple and cross have fallen forward to rest busted and blackened on grass so seared it resembles an oil spill. Tree branches which once shaded the yard are denuded and brittle, fried and betrayed. Gray trellises of smoke like little geysers rise from embers reluctant to die. From the car Nat sees odd bits of the church that have survived and stick up through the debris; some pews, the mint-colored lead tub of the baptistry, a swath of red carpet. The area is cordoned off by yellow police tape reading DO NOT CROSS. Several cars and pickups have parked along the shoulder. Gawkers gather along the road outside the perimeter. One of Talley's patrol cars sits in the gravel lot, the deputy stands with his arms crossed and face shaded under his firm-brimmed brown trooper's hat. His wide belt slants toward the pistol, a gunslinger pose. Beside him is a white van that has just arrived. The vehicle has Virginia State government tags. Nat watches two men in white short sleeves climb out of the van and start unloading equipment. These, Nat knows, are the arson boys called down from Richmond.

Nat drives on. In ten minutes he pulls up to Monroe Skelton's rancher. Monroe comes out to meet him. Nat thinks of a bear, but the deputy's handshake is gentle.

"What's up, man?" Monroe's face is puffy. He was sleeping when Talley called.

"Money. How've you been?"

"You know, same." Monroe shrugs. "What's gonna change out here? Nothing."

Nat glances up into the branches and the stipple of blue between the leaves. "Yeah," he says. "That's why I used to love it."

The deputy hooks his thumbs in his belt loops. "Yeah. I heard. Sorry, Nat. You left so quick I never got to tell you that."

Nat clears his throat. He says, "Well." He wants to talk about it, to draw support from this man whom he's known and respected, who has a good marriage and a proud son. Nat's head stays tilted to the trees. Maeve's not there, in the trees that do not rustle in the hot morning doldrums. He looks down, signs of her are not in the jots of sunlight on the grass. Where is she? She's here somewhere, she is here more than anywhere else in the world and that's why he told Baron he didn't want to come back. Before she can find him or he grows lost searching for her in the air and earth, Nat hurries ahead to talk business, though it feels like retreat.

He explains he is handling the Waddell arson case as appointed counsel. "Before I head over to Rappahannock to see him, I thought I'd talk with you first and get the skinny."

Monroe deposits his backside on his brick steps. "Shoot."

"What am I getting into?"

Monroe folds his arms in his lap, like two big sticks of wood.

"I'll tell you right now," he says. "Boy did it."

Monroe describes what Clare told him yesterday morning, that her husband had gone missing after the funeral at Zebulon Baptist. That Elijah Waddell was capable of "anything." Then the deputy tells what he saw just twelve hours ago in the early morning. Waddell drunk, pumping his fist at the fire, his statement that he was glad to God the Victory Baptist was burning.

Monroe asks, "You know about the baby?"

"Yeah. I know."

"Motive, opportunity," Monroe says, toting up facts, "arrested at the scene, and no remorse."

"No admission?"

"He's gonna tell you he didn't do it. Says he saw some guy do it. Can't identify him, says the guy was wearing too many clothes, a bandanna and a cap, so he doesn't know. Says he saw the guy just for a second. Claims he was just sitting across the street in the bushes watching."

Nat calculates differently from Monroe, not facts but other, human things. Bitterness, pride, the toppling of any justice. Elijah Waddell's child was rejected by that church, and so too it was rejection of him as a man and for what reason? That he had done something evil to them, that he had broken some law or promise? Omohundro's shovel—Nat knows it was Omohundro, who else but the timeless digger, the spade of death in Good Hope like the bogeyman since Nat was a child?—jabbed into the earth to remove the infant, but it may just as well have split open Elijah's heart, simply because he and his child are black. These people will blame Elijah and not themselves, for now Elijah has fallen from the good like the church steeple burned off its perch. They, the Victory Baptist folks and probably the rest of the town when they hear about it before the day is over, have not exposed themselves as Elijah allegedly has with an overt act. Instead, they'll hide behind their goodness and defend it with a fury as their safe haven. Nat knows the evil was done not by Elijah alone but also by those good people. Elijah's trespass was to strike back beyond the boundaries of society, and for this he will be punished. But his blow was against property. Theirs was an offense against a man and a wife and a pitiful baby. Theirs was the evil of racism, the halving of human beings into separate parts, soul and skin, an evil which—Nat thinks with a deflating sadness—is no longer in the hands of those who openly hate and destroy, where it can be fought openly. No longer. Wickedness has exhausted its efforts to grow among the wicked. Yesterday, in Good Hope, the town of Nat's birth and a town of good people, evil showed that its tendrils have gone underground, into the soil of goodness, where they have found fertility and welcome.

Nat cannot agree with the arson that Elijah is suspected of committing. But he understands that a man can draw a line, that he can react in an absolute manner against what he deems an absolute wrong done him.

"Come in and have a beer," Monroe says. The deputy appears to have noticed the sinking that must be on Nat's face.

"No," Nat says, "thanks. I'd better go see him. How's Rey Ann?"

Monroe jiggles on the steps. "Hmpf. Ornery."

Nat musters a smile for the big deputy who stands to say good-bye.

"This shouldn't take you too much trouble," Monroe says, following Nat to the car. He repeats, "The boy did it. I've seen this shit too many times not to know."

"Money," Nat says getting into the car, "I'm defending this time, not prosecuting."

Monroe closes the car door for him. He laps a big dark hand over the upholstered sill.

"Well, he's got a good man defending him."

Nat drives away. There is a blind spot, some tumor spreading. He wonders, What is a good man?

5

Nat sets his briefcase on the table. The thump echoes in the small interview room. He slides back one of the two metal chairs, the feet screech on the linoleum. The clicks when Nat opens the briefcase, the scrunch of his soles on the floor, he clears his throat; the cinderblock walls chastise every noise, nothing escapes, everything is repelled. The door opens, releasing more sound into the room like shards of glass. A guard's arm puts Elijah into the room, then disappears. Elijah stands near the closed door eyeing Nat. He wears the drab orange prisoner's garb and sneakers. The clothes and shoes he wore when arrested early this morning, Nat knows, have been impounded and taken to the crime lab.

Nat gazes back at the man. For seconds the room hears no sounds to censure. Over eight years Nat grew accustomed to viewing these people with the eyes of a prosecutor. Men and women in clownish orange and often manacles were brought before him first as suspects in file folders, squashed flat onto pages, their alleged violations accompanied by police reports, photos in black-and-white and color, witness statements, crime lab findings. It was never his job to think of them as fleshed-out people with names and stories and excuses but only as provable or unprovable acts. It was Nat's job to present the evidence against these men and women and reflect the county's and the victims' outrage with them through convictions. Whenever defense counsel could convince him they were wanting and deserving of leniency Nat recommended it, when they were co-operative he made deals, and when they were dangerous and unrepentant he bore down on them and always won. Elijah stands uncertainly by the door and he is a new format for Nat, he is Judge Baron's charge to him, to understand this single man in orange and protect him. But like an old bull Nat sees the color. He wrestles the deep-seated urge to view Elijah in one dimension, as a criminal act.

Nat draws out another noisy chair for Elijah. He looks over at the prisoner, who is still hesitant. Nat sits. He speaks. Elijah listens from the doorway. The man's face is dark and stoic, also scared and evasive, like a squirrel that circles a tree trunk to keep on the far side of you.

"My name is Nat Deeds. I've been appointed by the court to be your lawyer."

Elijah, without speaking, moves to the chair and sits. He does not slide his chair forward, as though the less sound in the room for him the better.

"I heard about your daughter. I'm sorry."

"Everybody's sorry," mutters Elijah. "I'm sorry."

Nat says nothing to this rebuff. He is still shuffling his gut for the instincts to defend this implacable man, to find things to believe in him.

"I know you," Elijah says. "I read your name in the paper before. You're a prosecutor."

"Used to be. I quit eight months ago. I'm your defense counsel now."

"How long you work for the county?"

"Eight years."

"And now, just like that, you're going to defend somebody."

"I'm going to defend you."

"Uh-huh."

Like Judge Baron. The "uh-huh" has the lilt of "ah-ha." Suspicious.

Nat reaches into his briefcase for a notepad and pen. "Tell me what happened last night."

Elijah shifts in his seat. He cranes his neck and looks away.

"Let me repeat," Nat says. "I'm your lawyer." Elijah purses his lips at the wall.

"Elijah," Nat says, "you're in trouble. I'm here to help."

This seems to kindle Elijah. "Tell me something." Now his hands join his face in animation. There seems to be an on-off switch to the man. He asks, "How can I be in trouble if I didn't do it?"

"Do what?"

"Don't play that bullshit with me. You know what. Burn that church."

"It doesn't matter whether or not you did it, Elijah. You need to understand this. It's simply whether or not the state can show you did it in court beyond a reasonable doubt."

"How are they going to do that if I didn't do it?"

"You were at the crime scene, so there's no alibi. As I understand, you had a pretty compelling reason for burning it. That's motive. You were drunk. Deputy Skelton observed you actually stomping back and forth rooting for the fire. You told him in the squad car you were glad it burned. Right now you're the only suspect. They're not looking for anyone else."

Elijah stands. He turns to face the cinder-block wall. He paces from corner to corner, it doesn't take but a few strides each direction. Nat's recital of damning facts seems to have filled up the chamber. Elijah searches for a place to conceal himself from them.

From his chair Nat watches. His intuition as a prosecutor tells him to go for it right now, hit him hard and in an unexpected place.

"Why'd you leave your wife by herself all day yesterday?"

With a hammer shot from his open hand, Elijah slams the wall. Again with a sudden swap in intensity, he eases his forehead against the wall, onto the back of his hand.

After a moment, he quietly says into his wrist, "You believe what you want. But I didn't burn that church."

"Who did?"

This question—it was not an act of belief but Nat, practiced in this sort of inquiry, made it sound like one—spins Elijah to face him.

"Some guy. Baseball cap. A long-sleeve sweatshirt. He was only in the light for a second. A rag around his face. I couldn't tell who he was in the dark."

"What else? Was he tall, short, fat?"

"I don't know. Maybe medium. It's hard. I was . . . you know . . ."

"How much did you drink?"

Elijah answers with some shame. "A six. Maybe some before I went there."

"How far away from you did you see him?"

"Across the road, then over to the back of the church. I guess a hundred fifty, two hundred feet."

"And then he ran off. Which direction?"

"East."

"And after he left you came out of hiding from across the street. Once the fire was going good, Deputy Skelton arrived and arrested you."

"That's right."

Nat pauses. He has taken no notes on his legal pad.

Then he says, "Some unidentified person did it."

Elijah's eyes narrow.

"That's your defense." Nat says this flatly, as though counting pennies, as if to say, That's all you've got.

Elijah lands in the chair and slides it forward now. He brings up a long right forefinger, points it between Nat's eyes.

"That's the truth. Mr. Prosecutor."

Elijah lowers the hand. He links his fingers on the tabletop and glares into them. The little hard-shell room seems to support only so much clamor in it before it takes a rest, like a battlefield. Nat looks at the top of Elijah's head. He hears the man breathe. He follows the mingling fingers. A knuckle on Elijah's right hand is puffy around a small cut.

"How'd you get that on the back of your hand?"

Elijah sighs, flustered, as though he has tried everything with this lawyer except patience and now he will give that a go.

"I punched a tree. I was angry. I was drunk."

"Why were you drinking?"

Elijah blinks. He licks his lips and his nostrils flare.

Nat presses. "Why did you leave your wife alone all day?"

Elijah opens his hands on the table. He stares into his palms.

"Look. I didn't know what to do," he says. "You should have seen what they did. What they did to Nora Carol. And to Clare. She, um . . ." His breathing is choppy, Nat sees how he fights for control.

"She what, Elijah?"

"Nothing."

Nat says, "Elijah, if I'm going to be your attorney, you need to tell me everything, even things you don't think might help. That's my job, to figure all this out and defend you. Tell me about Clare."

Without taking his eyes from his open palms, Elijah speaks. "She wouldn't cry. She just kept saying how stupidity and hate were just part of the world, you know, and we'd been lucky so far to have as little of it come our way as we did. Even after giving birth to Nora Carol and having her be the way she was, you know, even after going through that two days before, Clare was . . . she just wouldn't cry. She kept telling me all morning, Elijah, it ain't us, it's them. We're not the ones doing this, they are. We didn't dig up a baby, we didn't do anything unjust. She said maybe that's why God took Nora Carol from us. To show everybody what's going on, that there's still so much hate out there. Maybe it was time folks saw into their own hearts. Maybe that's what this is all about." Elijah shakes his head, unable to continue for a moment; the hard little room has again heard enough.

Nat considers the man across the table. His head is hung, his chest fallen, palms flat on the tabletop working his fingers, he looks like he is crawling in sand. Nat wonders if there are forms to a man the way there are to water: ice, steam, and liquid. Look at this man, stony and guarded only moments before, drunk and agitated last night at his arrest, now this twitching, talkative grief. Nat begins to apply this question to himself while Elijah lifts his head, but there is no time to delve further because Elijah asks, "Mr. Deeds?"

"You can call me Nat."

"Okay." Elijah nods, seemingly grateful for this small kindness, and Nat marvels at the swings in this man, in all of us. How can a man rely on what he will or will not do with all this inside him to guide, buffet, trip him? "Nat," Elijah asks, "you gonna talk to Clare?"

"Yes."

"Will you do me a favor when you do?"

"What."

"Tell her this is all going to be okay. Even if you don't think it is. Do that for me." His voice is soft, pummeled, another form of the man.

"I can't promise that."

Nat waits. Elijah seems not to comprehend this, that his lawyer cannot temper truth for him, not even to a woman who surely bears enough hurt. Nat has told him no to a precious favor. Nat sees on Elijah's face that he stashes this refusal in a deep place.

"Has she been in to see you?"

"Yeah. This morning. She brought me my sneakers."

"How was she holding up?"

"Okay."

"Have you talked with her since this morning?"

"No. I get one call a day, man."

Nat closes his briefcase. The clicks of the locks are like the slaps of a gavel.

"Elijah, I've got to ask you again."

The man closes his eyes with his answer. His face fades in the exact way an oil lamp is turned down.

"No," Elijah says. "I did not do it."

"Then why were you there?"

He opens his eyes. He has gone somewhere inside himself and ferried back this reply.

"Because somebody had to be there. Somebody had to sit out there and wish for that church to go down in flames. Somebody had to show what those people are and what they did. So, yeah, I was there and I was praying. And God heard me."

"And He sent the guy with the baseball cap." Now Nat does it, he hears himself utter the "uh-huh" that is really an "ah-ha."

Two hours from now, at four o'clock, Nat must enter Judge Baron's court, stand by Elijah, and hear the charges against him. Then begins the wrangle with Ed Fentress. The next step will be the preliminary hearing. This is the beginning of the commonwealth's effort to bring Elijah to trial. In front of Judge Baron, Fentress will lay out his case in minimal fashion, just enough to show there is probable cause to proceed before a grand jury, then to circuit court for trial. At the prelim hearing, Fentress will try to hide from Nat as much of the commonwealth's case as possible. Nat wonders, What will there be to hide? The plain facts as they stand right now are awfully incriminating. Maybe some circumstantial or physical evidence will come out of the sheriff's report to exonerate him, maybe the mystery angel will burn another church and get caught or someone will turn him in. Maybe a witness will show up; maybe, but Elijah looks guilty. In Virginia, the arson of an unoccupied house of worship is a Class IV felony. It carries two to ten years in jail. If Elijah will confess now, Nat can get him a much lighter sentence than he could after putting Ed Fentress through a big investigation in preparation for trial, and before the whole town gets whipped into a lather over the racial elements involved. He should get no more than a year in jail. Nat can even pull some strings with Fentress. He can apologize for leaving Ed in the lurch eight months ago. It's possible Nat can get Elijah off with no jail time. If Elijah will say in court he's sorry, it might save his mill job and ease the town off his and Clare's backs, considering everything. A small fine, a boatload of community service, and five years' suspended time hanging over his head. Elijah can win back these people, if he says he's sorry.

Nat explains this. When he is done, he says, "Think about it carefully, Elijah."

The man stands. Nat stays seated and asks, "Is there anything else you think I should know, Elijah? If there's anything at all the prosecutor might find out, you need to tell me first."

"Nothing."

"All right. Do you want me to talk to Fentress? For a deal?"

The orange outfit looms in front of Nat. It is the hue of tomato soup, a jack-o'-lantern, a faded ochery thing. Nat notes inside himself that his prosecutor's pattern to objectify has receded; it's there still but skulked off to a watching distance, to give this new, court-appointed regime of empathy and defense a chance to work. Nat looks into the orange tunic, then up to the iron-black face of Elijah Waddell.

Elijah answers. "An innocent man doesn't need a deal."

Nat says nothing to the orange, which Elijah has just chosen to wear.

The man says, "And he doesn't need to say he's sorry."

# Two

If it doesn't rain soon, the corn will be lost. The dust behind Nat's car is the only cloud in sight. Tall stalks file past in their thousands, withering from the top down. Inside their shucks the ears, swelling and flushed with juice last month, cave and wrinkle in the sun, which itself is not anymore yellow but white hot and dry. Nat sees beneath the ground, where the root systems reach like beggars and are turned away; I have nothing to give you, says the earth.

He slows at the mailbox. A short, gray dog with curly hair and a bobbed tail jogs to greet him. The shotgun shack is painted the ruddy color of a man flushed from the heat. Clare sits on the porch steps. She is barefoot in cutoff denim shorts and a loose white shirt. Her long, bare arms pull her knees to her chest. Nat stops and behind him the dust lies down like a mule in the road, so little breeze is there. He leaves his briefcase in the car. He walks up, the little dog pants beside him. Clare drops her heels to the ground, she does not stand. Her blond hair, the shade of dying corn, is not tied up or in tails to help keep her cool but runs down her back to the porch floor.

She says before he can introduce himself, "Hello, Mr. Deeds."

"Hello, Mrs. Waddell." He comes to the steps and smiles down on her. "May I call you Clare?"

"Please."

"I'm Nat."

She nods.

He asks, "How'd you know who I was?"

"I hear," she slowly says, gauging him. "Folks."

Nat sees in her face the bloodlines of the county. The moon over the harvest is there, and the flatness of the river, the occasional snow on the piney woods, and the forested back roads. Her legs are tawny, they are strong and lean though she bore a child three days ago. Below her neck, between her breasts where the cotton shirt opens, shine beads of sweat. The cotton shirt is sheer to suit the temperature and Nat sees the white straps and cups of her bra. Her breasts are large, out of place for her frame. At the nipples her shirt is wet. Nat thinks with a twinge this is not sweat but the dribbling of milk for which there is no child to suck.

"Come on inside," she says, standing. "I'm making sun tea."

Nat, in his gray suit and tie, is glad to follow her into the hum of the window air conditioner. The dog stays outdoors. Why, Nat wonders, with this heat? Air conditioning is an addiction, he thinks, it's a weakness, and looking at Clare, who can sit out in the heat and love a black husband and bear a child and wear the river and moon in her face, he feels she is the stronger animal, more primal and better suited for life on this planet. "Take a seat," she says. She disappears through the kitchen, out the back door. Nat sits on a plush sofa. He takes in the room quickly while she fetches the tea: low ceiling, she sewed the curtains, heart-pine floors carefully sanded and stained a deep rust; the furniture seems to have been bought from the same store all at once, chocolate fabrics and heavy-legged styles matching. Nat imagines the young couple shopping, a salesman making them a deal, easy credit terms, very little down, we'll deliver tomorrow. Clare returns to the kitchen with a gallon jug of tea brewed outdoors. She pours two glasses over crackling ice and drops in mint leaves. She sits opposite him and hands over the glass. The cold floods from his hand up his arm.

She holds her glass with both hands, drinking like a little girl. He sips his tea. Their eyes meet over the clear rims. This is some ritual of dawdling Clare conducts, Nat must be put at ease by hospitality, they must both swallow coolness before they can discuss the heated things, the fire, the arrest, death, malice. Nat wonders if she is stalling and thinks, No, he reads no reluctance or fear in the woman. She lowers her glass after several inelegant gulps. She says, "Ahhh," the way a small child finishes her swallows.

She says, "We need rain."

"Yes, we do."

Clare sets her glass on the glass-top coffee table with a clank and leans back. She pulls her bare legs up with her in the chair.

"Thank you for taking Elijah's case. I know you've got to drive down here from Richmond to do it."

"Judge Baron didn't leave me much choice."

"You could have said no."

"You don't say no too often to the judge."

"You don't live here anymore. You could've. Why didn't you?"

Nat looks at the floor. She's checked him out. Why is she asking this? Why do his motives matter? He doesn't know the answer.

He says, "Let's just figure I missed Good Hope."

She nods. Nat thinks she is just like Elijah, she stays back, wary, probing.

He asks, "You've got some time off from the mill?"

"They gave me three months' maternity leave. I'm gonna go back week after next."

Nat says what he can: "I'm sorry."

She nods again and her look tells him he cannot touch her there, even with his regrets.

He turns his eyes to his watch. "Court is in an hour."

"Do you think I ought to be there?"

"There's no need. You won't be able to visit with him."

"But he could see me there."

"I think it's better if you stay out here. The judge believes there's going to be a little uproar in town for a few days over this. Let's just keep you out of the way of that as long as we can."

"I don't care."

Nat smiles. "I believe you. But let's not make Elijah worry by putting you in the middle of it just now. All right?"

"All right."

"He's going to plead not guilty, Clare."

"That's what he told me this morning."

"What do you think about that?"

"What are you asking me?"

Nat sets his tea on the table. Now both of the glasses are down, the ceremony is over. "I'm only asking you if you think he ought to plead not guilty."

"Isn't that what you do if you're innocent?"

"It's what you do if you can prove it."

Clare lifts her nose and brow like a ship firming to wind. She sits motionless, as though to move would be to joggle and spill what she contains, what she has endured, what she will yet go through. She's full, Nat thinks, full to the brim. She keeps a precarious balance. But she will not spill. Her tears are only for her child, and they are wept only at her bosom.

"Clare, let me make this as clear as I can." She listens unblinkingly while Nat explains as he did for Elijah the potential risks and consequences of both innocent and guilty pleas. When he has done this, he lifts his glass for another sip of tea. This is to draw a line at the bottom of his observations, a pause, after which he sums up.

"If he admits he did it, if he tells the court he's sorry, I can maybe have him home to you tonight. In a few days at most."

She takes this in with a pacific bearing. Her stare is disconcerting.

He continues. "Things'll cool down pretty quick. You and your husband have been pretty good members of this community. I expect the mill won't fire him if he shows some remorse and explains he was just acting out of grief and anger. I can have the judge and the prosecutor talk with the managers over there. Even the great George Talley would go to bat for him if he spared them all a trial. Worst-case scenario? He might have to serve a year in jail, and I'll work real hard to keep that from happening. The court will lay a fine and some community service on him, so he'll be punished. And Elijah will have some fence-mending to do in the community. People are understandably upset. But if he'll just ask them to be forgiven, well, I reckon folks will. Those that won't forgive will forget. I figure some will probably pat him on the back for it, considering what you've both been put through."

She moves only her lips. "Considering."

For seconds, something silent congresses between them. Her eyes are focused on it, into a middle distance in the air. Nat knows what she sees: a tiny coffin, Mr. Omohundro and his shovel, deep night and the church fire roaring and her husband there, his fist balled and shaking. Nat sees this too. He watches with her like fireworks. And watching this image of fire and fireworks, mesmerized, a light flickers inside his dark vault—one of which is inside all of us, where the most precious and honest things are kept behind the thickest barriers—the safe door cracks barely open and Nat reaches in quickly with the flash and withdraws a truth he did not know before. Holding it now it disturbs him. And now that he has it he cannot put it back, that is the rule of our vaults.

He actually hopes Elijah burned the Victory Baptist.

He wants to believe the man has avenged himself against their cruelty to his child and his wife and the insult to his own African blood. Fuck them, Nat thinks. They dug up his baby. They spit on his heritage. An absolute response to an absolute wrong.

Nat's eyes plummet to his open palms. He hears his own breath and looks closer at what he has removed from his vault.

That was not the whole truth he withdrew. There is more. This.

He knows he would have done it himself.

"Nat."

Clare's voice startles him. He pulls a short breath and locates her in the room.

"Yeah. Um . . ."

She hasn't moved, this surprises him, it feels like a day has passed in those seconds.

She says, "You think he did it, don't you."

Nat blows out the breath, a little taken aback at her insight. "I know I'm angry at what was done to you by those people. I can imagine how Elijah must have felt."

Now she tilts her head. "Can you?"

"Yes."

Nat feels a chill and thinks, There she is. Maeve. She has followed me here, of course. She's shown herself, floating in the air where the fire was. She's the one who opened the vault and stuck my head in. Yes, Maeve, I burned our church. All right? I did it. But you disgraced it first.

Clare asks, "What's your advice?"

Nat tries to clear his head. He has not seen or spoken to Maeve in eight months. Three times he has heard her voice on his answering machine, asking, "Nat, will you call me? Nat?" and once concluding, "This isn't fair." Fair, he thinks. Fair is like good and evil, a moving target. It depends on where you're standing.

"What's your advice, Nat?"

Maeve will not step aside so he will speak through her. "Actually, I came out here to ask for your advice."

"My husband is not a fearful man."

"No, I don't think he is."

"If he'd done it, if he'd lit that church, he'd say so and take what was coming to him."

"Yes, ma'am."

"But he says he didn't. Now the question I have for you is, Can you defend Elijah without believing him?"

"Yes."

Clare stands. "Let me show you something."

She walks out of the living room to the hall. She enters another room, then returns carrying an amber bottle of pills and what looks like a clear plastic bicycle pump attached to a small funnel.

She shoves them at Nat.

"The doctors gave me these pills. Parlodel. They're supposed to dry my milk up. About two weeks, they said. And this. This is a pump to siphon off the milk until the pills kick in."

Clare drops them on the sofa beside Nat.

"I don't want them," she says. "I want my baby and I want my milk but I can't have them. And I want my husband. Can you really get him home to me like you said?"

Nat nods. "If he'll say he's guilty. If he'll apologize. Yes. I can do that."

Clare looks down at Nat, considering him and his ability to accomplish what he says he can do. She nods back at him, accepting him at his word.

Clare says, "You go ahead and tell him to plead guilty. You tell him to say he's sorry and do whatever else he has to do to get himself out of there. You bring him home to me. Just like you said. Make him do it, Nat. Make him say he's guilty. I need him."

Clare steps back. With that, she expects Nat to stand. He does. The pills and pump stay on the sofa.

She walks him to the door and onto the porch. The heat of the day flares at him. He strides into it, turning back to her before he gets into his car. She has taken her place on the porch steps, and a minute after he has driven off she will glisten again with sweat; how long will she sit there, until Elijah comes home? Something about her is closed off again, she and her home opened only for the minutes it took to speak to Nat and now that is done. Nat drives off from the shotgun shack. In his mirror, dust obscures her and the dog sitting on the steps.

The dirt road is cracked. With the cornfield around him scrolled out like an earthly parchment, he looks into the stands of thirsting corn. This takes him journeying further, into Clare's and Elijah's hearts and the hearts of the deacons of the destroyed church and up to the dry firmament and onward to God, who took the baby, and finally into himself. Nat Deeds finds everything unwilling. Unhappily he senses that not the arid earth nor the people on it will soon do what Clare wants and say they are sorry, to let things, if they will, heal.

2

There is a certain kind of light—and it is not always hot like today—when the sun widens its eye in surprise at what it sees. Edges are sharp, cut as if with scissors; colors seem electric and the human eye hurts to look at any one thing too long. In this light we squint and glance downward and away and we seem nervous. This is what is captured on camera of Nat Deeds moments after he gets out of his car in the parking lot of the Pamunkey County Courthouse, to be shown on the six o'clock news and again at eleven that night.

A dozen or more news people hustle toward Nat as though he is about to run away from them, and he is not, he stands still but they hurry anyway. They are like landing commandos streaming across a beach, jogging heavily over the grass in front of the courthouse, holding weapons of lenses and microphones, dangling cables and thick battery belts. Women in tight outfits and heels and men in smart suits run in the pack; alongside them are young men in jeans and sweaty armpits with cameras hoisted on shoulders like bazookas. Holding his briefcase, Nat leans against his car while they form a phalanx around him. He wishes they would come from the other direction, from the building side instead of the open grass where the sunlight is strong and will make him look beady-eyed in their cameras. In his years as assistant commonwealth's attorney he handled several noteworthy cases, a few murders, an abduction from one of the posh river houses. Ed Fentress usually dealt with the press. This is not Nat's first time in the spotlight but it is one of only a few and he is conscious of how he will look.

He does not respond to the first round of shouted questions. With astonishment he takes in the logos on the vans parked at the curb in front of the courthouse and the call signs on the microphones and on stickers glued to the cameras directed at his face. The three local network TV affiliates are here, also two reporters with cameras from cable news, and two radio stations. Nat thinks, just when he is trying to settle into a quiet civil practice in Richmond, he gets handed a very public criminal case in Good Hope. Judge Baron called this one right on the nose. Apparently it matters a great deal what color is the hand that lit the flames and what color are the faces that worshiped in the church. Nat notes that half the newsmen and -women crowding him are black. Color matters to them too, he thinks, but only as news, and he doubts if this is an improvement.

"Mr. Deeds? Is it true that Waddell was arrested at the scene?"

"Was there any racial motivation behind the burning of the church?"

"Is your client part of a hate group?"

Whichever reporter is asking a question leans in to shake his or her microphone, then pulls back when the next one cranes forward. They are like pistons. Nat raises a hand and tries to keep from squinting. He has one answer for all of them.

"My client . . . my client will be in front of the judge at four o'clock. We may have a statement for you after that."

This satisfies none of them.

"Can you confirm that your client was arrested at the fire?"

Another calls out, "There's a rumor that Waddell was arrested urinating on the church while it burned. Can you confirm or deny?"

Nat thinks, What a stupid question. Anyone close enough to pee on a fire that size would have fricasseed his peter. Nat shakes his head. "Until we get the sheriff's report there is no evidence even that a crime has been committed. This might have been a faulty fuse box at the church. Let's wait and see, all right? Now excuse me."

"What are you going to plead?"

Nat surges forward. The cameras and foam-padded microphones do not yield. Nat knows he is neither tall nor imposing, but he does understand words and inflection and has always vested his power there. He stops and glares into one large dark lens and says, "I have a client to defend. Unless you're a better lawyer than me, move and let me go do it."

A path is made. Nat presses through them. He notes they do not lower their cameras and mikes, the voracious press records images and sounds of the back of his head.

He walks up the nine granite steps to the courthouse front door. He observes there's nobody here from the church or the town, no protesters or placards, no blacks and whites shouting across battle lines drawn for them by color. The church burned early this morning so it hasn't made the papers yet, the county is still in the word-of-mouth stage. The Victory Baptist folks are lying low so far, with good reason. It's still calm, but if the press and their microphones have their way it won't stay that way: Local white Baptist church exhumes mixed-race baby; black father of child accused of burning the church, arrested cheering at the flames; details tonight.

At the top of the steps George Talley has placed a deputy—the man's brown felt hat brim pulled low to his eyes, arms crossed, a menacing mien—probably at Judge Baron's request to keep the press out of his corridors. By law Baron can't do that, he can only ban cameras in the courtroom proper. But the judge is never bound by convention. He dares you to have the fortitude to take him on, even advising you that you'd win if you did.

Inside, Nat sits on a bench across from the courtroom door. He looks at his watch. There's still fifteen minutes before court. They will have transported Elijah from Rappahannock by now, he'll be in the holding cells. Nat thinks he should walk over to speak with him before the hearing but he doesn't want to reenter the heat or the gauntlet of the press again. He'll talk with Elijah after they bring him into the courtroom, before the plea. He'll ask the judge for a minute, tell Elijah what Clare asks.

Nat stands to straighten his shirt and tie. He thinks to go upstairs, to confront Ed Fentress privately, take some ribbing for leaving the way he did eight months ago, then plumb what the commonwealth's attorney for Pamunkey County is willing to give in exchange for a guilty plea today.

Nat moves to the stairs. Outside, the sounds of another commotion rise up the granite steps. The press has its hooks into someone else. Nat hears the deputy tell them to back off and make room. One of the doors creaks open. An angular figure is silhouetted by the luminance behind him. Nat waits until the door closes and his eyes adjust from the shot of sunlight. Heel clicks bring the figure closer. The web of shadow unravels from the man's face and it is Thomas Derby, as it was twenty, more than twenty, years ago.

"Is that you, Tom?"

The man walks steadily forward. He moves in a narrow trace like on a rail, it is the charismatic gait of a cinema star, it was always so. Derby walked as though nothing could make him rush. Tom Derby does not rush now. Nat thinks this is the first time he has ever heard Derby's footsteps, we must be getting old, his feet are touching the ground.

"Nat Deeds," Derby says. "Nat Dirty Deeds."

Nat puts out a hand. Derby walks past it like a turnstile to put his chest to Nat's and his arms around him. Derby hugs first, then Nat wraps his old friend in response. Nat hugs two and a half decades. There's a time-machine quality to this encounter, unbalancing, though he feels through the blue coat and dress shirt that Derby is still as fit and straight and lucky as the teenager he was last.

The embrace is quick, as men's are. When they release Derby leaves a hand on Nat's elbow, as though Nat will disappear from him. This is familiar, Nat thinks, Derby holding on to his elbow like this. Something emotional, something that sums up twenty-five years, it feels now and then like need.

"Tom, it's . . ." Nat moves his arms out from his sides in the beginning of a flap, this takes his elbow out of Derby's hand, "it's good to see you. It's been a long time. Where've you been? What are you doing here?" This is all said quickly and sounds pat and hollow. Nat wants to exchange everything between them in an instant. Tom Derby is the mystery, the one who disappeared, the one with the brains and style, the walk and the sea-green eyes, the leather jacket and the girls. He was the one who didn't care, who looked like a greaser and topped the class in grades and apathy. He refused the honor of valedictorian, didn't attend graduation; that night of football field lights and gowns he was gone, the myth begun. Rumors of Hollywood, Alaska, Tibet.

For two years Nat was the editor of the Pamunkey High newspaper. Derby brought him poems to print, signed Anonymous. Nat never told who wrote them and so won Derby's trust, a trophy he wanted to crow about but would have lost in the doing. Derby used to come by his house late on weeknights. The two sat on the porch in any weather, cold, rain, smothering humidity. Derby told of older women and bourbon and vodka and made up poetry there on the spot about the stars and streetlights and headlights on cars. Derby said light was what moved him always, but not light alone and not darkness but the two side by side, coexisting and struggling simultaneously, enemies and cohorts. This was how Derby spoke then, and Nat asked his parents when they told him to come inside from the porch if he could stay outside a little longer, telling them later in privacy that Tom Derby needed someone to talk to.

Derby smiles. He points back toward the doors, out into the world where time does not stand fast the way it does in recollection. "The Victory Baptist? The church that got burned down?"

"Yeah."

"I'm the pastor."

"You?" Tom Derby, the boy of tales and hot breath sour with liquor and cigarettes, a man of God? Yes, and the boy of poetry and stars plucked out of the night.

Derby draws back his head. "Don't look so shocked. That hurts my feelings."

Nat laughs. He wants to touch Derby in congratulations—for what, he does not know; it seems that being a preacher does not suit what Nat thought would befall Derby in those early years when Nat and others wondered where he'd gone and what he'd achieved, and so it appears Derby has moved outside those limits and that, probably, is what Nat wants to commend. Derby is free, the thing he always seemed to want most—but Nat has historically waited for Derby to reach to him, it's a habit even now. "That's good. Good for you. I mean, well . . . sorry about your church."

Derby shrugs. "And you're the lawyer for the fella they're saying did it."

Nat puffs his cheeks. "They're saying. I can't comment just yet."

Derby lampoons Nat with a comic face. "You? A lawyer?"

"It was either that or the mill."

Derby indicates with his chin the cameras and crowding faces outside through which both of them had to wade. "At least at the mill you wouldn't have had them to worry about. Bedlamites."

Nat asks, "When did you get back to Good Hope?"

"Four months ago. Mrs. Epps, you remember her from third grade? She's a deacon at the Victory Baptist. She brought me back to be pastor."

"Back from where?" Nat wants to comment on this, keeping in touch with your third-grade teacher for thirty-five years, but he does not, because this is Tom Derby of rhymes and tales, from whom you learn a lot about life—pieces of life you will never lead and now he has twenty-three years more—if you will just listen and not comment. Nat backs to the bench and sits. He looks at his watch. He'll talk to Fentress in the courtroom before they bring in Elijah. Nat sets his briefcase on the tile floor. Echoes race off down the hallway; it is a long hall like memory and the echoes fly a long time into it. Derby sits beside him and they are on the porch again, Derby tells a story the way he always did, forming with his fingers and eyes people and things out of the air.

"You remember my next door neighbor, Mr. Jacobson." Derby jerks his thumb past his neck, as though the neighbor were there, across the yard. "Remember he had MS?"

"Yeah. Nice guy, I recall. Worked at the mill 'til he had to retire from his legs."

"And no matter how bad it got, he never went into a wheelchair. From seventh grade on, every time it got so bad and it didn't look like he was going to be able to keep on walking, before he'd head off to the hospital he'd tell me don't worry, he was going to walk out. And a couple weeks later, every time, when he'd come home from the hospital, he'd still be on his feet, somehow. He went from a limp to a cane to a walker to hand crutches but he walked out just like he said he would. Then a few days before graduation I come home from school and Mr. Jacobson is in his driveway in his car. But the motor's not running. I walk over to say hello and he rolls up his window. I tap on it and say Hi, Mr. Jacobson, but he shakes his head at me.

" 'Mr. Jacobson, what's the matter? '

" 'I'm okay, Tom,' he says, 'go on ahead.'

" 'No, sir. Something's the matter. Tell me what it is. Maybe I can help.'

" 'No, son, this is personal. It'll keep. You go on.'

" 'Mr. Jacobson, it's just you and me. If it's personal, I can keep a secret.'

"And with this look on his face like he's got to tell me the worst news in the world he rolls down his window. The smell of shit jumps out at me like a cat. He'd shit himself sitting in his car. It was the MS. He'd lost control and he was so weak his legs couldn't get him into the house, and he was just sitting in it. Nat, I'm doing everything I can to keep from curling my nose, because it's coming at me.

" 'Mr. Jacobson, you've got nothing to be ashamed of, sir. You're the single bravest man I ever met. If you don't mind, let's get you into the house.'

"He just shakes his head, he can't look at me, but even so, I won't let anything show on my face. I open the car door and grab his keys from the ignition. Then I slide my hands under him and pull him to me out the car. I hoist him up. He's looking around over my shoulders to see who's watching in the neighborhood but no one's out on the sidewalks and it's okay. The shit has soaked through his pants seat because he took a piss too and it's getting on me and he starts to cry in my arms while I'm carrying him to his front door. He's light, a lot lighter than you would have thought by looking at him. And I think something in this man has departed, something which gave him weight has taken advantage of his tears and the smell of his own shit to skip out on him. And I think I'm going to stay right there by him until he gets it back. This man, this good neighbor and honest man, should not be this light.

"He says to me, 'Tom, you don't have to do this.'

"He's wrong. I do. It was the first thing in my entire life I knew I had to do. So I carry him through the house like some bride and set him on a plastic stool in the bathroom he keeps in the shower. I strip him out of his shoes and socks, they're soaked, and pull off his shirt and pants and undershorts. I bundle them all up and they are making a smell, God Almighty. I turn on the shower for him, I pat him on the shoulder. He still can't look at me. I take the clothes to the laundry room and dump them in the washing machine. I got the man's shit under my fingernails and on my arms. I wash real hard. Then I go and set out some fresh clothes for him out of his dresser. I shout out 'See you, Mr. Jacobson.' I take a sponge and clean the front seat of his car. And I leave."

This is the storyteller Derby. Nat thinks someday he might enjoy watching the verve of his old friend's craft in church. He must keep his flock spellbound.

Derby continues. "So I left Good Hope. Because something had hit me, Nat. Some energy let me pick Mr. Jacobson up like he was no more'n a rag doll and carry him like that. And I was strong, boy, I was strong. I went looking for it, to see if I could find it again. I borrowed a couple hundred bucks from my folks and hitched down south and ended up in New Orleans. I worked for two years on the rigs, sucking oil out of the earth like some mosquito. Sometimes I could feel it again, almost hear it, at night with the big stars, a needle stuck five miles into the earth and a horizon of water and the men singing. But most times I didn't hear anything but the rig pumping and the world was just the world. And believe me, New Orleans is not a place to go looking for much inside yourself, there's too much coming at you from outside."

A deputy opens the courtroom door just as Derby says, "Then one night down in the French Quarter in a bar, I heard my call. I knew all of a sudden. That power I was looking for was God. It just opened up to me." Listening, Nat thinks the swinging wide of the courtroom door is a well-timed and beautiful physical metaphor. Derby continues. "It's like that story where the man dies and walks with God and looks back over his track of life. He sees two sets of footprints and asks God, What is that? God says to him, That's where I walked beside you during your life. Then the man points at a place where there's only one track and asks, Why weren't You walking beside me then? God said to him, That's where I carried you."

Nat's watch tells him it is time to go inside. He stands.

Derby stands too. He extends his arms like two tusks, reenacting God's shouldering of the man in the fable or his own strength to lift the neighbor. "That's what I heard in my call, Nat, that night in New Orleans. And you know what? I'd been wrong the whole time." He drops his arms. "I left home to go looking for that power again. I wanted the strength to carry. What I found is that it's not about carrying at all. It was never me who had the power, you see. It was Mr. Jacobson all the time. The power is to accept being carried."

Derby is taller by two inches. Just as he did when he spoke to Nat long ago in their teens and now again as men, Tom Derby seems to speak from on high, a natural pulpit. Nat begins to understand how perfect it is that his friend has become a preacher.

Derby smiles. "You know what I did first thing after receiving my call?"

Nat returns the smile. "No."

"I finished my drink."

Nat savors the finish of the story, but now cannot show more appreciation or curiosity. The open courtroom door draws him. He moves toward it. Derby's hand stops him.

"Nat, what are you going to do with Elijah Waddell?"

"Plead him however he wants to go with it."

"What do you think he ought to do?"

"I can't discuss that with you. I'm sorry."

"He's innocent, isn't he? I can't believe he did this."

Nat licks his lips. He is not comfortable with what he has to say. "Tom, from what I understand, I can't believe what your church did to his little girl."

Derby hangs his head, nodding, tasting this bitterness.

He raises his head. "I want you to know I fought it. But the pastor doesn't get a vote. That's the truth, Nat. I was against it and I still am."

Now it is Nat who takes the other's elbow. Like a flipped switch the waiting courtroom door has reversed their roles, for the law is the one place Nat can travel where Derby must ride along. "I've got to go in now, Tom."

Nat turns. Derby lags. Nat looks back to see the need conveyed on Derby's face, the old need by the porch light or delicate moonlight or barely outlined by dim night with green ponds of eyes that beg— then and now—Swim in me, ripple me, I must have you, eyes that are reservoirs where Derby's sadness is dammed, swim in me and love me in my sadness when I cannot.

"I was against it," Derby says again.

Nat has to enter the courtroom. He says, "I'm sure you did the right thing."

3

For eight years Nat sat to the right, at the prosecution table. This afternoon for the first time he pulls out the chair at the defense table, to the left. He lays down his briefcase and stands beside the chair, taking in the contours and colors of the old courtroom. From this angle, after his eight-month absence, he sees the chamber is stately and dull, three shades of brown: mahogany rails and bench, chestnut carpet, and tan wallpaper, like an old sepia photograph. The county symbol hangs on the wall behind the judge's leather chair. Nat feels an unpleasant tingle noticing all this as though seeing it for the first time, as though a visitor. His tingle is his realization that he is only visiting, a defense lawyer from Richmond making an appearance at the left-hand table in the Pamunkey County Courthouse. This is not his home court any longer, though from beside the judge's door the thick-waisted bailiff waves in recognition.

Through the door on the opposing wall Ed Fentress enters. Dapper in a charcoal suit, Fentress is a pillar of composure, his hands and legs are jaunty, even his salt-and-pepper hair is relaxed in perfect layers, as though the world were a square hole and he is the square peg. He slaps his own briefcase onto the right-hand table and glides toward Nat. It is as impossible for Nat to dislike the man as it is to respect him. Fentress holds his hands out from his sides in a mute "hey-hey," or maybe it is a "ta-dah," Nat cannot tell, and he thinks of George Talley, the other hale bookend.

Fentress seems to cock himself, posing with his head tilted. There is something bizarre, of the puppet, in this. He says, "Welcome back, stranger. We missed you." Fentress checks the courtroom gallery. The room is empty except for Tom Derby seated in the rear. He lowers his voice to keep the pastor from hearing. "You son of a bitch."

Nat extends a hand. Fentress swoops his grip inward for the shake like a tennis forehand.

Nat says, "Ed."

"Look," Fentress says, bringing his other hand to Nat's shoulder so that Nat, the smaller man, feels as if he is being set up for a judo throw, "you know I'm sorry about you and Maeve."

With a different tone, Nat says again, "Ed," but Fentress presses on. "We can catch up on all that later. But I'm your friend, you know, you could have confided in me you were having problems before they got out of hand." Nat thinks he didn't know he and Maeve were having such problems; is that what the rumor mill is spreading? What has Maeve been saying here in Good Hope? Problems? Fentress says, "But for right now, what are we going to do about your boy Waddell? I don't want to bring the hammer down on him. He's had a rough few days."

Nat disengages himself from Fentress's grasp. "Yes, he has. You've heard."

"Yeah. Talley and Monroe just left my office. They found Elijah's shirt and some beer cans across the street in the bushes. When Monroe took him in last night the guy's blood alcohol was two times over legal. The arson guys called me from the site a few hours ago. They're saying the fire was started with an accelerant, they think it was kerosene-based. Your guy's boots are coated in kerosene. He was drunk. He was mad. He was there."

"He works at the mill. He's a mechanic. Christ, of course his boots have got kerosene on them. It's what they use for degreasing. Anybody can get kerosene. That doesn't single out Elijah."

"You're an ex-prosecutor. You tell me how much slack that cuts with a jury. The shit was on his boots, whether he works with it or not. He had access to the stuff is all it says to me."

"Look, I'm talking to him about a guilty plea. What can you give me?"

"You're direct, Nat. That hasn't changed. I like it."

"I told him he might get all suspended time and probation. You can name the term, Ed. This guy's a first-time offender. He's not going to be getting into any more trouble. He blew a gasket once, that was it. Give him five years' probation, a fine, but don't break his back for me. Community service, we'll call it a day and I can get back to Richmond."

"All suspended time? No jail? Let me repeat. He was drunk. He was mad. He was there. Why should I let him walk?"

"Come on. This is a good guy, hard worker, husband, grieving father. Cut him a deal. You don't need his head on a platter."

"So you can get back to Richmond." Fentress examines him, puts on a sympathetic face, slaps it on like a bumper, something to give and absorb shocks, and says, "How come? To go and lick your wounds?" Nat blinks at this but Fentress says more. "Look, we're old buddies, but you know I think you're an idiot for walking out on everybody the way you have."

Fentress means this to be companionable and urbane but he has overestimated their friendship—"Hey," he adds, sensing Nat's discomfiture, "I'm just telling it the way I see it"—and he has been insensitive, as though seeing warrants telling, like a parrot or a fool. Nat, who has been agitated and on his heels all day long since he got Baron's call this morning and especially after entering the courtroom, feels Fentress's cavalier words as salt in the open wound of his wife and his separation from her. Internally he thanks the prosecutor for this blunt reminder. This is a court of law, and it is his singular domain, the one place Maeve never came. Maeve cannot come in here now, even though Ed Fentress tries to conjure her. Nat fights her off, and though she is near him—he cannot ever push her so far away that she is not close—she is not enfolding him as do the shades of brown and the ornate woodworking and the hovering county symbol. The fight against Maeve in one violent, quiet moment metamorphoses easily into a fight for Elijah.

"No time served," Nat says.

The commonwealth's attorney wags his head. "I'm getting phone calls."

Nat slacks his jaw. Fentress answers before Nat can speak, saying, "From the Feds, for one. This is a black man burning a white Baptist house of worship. It's got hate crime written all over it. That makes it Fed. If Justice doesn't see me get tough enough on Waddell, they step in and hang a civil-rights violation on him. That looks bad for my office, Nat. And I'm getting local calls too."

"From who? The rednecks who dug up his baby?" Nat lowers his voice, but thinks perhaps Tom Derby heard him. "Look, Ed, you don't want me to put that on the stand. You want to talk about looking bad? I stick his wife up there and she tells the court what she and her husband went through with the birth, just to have the church go and exhume their infant out of the church graveyard the morning after it dies. When the goddamn jury stops crying they'll go over there and kick the burned-up pieces of that church around themselves. No one wins if I do that. The whole town will split right down racial lines over a trial, and when your precious media gets done with it Good Hope will look like some bullshit racist backwater. Let me plead him out. I'll take care of the Feds. This was an isolated act of passion in response to the church's own race-motivated and, frankly, despicable act. I'll make sure Justice won't touch him. And I'll make sure you don't look bad. You'll be the big peacemaker, all right? Just give him a deal that lets him go back to his wife and his job."

Fentress looks to the ceiling. "And what do I tell the people calling me?"

"You mean the voters calling you."

"Touché. But it's not my fault the people are the voters. They're still calling me, lad. What do I tell them. It's still arson."

Nat sends his eyes to the courthouse walls, beyond which the press waits.

"Ed, this could get ugly."

Fentress examines the quiet courtroom, then sends his own gaze out through the walls to the cameras and microphones and pretty female news anchors.

He pokes out his lower lip, then says, "Once in a while, ugly's not so bad."

The bench where Thomas Derby sits in the rear of the courtroom creaks, like a church pew. He stands, tall and golden. "Tell the people calling you," he says, walking up the aisle, "to hang their heads in shame the way Elijah must. Tell them to rebuild the same way Elijah and his wife must." Derby's voice, without rising, fills the courtroom, which is only slightly larger than the sanctuary of the Victory Baptist had been. He is beside them now with the bar rail at his knees, he is above them like a cascade, his green eyes like water and white teeth like froth pour down. "Tell them there's been enough anger. It's time to mend."

Ed Fentress does not respond but lifts his eyebrows, bemused. He is not the sort of man, Nat knows, to acknowledge Tom Derby. Derby is handsomer than Fentress, he is more articulate, he commands the same type of attention—and there is only so much of that to go around; whenever there is a selection, Fentress votes for himself—and besides, Tom Derby is a preacher. The law is godless.

Fentress stirs his hand in the space between the three of them.

"Pastor Derby. Do you know Nat Deeds? He's defense counsel. Nat, Pastor Thomas Derby from the Victory Baptist."

"Mr. Deeds and I are well acquainted with each other, thank you."

"Pastor," Fentress says, "maybe you know I've been contacted by a few members of your church. They seem pretty upset about all this."

"I know the ones who've been calling you, Mr. Fentress. They're deacons and they're responsible for the decision to remove Elijah's child from our cemetery. They're hoping for you to throw the book at Mr. Waddell and cover their own perfidy with his. That way they get to look righteous by decrying another man's sin. It's an old ploy and not unexpected."

Derby holds his palms up to Fentress. It is a defenseless posture, a sort of surrender in miniature: They're my flock, he seems to express, and I'm sorry for them. Nat notes with interest the austere, sermon language Derby uses with Fentress. He is in his role of pastor now.

Derby continues. "But I've also spoken with every other member of the church I could reach today and that's been quite a few. I can tell you they, particularly the younger members, are just as disturbed by what their church elders did to the Waddell family as they are with what Elijah is accused of doing to their church. I'm certain I can stand here and represent a great many of the Victory Baptist Church members when I say we plead for your office to show forbearance towards Elijah. We can't ask his grace without first giving him ours."

Fentress nods and considers. "Well, that sounds mighty Christian."

Again Fentress says something meant to be clever and Nat watches it fall like a shot bird. Nat has never thought of Ed Fentress this way, as inappropriate, a buffoon. He'd always bought into Ed's act, measured him and found him at most entertaining, at least political. He was Nat's boss and generally stayed out of the way to let Nat do his job. Now he is an opponent. Nat feels disjointed by this, but also revved.

Derby calmly says, "It is."

The bailiff calls into the courtroom, "All rise. This General District Court is in session. The Honorable Judge Malcolm Baron presiding."

Without a look at them Fentress turns to his place. Nat quickly runs his hand to Derby's sleeve. "Thanks, pastor." Derby smiles at the grant of his title and takes a seat.

Judge Baron flurries in behind the bench. His black robe furls to his gait. He swivels his leather chair to him and takes his place beneath the big county emblem. The judge glowers over his courtroom like a raven over his field, he has a dark veneer, jet hair, ebony framed glasses, and a mustache hiding his lip. Nat sits at the defense table. He rides again a small crest in his chest at seeing everything from this unaccustomed angle of the courtroom. Judge Baron himself lets his blackbird eyes crinkle behind his frames only for a moment at Nat seated over there.

"Good afternoon, gentlemen," the judge says.

Fentress and Nat say in unison, "Judge."

"Sheriff, bring in Mr. Waddell."

The clerk reads from a sheet. "The Commonwealth versus Elijah Waddell."

Through the same door Fentress entered, Elijah is brought into the courtroom by a deputy. Elijah's pumpkin-colored jail clothes and dark skin digest into the drabness of the courtroom, as though he has already been swallowed by the system. There are no chains on him and his head is erect, his hands are clasped behind his back. The deputy walks him directly beneath Judge Baron's gaze. The deputy removes his hand from the crook of Elijah's arm and retreats two steps, as though he has brought the judge a sacrifice, an unafraid one.

Nat rises. He walks to stand beside Elijah, who turns his head to Nat but otherwise makes no sign of recognition. The judge peers over his black rims and says, "Good afternoon, Mr. Waddell."

Before Nat or Elijah can say anything, Fentress gets to his feet.

"Your Honor, if I may. I've had several requests from the press to prevail upon you to allow them into the courtroom. Just reporters, no cameras or mikes, of course."

"Mr. Fentress, you know my dislike for circuses."

"Yes, sir, I know it very well. But if I may remind the court . . ."

"Don't remind me of anything, Mr. Fentress. There's nothing I've forgotten. We'll leave the esteemed press corps to stew outside for this afternoon, it's just an initial appearance and you can brief them yourself, if you like. Later on, you and me and Mr. Deeds can discuss how we'll handle them for the duration of this case, such as it will be. Agreed, gentlemen?"

"Yes, judge. Thank you," Fentress says, unctuous and smiling, pretending this was just what he wanted to hear. He sits. Nat nods.

"Now," the judge says, "good afternoon, Mr. Waddell."

Elijah says, "Judge, good afternoon."

"Mr. Waddell, I'm going to read the charges against you. If there's anything you don't understand or you want me to stop and go over again, you just say so. All right?"

Elijah says, "Yes, sir." Nat watches Elijah's face. The man does not flinch or blink.

The judge reads from a sheet. "Elijah Waddell, you are charged in the county of Pamunkey, Commonwealth of Virginia, with the arson of a house of worship." The judge reads the date, time, and location of the arson, and the specific section of the criminal code violated. Throughout, Nat follows the lines of Elijah's cheeks and chin, his eyelids, and sees nothing to reveal that Elijah realizes the predicament he is in, as though the night he spent in jail, the jailbird garb, and this proceeding are a dream. Nat ponders where Elijah's thoughts are: on the soul of the child Nora Carol, on his wife and his dog ensconced alone in the dry cornfield? Wherever the man's mind is, it's not on himself and in this courtroom. The judge glances up from his page. He looks again at Elijah over the dark top of his glasses.

Judge Baron inclines his head. He sees Elijah's impassive face. "This is a serious charge, Mr. Waddell. It's a felony. It carries a penalty of two to ten years in prison and a fine of up to a hundred thousand dollars. Do you understand all this?"

"Yes, sir."

"Mr. Deeds."

Nat answers, "Yes, judge."

"Have you had ample opportunity to discuss these charges with your client?"

"Actually, Your Honor, I'd like another couple of minutes to talk over a few more things with the commonwealth's attorney. We haven't had much time this afternoon."

"How long will you need?"

"Just five minutes."

The judge rises. "I'll be in my chambers. Tell the bailiff when you're ready."

When Baron is gone, Nat sits at the defense table. He indicates the chair beside him for Elijah. The deputy guarding Elijah moves to lean against the wall.

Nat whispers, "I'm going to talk to the commonwealth's attorney about a deal. If I can get you off with no jail time, a fine, and probation, will you take it?"

Elijah looks straight ahead. There is some girder in him, some steel thing that will not let him bend or even turn his head to Nat when he says, "No."

Nat sits back. At the next table Fentress looks impatient and forlorn without the cameras he knows are tantalizingly close, just outside on the courthouse steps.

Nat releases a sigh. "You want to tell me why?"

"Because I didn't do it."

This irks Nat. Quickly, he puts his hands on Elijah's shoulders and turns him to face the prosecutor drumming his fingers on the right-hand table. Nat does not whisper, he ignores the fact that Fentress will hear him.

"Look. You see that man right there. He thinks you did it and he thinks he can prove it in court." Nat lets Elijah loose. "And the judge? He thinks you did it, or else he wouldn't have called me in from Richmond to take your case." Elijah pivots his head slowly to Nat, it is like a gun turret, round and metallic hard and at its far shaft bottom lies an unseen charge, something that can explode. Fentress stills his hand on his table and looks too. Nat goes on. "That man in the back of the courtroom? He's the preacher from Victory Baptist. He thinks you did it. Elijah, I visited Clare after I saw you. She wants you to plead guilty. She wants you home where you belong. And I can send you home. Today."

Nat flings his gaze at Fentress. "Ed? Tell me right now. Do we have a deal?"

Fentress does the ta-dah gesture again with his arms. He nods yes and says, "Sure. I'm the big peacemaker."

Nat looks at Elijah, who has dropped his eyes into his lap.

Elijah's voice is weak. "Clare told you she wants me to say I'm guilty."

"She just wants you with her. But she knows I can't make that happen for sure unless you take a plea of guilty."

Now Elijah elevates his gaze to Nat.

Nat continues. "Think of Clare. How hard this is on her too. If we go to trial, it's going to take months, and there's no guarantee you're going to be found not guilty. You could get years, away from your wife, your home, your work. Fentress isn't offering you a deal because he thinks he won't win. He's cutting you a deal because I asked him and you deserve one. Take it, go home, and start over."

Nat hears how insistent he sounds, how transparent to himself. He knows he is a shill; his passion for Elijah is simply the wish for himself to be forgiven without forgiveness, to accept fault without blame; anyone, he thinks, could see this if they only looked, if they listened to him for a second. If Elijah will just confess he burned the church, tell the judge he is guilty and sorry, he will be punished but lightly, Nat has seen to that; Elijah will—in effect—have gotten away with it. As he should, because he is their victim more than they are his. Nat admits this to himself: He badly wants the same, to have separated from Maeve as her victim, to have burned her down with coldness the way the church met its end in fire, and so too to be punished lightly, to get away with it. As he should. Nat has swung the deal for Elijah with Fentress; with whom will Nat make the deal for himself? With God? God lets things happen to babies, churches, love, innocence. God does not make deals. And all this is an anguish for Nat because he has long considered himself to be equitable and measured. A man should not get away with it.

Elijah draws a deep breath, as though he is going underwater to bring something up to show Nat. He closes his eyes, making visible the idea of some internal descent. In a moment, he lifts his lids and takes his voice low. What he has to share is pressing and private, it is not for Fentress or the man in the rear of the court, even if he is a preacher. Elijah brings his face close. Nat can smell his breath, hear his lips and wet tongue working the words.

"Let me tell you something. I'm named after a prophet in the Bible. My mother, she always wanted me to be like him. That's what she always said to me, live up to your name, even in the face of trouble and death. So how do I do this, Nat? How do I take the name my mother gave me and stain it with this for the rest of my life? Guilty. That's what you want me to say I am. Guilty. You and Clare. I won't lie to you, I sat across from that church wanting it to burn down. But I didn't do it. Understand this. I could've burned that fucking church down for the insult to my color. I'll tell you right now I could have used that as my way of getting even, of letting everybody know what those white folks did to me. But in the end there was no way I could do it."

Elijah shakes his head. It is a stately, solemn movement, freighted with dignity and honest fear. "No, Nat. I am innocent. And because I am, you're gonna prove it. You tell Clare that."

Without a smile, Elijah says, "Now go ahead and tell the big peacemaker."

Fentress, who has relaxed the ta-dah posture, hears this and flaps his hands flat on the prosecution table. He turns his nose to the front of the court.

Exasperated, Nat says, "I hope you know what you're doing."

Now Elijah can't help a nervous laugh. "Man, I hope you know what *you're* doing."

Nat brings his fingers to his eye sockets and rubs. This is not what he'd expected. Drawn into a trial in Good Hope. Dealing with the press. Spending more time here in the town where his memories and thoughts of his wife are still molten. Representing a client who the facts indicate is guilty as sin but who makes it a point of honor to say he is not. And, like the judge warned him, the pressure hasn't even started yet. Nat pushes in on his eyes, unleashing a kaleidoscope of colors and bolts beneath his lids. He crams harder and the false lights reach a pitch. He pulls down his hands, the flashes dissipate, his eyeballs ache for a moment. Nat says, "Bailiff."

The bailiff knocks. In a moment Judge Baron enters. The bailiff intones, "All rise." Baron quickly steps to his leather perch. He looks down on Nat.

"Mr. Deeds, have you finished your discussions with the commonwealth?"

Nat remains standing. "Yes, Your Honor."

"And did you gentlemen reach any understandings this court should be informed about?"

Baron looks hopeful of a deal. He purses his lips in a clear sign of puzzlement when Nat makes no answer. Baron looks to Fentress. The prosecutor shakes his head with the mock, irritating patience of a parent. He adds a condescending shrug with closed eyes.

Baron sighs. "All right," he says. "Let's get this on the calendar. What's good for the sheriff's department, Mr. Fentress? How long do you need to get ready for the preliminary hearing?"

Fentress digs into his briefcase for his calendar. Quickly, he says, "Monday ought to do it, judge. Or we could go right now, to tell you the truth. We've got all the probable cause we need."

"Mr. Fentress, I appreciate your enthusiasm but please keep it to yourself. Mr. Deeds, how do you feel about Monday afternoon?"

Nat thinks Fentress is right, the commonwealth has enough to satisfy probable cause to get an arson case to a trial. No need to drag things out. "Fine, judge."

"All right. Please so advise your client. Gentlemen."

Nat lifts a hand. "Judge."

"Yes?"

"About the bail. I'd like to move for a reduction."

"I've set it at fifty thousand, Mr. Deeds."

"Yes, Your Honor, but Mr. Waddell signifies no risk of flight. He has a wife here who needs him. He has a job at the mill he'd like to keep. He has no record of prior offenses."

In the back of the court Thomas Derby rises.

"Your Honor? May I say something?"

Baron appears piqued. "Sir, I've been wondering what you are doing sitting in my courtroom. I thought I closed this hearing."

Derby speaks clearly. Baron does not intimidate him. "Your Honor, my name is Thomas Derby. It was my church that burned. The deputy outside let me pass through."

"Pastor Derby, sir. Well, I suppose you have a vested interest in being here. All right. You have something to add, pastor?"

Derby's voice, against those of the three lawyers who have been speaking in the court, is like velvet. "Yes, sir. The Victory Baptist Church concurs that Mr. Waddell should be allowed to return to his wife if at all possible. We think it would begin the healing process for all concerned. We are not seeking retribution, Your Honor, only reconciliation."

"Pastor, with all due respect, sir, that is why there is separation of church and state." Baron fidgets when he brings his eyes down to Nat. "Mr. Deeds, I consider the matter of bail settled."

Nat lifts his brows. "Judge, you're the one who asked me to take this case. You had to figure I would represent him as best I could."

Judge Baron takes this in. He lifts his gavel. On the upswing, he announces, "Bail stays at fifty thousand." The gavel strikes. "Court adjourned." The judge stands. With a disapproving glance at Nat, then another at Derby, he says again, "Gentlemen." The bailiff holds the judge's door open. Baron steps down from the bench and with a black flurry he is gone, the bailiff in his wake.

Elijah's guard moves up to lead him back to the holding cells. Elijah and Nat rise.

Nat says to Elijah, "I'll meet you in a minute and walk over with you." To the guard, he says, "I'll be right there. Don't take him out through the press until I'm with him. And don't cuff him, okay? He's not going anywhere."

The deputy says, "Sure, Nat," and guides Elijah through the door. Nat pivots into the courtroom to where Derby stands. "Tom, I'll find you later on."

Derby calls back, "I'm going to talk with some of the church members about helping with the bail money." Derby waggles a hand and walks out. Nat can't resist but replay Fentress's remark, That is mighty Christian. Tom Derby has become a Christian. This must be tearing his congregation right in half, Nat thinks, some forgiving, some wanting Elijah's eye for their eye. Baron was right.

Ed Fentress plays a bongo beat on the prosecution table in the emptied courtroom. He continues to look straight ahead where the judge had been. He says, "That went well. Don't you think it went well?"

Nat eases his rump onto the table. He feels Fentress's rhythm in the wood. Nat too looks at the empty bench. The men are like two musing boxers visiting the silent ring hours before their fight.

Fentress says, "I'll let the deal stand a little while."

"Thanks."

Nat swings his legs.

"Ed," he says, smacking his lips, "I think what we might have here is the criminal defense lawyer's worst nightmare."

"Yep." Fentress slaps the table. "Seen 'em before."

"Yep," Nat says.

"Right out of the box, too, on your first case for the defense. That's tough luck."

After moments Nat puts his feet back on the ground. Slowly, he walks to the left-hand table and takes up his briefcase. He strolls past Fentress, without looking at him, to the door where Elijah waits.

"Yep," Nat says again. "I think what we have here is an innocent man."

## 4

Members of the press have set up a reconnaissance perimeter, watching all the doors to the courthouse and ogling one another. When one of their number moves, they like the coils of a snake move in unison. A cameraman sees the deputy open the side door and Elijah and Nat follow onto the hot sidewalk under the metal awning, which runs a city block to the sheriff's office. The cameraman jogs forward, and with no signal to the others the rest are at his back, lugging their circles and squares and lines of equipment. Nat tells Elijah to say nothing and keep walking past them. "There's going to be cameras," Nat reminds him. "Keep your head up. You're innocent. Look it."

The press forms a skirmish line across the sidewalk. The deputy wants to push through them. The newsmen and -women give way, shouting questions, then re-form along the flanks, keeping pace, the microphones and cameras and hands like a thicket of flesh and metal thorns growing in Nat's and Elijah's path. Their closeness makes the heat of the afternoon after the cool of the courthouse almost unbearable.

Walking, Nat holds up his hands. "All right, all right," he says.

The cawing of the press falls to a twitter. The suited ones pipe urgently, "Get this," to the sweaty bearers of the cameras. "Are you getting this?"

"Folks," Nat announces, "ten minutes ago Mr. Waddell was charged by the commonwealth with one count of arson. We've got a preliminary hearing scheduled for Monday. At that time we'll have a plea for you and more information, okay? That's all for today. Thank you. Now if you'll excuse us."

Nat's words are nothing more to the press than an opening salvo; they fire tumult back at him and at Elijah. "Did you burn the church, Elijah?" "Was it motivated by race?" "Are you talking with the commonwealth's attorney about a deal?" "Was there anyone else involved?" "Are there any other suspects?"

Nat makes no response but keeps striding beside the deputy and

Elijah. The deputy has his head down, no concerns of appearance for him, he resembles a battering ram. Nat sees Elijah's head is not hung in a shameful attitude but is erect, though his gaze is not on the press but over their heads, to the court parking lot. Two dozen people, all white men and women, flock there, many with placards hoisted:

**CHURCH BURNER, BEWARE.**

And

**OUR FIRE TODAY, YOURS IN THE AFTERLIFE.**

And

**WE'LL REBUILD, YOU'LL ROT IN JAIL.**

When they see Elijah, they churn their signs. Nat instantly thinks the color white, of the shaking paperboards and the flushing skins holding them aloft, can look so enraged, it can be the harshest of all colors, of white heat and infection and angry bulging eyeballs.

The door to the sheriff's office is ten yards off. The deputy leans forward, lugging Elijah with him through the moil of the press, who have not relented in their clamoring for answers, who seem to figure if they bang long and hard enough something will give. Nat takes Elijah's other arm and forges ahead with the deputy in breaking through the last few steps. Elijah's eyes are riveted on the church protesters. He seems to want to hear what they are shouting at him over the din of the press.

Just before reaching the sheriff's door, a pretty woman with a microphone boldly leaps between Nat and the door handle. She rams her mike at Elijah's lips and demands, "Did you burn that church?"

Elijah stops. At first Nat thinks it is to avoid running the woman down. Then he realizes that Elijah is going to say something. Nat pulls hard on Elijah's arm but the man is rooted, only three feet from the safety of the door, the woman poised in front of him. The other members of the press see Elijah's feet stilled. They try to squeeze in front too, where the lone woman holds Elijah back, her microphone up like a cross to a vampire.

"Did you?" she insists.

Nat says, "That's enough." He puts the back of his arm against her shoulder to shunt her aside and grab for the door, but the deputy has already put his elbow over her mike and shoved it down, slipping his backside in front of her, shielding Elijah from her. Nat grabs the door handle and opens. He pushes Elijah in. But Elijah turns his head over his shoulder, past Nat's shoulder. Nat cannot stop him. The door is still wide open, Elijah's mouth is open.

"Those church folks," Elijah says to the newswoman, who is stumbling back into place, "they shouldn't have done what they did to my baby."

Nat slams the door behind him, not caring if mikes or fingers get in the way. Through the door he hears their voices, "What baby? What'd they do? Did you get that? Yeah, yeah, I got it! Go, go!"

Nat stamps his foot. "Dammit!" He stops and leans against the wall, smacking it with the flat of his hand. Elijah and the deputy face him. Nat looks away. He says to the deputy, "Put him in the cell. I'll be right there." The deputy turns Elijah down the linoleum hall. Nat takes a deep disgusted breath. He looks through the vertical window slit in the door. The intrepid newswoman smiles at him and shrugs. Nat does his best to return her a glare of revulsion. She tilts her head and scurries off with the rest of the press pack to speak with the people hefting the signs in the lot. Nat bends to see her run off. Already in the parking lot several black passersby have gathered in their own clot, to question or balance what is going on.

Nat walks down the hall to the holding cells. The air conditioning brushes past him, it feels arctic on his cheeks, he realizes he is sweating. His briefcase seems to stretch his arm with some new and baffling load. Nat's leg feels stiff after his angry clout against the floor. The hall is narrow with a low ceiling, the green linoleum tiles are waxed to a hard shine. His amplified footfalls sound in his ears like blows from an ax against a trunk. He imagines his ringing steps to be the chatter of chunks hacked out of his own flesh; when there are enough of them he will lean and fall, maybe fill up this tight hall with his upside-down leaves and broken branches. He does not want to be in Good Hope, there's too much unresolved here. *Clack.* Elijah's claim of innocence has—had?—Nat believing he just incriminated himself in front of a dozen cameras and microphones. *Clang.* He is about to get mired in a racial and religious crossfire because Elijah refuses to take the easy way out and go home to his wife. *Whack.* When this scalding day is over, when the damage of it is toted, Nat will sleep in an empty bed in a dull apartment an hour away in a city he does not like. *Thud.*

The hall leads past a plate glass window, behind which are the sheriff's office and several deputies' paper-strewn desks, file cabinets, FBI Most Wanted posters, and a box of doughnuts. A smaller window on the far side of the big room looks into Talley's office through half-drawn blinds. Talley is in, his boots up on his desk.

Nat continues to the door leading into the three holding cells. He pauses. He has more of himself left, it is not yet time to holler Timber. Instead, he's going to shave a few pieces out of Elijah.

He pushes open the door. Elijah sits in the last green cell to the left. The deputy stands beside the bars, holding the cell door open, waiting. Nat steps into the cage. The deputy slides the door to with its heavy and secure jail-door click and echo.

The deputy leaves. Nat tosses his briefcase on the cot. Elijah sits on a stool. Nat has looked into these cells many times from outside the bars but has never been on the interior with an inmate, there was never any reason when he was prosecuting. He feels how oppressive this is, a straitjacket of green metal and cinder block. He takes in the dimensions, tiny, one Spartan bed, a stool, and a stainless steel toilet with banged-in dents. What kind of person dents a steel toilet? Nat's anger at Elijah wanes with empathy; he imagines there is only one thing worse than to be locked inside these bars as a guilty man and that is to be locked in here innocent.

Nat eases onto the edge of the mattress, the old bedsprings squeal. He looks into Elijah's round ebony face searching for clues, ways to help this man, ways to feel sorry for him and so better fight for him, but there are none, his face is cloaked.

Nat addresses himself right into Elijah's eyes. "Do you know what you just did?"

"What."

"You just made both of our lives a lot more difficult. Frankly, you made yours worse than mine."

"How?"

"That woman asked you, on camera, on tape, if you burned the church. You should have said nothing, like I told you. What you did say was they shouldn't have done that to your baby. In effect, you said, on TV, 'Yes I did burn that church, because they deserved it.' "

Elijah stays plain-faced. "They did." Even so, his voice has a surly bite.

"I know that. But now you've done several things. You've made a public incriminatory statement. That's going to be hard to undo at trial, we'll see that videotape fifty times in court. And worse, you've set loose the dogs on those church people when you didn't have to. The preacher at Victory Baptist, Tom Derby, is an old friend of mine. He told me a lot of the church members were upset and sorry when they found out what the deacons had done to you and Clare. He said he was even going to find help for you with the bail. This all could have been handled privately, Elijah, maybe we could have made some allies. But now you've gone and called everyone at that church a racist just because a few assholes were carrying signs. By the time the press is done with this, all of Good Hope and probably the rest of Pamunkey County is going to look like a bunch of hate-filled rednecks because of what you said."

"It's not because of the signs and it's not because of what I said. It's what they did. I told you, Nat. I had to speak up. Somebody has to show what they are and stop them from getting away with it. I didn't burn their church but I got 'em anyway. Wait'll the newspapers are done with them. Look, man. It wasn't your baby they dug up."

"No, it wasn't."

"It wasn't your wife they hurt."

Nat rubs his neck. He waits, then says, "Well, the good news is you'll probably look like a hero outside of Pamunkey County."

"Yeah."

"The bad news is your jury is going to come from Pamunkey. And by tonight there won't be one person in this county who hasn't heard what you said and what they did and isn't pissed at someone over this. My guess is that most of them will be pissed at everybody involved. I can't wait to hear what Baron has to say about it. Fentress is probably drinking a toast to you right now."

With this, Nat stands. He takes up his briefcase. He looks down on Elijah.

"Okay, now tell me you got that out of your system. Tell me you're going to keep your mouth closed from now on like I say, or is this going to happen again? We can't have it, Elijah. You've got to listen to me if I'm going to be able to help you, all right? You don't dream and talk in your sleep about this case. You don't even talk to Clare about it. You talk to me and no one else. Got it?"

Nat doesn't want a response. He wants to get out of this cell and Elijah's world, both of which seem to be crushing in. Nat needs to step outside and be shut of it for a while. Even the heat outdoors and the lurking press is better than this dungeon and this occupant so willing to be bottled inside it. Nat has his own close walls to deal with. Tomorrow is Saturday. He'll rest and compose an answer for the press—and the judge—as to why Elijah, a man in custody, spoke to the press.

Before Nat can shout for the deputy to come open the cell, the door from the hall is flung wide. Nat hears agitated and loud voices before he sees George Talley storming along the green bars to Elijah's cell. Talley is followed by the deputy with the keys and, in street clothes, Monroe Skelton.

Talley's mouth is tight in a bitter streak. His face and forearms are red, veins all over him pop up like swollen rivers. Through clenched teeth he speaks to the deputy. "Open it."

Monroe lays a hand on Talley's big shoulder. "George, let it lay." His voice pleads. "Please."

Talley repeats, "Open it."

The deputy fumbles, nervous with the keys, they jangle until he finds the one to Elijah's cell door. Talley waits beside him. Nat hears the man's breath coming, it sounds like the wind of a locomotive, *shu-ushhh, shu-ushhh.* The deputy finally works the lock and slides the door open. Talley breaks from Monroe's grasp and treads into the cell. Monroe steps in behind Talley, the cell is full of men and something else, fury and fright.

Talley's eyes slash at Nat. "Out."

Nat sets his jaw. "George. What's up?"

Talley's lips fleer back, baring his teeth. He grabs Nat's lapel in his fist and propels him backward, the sheriff is much stronger; this is not the first time Talley has laid hands on Nat, but his pranks in the locker room as kids were nothing like this. Talley moves quickly before feet can be set. He forces Nat back against Monroe and the deputy, using him as a ramrod to shove them all out of the cell into the hall. Talley slams the steel door. Elijah, who has not stood from the stool, rises now. Talley flings himself the short distance forward. He wraps his hands around Elijah's neck to jolt him against the cinder block wall. The bars in all the cell doors and the lamps overhead rattle.

Talley snarls, "You son of a bitch!"

The keys to the cell door are still in the lock. Monroe reaches and turns.

"I'll kill you right now," Talley hisses, his face fixed only inches from Elijah's. Elijah has clamped his hands over Talley's wrists but he stands no chance of releasing himself, Talley is much too powerful. The sheriff thrusts all his mass into Elijah's neck, his elbows and blanching knuckles pin Elijah bug-eyed to the wall. Monroe throws open the door and rushes inside, Nat behind him, the deputy stays in the hall. Elijah has locked his eyes onto Talley's so that if you passed your hand between their glares you might feel death.

Monroe pries on one of Talley's straining arms. Nat pulls at the sheriff's fingers around Elijah's neck. Talley never looks from Elijah, growling, "I'll kill you, I'll kill you . . ." Monroe slips his large frame between Talley and Elijah and breaks the clutch with his body. Monroe and Nat wrap Talley in their arms and wrangle him against the opposite wall.

"No, George!" Monroe yells into Talley's face where still the death stare resides. "No! This ain't right! No!" Monroe blankets Talley against the wall with his body as though defending his boss from an assassin's bullet. "Leave off, George. Come on, man, leave off."

Elijah stays plastered against the opposite wall, running his hand over his throat, which even beneath the impenetrable black of his skin glows with crimson handprints. Nat stands in the center of the cell. He does not know what he will do if Talley escapes Monroe and another attack commences. He was helpless in the last one but he stands there as at least a smallish impediment.

Nat senses that his position in the center, not gripping anyone else or himself, makes him the one to speak amid all the heaving breathing of the men.

"George? You want to tell me why you just went apeshit?"

"Let me go, Money," the sheriff says, tersely calmer. "I'm all right. Let me loose."

Monroe takes half a step back, blocking Talley's path to Elijah. Staying between the two, sheriff and prisoner, Monroe herds Talley out of the cell and into the hall. Once the two big lawmen are out of the cell, the deputy closes the door again, locking in Nat and Elijah. Talley hulks off down the hall, slumped and drained. The deputy takes his keys and goes behind him. When they are gone, Monroe leans against the cell door. His big brown face and wide chest fill the spaces between many bars. His civilian shirt is untucked. The cell is quiet but Nat feels the reverberations of the struggle still in the walls and stark light, in the sharply drawn breaths.

Elijah sits on the bed. He seems to have descended again into his solitary place. He does not look or seem to listen when Nat asks, "Money?"

The big deputy wraps his mitts around the bars. This makes him appear to be inside, looking out, and something in his face has the quality of the prisoner's gloom.

He says, "It's not good."

"What."

"Maybe we ought to talk in private."

"Tell me here."

Monroe chews on a thought for a moment, it is a thick wad he almost cannot bite through.

He inhales. "The arson squad called me at home about thirty minutes ago."

The big deputy shakes his head, forlorn.

"Nat, they found a girl in the Victory Baptist. I went by to see the body. Then I went to tell George."

Elijah does not move save for the clench of a fist and the plunge of his eyelids.

Monroe looks straight at Elijah when he says, "It was George's daughter, Amanda."

GOOD HOPE

# ONE

On another day, Monroe might have opened a beer and sipped it on the screened porch. Rey Ann might have joined him or not, she has a way of sitting near him that leaves him comforted and alone. Couples who have been together since teenagers can do that. Or he might have been in his county car listening to squawk or walking downtown, pushing through the cottony heat. This is what he thinks of, other days.

On other days longer before, in another country, in the crevices of a jungle, he witnessed this sort of thing. He shared his sweaty, scared, disgusted face with other young soldiers he hunkered with at a safe distance while American jets plowed fire into the soil. Afterward, his Ranger unit walked through the villages with rifles pointed down, at ease. Nothing was alive ever in the dirt streets and alleys still radiating heat. But as a reconnaissance squad they had orders to walk among smoking blistered plants and blasted huts to find roasted bodies of humans, bodies cooked past meat, cooked to brittleness more akin to the charcoal of sticks than flesh. Also there were dogs, apes, chickens, all murdered in flame. The Rangers called these eerie strolls the Valleys of Death. Those bodies in the ruined villages thirty years ago looked no better than the one Monroe saw this afternoon at the Victory Baptist Church.

Rey Ann comes to him now in the late day after he has made it back to his screened porch and his beer. The cold bottle sweats in his fist. He puts it to his forehead, the chill strikes him between his shoulder blades. He closes his eyes. Her hand runs over the nap of his hair, once, twice. He has the strength to open his eyes and look at her and tell her but Monroe wants these strokes, even without needing them.

"Hey, baby," she says.

"Hey."

Monroe hears other men's wives in his head say something stupid like, Bad day? but not Rey Ann. She gentles his brow and waits.

She takes down her hand. Monroe opens his eyes to her. She sits, elbows on knees, hands clasped. He wonders how many hours she has spent like this, waiting for him. He thinks how much he loves her. He blinks to plug a tear he senses wants to bail out. Monroe knows it is the corpse of the girl making him emotional like this.

Monroe is the arresting officer for this case that began as arson and is now homicide. The young deputy accompanying the state arson squad followed the sheriff's protocol by calling him in first, even though Monroe was off duty.

"Jesus," the kid said up in the church lot, meeting Monroe's car, the kid's eye sockets still gray, "I fucking tripped over her. I thought it was a piece of wood."

Monroe greeted the arson team, three men in shirts and ties, emblemed caps and rubber gloves, state cops. He stepped behind one of them through the black rubble while the young deputy hung back in the lot. They did not go deep into the wreckage. The girl was near the doors at the rear of the sanctuary. The flames had scoured from this church every bit of man, leaving nothing but God, His building blocks. The heat had vaporized the water in the timbers, erased all the colors into ebon, ruptured the carved and hammered shapes into powder ash and jagged broken edges. The girl too was not of man any longer but had been re-formed by God and fire.

She lay facedown. All her clothes had burned away but Monroe guessed it was a girl from the remaining shape of the buttocks and the thin waist. The color and texture of her back and legs was not distinguishable from the cinders on which she lay. The heat of the fire around this girl had been horrific, the scourging grisly. Both feet were burned away, as was the whole right hand, which lay beside her trunk. Across her shoulders and over her head was a charred pew. She must have crawled under it before or during the fire. The arson investigator and Monroe carefully lifted away the etched slab of the bench. Her head lay in the crook of her arm as though sleeping, or crying. All her hair was purged, her scalp bubbled like road tar. Monroe moved around to kneel before her. He lowered his face to the ground, she did not smell different from the fire; he looked closely where the skin had been protected by her bent arm and the pew. He recognized Amanda Talley. Beneath the fingers of her left hand lay a Baptist hymnal. One of the church's fans made from popsicle sticks and greeting cards was stuck in the hymnal as a bookmark. Inside this little ring made by the girl's arm—the flesh on her face, her parted lips, the songbook, the paper cards stuck in the pages—seemed to be the only region in the entire church not savaged by the fire.

Monroe stayed a few minutes more. The other investigators showed him what they had found on the grass behind the church, a melted plastic milk jug smelling of kerosene. They were pretty sure the fire was started from the outside at the church rear with the fluid; the girl or someone else had not done it from inside the church. A quick search of the immediate area yielded nothing more, with the exception of the white T-shirt and beer cans found that morning across the road in the bushes. The church grounds were too hard and dry from the drought to look for footprints and they could find nothing else that could be considered a clue. Besides, they'd heard that Pamunkey County had the arsonist in jail already, arrested at the site during the fire; "Dumb shit," one of the investigators snickered.

Monroe prevented the investigators from calling the sheriff's office. Let me, he told them. It's got to be done by me in person. Instead he gave them the name and number of the local medical examiner, who would come out and file an initial report, plus arrange transport for the body up to Richmond to the state M.E.'s office. Monroe cast his eyes once more over the carnage. He saw in his mind Elijah Waddell pacing and wobbling beside the steeples of flames. He thought of Amanda frying under a pew inside, and once more he felt an old anger at the unseen which targets the young. Come at me, he thought, walking to his county cruiser, come at me you bastard and see how easy I go down. Monroe wanted to strike something with his fist. The feeling swelled in him enough to make him hit the steering wheel. The horn sounded and the investigators waved goodbye, apparently believing he had tossed them a beep in departure.

Monroe has finished his beer. He does not concern himself with the question of Elijah's innocence or guilt. He has done what the county asks of him, he has put the principal suspect behind bars. If the man stays jailed or gets out, it is others who will decide. It's a shame what's been done, no matter who's done it. If not Elijah Waddell, then someone else, it's all the same after a point. Rey Ann rises to fetch him another beer. He says, "No, thanks, baby. If I have one more I'll have fifteen and I got to go back in after dinner."

Rey Ann sits in the identical posture she held before, on the edge of the lounge cushion, fingers joined under her chin, a rapt pose. She's not to be believed, Monroe thinks. She's everything. She listens when he needs it. Talks when he needs it. Hollers when he needs it.

"George," he says. "George didn't take it too well, you can imagine."

"No. I guess not."

Nothing in his wife's voice says, Tell me, I'm curious. She is there only as receptacle for him, a basin for whatever he needs to wash, cistern for whatever he cannot contain and must spill over. He decides not to describe the violent scene in the cell, let Talley have his heartache in relative privacy; if others find out the sheriff threatened Elijah Waddell, it will have come from someone else. Besides, Monroe cannot say he would have handled himself much better in similar circumstance, though Talley never seemed that attached to his daughter when she was alive.

Considering similar circumstance—that of a murdered child,

which also brings to mind the twice-buried infant Nora Carol—Monroe thinks of his own child and like an animal smelling man he senses the unseen again, catches a stench of ill on his own porch, in his own house. He stands, teeth gritted, big chest out, and, empty beer bottle in his mitt as a cudgel to fight it off, Come on, where are you? Get away from my family, get away!

"Money?" He does not look down at Rey Ann's voice. He is afraid the unseen is in his eyes—it was there before on the times when he killed those whom he saw and when he put his eyes on the aftermath of killing, his own and others' work—he is afraid the unseen will alight where he looks, so he turns his face from his wife. He drops the bottle on the plastic cushion behind him and goes inside the house.

Monroe knows there is only one way to fight the unseen. Maybe that is what George Talley did not do, that is why his daughter fell prey, and now it's too late for both of them. Monroe picks up the phone. Rey Ann stays on the porch in the first signs of dusk fluttering through the screen, when the heat has peaked and the birds sound off to begin their last meal of insects before their evening roosts. He dials.

He says to the woman answering, "Sergeant Grover Skelton, please. Yes, it's his father. Yes, I'll hold."

A recorded schedule of events at Fort Bragg plays through the receiver. Monroe ignores it until he hears his son's voice.

"Dad? Is everything all right?"

"Yeah, yeah, Grove, nothing's wrong. Your mom and me are fine."

"Then what's up?"

"Just wondered when you're coming home for a visit."

"Dad, you called me for that? I'm on the drill ground."

"Good. Work 'em hard. When."

His son takes his laugh away from the phone, disbelieving. Monroe thinks, He's looking over his recruits.

"Grover, come home."

"Soon as I can, Dad. What's the matter, Mom missing me?"

Because Monroe is aware the unseen feeds itself in part on the unspoken, he says with certainty, "I miss you, boy."

"Okay." The voice is confused, but Monroe hears his son's smile stay in place, at attention.

Monroe thinks now of the rule learned long ago in a hostile land walking side by side with other boys, the alone ones who took the point, who encountered the unseen first, who spied it in its lair or caught it out on the prowl, they were the ones who assessed its strength and position.

"Grove?"

"Yeah?"

The rule of recon. Warn the ones behind you. Then—if you must, if you cannot run—fight it the only way you can. Together.

To his son he says, "Boy, your mom and I love you. More'n we can say. That's all."

2

Nat pulls his car onto the shoulder of the narrow road. He shuts down the lights and engine and gets out. Instantly the night prickles his skin with moist heat. The air out here in the country where the earth is not slathered with concrete and brick but is shaved down to the dirt then matted with crops, where trees and not man's stacked stones eat at the sky, where no masses rub shoulders only crickets their wings, out here the air is like the air that passes over a tongue, it has a pith and a fecundity you feel, you smell the breath of the planet, hothouse life. Nat mops his brow with the back of his wrist; he's only been out of the car's air conditioning a minute. He stares under star and moonlight over the field where nothing has changed in thirty years.

When he was a boy, he had a metal detector. In the planting time of spring he followed tilling tractors across this field to locate Civil War artifacts turned up by the cultivators. While other boys collected and traded baseball cards, Nat Deeds kept a shoe box of CSA belt buckles, brass buttons and coronet insignias, minié balls, rusted bayonets, and even a flintlock. He read about Ulysses Grant's Peninsula campaign, the Federal's tramp westward from the Chesapeake Bay to take Richmond, the Confederate capital. A fierce skirmish was fought in this field two miles from the river; back in the woods on the other side of the road is a long berm beside a scummy creek that 150 years ago was a Rebel redoubt. Nat played there, spread out his treasures behind it, shot imaginary advancing bluecoats, retreated to play another day. Now he is older and burdened, the shoe box lost and unimportant, his parents passed on. But the pearly field is planted with alfalfa the way it used to be and the moon is in place, the berm is still back there in the trees, and these are what Nat came here for.

He gets back in the car and drives off. The moon lights the backs of his hands on the wheel with a gray wash. He has been driving for over an hour—like the moon, on a tether—first around town and then the quiet county. Nat needs to move. The world appears bigger when the scenery changes, and though he is intimate with everything he has seen tonight, it all has grown larger because he has missed it. Nat wants the world to seem large right now, to push away the claustrophobic dimensions of Elijah's predicament. Nat is being drawn into Elijah and he must combat that. He can do the man no good as advocate if he cares too much about Elijah's innocence or guilt, if he continues to see parallels between himself and Elijah. It is Nat's job only to provide the best legal representation he can, to coldly assess the man's chances and risks, and that gets compromised if you identify too strongly with your client. So that is what Nat is doing tonight after learning that Elijah will appear in court again Monday morning to hear a charge of murder. He sat through one more round of Elijah's terse denials before the man was shipped back to the Rappahannock lockup. Tonight on the road perambulating through his home county Nat reclaims the proportions of his own world, stretching it in sight and memory back to its original size, outside of green bars and the threat of years spent behind them.

He drives east past the burned, humbled hulk of the Victory Baptist. He does not slow down, the place is already part of the night, twilit and untouchable. A quarter-mile up the road he pulls into the gravel driveway of the church's parsonage. Before his tires stop crunching, Tom Derby is at the screen door.

Nat lowers his window. "Tom. I was out driving. Is it too late to drop by?"

Derby lifts a finger to say, One minute. He disappears from the light of the doorway, then returns carrying a bottle. He pushes open the screen door, lets it slam, leaves his front door unlocked, and climbs into Nat's car.

"Drive," he says.

Nat takes off toward town. He watches the pallid moon on Derby's knuckles while Derby unscrews the top from the fifth of scotch and tosses the cap out the window.

Derby has a dour look on his face. He raises the bottle.

Nat asks, "What are you doing?"

Derby jiggles the bottle.

"It's Friday night, Nat. We've done this before, I believe, you and me."

"I thought if you were going to be a preacher you had to give that up."

Derby takes a pull on the bottle. He winces and licks his lips.

"Don't judge me too harshly, son. I consider it my duty to share everything my church endures. I figure I can best guide them if I understand them."

Nat reaches for the proffered bottle. Before taking a drink, he says, "You should be the lawyer here."

"I'd be a waste as a lawyer," Derby says, watching Nat's swallow. "I make a much better sinner as a preacher."

The two drive in silence past the charred church and the fields, into town. They nurse the bottle with small nips. Nat turns up the air conditioning, donning bit by bit the coat of scotch inside him and its warmth. They do not converse but watch the passing road and each other's dim profiles. Nat senses the mute agreement of patience until they are at their talking place.

They enter the town, past the Rotary Club sign. The night shift at the mill keeps the boiler steaming and the gargantuan gobs of pulp baking into spools of paper. The river is flat, muddy under the moon, only a few spotlight fishermen bobbing on it. Bats buzz the marsh grasses. Nat turns off Main Street for five blocks and comes to rest at the curb under a thick hickory tree that was fat and solid too the last time Nat and Derby sat under its branches on the porch of his parents' old house. This time they stay seated in the car with the windows down.

Nat takes the fifth. They've gone through about a quarter of it already. He downs a sip and hands it back to Derby. He waits for Derby to say something. But the preacher only makes the bottle gurgle. The silence of their passage into town seems to have gained a momentum, still traveling though the car has stopped. The shuttling bottle suffices for discourse right now. Nat waits another minute while Derby stares through the windshield, spellbound by his own thoughts.

Derby says, "I heard about the girl in the fire."

Nat is not surprised by this. You grow used to news spreading like dawn in a small town. He wonders first if Clare knows, then figures she does, the word has swept across the county by now, it'll be statewide and maybe national in the morning. But for now it is only here in this car tucked under the dark calm hickory.

"How?"

"One of George Talley's deputies is married to the daughter of one of our members."

Nat asks, "Did Amanda ever come to your church?"

Derby purses his lips and gives a small nod. "Just once that I know of."

Nat perks up. Here is a connection. "When?"

"Three or four weeks ago."

"Who brought her in? You know her father's a big Catholic."

"Nobody brought her in. She just walked in on her own. Came up to me after the service and said she enjoyed herself. Had a pretty smile on. Said who she was. That was all. Turned around and strolled out like she came in, by herself."

"You didn't see her after that."

"No."

"What do you think she was doing in the church last night?"

"I have no idea. I was in Williamsburg last night 'til after midnight."

"Doing what?"

"This has all been kind of hard on me, Nat. It wasn't easy getting turned down like that by the deacons. It brings up some bad memories."

"You were drinking?"

Derby uncorks a smile. "A little."

"How'd the girl get into the church?"

"I leave the doors unlocked. Anybody can come in, day or night."

Nat mulls this over. Why would George Talley's daughter be in a small Baptist church three miles outside town at one-thirty in the morning? At the jail, after Talley's outburst, Monroe told Nat what he'd seen at the fire site, that under Amanda's hand there'd been a hymnal with a bookmark in it. Had the girl been reading it? Did she wander in the open doors the way Derby suggests, like she did weeks ago for one Sunday service? Was Amanda Talley trying to break away from George's avid Catholicism? Did she walk out to the Baptist church in the night to sit and consider, did she take up the hymnal in failing light to practice singing sacred songs, made even more sacred because they were her last? Did she fire the church herself then run inside to die, some symbolic suicide? Or did Elijah or someone else throw her into the building and burn it down around her? Why was she found lying under a pew? What happened in those early hours? With a churn in his gut, Nat anticipates the medical examiner's report. He knows it will be awful, but it may also shed some light, maybe something to clear Elijah. Maybe not.

Nat begins to describe to Derby what he knew of Amanda Talley. He doesn't have a reason for doing so—he didn't know the girl that well, he thinks no one in Good Hope did, perhaps not even her father—other than it feels seemly to Nat to speak of the dead soon after their passing. He observes while he speaks that he is almost superstitious about this, as though it is a way of appeasing the powers that pull the destiny strings, for the purpose of building a good account to help ward off a dreadful fate such as Amanda Talley's for himself. The worst part of death is the attendant silence, he thinks. Words are a gift to the dead, to alleviate their silence, at least for the short while until they are forgotten.

Amanda Talley was seventeen, a rising senior at high school up in Maryland. She lived there with her mother. She liked horses and all animals, but George could not keep a horse here for the girl to ride. Amanda never seemed to have a boyfriend during her summers in Good Hope, though she came every year since the divorce. She let her ginger-colored hair grow long, it had a natural curl that the humidity of the river made tangly. There was something quietly feral about her, she was leggy and loose-limbed so that when she strode on her lonesome walks she seemed like a young coyote, wary of man. Some in the town said she was aloof, others said lazy and uninspired, still others remarked they felt bad for the gangly girl, she had a well-known father who spent most of his time at work and at church and she must have just decided to stay out of his way. George has a loud greeting and a slap on the back for everybody in public; what gentleness did he have in private for his daughter? Nat concludes, "I guess I could have gotten to know her better."

Derby lets that hang a moment. Then, without turning to Nat, he asks, "Why do you say that?"

"I don't know. I just could have. She was a kid. She could have used friends."

Derby looses a small, sardonic laugh. "Truth is, she was nothing to you. She was nothing to nobody around here."

"Maybe so." But this seems unkind and the dead and their overseers will not enter credit into your account if you speak of them without charity. Nat pushes his vision past Derby across the dim lawn to the unlit front steps of his childhood. The light in the living room window goes out. The folks in his parents' house are retiring for the night. Nat recalls himself and Derby on the porch steps twenty-five years ago, young, hungry men. Derby was like a dynamo then, spinning off energy and ideas. Nat asks his friend a question the way he would have then.

"How does this happen? How does the birth of a mixed-race child lead to all this?" Nat ticks off on his fingers. "Fire, revenge, murder? How? These are all good, average people. These aren't criminals or racists."

Derby says, "You're asking me to explain God to you."

"I'm not sure what I'm asking."

"I can do it. Something has come to me. Today."

Nat says nothing, which is his role once the question is presented to Derby. He reaches for the bottle. Derby hands it over with the start of his answer.

"Tell me," Derby says. "What is the one thing God knows the least about?"

"God's supposed to know everything."

"Know everything. Be everywhere. Do anything." The preacher's voice climbs as though up the steps to the lectern. "So what does God not know? See, I've been wondering about this for a while now. I've been needing to find a way to forgive God. But I can't forgive Him if He's all-powerful and all-knowing. If that's the case, we've got no choice but to blame Him for everything we think goes wrong, because He could have stopped it. So if God maybe doesn't know something, just one thing, then we can understand and forgive. Perhaps the one thing God Almighty is ignorant about is what it's like to not be almighty. Look at it. God is immortal, so He obviously knows nothing about dying. He's without flaw and can't conceive what it would be like to have faults, temptations, wants, greed, remorse, suspicions. He's loved by all that is, therefore He doesn't understand a thing about loneliness and desperation and rage. He created a universe, so we can assume He has no real insights on being weak. In short, God does not know what it's like to be human. That's our job. To be impotent and tiny, vicious and scornful and mortal. We educate God in the one black hole of His knowledge. He won't stop us or save us or ease our pain, Nat, not for a minute. We suffer and perish in front of Him to school Him about suffering and perishing, which God can't do for Himself. He let that poor baby girl come into the world to Clare and Elijah in a terrible fashion, then took her away. Then He sat back and watched what happened afterwards. He watched my hateful deacons, Elijah's pride, that fire, innocent Amanda Talley, me, those folks with the signs, the TV people. He even sent down His only son Jesus Christ to go through the racking of life, same as the rest of us. So, in a way, we're all like Jesus. We're all God's children and teachers."

Derby tips the bottle. This swig is like water to him, nothing on the man's face shows it is liquor, there is no gasp or crinkling eyes.

"Don't look to God for answers," Derby says, handing the bottle urgently over to Nat as though it were medicine. "Don't. Because He's looking to us for them."

That is enough scotch for Nat. He waves off the bottle. Derby shrugs and keeps it.

"That's kind of bleak, isn't it?" Nat asks. "I thought God was supposed to love us."

Derby speaks more softly now, he has pulled out some burr. With the oratorical edge gone, Nat hears a sorrowfulness like a pall over his friend's voice.

"He does, son, He does. He loves us too much, in fact, and that's why He can't touch us. If He lifted one finger for us He'd go too far and spoil us, He'd take away all our pain. He'd make us angels if He could right here on Earth, but He can't. That would stop us from instructing Him. He suffers with us, remember. And it's not all bad. He sees everything we do. That includes the goodness, the courage, the selflessness. He sees you, my friend Nat Deeds."

"Yeah, right. Me." Nat snorts, it is a misplaced funny sound, it is the alcohol. To make himself feel more sober, he jerks his thumb at the bottle in Derby's grip. "You're hitting that a mite hard, aren't you?"

Derby ignores this. "He sees you, Nat. You're a good man. You didn't have to take this case. You don't have to be here at—what time is it?—drinking with me, worrying over what to do and why all this has happened. You care a great deal."

"I know. I gotta stop that."

"If that's what helps you do your job. But I know you, Nat, you haven't changed that much. I don't know what your life has been like for the last twenty-some years but it hasn't taken this away from you. You've still got the gift, the fearlessness that lets you commit, makes you care. And when you care about something, I know you, you go all out. I still see it right where it always was." Derby pokes a finger, too steady for the scotch he has consumed, over Nat's heart. "That's what Elijah's going to need from you. Right there. So even if it costs you, even if it hurts you, keep caring. Anything less and that boy is in deep shit."

Nat wants off this particular hook. He doesn't wish to explain to Derby all his issues right now. It's late and he has to try to drive to Richmond. He and Derby can trade histories later, in the daylight, straight. Now he wants to deflect Derby away from Elijah and that bridge which has built itself in his heart—where Derby's finger presses, his heart seems to push back, it is that full—from Elijah to Maeve.

He says, "I thought preachers couldn't cuss."

Derby withdraws the poke. "Preachers can't do nothing. I'm the weakest of the weak. That's why God values me so highly. I'm His best tutor."

Derby holds up the bottle, uses the streetlight to measure the remaining liquor. An inch of crystal brown swishes inside. He seems to struggle a moment whether to down it but does not drink. Nat thinks it is to show that Derby does not have a drinking problem, that he can resist the last bit. It is a trifling display of command. Nat decides to address this another time, not while he has plenty of that same bottle washing in his own veins.

"I want to help," Derby says. "I'm going to raise money among our membership for Elijah's defense. You'll need expert witnesses, investigators, whatever, I don't know, but I'm going to get you the money for it. I got plenty of people who feel bad about what our church did."

"Tom, you don't have a church."

"No, Nat, no," Derby sings sweetly, his head sways now just perceptibly. "That was just a building. You got to understand, a church is a community. For instance." Derby taps the front of his shirt over his chest. "When I first came back Rosy Epps gave me a silver crucifix she wore for seventy-eight years. She figured her husband is dead, her daughter is dead, and her granddaughter don't care much about church anymore. So she gave it to me. She said she wanted it to stay with the Victory Baptist after she was gone. But when the baby died, we agreed we should give the cross to Clare. Maybe it would bring her closer to God, maybe not. But even if Clare doesn't ever come to the new building, even if she never worships one day in there after it's built, that cross which was given between Rosy, me, and Clare is a church. Our own little church. See, it's a community, Nat. Sometimes it's two or three people, sometimes it's hundreds, sometimes it's just you and God by yourselves."

Derby pivots a shoulder into the car seat, to face Nat. His voice relinquishes the tone of the preacher. But the Rock of Ages voice, the unshakable faith, is still there. It's the old visionary Tom Derby, the young man on the front porch who could and would do everything in his life.

"I still have a church. I still do. The younger members are furious at the deacons. I've talked to fifty of them today already. They agree that Elijah was done a dreadful wrong. I think even when they find out about Amanda Talley a lot of them are still going to feel ashamed for what's happened. We're going to rally around this tragedy, Nat. We're going to rebuild Victory Baptist more beautiful than ever it was in the last two-hundred-odd years. We're going to have pig pickings and bake sales, raffles, fish fries, I'm going to try and get the mill to contribute. I've already got a call from the Virginia Council of Churches for funding. We'll get prayers and money and we'll remake Victory Baptist with new values, younger blood. We'll put God up front and leave man to second place like he's supposed to be. And we'll build her right on top of the ashes of the old one because that's what ashes are for, to cleanse the earth for the new."

Derby has emptied his last dregs of sobriety on this speech and now his body switches tanks, to the full tank, the scotch. Gone is the firebrand Derby, doused by the liquor, smothered by an unhappy weight. His head and shoulders loll back against the seat. He closes his eyes.

"The greatest shame," he says, "is mine. I had the chance to stop all of this and I couldn't."

With his face pointed to the car roof, eyes folded shut, Derby lifts an open hand. His voice takes on the intoning of a benediction, his palm pointed at Nat is like a small white lens, one of the watchful eyes of a studying God.

"You defend Elijah. You give it your absolute best shot. I have faith in you. You care about him all you can, because there's going to be a lot of folks who just won't."

Derby says no more. The hand furls and flops into his lap. Nat drives out of the neighborhood and out of town to take his friend home. He leaves his window down to help shake off the scotch. On the back roads he listens, that is what he did with Derby, what he has done all day with others, and he keeps doing it now with Derby subdued, or asleep. Nat listens to the wind; tonight it is a honey-suckled lullaby, hushed, a warmed whisk that knows his name. His tires rub the willing road. Nat wonders under the dodging moon, beside the silver fields and marching trees, even sliding past the black death place of Amanda Talley, if tonight after leaving Derby he will cross the bridge above the river, westward to his bed, or if he will cross instead the secret span in his heart, to sit hours more in his car on vigil at Maeve's dark and familiar door.

3

It is not midnight but that is the next destination for the night. Clare squats on her front porch. The moon is flung as high as it will go. Clare cannot see stars, just moonlight, as though the moon is jealous of other lights, almost panting beams into the sky to blot out all but itself. On the earth, the cornfield is milky. Illumed by the moon, the stalks seem to Clare's tired eye like gray wraiths in their thin millions gathered about her house to see her on her porch, come to lend an ear or jeer at her. She waits for that, but the ghosts are just corn and crickets. Clare licks salt from her upper lip.

The telephone rings inside the darkened house. It has rung all day. Folks from the mill. Newspaper people. A television camera crew drove out here and Clare tried to sic Herschel on them as soon as they got out of their white van but the dog is too playful. She went inside and refused to come out. The intruders called to her and came on her property and actually knocked but Clare sat inside behind closed curtains curled on the sofa with the phone ringing.

Now the phone beckons Clare inside from the porch. The house is lightless because Clare has sat out here since nightfall. The phone rings for a full minute. Clare rises to see who it is—these things in our hearts are random; five minutes before and perhaps five minutes after she would have let it ring, measuring her resistance against the stamina of the midnight caller. Herschel stays on the porch, asleep on his side.

She does not turn on a lamp. The moon is in the house, spilling its milk on everything, on the corn outside, the carpet, the phone.

"Yes?"

"Clare. It's Gran."

Clare is wordless.

"I know it's late. Don't hang up. Please."

The old woman's voice is a stab in Clare's breast. Every second since yesterday morning when Nora Carol was moved from the Victory Baptist, Clare has careened between sharp feelings for her grandmother, feelings that do not easily stand alongside each other, furious anger, tender grateful memories, estrangement, befuddlement; each consideration of the old woman's betrayal among the deacons pitches Clare headlong into her own wounded heart as into a briar patch where every thought of her grandmother is barbed and jabbing. The old voice on the phone—Clare has been waiting for a moment—brings her to calculate the stack of loved ones she has served over in the past three days to some evil and ravenous fate: her daughter, her grandmother who raised her, her husband, perhaps even herself before all this is said and done. And for what? Why? What has Clare done to be singled out like this? She wanted to have a baby, that was all, just a man and a child and a joined future like other women have. A simple desire. But for some reason she is being tested. She has been found strong, she knows. She was strong when she bore Nora Carol, strong when she buried the child then buried her again. When she visited Elijah in jail this morning, when Elijah's lawyer came to call in the afternoon, when she heard about the sheriff's daughter in the fire, strong when the night fell and brought nothing to a close but the day, not its sorrow. With Gran Epps on the phone Clare senses now what the aloneness and woe and constant strength are doing to her. She is changing. She is becoming one of the wraiths of the cornfield. The moon through the window draped across her bare arms drains her flesh color, she is turning not of this world. The old voice on the phone belongs to the rainbow world and its dear past, before death stole Clare's color and her life.

"Clare?" Gran Epps's voice is timorous. "I'm sorry."

She pulls the phone from her ear. She looks at the receiver, it is a bone-shaped and -hued thing, like part of a skeleton in her hand. Gran Epps's voice rattles from the bone. "Please believe me. I'm sorry. Clare? Will you talk to me?"

The old voice wants pardon from Clare. The voice does not understand that Clare can grant that easily and it will change nothing. Clare forgives Nora Carol for being born so poorly and leaving so soon. She forgives her husband for having been at that church last night, the wrong place at the wrong time. But Clare's forgiveness will not unlock the fresh grave or the jail door. Likewise her forgiveness will not open her choked heart to Gran Epps.

She brings the phone back to her ear. The receiver is oddly cool on such a warm night. Bones are cool, she thinks.

She does not speak yet. Gran Epps continues to wangle. Clare, sweetheart, she says, you don't understand, the others in the church, she'll make it up to Clare, she knows in her soul Elijah didn't do this, she's so sorry the way things have turned out, she never dreamed. Clare senses the otherworldly strength in her arm supporting the phone; the receiver soaks up Gran Epps's speech and grows heavier word by word in her hand but Clare holds the receiver and her tongue with the endurance of stone. Finally, not because it is too heavy but simply to come to an end—which inevitably is what strength is, the power to be the one who finishes—Clare speaks.

"Gran?"

"Yes, dear? Yes, sweetheart?"

"I've got too much to say to you."

"I know, I know. You must."

"So I'm going to say none of it. Good night."

Clare lays the receiver in its cradle.

## 4

It has begun, the stripping away. So quickly, it surprises Elijah. This is his first full night in jail. He does not know the time. It is late, but how late? Two, three in the morning? Returning from court in Good Hope this afternoon to the Rappahannock Regional Jail, he was moved from general population to isolation. His cell resides at a far end of the second-story tier, the last cell before the high brick wall. Not even the light from the Exit signs reaches his bars. He has no window. It is so dark where he lies on his cot he could be floating in space. Faraway sounds come into his small hard space but they are indeterminate, echoed off so much brick and metal, flying and bouncing through so much open air he cannot tell what they are or where they originate. Footsteps? Voices or snores? Mechanical, like fans or water pipes? The world stumbling through his bars is blind and crippled and confounded, it comes at him all woven together, sound and time and heat and distance corded up like a noose. This is the stripping away, for if you must fight to know when and where you are, you will soon do battle for who you are.

Elijah does not sleep. His pulse is like a hand that nudges him, Hey buddy, you sleeping? every second. His eyes are open, he thinks his eyeballs should parch and scratch he blinks so little. He searches for sensation: shreds of light on the ceiling, the thick warm sheet under his fingers, a button in his back from the cheap mattress, a cotton-wad dryness in his mouth. He casts for thoughts too, but they are all of fire. He suddenly can think of nothing else, as though he has looked into a great beacon, then looked away and the image is burned there overlying everything. In his mind he watches the church fire leap, joyous in its freedom like a genie unstoppered, the fire gorging but wanting more, he looks away from the flames to the little graveyard, but his eyes like a brazier carry the flames with them to the grave, and the red clay over Nora Carol ignites and has flames prancing on it too. Then he looks to Clare standing beside the burning church and the grave and she is set ablaze by his vision. He glances around in a panic and so ignites the trees and the road, the big brown police officer come to arrest him goes up in flame, the grass like a lake in Hell burns, and Elijah stands in the middle of the inferno, shirtless and drunk and weeping tears that hiss and boil on his cheeks.

Elijah yanks open his eyes. He fell asleep. That nightmare awaited him. A moment's relief that it was just a vision is sunk instantly by what he awakes to, jail. Now, because he is in an ethereal darkness of prison that he is not sure is the end of the nightmare, he hears a voice, tiny, fluttery like a candle in wind. The voice is not a part of the place or time of his incarceration. Daddy, it says. Daddy.

Nora Carol?

Daddy. Daddy.

Oh, child. Oh, child, I want to undo everything.

Daddy.

And the voice walks, it has feet and footsteps. It comes nearer through the absolute black to his cell.

Elijah opens his lids again.

Floating outside his bars is one red eye, an orb of anger and fire. In a moment the orb glows hotter, almost orange now, then dulls. Smoke, just barely lit, flumes in curls around the dot.

Elijah does not lift his head from the pillow or move on his cot. The red point, like a dragon's eye, gleams hot again, then cools.

The dot hangs outside the bars for a minute, glowing and dimming, smoke attending its dwindles. Elijah waits, he does not let on that he is awake, watching as he is watched. Then the dot glows its brightest, a deep breath from the dragon, and the eye is tossed tumbling end over end at Elijah on the bed, who swats the cigarette off his chest. A cloud of smoke drifts past the bars when George Talley walks away.

AMANDA TALLEY

# ONE

The death of Sheriff George Talley's daughter has brought out the crowds. Nat does not attend the memorial service at St. Bede's though he drives down Main Street and looks up the church steps into the open twin doors. The church is packed to the rafters. People stand on tiptoe in the vestibule. On the sidewalk outside the church wait several photographers and cameramen. Keeping an eye on them, pacing the sidewalk in uniform, is Monroe. He waves Nat over to the curb. Nat stops. Monroe leans in his window.

"Damn shame," the deputy says.

"That it is."

Nat sends his gaze up the steps, into the church.

"How's George taking it?"

Monroe shrugs.

Nat has long noted an ambivalence in Monroe Skelton, the ablest of all the county deputies, for George Talley. Monroe does his job, keeps his nose clean. He grins whenever George whaps him on the back but there is always that something of the grizzly about Monroe, the big creature whose power you'd best respect.

Monroe relaxes the pinch of his shoulders. "Man, it's crowded in there. You goin' in?"

"No. I don't think so, Money. I'm the lawyer for the guy accused of killing the girl. I think I'll keep a little distance today, you know what I mean. I'll wait and go out to the cemetery after church."

"Yeah. Gutty of you to come at all, Nat."

"Maybe. I've known George a long time."

Monroe tells Nat how Talley went to Richmond yesterday morning to the medical examiner's office to identify the body. Monroe concedes that must have been awful. Talley pulled some strings with the state people to push the autopsy through so he could bury his daughter after Sunday services today.

Nat asks, "You see the newspapers?"

"Yeah. Your boy Waddell's well-known by now."

The story of the church arson and Amanda Talley's suspected murder was bruited in the Saturday and Sunday news in Richmond, on TV and in print, probably around the state as well. Photos and videos sprayed the image of the charred church across the public eye like graffiti. Details were paraded of Nora Carol's tragic birth and death, her exhumation at the hands of the Victory Baptist deacons, the early morning church blaze, Elijah's arrest, the discovery the next afternoon of the teenage daughter of the Pamunkey sheriff in the ashes. The whole county takes lumps in the articles. The words *black, white, racial, hatred, troubled, alleged* crawled over the reports for two days like angry ants and there will be more, Nat knows. He stares past Monroe to the open church doors. From inside he hears dirgeful organ music. He thinks of the sweaty people crammed in there in aisles and benches with wreaths and a flower-draped closed coffin, he envisions a potent mix of reporters, lamenting Catholics, repentant Baptists, loyal debtors and cronies of George Talley, bawling or sniffing and united in righteousness, all quite horrified at the circumstances of the girl's demise and vexed at reading in the statewide papers that they are such small-town hicks with arcane Jim Crow ways. All looking for someone to blame, so long as it's not themselves. Nat hopes Tom Derby is inside whispering to them of contrition and forgiveness.

One of the reporters lurking on the church steps begins a walk toward Nat's car. Monroe sees the look on Nat's face. He turns to stem the man's advance.

"It's Sunday," Monroe says to the reporter. "Give it a break."

The newsman speaks over Monroe's blocking shoulder. "Mr. Deeds? Can I have a word with you?"

The other newspeople hear this and come like pigeons to popcorn. Monroe sets himself to contain them. He waves Nat on. "Later," he says.

At one o'clock Nat parks his car in the large Catholic cemetery outside town. The place is well kept, potted flowers adorn most of the graves. The pale headstones are set flat in the ground to maintain the feeling of a grassy pasture. Atop a low hill in the center of the cemetery stands a tall stone cross. Nat walks up the crest to stand below the cross, which casts no shadow, the light beats almost straight down now. From here the view beyond the assemblage for Amanda is of the river bend where the green waters run away to join the Chesapeake Bay.

Nat wears a black suit but there is not much black at the funeral. The heat greets everyone around the grave site as though the heat itself is the shimmering host and not George Talley or St. Bede's. Nat guesses there are four hundred people spread over the lawn. Many of them are cloaked in cooler tones, the women in carnation pastels, the men in seersucker blue and white twill or tan cotton khaki. Black is a formal color; the folks of Pamunkey County are largely working-class, they do not wear a lot of black. This looks more like an Easter gathering than a burial.

Maeve wears black.

Nat sees her standing alone under an ebony broad-brimmed straw hat. Her hair, dark as the hat, falls straight onto her back, so that from this distance she seems to wear a black cowl. This is the first time he has seen her since Christmas week eight months ago. For a moment seeing her he senses snow, that cold day. She is surrounded by four hundred others in close quarters and even so, even clothed in mourning, her face turned down, from a hundred yards away on a hilltop his eyes light on her easily.

Nat leans back against the stone cross. The thing has the day's heat coursing through it, it feels unliving but alive all at once. Nat has not been inside a church to pray since a teenager, and only then infrequently with his parents for the holidays to keep pace with other management families. Once inside his family's Presbyterian church, he did not pray under his breath to God asking for things like he was taught, beseeching for wisdom or patience or toys or relief for some relative who lay sick; Nat simply said Hello to God. How are you, God? What's it like up there? Nice, I hope. Nat always figured it was wrongheaded to bother God for help or rewards. Nat decided as a child he already had everything he needed, so he resisted asking God for extra portions. This became his way and it robbed him of faith. Looking down from the hill he wonders what it is like today to be George Talley. To have such faith and such need for a kind, generous God and to have at the same time a dead daughter. How do these reconcile? This thought leads him to Clare and Elijah—to have such love as they and also a dead child, and to have jail bars between them; to own such a dangerous future. These thoughts come with his eyes fixed on Maeve, and he wonders what it is like to be her. As if on cue to this, she lifts her head to the hill. To be her right now. To have your husband leave so absolutely, to have no response to your entreaties for him to come home. To see him watching you from the top of a hill in a graveyard. To admit you are wrong and say you are sorry—what more can you do?—and still be without your husband.

Nat wants to create some motion, a wave, a show of looking away, even scuff his feet in the grass. But he stands stock-still and Maeve breaks off first. She lowers her face and drops the wide black hat brim across her countenance like night.

From his perch Nat sees three black vehicles pull up. The first is a long hearse, followed by two Cadillac limousines. The colorful crowd senses their arrival and presses closer to the lip of the grave. A short row of metal chairs is arranged there. Maeve fades back from the hole. Nat catches now only the top of her hat. The three cars stop. Four dark-suited men, funeral home employees, get out of the hearse to unload the casket. George Talley exits the first limo. His ex-wife and a man, probably her Maryland husband, get out of the second.

Nat wonders if it was generous of Amanda's mother to let her child be buried here in George's hometown and Amanda's birthplace, or if there was a fight. George and she arrive at their daughter's grave in separate limos. Nat guesses this day in the sun on this crowded lawn was a victory for George.

Nat watches the procession to the grave. It is time to go down from the hill. He stands away from the cross; the thing has made his back sweat.

He takes a step and stops. There's a spate of reasons for him not to go down there. He is the attorney for the accused killer of the girl buried today. He is Maeve's separated and unresolved husband and he is not ready to encounter her. But the hill slants down and the walk is eased. Nat has friends down there, people who will be glad to see him. He has known George Talley for many years. He will not go too close, just near enough to the rim of the crowd to show his support and condolence for George, then quietly slip away.

Coming down the hill, he watches George Talley. The sheriff hugs, pats backs, and shakes hands, it is a campaign stop for him without the jocularity. The ex-wife and her husband somberly wait in the metal chairs beside the grave for George to join them. Nat cannot find Maeve.

He moves to a position where the mourners are spread out, barely within earshot of the priest. So many people fan themselves and fidget in the heat, he cannot make out the words of the memorial service. He stands alone.

Standing at the edge of the assembly, Nat realizes he has underestimated its size. There must be five hundred people here. He sees no common walk of life among the gathering, there are rough-hewn farmers, thick-handed mill workers, double-chinned men and women office workers, there are uniformed law folk from four counties. He spots several people he knows. Judge Baron wipes his glasses on a kerchief. There are Nat's neighbors from both sides of his and Maeve's house. Old friends of his parents. He sees his former accountant standing near Ed Fentress's secretary. There are Monroe and Rey Ann Skelton. Dr. Charles Jorgensen, his former physician, also the local medical examiner, the one who would have been called to Amanda's body after Monroe. As local M.E., Jorgensen will have filed a short narrative report to accompany the body to the state M.E.'s office, describing obvious facts, white female, dead in church as result of probable arson, a diagram showing where the body was found. The doctor gets fifty dollars for going to the scene and fifty for filing the report. Nat will receive that report probably on Monday, before Elijah's new charge for murder.

Nat thinks, George Talley is the law. The law touches every household and today that touch is a beckon, they have come. Nat winces into the sky, the place where Heaven is kept. He imagines Heaven up there and is glad for Amanda that she has such a clear day to ascend. But the crowd around her grave is her father's, sure enough.

He tries to catch a few eyes; out here far from the priest's voice there is not much to do other than look down or around. The accountant notices him, nods without changing expression, and looks away to mutter something to his wife. Nat sees Dr. Jorgensen, and the old doctor does the same, whispers to his wife, who listens to her husband then coldly levels her eyes at Nat and leaves them there until Jorgensen takes her by the arm and turns her. The doctor and his wife step together so they face another direction.

Nat stares off through the host of people. On the opposite side of the circle around the grave he spots a couple he and Maeve were friendly with. He thinks to walk over to them but figures he'd best just stand still. He stops trying to get anyone's attention and looks at his shoes. He admits he is frustrated, he is feeling a bit disjointed and exposed; he wanted someone to greet him well.

Slowly, without looking up, Nat notices a shifting in the people around him, a noiseless ebb, as though he is a stone dropped into a pond and rings slide away from him at the center. He lifts his gaze. Many eyes are on him now, whispers he cannot hear tilt from shoulders to shoulders. Within a minute all the folks standing nearest him have actually stepped away. Nat tries to curtail himself but he cannot; disappointment and indignation inform his face. Beneath the warm wisps of the priest's oration, Nat thins his lips and swivels his head at the retreaters.

From behind, a hand touches his sleeve.

Nat pivots. Mrs. Rosalind Epps recoils a step. Something on Nat's face gave her a start when he turned. The old woman puts a hand to her starched blue hair to compose herself.

"Excuse me, Nathaniel." She speaks too loudly. She does this with all her former students, Nat recalls, as though she is still in front of the chalkboard, no matter it was thirty years ago. She catches herself and lowers to a stage whisper. "I'm sorry. Did I startle you?"

"No, ma'am, Mrs. Epps. How are you?"

The short woman extends her hand. She wears a peach dress patterned with vegetables. It is not funeral attire, she is another of the walking flower arrangements. Nat takes her hand softly, his fingers beneath, thumb on top, as one does with matrons who taught you in third grade, it is a cotillion touch.

"Fine as can be expected, for all the sorrow that's been brewing. You know I'm Clare Waddell's grandmother."

"Yes, ma'am. I'm sorry for your loss."

"Thank you. And now this poor girl."

"Yes, ma'am."

"I don't recall this town ever seeing this amount of tragedy all at once."

"No. Me neither."

"You're Elijah's lawyer, I understand."

"Yes, ma'am, I am."

"Well." Mrs. Epps carries a hanky in her other hand. She mops it across her brow. Nat thinks she is not taking the sun very well. Her hand is clammy. He sets it loose and her arm stays up as though he still grasps it, it is a canine pose, like an old pointer. The folds of skin in the bend of her elbow are pink, her blood is up.

"I am sure he didn't do it, Nathaniel."

She seems to want to say a lot more. She looks at him, works her tongue over her lips but says only, "I saw you over here by yourself and I thought I'd come stand with you. If you don't mind."

"Not at all, Mrs. Epps. Thank you."

The old woman turns her face to the ceremony. She has planted

herself beside Nat and says no more. Nat looks down over her; the
base of her neck where it shows above the cut of her dress has red-
dened also. She is cooking in the heat.

Nat leans down. "Mrs. Epps, why don't we try to find you some
shade and a place to sit."

She gives him a resolute smile. "I'm all right. It'll just be a little
longer. But thank you, Nathaniel."

She returns her study straight ahead. Nat senses that Mrs. Epps
has somehow become his sentinel. The subtle cool glances have
abated, no others nearby try to distance themselves with tiny steps.
He watches Mrs. Epps slyly shift her focus between the grave and
their restive neighbors.

She holds like this, erect, mute, and watchful. Though she is squat
and old, she preserves her teacher's presence, at the head of the
class, daring you to let her spot you cheating. Periodically she mops
her forehead. The priest quits talking. George Talley rises, his voice
is commanding. Nat thinks there might be some quiver in a father's
words beside a daughter's grave but George speaks loudly and well.
Nat notices and forgives this, it's just George's nature to be so comfortable in public.

Listening to Talley, Nat catches something stir in the crowd
around him. They are far enough away from the grave that it does not
disturb George's speech. Rosy Epps's bosom rises.

She asks Nat, "Do you know a local man name of Mr. Snead?"
Nat sees both of her hands are balled. The hanky sticks out from one
fist. Along her neckline her color swells.

"No, ma'am. Is anything wrong?"

She says, "Nathaniel Deeds." Her face is sweet and gloomy.
"We'll talk again soon, I trust. Thank you for keeping me company."

With this Mrs. Epps strides forward into the crowd, brushing past
people with some urgency and clumsiness. Nat watches her go and
sees her collide head-on with a thin older gent who Nat guesses must
be Mrs. Epps's Mr. Snead. The man appears to be at the lead of a
train of folks snaking in his wake. Rosy Epps's red balled hands go to
her hips. The man stops, the line behind him bunches. One of his
skinny fingers jabs toward Nat, but Mrs. Epps says something and

the finger recedes. Several folks on this side of the crowd turn from George's eulogy to see what is the fuss. Nat shakes his head, thwarted and uncomfortable. Eyes are on him again, hot, rejecting eyes. He spins on his heel to go.

There is Maeve.

She stands the way you would draw her if you had but a sheet and a pencil, all in black, smooth lines, white skin. She lifts a palm to him. Nat cannot tell if it is to say Stop or Hello. She is ten feet away. Three strides. But three strides will not be enough.

Nat lifts his hand to mirror hers. His gesture is to say Goodbye.

## 2

A man who tosses a ball high into the air cannot concentrate on much else waiting for it to fall to his hand. This is Nat's Monday morning. His whole day is unsettled, spent trying to work while anticipating a call from Ed Fentress.

Nat expects to hear that Judge Baron has canceled Elijah's preliminary hearing on arson and is bringing Elijah in for his second appearance, this time on new charges. Nat figures he'll have to jump up at a moment's notice when the call comes to drive to Good Hope. This prevents him from reaching any depth into the legal matters cluttering his desk—a divorce, a contract dispute, a real estate closing. Every ring of his phone, no matter what it is about, is not about Elijah. Nat lunches alone, he cancels an afternoon appointment. He deals with several calls from the press, statewide, all the way from Virginia Beach to Fairfax out to Roanoke. He has no comment for them, he tells them all the trial is public record and they can gather their own facts as they see fit. One reporter who calls is a man Nat knows, Sam Worth, a writer from the Williamsburg paper who covered some trials in Good Hope when Nat was prosecuting.

"C'mon, Nat, talk to me," Sam says.

Nat responds. "Off the record."

"Okay. Off the record."

"You're making too much of this case, Sam."

"Nat. It's murder."

"It's not murder until we see the medical examiner's report."

"It's a dug-up baby. It's the angry father standing next to the flames of the burning church. It's the sheriff's daughter."

"Why don't you just say it. Be honest. It's about race. The press is whipping this up out of proportion."

"It's news, Nat. Hello? It's about what people want to read. If that turns out to be about race, what the hell. It's not our fault if people are willing to pay us to have their stereotypes confirmed. Your every-day man on the street thinks he's threatened on all sides, from blacks or whites to crime and terrorists to the IRS to politicians. He doesn't think he's safe anywhere or that his money or his vote or his health will be any good this time next year. What do you want the press to do about it? It's an industry, Nat. You want to sell papers? Get folks to watch the evening news? Fuck." The reporter chuckles. "Exhume a black baby. Burn a white church. Kill a teenage girl. Come on, man. It's only real life to the people who do that stuff or get it done to them. To the rest it's just good theater. And it's not going to go away just because sometimes it's unfair and sometimes it's hysterical. And sometimes, you got to admit, it's right on the money."

Nat asks, "What if he's innocent? You think about that?"

Sam Worth laughs again, easily. "That's news too."

"You can't lose, can you?"

"Nope. Everybody can but us."

The reporter waits, considering something. Nat makes ready to hang up. Then the newspaperman says, "And now I'll be honest. We don't lose because we don't play. We don't bet. We just keep score."

At five o'clock Nat goes home, thinking he ought to hire a secretary as soon as he can afford one to handle the phones. He is tense. His neck hurts, just as though he'd spent his entire day at the office looking up, clenched, waiting for the ball.

He exposes himself to the heat only for moments, walking to his car, cranking the air conditioner. After a ten-minute drive he hurries up the sidewalk to his apartment. He slides in the key and is greeted by beige. He closes the door behind him, grateful at once for the cooled interior but that is all he likes about this place. His apartment is in a complex, a bland hive of professional people around a swimming pool and two tennis courts. His furniture is rented. It was delivered to him in shades of brown, tan, off-white, overstuffed and striped. The coffee table and end tables are faux mahogany, the matching lamp shades are mottled and just look dingy. The apartment is carpeted in high-traffic pile the color of dry sand. The kitchen Formica is flesh-toned. There is nothing hung on the antique-white walls. Nat pitches his briefcase onto the sofa and plummets beside it.

He casts his tired eyes around a space that is devoid of him, nothing of Nat Deeds is in this dwelling but his body; out of sight there are clothes in a closet and a dresser, some old food in the fridge. It's like an asylum. He imagines ramming the walls with his shoulders, his arms bound about his waist. But that is the wrong reaction to this place and his mood; they are oppressive so he sits beneath them as if under a boulder.

Nat feels again the weight he sensed yesterday at Amanda Talley's funeral, the burden of abandonment. He is lost. He feels that in the eight months since leaving Good Hope he has had ripped away all his old boundaries, he is left to meander in a world without demarcation. He has no wife, no friends, no home—this apartment can never be home, not rental furniture—little satisfying work. The case of Elijah Waddell. Something is awry: Why wasn't Elijah brought in on murder charges today? The autopsy is finished, the body is buried. What's the holdup? The whole case has a rotten bunch of facts to it, something is wrong in the roots, and so the case, like Nat, is unanchored and wandering.

On the table beside the sofa and on the dull walls throughout the apartment there are no photos of Maeve. Because this is a conscious choice, Nat is aware of her absence eclipsing every inch. Beside my hand, he thinks, this is a table where there is no picture of Maeve. There is another table in the bedroom without her, and a bed there too. She is not here anywhere, purposefully, so she is infinite and everywhere. Nat does not struggle with this thought but sits and bears it, like some brand of justice meted out to him, and he is a believer in justice.

She is not here. Perhaps, he thinks, that is the reason why he is barely here himself.

An office without a secretary. A solo civil practice that he can fold up quickly if he decides to. A bloodless apartment filled with temporary furnishings. A case he accepted that takes him back to Good Hope.

Plenty of evidence.

Nat wants to go home.

But he can't.

What is there for him in Good Hope? Alienated neighbors upset over the Waddell case, which promises only to worsen. Friends he's let lapse with his stricken eight-month silence. Maeve's long shadow. Would Fentress give him his old job back? Likely not, after the cursory way Nat left.

How can this be? Nat wonders. To have nothing left in the town of his birth? Where he'd lived most of his professional life, where he'd married? Nat thinks of himself as a friendly enough man, not garrulous or chirpy but certainly approachable. How could those folks actually move away from him at the funeral yesterday? He's just doing his job, like they do theirs. Didn't he generate any loyalty at all in his years in Good Hope? Or was the whole community so banded together in their anger at Elijah, even before his trial, that they can forsake his lawyer too, even if that lawyer is local boy Nat Deeds? Baron knew this would happen. He picked Nat because he figured Nat had already lost all he could lose of Good Hope.

Nat realizes the town has rejected him. This disheartens him. But it's fair, he rejected them first. The notion bows Nat's head, it is a heavy crown. Again, because it seems just, he abides it.

Maeve.

When he saw her yesterday, she had not changed. Nat wonders how long that will last. How long can he imprison himself apart from her with only an image of her beauty, until one day he sees her again and discovers that it has changed from his image? Though she may still be beautiful it will no longer be the soft kind you draw with a pencil, but rather a beauty that you pour of cement, a hardness to her, hard to him. When that happens they will be more than apart. They will be done.

That day, Nat knows, is coming.

Why can't he forgive her?

Other couples survive an affair. They move past it. Nat even understands he may bear some responsibility for her infidelity. Perhaps he was inattentive to love, centered too much on his work. He drove her to it somehow. Whatever. But in his mind he hears her vows, takes her hands in his, she wears white, he lifts her veil to kiss her.

He loves her, will always. But he cannot trust her now. She says she only did it once, then broke it off. This is the same as saying, I have lied to you and betrayed you, but now you can believe me. Nat has seen enough crime, heard too many liars, not to know better.

He does not know whom she slept with and doesn't care to know. It will just install another face in front of him to target and agonize over if he knows the man. The nameless man is not to blame. He bears no allegiance to Nat. Maeve does, she is the one. Nat understands this is caveman and sexist thinking, yes, it is possessive and politically incorrect and unforgiving and un-Christian. But he is feeling beat up enough right now and so does not reproach himself for it.

Because he is astray in his head and in the cool desert of this apartment, Nat's thoughts stumble to his parents. The topic in his mind, like a game-show category, is constancy. He's sure his father and mother would have viewed his wife's tryst with his same aversion. They were married for thirty-two years, separated only by death two years apart. They had discipline and restraint, Nat thinks, dammit, they didn't screw around on each other. Some cynic on vigil inside him asks, But what if they did and you just didn't know about it? What if they hid it from you like good parents? Nat thinks to the prosecuting voice, Shut up. Not now. Not ever, in fact.

Carefully he opens his memory to recall sitting on top of a fire-engine red Coca-Cola icebox inside Utz's Esso station, where his dad, Billy, played pool every Saturday afternoon. The men played eight ball and cutthroat. They flipped dimes to Nat on his perch. He cupped his two palms to catch them until he was big enough to snatch the coins out of the air with one hand and never miss. He slipped the coins into the box and pulled cold drinks for the men through the gray jaws of the machine. Sometimes a dime fluttered to him, Nat would snare it, and one of the men said, Keep it, kiddo. His father was the best pool shot, not because of talent but as a result of playing every Saturday, rain or shine; always he lifted Nat up to sit on the Coke box. Over the years his father got in a few scraps at the mill, not often, but in the early 1960s there was a move to unionize, and at home in the kitchen with a blue ice pack to his cheek he told Nat, Son, in this world you gotta stick up for things. Don't ever be afraid to do that. When you're right, you're right. That's all there is to it. His father kept a black leather belt in the drawer at the bottom of the stove where his mother stored the iron skillets. The thing nested in there like a snake, black curled among black. Most times he had only to refer to the belt to get Nat to quiet down. His father's idols were Lou Gehrig and J. Edgar Hoover, men of accomplishment and longevity. On weekends he hit grounders to Nat in their uneven backyard, smacked them hard, the balls bounced unpredictably on clods of crabgrass and dandelion. He shouted at Nat, Stay down, keep your head on it. If you're scared, the best thing to do is catch it. No one ever got hit in the face by a ball they caught. Nat hears his father's voice mingling twenty years later with Maeve's vows, Don't pull away! Bear down, boy. To honor and cherish! Stay put! For better or worse!

Inside the house, his mother, Jane, never let the tin container on top of the Frigidaire run out of home-baked sweets. Chocolate chip or oatmeal cookies. Brownies. German chocolate cake in wax paper. Rum balls rolled in powdered sugar. This was one of her pacts with Nat, never to let the tin be empty. Every day after school or play when he took the tin down, the heft inside was better than any hug or smile, it was a promise kept, a tender lesson in dependability. His mother was the one who passed on to Nat the family catalog of story and legend, of Irish, Polish, and Scot great-grandfathers coming to America with only hardy backs and wills, never much mentioning the women who married those men and bore their children. She took Nat to movies. She loved the epic heroic films, *El Cid, Doctor Zhivago, African Queen, Lawrence of Arabia*. She laced her arm around her son in the dark movie houses and squeezed him, whispering to him of the virtues the movie heroes put on display, their intrepidness, their honored oaths; she was moved by the same traits of manhood that moved his father and in her softer ways she taught Nat the same lessons. Like this Nat was ushered by his mother and father into the world of men, an unbroken past, present, and future of valiant and headstrong men, unflinching in the face of peril, gallant, virile. Heads of households. Respectful of their women. Unbending in their convictions. Giant in their myths. Punishing.

### 3

The call from the Pamunkey court clerk comes at nine the next morning. Judge Baron has set Elijah's initial appearance for ten o'clock.

The drive takes Nat forty minutes. The time passes like a memory lapse, he is on the Mattaponi River span before he knows it. He cannot recall much of the drive except for the glare of the sun beaming straight out of the August morning through his windshield.

Parking at the courthouse, Nat sees a larger contingent of news satellite vans than there was on Friday. Several of them have their dishes raised high overhead for on-the-scene transmissions. There are no reporters roaming the green and the sidewalks between the cannons and there are no locals waving placards. This is a bad sign. Fentress must have persuaded Judge Baron to let them inside the courtroom.

Nat does not have time to visit with Elijah before court convenes. They'll sit together in court, hear the commonwealth's murder charge, almost certainly second degree, then they'll set another date for the preliminary hearing, probably again for tomorrow. Nat will get a copy of the medical examiner's report from Fentress. He'll go over the report with Elijah before they transport him back to Rappahannock.

Nat pushes open the courtroom door. The room is brimming. He pauses, taken aback by the size of the crowd. With a breath he proceeds down the aisle to the defense table as quickly as he can. The rows of benches on either side of him are packed. Hands clutching pens and notepads reach to flag his attention, other arms—mostly bare, locals in short-sleeved shirts or dresses—point and wag fingers. Along one wall stands George Talley, big arms folded, his eyes zeroed in on Nat. Fixing his gaze ahead, Nat tries to advance with some lawyerly bearing but he knows he lacks the physical stature of Ed

Fentress so he just shoves forward through the limbs and fluting voices. At the defense table he slaps his briefcase down hard and glares at the seated commonwealth's attorney, who sits felinely in his composure.

"What the hell is this?" Nat shoots at Fentress.

The well-groomed prosecutor shrugs. "The public's right to know."

Nat slacks his jaw. "Know what?"

The deputy standing beside the judge's chamber door barks, "All rise. This general district court is in session. The Honorable Judge Malcolm Baron presiding." All the benches in the courtroom creak, shoes scrape the floorboards. Even with the voices quelled, the room at Nat's back makes a ruckus, this many anxious bodies can be only so quiet.

The judge streams in. He quickly takes his chair and says, "Be seated." With the room attending him, Baron sends a glare over them all, left to right. "Before I call the first case this morning, I want to make one thing clear. I expect a ruly courtroom. There will be no outbursts or noise. Anyone in the gallery interrupting my proceedings will cause the lot of you to be removed. All right?"

Several voices, most of them locals, answer, "Yes, sir."

The judge raps his knuckles on his desk. "People, don't answer me! Don't say or do anything! Just sit there. I don't care what you hear." He digs his rump deeper into his chair. "Now."

The woman seated in the box below Judge Baron announces loudly, "Elijah Waddell."

Nat looks past Fentress to where Elijah is brought into the courtroom. A deputy escorts him by his elbow through the side door. Elijah appears haggard. His head is bent, some glow seems to have faded from his orange prison garb. Instantly Nat feels petty, the way he has mulled over his own problems.

Nat stands when the deputy deposits Elijah beside the defense table. Elijah slips behind Nat to sit in the second chair. He does not wear handcuffs but even so Nat sees his movements are fettered, he shuffles.

Elijah settles. Nat leans over. "You okay?"

Elijah lifts only his eyes. "Man."

"I know. I know."

Elijah shows his teeth. "What do you know?"

Nat accepts the bitterness. He lays his hand on his client's back. There is the man beneath the jail tunic.

Nat says, "I know you didn't do it."

Elijah's chin comes up with his eyes. A corner of his mouth curls. "Yeah? How do you know that?"

Nat indicates the commonwealth's attorney. "The same way he knows you did it. I'm guessing."

Elijah pushes a short breath out of his nose. He shakes his head. Nat has amused him.

"Counsel?" Judge Baron is ready. "May we proceed?"

Nat and Fentress say together, "Yes, Your Honor."

"Good. Mr. Waddell?"

Nat rises. He whispers to Elijah, "Stand."

The judge says, "I must say I'm very sorry to see you here this morning, Mr. Waddell. Very sorry. I have a few questions to ask you."

Elijah nods.

"Are you still satisfied with the services of your attorney Mr. Deeds?"

"Yes, sir."

"Good. I presume that your financial situation has not changed, so the court will appoint him to continue to represent you on these new charges. All right?"

"Yes, sir."

The judge pulls his glasses to the edge of his nose. He lifts a sheaf of papers from his desk. The gallery behind Nat hushes. He hears the papers ripple in the judge's hand, a small thunder.

Judge Baron reads. "Elijah Waddell, you stand charged in the Commonwealth of Virginia, county of Pamunkey, with the crimes of capital murder and rape. Bail is revoked."

Nat is rocked, his lungs wrench. Capital murder? Rape? When did these charges come about? There was no word, nothing . . . the M.E.'s report!

Fentress, Nat thinks, that son of a bitch. Fentress knew. He sandbagged me.

Nat turns quickly to Elijah. The man's legs have buckled beneath him. He falls backward, caught by the chair. He seems not able to breathe, his mouth hangs open, his lips work wordlessly. Elijah's hands are up off the table as though holding something invisible. He stares into the open space between them, as though to identify what horror he has been handed.

Nat finds his voice.

"Your Honor!"

Judge Baron bangs his gavel. The report snaps in Nat's ears and now he hears how the courtroom has erupted at the announcement of the charges. The gavel continues to pound, piercing the room's commotion, which has in it some cheers, some wails, and much rustling of whispers.

"One more sound," the judge shouts, the gavel coming down again, "one more peep out of you folks," and Nat notes the noise break and withdraw like a wave hissing over sand, "and I'll clear the room." A final strike from the gavel and Baron has the courtroom quiet. His voice seals the silence. "You best believe I mean it."

Nat reaches behind him to put a hand on Elijah's shoulder. He feels bone more than any flesh or muscle, so collapsed is Elijah.

"Your Honor."

Baron glowers down. "Mr. Deeds?"

"May I approach the bench?"

"In my chambers." Baron flings his eyes, wide behind the glasses, at Fentress. "Let's go." Baron raises his voice. "Court will recess for five minutes. And when we come back, ladies and gentlemen, be advised that you have already worn out your welcome."

The deputy approaches to take Elijah out of the courtroom. He does not stand to receive the deputy's hand on his elbow. The deputy lifts him. Rising on shaky legs, Elijah says only, "Nat."

"I'll find out what's going on, Elijah. Stay calm."

The deputy leads him away. Elijah keeps his head turned to Nat.

Nat walks past the deputy standing beside Baron's door. He follows Fentress's back through the doorway, the prosecutor walks with his head high, he pats the deputy on the belly when he passes. This is his home field, Nat thinks, but that doesn't mean he can play this dirty. Capital murder. This was supposed to be second degree, anything else and Nat should have been notified. But rape and capital. Fentress has never had a capital murder case. This is his first, and he's going for it, for an execution, on Elijah.

The judge's chamber is windowless, paneled in dark woods with lots of molding. Pen-and-ink caricatures of lawyers break up the wall space. Sweeping into the room, the judge has his back to Nat. He hangs his robe on a coat tree. Fentress is already settled into one of the cinnamon leather club chairs.

"Judge," Nat says before the judge can turn around.

"Be quiet, Nat." Baron eases himself into his big wingback desk chair. "I already know your position. I want to hear Ed's."

Fentress quickly says, "Your Honor, what else could I do?"

Baron utters the "uh-huh" that means "ah-ha." Then he says, "Well, for starters, this morning at eight-thirty when you came in here and told me you were charging Elijah Waddell with capital murder and rape, you could have also informed me that you hadn't yet told his lawyer."

"Judge, Monroe drove up to Richmond this morning to get the preliminary medical examiner's report. I just got it myself fifteen minutes before I spoke to you."

"That was enough time to call opposing counsel."

"Maybe, judge. But that's what the initial appearance is for, to inform the accused of the charges against him."

"It's a courtesy, Ed. This is not the first time you've heard from me that I insist on decorum and courtesy between attorneys in my court. Am I correct in this?"

"Judge, Nat's case was not prejudiced. He was apprised of the charges in a timely fashion."

Nat continues to bite his tongue.

Baron says, "It was done in a showboat fashion. You talked me into letting the press in the building and then you pandered to them. You gave them a nice little moment of shock and dismay they can report on. I know you're an elected official, Ed, and the press has to be your friend but that was over the line."

Fentress works his tongue inside his cheek.

"Yes, sir," he says.

"That," continues Baron, "is the last time I expect to see this kind of brinkmanship in my courtroom from you, Ed. And, Nat, I don't expect any paybacks. This is a one-off, you got me?"

"Yes, judge."

"All right. Now, Ed, are you prepared to conduct a quick and efficient preliminary hearing in my courtroom this afternoon?"

"Yes, sir."

"All right. Nat, now you understand me. Ed thinks he's got enough already to show probable cause, so I'm going to let him have his way and we'll go at four o'clock this afternoon. If Ed's right—and I'll tell you both right now, he probably is—then I'll be sending this case up to Judge Hawk for trial and you two can become her problem. But while you're still mine, this is how we're going to conduct it. Nat, you are going to sit in my court and listen to the commonwealth's case this afternoon and you will do so without rancor. Ed, one more piece of horse hockey out of you and you'll find yourself in contempt. We are going to put this matter on a smooth and fast track, gentlemen. Am I understood?"

Both men nod, Nat with a sullen mien.

To Fentress, Baron says, "Go get some coffee." The prosecutor rises with a disarming smile at Nat. "Sorry, buddy," he says. "You want some coffee?"

"No."

When he is out the door, Judge Baron tosses a manila envelope onto his desk. It skitters to a stop in front of Nat.

"Here's my copy of the prelim M.E. report. Keep it, I'll get another one from Fentress. Take five minutes to look it over." The judge rises. "I'm going to take a leak." He grabs up his black robe, tosses it over his shoulder like he has skinned some creature, and leaves through the inner door.

Nat opens the envelope to slide out the three typed pages. The first page is the report from Dr. Jorgensen, the Pamunkey County local M.E. The second two pages are from the state's medical examiner in Richmond. Nat checks the last sheet; it's signed by the assistant chief medical examiner, Dr. Jacquelyn Kline. He knows Jackie, her forensics work is thorough, unimpeachable. He scans the conclusions paragraph. She lists the provisional cause of death as smoke inhalation. She is waiting on toxicology for carbon monoxide levels. Amanda's jaw was broken on the left side. Then these words, highlighted in yellow marker: "Preliminary report from serology indicates presence of semen. Full report to follow."

There it is, Nat thinks. A broken jaw and sperm. Fentress's rape.

In Virginia, murder in the commission of a felony makes the charge a capital crime.

Nat does not have time to examine closely the rest of the report, that will have to wait. He slips the pages back into the envelope and returns to the courtroom. The walls are buzzing. Fentress stands with arms folded, looking with his satisfied grin over the crowd of newspeople like an Arab prince choosing his ponies. Nat sits. Fentress sits, then swivels to Nat. He holds up his hands at his sides, Don't shoot, the gesture says, I'm unarmed.

"All rise."

Baron enters, as always, like a flight of crows, inky and flapping. Flying up the steps of the bench, he impatiently says to the courtroom, "Keep your seats," as though their offering of standing respect does not move him. Many in the courtroom have already jumped to their feet, the rest have not yet moved, and the effect is confusion. "Settle," the judge instructs, taking his seat.

Baron pushes his glasses up. "Bring in Mr. Waddell."

The side door opens. Elijah appears behind his deputy guard. He looks bewildered. The slow ritual ensues, he is walked to the defense table and released. Nat stands and before Elijah can move to his seat the judge says, "Mr. Deeds."

"Yes, Your Honor?"

"Did you have a look at the report?"

"Just a glance."

"Enough of a glance?"

"Yes, sir, for now."

"All right. Can we proceed?"

Nat turns to Elijah standing beside him.

He remembers the remains of the Civil War fortifications in the forests outside Good Hope, green and woody places he roamed in his boyhood with a metal detector finding old pitted evidence of battle. He recalls the romance of the trenches, the fight in the earth, the will of men to survive other men, the resolve in the mounds themselves to survive nature and time. Nat lifts his voice in volume and steel, to throw up a bulwark, to announce to the judge, to Fentress, the press, and to the townspeople, that Elijah Waddell is defended.

"Yes, Your Honor. We can proceed."

# Two

1

At ten-thirty old West Redd flips the Open sign in his restaurant door around to read Closed.

To Nat he says, "I could give a shit about them fellers." He refers to the press shadowing Nat up Main Street. "Go ahead, take a booth. I'll give you a half hour."

Nat smiles at the ancient cook and diner owner. "You're going to lose business."

"Come on, Nat." The man wipes his hands on his apron. Nat has no guesses about what made the stains on the white cloth or how long ago. "How many cups of coffee you had in here over the years?"

"Ten thousand. More."

"You see a Closed sign in my door, you see me inside, you gonna stay out?"

"No."

"Ain't nobody else who's a regular gonna stay out neither. Just them outa town pests. Go ahead. Have some peace. Java'll be right up. Toast?"

"Whole wheat."

Nat slides into a worn, familiar booth. This little eatery is one block from the courthouse. It is empty right now but by eleven the retirees will start to filter in, then the courthouse lunch crowd, then the mill workers, and finally the farmers who come to town for supplies. But right now West has made it a safe haven for Nat to look over the medical examiner's report in his hands. Old West sets coffee and cream on the table and ambles off with no interest about the case or the three white sheets Nat spreads out. West has served lawyers for thirty years and knows to leave them alone. Nat watches the white-haired old man limp behind his counter to make the toast. He thinks, Here's an ally, when he believed he had none left in Good Hope. He sips the coffee and brings his head down to the three pages.

The body was first examined at the fire scene by Dr. Charles Jorgensen. Nat looks at the man's report, labeled CME #1. A hastily drawn map of the site is marked near the church's front doors to indicate where a white female body was found. Jorgensen's remarks detail the condition of the body, the ghastly percentage covered in char, both feet and the right hand burned away, the girl's protected face, a Baptist hymnal found under her preserved left hand. Jorgensen concludes his report with the statement that arson is suspected in the girl's death.

Before he peers at Jackie Kline's preliminary report, Nat wonders again about the book under Amanda's left hand. It's a simple fact but it leads Nat's mind on a careering chase.

If Elijah had raped her, knocked her out breaking her jaw, then thrown her into the church before torching it, how did she end up under the pew clutching the hymnal? The church doors were not locked, Tom Derby said so. The girl was not tied up. Her face was protected from the flames because her head was found resting in the bend of her left arm, the fingers of her left hand were on the hymnal. All this taken together suggests that she was conscious at some point in an attempt to make herself comfortable, perhaps even reading by the dim light of stars and the Exit sign; it's inconsistent with someone who's been beaten and thrown insensible into the church. If she was conscious when the fire broke out, she could easily have escaped, because the blaze started at the opposite end of the building from the spot where she was found. But the broken jaw and her death certainly indicate that she was unconscious when the fire began.

So what about the hymnal? Did she awaken from being knocked out by whatever or whoever broke her jaw, but come to her senses too late to get out? Was she already too weak from breathing fumes, the flames too high to dash through them? Did she take up the hymnal as some last passport to Heaven and crawl under the pew in a pitiful, feeble try at shelter?

Nat quickly rules out suicide—lonely Amanda lighting the fire herself, entering the church, taking up the hymnal, and lying down to die. No suicide note has been found anywhere. Why burn a Baptist church down around yourself? Who was it Elijah claims to have seen run off through the church graveyard? No, she didn't kill herself.

Nat's head clicks through more scenarios like a slide show, scene after possible scene. He is building his defense bit by bit, probing, poking holes, filling in others, trying to stitch together a crazy quilt of unmatched patches of fact and conjecture.

Bewildered, he pushes aside Jorgensen's single page. He turns his attention to Jackie Kline's preliminary medical examiner's report. Her work is clear and perfunctory. The cause of death is listed as smoke inhalation. Soot and scoring were found in the trachea. Blood alcohol level was .03 percent.

Nat stops. Amanda had a couple of drinks that evening. She wasn't drunk when the fire started around one-thirty in the morning, the alcohol level isn't high enough. But she was only seventeen so she couldn't buy her own alcohol. Sometime earlier that evening, she drank with someone who gave her the liquor. Who?

Sperm was found on the cervix at the back of the vagina. "Full report to follow," Jackie writes. What she means is a DNA test.

As bad as it looks now, the sperm found inside the girl is a good thing. If Elijah didn't have sex with her, either consensually or forced, a DNA test will demonstrate conclusively his innocence of rape. And that would put a stop to the capital murder charge. The test results will take six to eight weeks to come back. But this will give Elijah hope. He can hang in there for two months.

Nat drums his fingers. West appears at his side holding a plate of warm buttered wheat toast. Nat shoves a page out of the way of the descending dish. West trundles off.

Halfway across the floor the old man shouts, "Read the sign!" Nat jumps, then turns in his booth. Outside in the heat a sweating woman and her attendant cameraman stare through the glass door. Her face goes forlorn looking at Nat, like a puppy at the pet shop that wants to go with you. Nat pivots back to his papers and toast.

So Amanda Talley drank alcohol with someone the night of her death. She had sex. She got her jaw broken. She wound up burned alive in the Victory Baptist.

Nat wonders, did she do all these—the drinking, sex, and fighting—with just one person? Or several, each one leaving a mark? Did she walk out to the Victory Baptist by herself, or did someone take her?

Jackie Kline x-rayed the remains. She found two broken bones in addition to the jaw, neither of which she believes contributed to the cause of death. She speculates in her notes that these bones, the femur of the left leg and the radius in the right forearm, were snapped as the result of brittleness caused by the extreme heat and an intense involuntary contraction of muscles, which commonly occurs in fire victims, even when unconscious.

But the assistant chief medical examiner did not x-ray the girl's broken jaw. Why not? Jackie's notes simply mention that the jawbone was "loose to the touch, with edema apparent in the flesh of the left jawline." Because Amanda's body was found with the pew across her upper back and the facial swelling showed no break in the skin, Jackie believes that the jaw was not broken in the fire but probably before. She writes that the injury "is not inconsistent with a hard punch from a right-hand fist."

Nat recollects the small cut and swelling he saw along the knuckles of Elijah's right hand. The welt and cut could easily have come from striking a tree as he claimed. Or not.

Nat totes up these surmisals, chewing on wheat toast and probabilities. A hazy snapshot of Amanda Talley's last hours forms for him. She had a few drinks earlier in the evening. She got into a tussle, taking a hard shot to the jaw from a right-hander. She had sex. She went to or was taken to a church three miles outside town she had attended only once before, recently, a Baptist church that is far removed from her father's fervent Catholicism. There, in the early hours of Friday morning, she had some period of consciousness inside the church before she met a flaming end, unconscious, on the floor beneath a pew, her fingers across a hymnal.

None of this points directly at Elijah.

None of it points away from him.

Nat finishes the toast. He glances at his watch, his thirty minutes of sanctuary in the little restaurant are almost up. He stands and leaves the price of coffee, toast, and tip on the table. He knows the total well. It is $2.50.

"West," he calls, "thanks for the break." Nat looks out the windows to Main Street. The sidewalk is clear. "You can open back up to the hordes."

West Redd heads to meet Nat at the door. With his hand on the knob, he pauses. His crinkled gray eyes look at Nat with kindness, they are like two robin's eggs on straw.

"So you thinking about comin' back to town?"

Nat thins his lips. With a headshake he says, "I can't tell. I miss it, that's for sure. But things are changing on me."

West nods sagely. There is snow in his hair and beard, the man is in his winter. He softly says, "Are they now?"

Nat says, "Yeah."

West turns the doorknob. Shafts of heat jackknife around the edges of the door. He says, "You know I've lived here all my life. Owning this place, I have heard against my wishes and better judgment everything people have said about me, and about you and Elijah Waddell, about everybody and every damn thing in this town and country and planet. You want to know how I've managed to live in peace with these people all that time?"

"Good coffee?"

"Yep. That and one other fact."

West Redd opens the door wide. He plants the flat of his hand squarely in Nat's back, forcing Nat to take a stumbling step outside the restaurant.

West grins and there is something in the aged cook's eyes after all, not baby bluebirds but an old, dark river heron.

West closes the door, saying before it shuts, "I don't give a shit. Never have. Never will."

2

Nat is winded at the top of the stairs. He has hustled up to the third floor too fast, too fired up. He pauses to catch his breath; he does not want to walk into Ed Fentress's office wheezing.

The receptionist is new. She does not recognize Nat from his eight years in the small office to her left. The door to it is open. Nat glances in before he announces himself to the secretary, no one is in but some new career is taking place in his chair and spread over his desk. The back of a frame says someone else's family watches him, or her, work. Nat pulls his eyes out of the room. It's not his concern anymore, his life is not in there anymore. He pushes memories down, they feel like the hands reaching for him in the courtroom downstairs an hour ago. They make Nat mad. Without a word to the openmouthed reception- ist he pushes open Fentress's door.

"What the hell was that, Ed?"

Fentress swivels in his leather desk chair from gazing out his win- dow. Below, around the courthouse green, a half-dozen satellite vans have hoisted their transmission dishes high, almost level with Ed's window. It's an eerie sight, they look like eavesdropping heads.

"Nat. Come in."

"I am in. I said, What the hell was that?"

"Oh, for Christ's sake." Fentress waves the back of his hand at an open chair. "Close the door. Sit down."

Nat shuts the office door. He takes the offered chair.

Fentress smooths down his hair, though it does not need it. It's his way of moving first. He says, "Come on. You were a prosecutor for a long time. Don't tell me you never pulled that trick."

"No. Never."

"Well, you should have. It's a good one. It's mean, but if you time it right it's ethical. Bang 'em with a new charge right in front of the judge. Bend a few knees. It tells the defense lawyer right off that he can kiss your ass, you're not giving him or his scumbag client an inch. He's in for a fucking dogfight."

"Is that what you're telling me?"

Fentress dons a comic, stultified look. "Yes, Nat. I am. Aren't I in for the same?"

"Yes. You are."

"There. See? Baron didn't drag you into this because you're going to roll over. I know you. I trained you. You're a hard hitter. So, I figured I'd give you a little shot in the gut first to remind you who taught you. That's all. No harm done. And no kid gloves because we're old friends. Get over it."

Nat studies his former boss. Though he's known Fentress for years, he's never seen this side of the man. Nat always figured Ed was too concerned with being popular and attractive to ever develop an edge. But behind closed doors, where Nat sits now for the first time as a defendant's lawyer, he sees the commonwealth's attorney can be canny, formidable. Turn your back and the cloying, preening cat Ed Fentress will eat the canary.

Nat asks, "Why'd you go capital?"

"Wait on that." Fentress digs under a stack of papers on his desk for an envelope. He spins it through the air onto Nat's lap. "Here's the arson report. Read it first. I don't want any more trouble with Baron today."

Nat opens the envelope. He unfolds two typed pages of diagrams and dense paragraphs.

"I'll read it later. What's it say?"

The prosecutor points a shiny fingernail at the sheets in Nat's hand. "It says the fire was definitely arson. It was started at the rear of the church with an accelerant they've identified as kerosene. The arsonist splashed the stuff all over the back of the church and the ground. No other evidence was found at the site."

Fentress waggles the finger in the air. "And you'll see there, on the second page, that your boy's boots are covered in kerosene." Fentress uses the finger to scribe a slash in the air, like a point on a scoreboard.

"I told you," Nat says, "he uses the stuff at the mill. It's a degreaser."

"And I told you I don't care where he got it. He got it. His boots, the circumstances regarding the exhumation of his baby from the Victory Baptist, and the fact that he was arrested at the burning church where Talley's daughter was found dead are all I need for probable cause. That's all I need to show you today."

"Why'd you go capital?"

Fentress leans far back in his tilting desk chair. He laces his fingers over his belt.

"You said you read the M.E.'s report."

"Yeah."

"All right. Off the record, I'll tell you a little more. Make it up to you for this morning. The M.E. report says the girl had been drinking. Good. I got six beer cans across the street from the church in the bushes. No prints on them, too much sweat and condensation on the aluminum. The girl had a busted jaw. I got photos of Elijah's right hand the night he was brought in where he hit something. A swollen knuckle, a small cut. I got kerosene at the fire. I got Waddell's boots. I got an incredibly incriminating statement on three TV stations and in four newspapers made by your client about how they shouldn't have dug up his baby. 'They' meaning the deacons of the burnt church. I have absolutely no witnesses who have come forward to locate Elijah Waddell in the hours leading up to the fire. Not even his wife, who called Monroe late that night to say her husband had disappeared, and that in the state she suspected he was in he was capable of anything. Anything, she said, her exact word. I have no witnesses who can tell me where Amanda Talley was that night, either. George says she left the house on foot around eight o'clock and that was the last anyone saw her. So, the presumption can be made that Waddell and Amanda were disappeared together. I've got semen. I've got the very well-known Sheriff Talley's daughter murdered in a miserable fashion. I have a suspect who was an angry and vengeful man, who was at the crime scene, who cannot account for his whereabouts, who has alluded to his likely role in the crime in a public statement. I have forensic evidence. I have circumstantial evidence."

Fentress unclasps his fingers. He lifts them at Nat, showing his claws. "What have you got?"

Nat nods. "You'll be the first to know when I get it."

Fentress digs out another manila envelope. He holds it up. "It's not going to be the DNA, Nat."

The prosecutor drops the envelope at the edge of the desk before Nat.

"Go ahead. Look at it. It's the forensics lab report. I don't know how George Talley got them to move so fast, this shit normally takes a couple weeks. But it was the guy's daughter, so I guess he leaned on them and Richmond climbed all over it for him. He's got a way about him, you know?"

Nat opens the envelope. Inside is a single faxed sheet of the state's Forensics Biology stationery. A lone typed sentence spoils the paper's clean white face: *"Insufficient semen sample submitted for DNA testing."* The page is signed by Don Lee, the forensics lab's DNA specialist.

Fentress pats together the fingertips of his paws over his waist.

He takes a sympathetic tone, which annoys Nat. "This came while we were in court. I called Don twenty minutes ago. Apparently, you need at least fifty viable sperm to conduct an I.D. on DNA. Amanda's body was burned pretty much all the way through from the shoulder blades down. That must have been some fire. The semen sample the M.E. sent over didn't have enough surviving sperm in it for Don to work with. They got cooked."

Again Fentress opens his hands. The prosecutor pronounces the pun with a grin. "And so is your boy's goose."

Now Fentress puts his hands on the arms of his chair and tips it forward. The meeting is drawing to a close. "Look," he says, and there is still an understanding lilt to his voice. "I'll have the serology and toxicology reports in a day or so. I'll get them right over to you, okay? But, Nat, if I were you I wouldn't hope for a magic bullet to come out of them. You know what I'm saying."

"You're saying he's guilty."

"I'm saying I'm going to do everything in my power to make him look that way to a judge and jury. I have a lot of ammunition already.

I suppose I'll get more. Nat, don't assess the man's guilt. Assess his chances. That's all."

With this Fentress stands. Nat keeps his seat.

"Ed, don't do this. Don't go capital."

The prosecutor slides his hands into his pants pockets. He turns his back to Nat, to look out his window over the beaming satellite dishes and the trees and streets of the town.

"Do you know it'll be ten years before another capital murder comes my way in Pamunkey County? Maybe never. Thank you for your advice but I'm going to play it where it lays."

Nat says to the man's back, "You can't make it stick."

Fentress draws a deep breath of his county. "Why not?"

"Sex and drinking and a broken jaw are personal. You've got no immediate connection between Elijah and Amanda Talley. No witnesses, no forensics. Elijah's statement to the press was vague, it proves nothing. No way will you make murder with rape hold up. No way."

Fentress seems to take this in. In a moment, still facing the window, he says, "Don't worry. I have a connection. And I'll have something better."

Nat lets it come without asking.

Fentress pulls his hands out of his pockets. He holds them up at his sides as though a crowd is gathered below his window and this motion is his greeting of them.

He says loudly, almost directing his voice through the glass panes, "I'll have a jury selected out of this county. This old, somewhat backward, very insulted and bereaved county."

Now Nat stands. He gathers the reports in their envelopes.

"I'll ask the Hawk for a change of venue."

This is Circuit Court Judge Imelda Hawk, whose court will assume jurisdiction after Baron certifies the case following the showing of probable cause at this afternoon's preliminary hearing.

"Go ahead, knock yourself out." Fentress turns from the window now to make this point. "The Hawk grew up here, just like you did. She's a Pamunkey Indian, for Christ's sake. She's not going to slap these people in the face. I'll object and she'll agree."

"I want Elijah transferred out of Rappahannock. I don't want him where Talley can get to him."

Fentress exhales. He is tired of giving the same answer, No. The man's sigh seems to convey, Ask me for something I can give you.

Fentress says, "And I'm not going to slap George in the face."

Nat considers telling Fentress about Talley's attack on Elijah in the jail, but Fentress will just defend the sheriff. He was upset, he'll say. Let it go. These two men, Nat knows, are longtime elected cohorts.

Nat tucks the envelopes into his briefcase. He opens the office door and stops. The receptionist has gone to lunch. Nat's old office is still empty.

"What's your connection?"

Fentress takes his seat. Nat admits he looks assured, powerful. He wonders if, in his own years as a prosecutor, he made other defense attorneys leave his office—that little room ten feet away—feeling like he does now, over his head. He hopes so.

Ed Fentress says, "Here's how I figure it. I got me a black man accused of raping and killing a local white girl, one of the community's better known white girls. The connection I see is this: We know the white folks took Elijah's child out of their cemetery."

Nat feels a chill beyond the air conditioning. He says, "Yes."

"So it looks to me like ol' Elijah figured he'd return the favor."

Nat's mouth goes dry. "What are you saying?"

"I'm saying it looks like an eye for an eye. Out of revenge for his black child being pulled out of the ground, Elijah Waddell took a white child and put her in the ground. In a damn nasty fashion, I might add."

The floor sinks beneath Nat's feet. The chill he felt has gone frigid. Prosecutor Ed Fentress is saying he will use race in court as a way to show how plausible it is that Elijah is a rapist and a murderer. A predator because he is black. A monster who selected Amanda Talley as his prey because she was white. It is baseless, outrageous conjecture. Pure nonsense. But—Nat understands, sadly—with the aggravated mind-set of the people of this county right now, with Fentress and Talley and the press fanning the embers, it will carry influence.

Aghast, staring, Nat looks past Fentress to the windows, out into the blue hot sky. He sees the disembodied noggins of the satellite dishes; their reach is global, their voices immeasurable. This is just one murder case in a small rural Virginia county, Nat thinks. It will be won or lost here. But when, he wonders, where, will the greater battle ever be won in America?

"Ed, you can't believe that."

Fentress smiles.

"Doesn't matter." The prosecutor leans back in his chair. "Ask me if I can make a jury believe it."

Before Nat can say anything, before he can choose whether to step back into Ed Fentress's office to plead or bluster at the man, or spin himself away to the cell where Elijah waits, to begin what now looks like a desperate defense, the prosecutor pushes forward on his desk a white envelope.

"Oh, and Nat. I almost forgot. I got this little present on my fax machine a half hour ago. I don't have to show you this just yet, but I thought I'd try to make amends for the little trick I pulled downstairs. Read it at your leisure."

Nat steps into the office and lifts the envelope. The room feels like a lair, with Fentress preening at the center of it. With the envelope in one hand, his briefcase weighing down the other, Nat backs out of the room.

3

Even before he walks far enough down the hall to see Elijah in his cell, Nat glimpses the burls of the man's fists clutching the bars.

The deputy unlocks the door to let Nat in. Elijah does not react, does not release his grip on the peeling green rods of his cell. Nat walks past Elijah to sit on the cot at the man's back. The deputy departs.

"Elijah. Talk to me."

The prisoner does not respond. Nat notes the muscles working in Elijah's forearms and wrists, squeezing the shafts.

"Elijah."

"They're saying I raped and killed her."

"Yes."

"And that's a death-penalty crime."

"Capital murder. Yes."

"How can that be?" Elijah gives the bars a yank. They do not move or even sound off.

He says again, "How can that be? I was just sitting there. How can they say I burned the church down? That I raped and killed a girl I never even knew?"

The man turns. The shock of hearing these charges has worn off him. Elijah's face now is grim and set. His eyes are clear. He looks ready for a fight.

"Show me what they've got."

Nat unsnaps his briefcase. He stares into its contents.

"Elijah, do you remember when I asked you to tell me anything you think might come up, anything the prosecutor's office might find out about you? You told me there was nothing."

Elijah looks down at Nat.

"Why'd you leave Norfolk five years ago?"

"Came here for the job."

"They have jobs in Norfolk. Why'd you leave?"

Elijah says nothing.

"This morning Fentress got a fax from a lady in Norfolk. A Mrs. Wingo. You know her? She knows you."

"Yeah. She was a neighbor lady."

"Well, your neighbor lady sent the prosecutor a note after seeing a report about you on TV." Nat handles the fax sheet in his briefcase. "Mrs. Wingo was sticking up for you. She says there's no way you could have hurt that girl or burned that church. You weren't the type."

Elijah waits. Nat changes his voice, he becomes prosecutorial.

"I'll get to the point. She says you stood up to some drug dealers on your block. You got into a fight. Then you left town. She says you were a good man."

Nat lifts the fax sheet out of the briefcase. He holds it up for Elijah to see.

"Why'd you leave Norfolk?"

Elijah's fingers work, he rolls something invisible on his fingertips as though there is blood on them. Then he says, "I busted one of 'em up pretty good. We got into it and he pulled a knife. I took it off him after he cut a piece out of my leg. I took him down pretty hard. I was pissed. I didn't kill him or nothing. No cops. But I left town before they came back."

Nat shakes his head. "You beat a man almost to death. Is that what you're telling me?"

"He was a drug dealer."

Nat slams his briefcase shut.

"Goddammit! I don't care! I told you to tell me everything! Everything, Elijah! Now what else is there? What else am I going to find out from the prosecutor that I should have fucking found out first from you?"

Nat jumps to his feet. He stomps the two short steps to Elijah and confronts the man's dark flesh with his own reddening skin.

"Huh? Tell me right now, Elijah, because there is no chance in Hell of you ever walking out of here a free man if you don't!"

Elijah lets a few seconds heave between them, they are tossed and stormy moments. He says, "That's it, Nat. Nothing else."

Nat searches for the truth on Elijah's face but there's no chance he can find it there, just as he could not find Elijah's lie.

"All right," he says, and backs away to take a seat again on the cot. "All right." Leaning back against the green bars, Elijah jams his hands in his pockets and hangs his head.

Nat totes up the damage of the revelation. "Well, this probably won't hurt your case. The woman didn't see anything herself, she just heard what you did and that's not admissible. The guy you beat up isn't going to come forward. He's a drug dealer, and that'll probably keep Fentress from going to get him to put him on the stand." What Nat does not say, but nonetheless lays onto the scale of damage, is that he cannot now completely trust Elijah.

On the cot, Nat spreads beside him the state's reports. He reclaims his calm, then begins his explanation to Elijah of the prosecution's stand on the capital murder charge. Elijah listens with his ebony eyes on the concrete floor. Nat lays out for him the awful luck about the sperm destroyed in the girl's body from the intense heat, leaving mere traces of semen. The position the body was found in, and the questions Nat has about that. The kerosene, the hymnal, the alcohol in the girl's blood. The evidence is all circumstantial. But there's plenty of it and, in the absence of an alibi, it stacks up against Elijah. Add to that now the revelation that Elijah left Norfolk because he took justice into his own, violent hands. The prosecution's case is predicated entirely on Elijah Waddell having done the same thing here in Good Hope. It doesn't look good. And Nat's fresh concerns about his client's veracity cause him to wonder what more that deep and taciturn face might conceal.

He asks Elijah to carefully recollect his whereabouts the evening of the fire, where and when he bought the beers and anything else he drank that night. Did anyone see him walking? Did he speak to anyone? It seems Amanda Talley was also wandering the town and county that night. Nat describes her in detail. Did Elijah see her? Did he talk with anyone who might have seen her?

None of Elijah's answers sheds any light. There are too many hours and gaps where he was out of sight, sitting alone by the river, walking in the woods, drinking and brooding in the bushes off the road across from the Victory Baptist.

"It's okay," Nat tells him. "If you were out of sight, then no one can say they saw you with Amanda."

Nat inquires approximately what time Elijah arrived at the Victory Baptist and started watching.

"A little after midnight."

"And you saw no one go in or come out of the church after you got there. Other than the person who burned it around one-thirty."

"No."

This means Amanda was inside the Victory Baptist by midnight. And she likely was not punched and raped while inside, or Elijah would have seen someone leave before the fire.

Nat asks if it could have been the girl herself whom Elijah saw run from the church through the graveyard after the fire was set. Again, Elijah says he was too far away, the light too dim, the beers too strong, his surprise too distracting. He just knows it was some-one else, not he.

The swelling on his knuckles? Nat wants to be sure the answer stays the same.

Again, Elijah struck a tree, angry, drunk. Good.

Nat starts to pack up the documents.

"All the forensics aren't in yet," he says. "I'm still waiting on more blood work. I'm going to talk with the state biologist about the DNA test. I'm interested in the broken jaw, too. I'll go see the medical ex-aminer. And if someone in this county saw Amanda Talley that night after she left her father's house, I'll find them. Plus, there's a link be-tween the girl and the Victory Baptist. I'm going to look into that."

Elijah says, "Before you go, tell me one thing."

"What."

"Tell me you're gonna get me out of this."

Nat watches his client move closer, to sit on the cot beside him.

"After you tell me one thing," Nat says, "and I'm only going to ask you this once. Tell me you had nothing to do with any of this. Because if you did, if you knew this girl at all, if you ever talked with her or were seen with her, if you ever had a drink with her, anything, Elijah, anything at all, then you tell me right now. I don't want to hear it from one of Fentress's witnesses. I've got to walk out of here sure that I know everything."

"I did not know Amanda Talley. Ever."

Nat waits, and there is nothing more from Elijah.

"Then," he says, his voice even, "somehow, I'm going to get you out of this."

At this Elijah bows his head. A hand comes to his face. He digs a knuckle into his eye socket. Nat feels uncomfortable this close to Elijah's sudden emotion. He knows the man is struggling—every sec-ond, it seems—for his dignity, probably even his sanity. Nat regrets telling Elijah he would somehow set him free. That was unwise. He knows Elijah and Clare will cling to that statement and it may prove to be a thin lifeline. Nat realizes he spoke out of simple pride, a fool-ish reassertion of his shaken confidence after the pummeling he en-dured thirty minutes ago in the meeting with Fentress. Nat is puffing himself up, the big lawyer in front of Elijah, the knight in shining armor, even the parent demanding he be trusted. And right now he does not know how he will deliver on that promise.

## 4

There is a River Styx in this domain of the dead and it is of cement. Cross it, the gray broad flat expanse with silver drains puncturing its plain, and you are among the departed. This underworld is not deep in the earth but below the street. It is not murky but lit almost blindingly, the odd incandescent bulb jitters like a soul nervous to be descended to this place. It is not hot and steamy, not rippled in stench, but cool and clean, the air recycled and antiseptic. The caretakers here are not demons but the quick, they are administrators and doctors.

Nat sits across a cluttered desk from Jackie Kline. Right now he does not want to ask the assistant chief medical examiner about her autopsy findings regarding Amanda Talley. He wants to ask how she can do this job. He wants to point not at the files on her desk but at the silver refrigerator doors arrayed on the wall behind her, and at a sheet plainly covering the contours of a corpse on a chrome table in the middle of the vast gray floor. Nat came to this basement department in Richmond more than a dozen times in his role as prosecutor, and each time he felt the same curdles he does now, ghoulish, childish curiosity and mortal repulsion.

Jackie Kline finishes an entry on some form while Nat waits. She is plump and pink, jolly and very alive, as though God put her here at the end of the road on purpose, as a billboard of what we could have been in life, content and relaxed, no matter what our work or hardships. In her mid-fifties, Jackie Kline is the anti–Grim Reaper. She chuckles to herself, pushes white hair behind her ear, adjusts her glasses.

"What?" Nat inquires.

She does not look up from her scribing. She says, "I can tell just sitting here this place still creeps you out."

He lies. "No it doesn't."

Jackie looks up now. Her eyes sparkle. How does she do that? Nat wonders. She says, "It's okay if it does."

But he thinks it is not okay. Nat is not pleased to be caught in his discomfiture. It feels somehow unmanly to be seen nervous among the dead.

Jackie finishes her writing. She takes up the pages of the report and taps them on the desk to even their edges. "Okay, it doesn't." She slides the sheets into a folder. Her eyes take on a puckish gleam. "So, you want to poke around some. I've got some very cool bodies down here, pardon the pun."

"No," he says, his voice level to show he does not appreciate being made fun of, "thanks."

Though jabbed, Nat smiles. He figures Jackie is glad to have someone to spar with down here in her cavern of scalpels and silence. He opens his copy of her preliminary M.E. report.

"May we?" he asks.

She sits back. "We may."

"Amanda Talley."

Now Jackie's expression takes on a look of genuine distaste.

"George Talley," she says.

"What about him?"

"Look," Jackie works her stout hands over the table, "I know the man lost his daughter and all. I'm not trying to be insensitive but he made a colossal butthole of himself here this past weekend. I couldn't get him out of my hair. Do this fast for me, get this done, like his poor kid was the only case I had. Well, I figured he's a sheriff and I've got to stay on good terms with all the law folk in the state. The best way to get rid of him was to give him what he wanted, so I moved her to the top of the list."

"You mean he was here for the whole autopsy?" Nat winces at the thought of watching your own daughter go under Jackie Kline's knives.

"No, he didn't stay for that. But after he came down Saturday morning and identified the body, he insisted on hanging around for the x-rays. All I'll say is he was mighty damn pushy."

Nat is prodded by the urge to defend George Talley; he is, after all, a part of Nat's history. "That's just George's way of grieving," he says. "He wants to know what happened. George hates sitting back. And he wanted to bury her on Sunday after church. He's kind of addicted to the public."

Jackie reaches into another manila envelope. She pulls out a short pile of Polaroids wrapped with a rubber band. Nat sees only the blank backs of them until Jackie tosses one on the desk in front of him.

She asks, "Could you have hung around very long if this was your daughter?"

Nat cannot touch the photo. The portrait is too gruesome, an excoriated mound, as though black leaves have been raked into a pile human in shape. Even after his years as a prosecutor, Nat thinks this is the most final thing he has ever seen.

He takes a shaken breath and looks up at Jackie.

"No. No, I couldn't." His mouth is very dry.

She puts the square away with the others. Nat will not let himself imagine what is on the other photos. He blinks many times but the image will not rub away. His mouth will not moisten.

"Odd way of grieving," she says.

Nat nods, not knowing what to make of this.

"Oh, well," she says, and adds in a singsong, "any day above ground is a good one."

Nat sees with this little maxim she has shifted past George Talley. But Nat remains ensnared in the picture. He cannot move his spirit so mercurially as she. Jackie takes up another folder.

"I've got some more info from serology."

"Show me." Nat holds out his hand for the papers, glad to be in motion.

"Save yourself the trouble," Jackie says, not handing the folder to him. "The info I got back is that there's no more info."

"What do you mean?" He lowers his hand.

"Listen, the girl's body was subjected to temperatures in excess of fifteen hundred degrees. She was left in the ashes for another sixteen hours. Nothing much escapes that. Blood serology exists at the chemical level. DNA is at the molecular level. If the heat in that church was severe enough to score away any trace of DNA from the semen in her cervix, you can be sure there's nothing left of the guy's blood type or whether or not he's a secretor. Everything alters under that kind of heat, Nat. Sorry to be blunt, but from the shoulders down the girl was steak. Not much more."

Nat reviews quickly in his mind the CME #1 report from Jorgensen, how Amanda's face and left arm were protected. How both feet and her right hand were incinerated. If Amanda had been in a struggle, maybe she clawed her attacker with her left hand, tore off some skin cells or clothing fibers that might have survived the flames under her fingernails.

"How about fibers, Jackie? Skin cells? On her face or her left hand. Anything."

"Zilch. And don't read anything into that. It's not unusual at all for there to be no evidence under a victim's nails. She still could have been attacked, just like it's still possible the sex was consensual. The absence of evidence in this instance means nothing."

She lays the folder from Don Lee's forensics lab on the desk. Nat does not take it up. It may as well be an empty folder.

"We were lucky to get the blood alcohol reading out of her left arm. Beyond that and the dried residue of semen in her vagina, the girl did no talking."

Nat nods at the unwitting aptness of Jackie's statement. In life and now in death, Amanda Talley remains an enigma, tight-lipped.

"What about the x-rays?"

Jackie rises. She turns to a wide cabinet behind her. She slides open a drawer and fingers through the alphabet to Amanda's file. The x-ray sheets rumble while she arrays them on the desk for Nat.

"Nothing here. The two breaks I found in her leg and arm had the classic marks of postmortem heat snapping. Anatomically, the rest of her was clean."

"Except for her jaw."

"Left side. Clean break. Slight contusion and swelling. Like I put in the report, it looked like a right-handed punch. The jaw wiggled in my hand."

"Why didn't you x-ray it? You did the rest of her."

The medical examiner takes her seat.

"Your Sheriff Talley stood over me every minute I was doing the x-rays. He said he wanted me to focus only on the cause of death. The girl's busted jaw clearly had nothing to do with what killed her, so I asked him if he wanted me to skip it and he said Yes. I did a visual inspection only on the head. I saw the edema and the bruise on the protected part of her face. I put the jaw in my hand and it moved side to side. So I noted that it was broken and moved on."

"Can you make a guess about how long it was before she died that she might have taken that punch?"

Jackie gathers the spilled x-rays into a neat batch. She puts them into their yellow folder, assembling Amanda's skeleton in one dimension, thinking.

"Judging by the swelling, probably three to six hours before the fire. That puts it between six and nine o'clock that evening."

"You're sure about that?"

"It's my best guess."

Nat calculates. If Amanda was punched sometime in the early evening, then perhaps the fight was a separate event from the sex. Fentress said that George Talley reported the girl left their home on foot at eight the night of the fire. No one has come forward yet to say they saw her at any time after that.

Jackie's guess still leaves room for Elijah to have hit Amanda at nine o'clock, raped her, and put her in the church before one-thirty. But if that's the way it happened, the girl regained consciousness after she went into the Victory Baptist. If she wasn't bound—and the position of her arms and feet indicate she wasn't—why did she stay there, with a broken jaw, after a rape, with a fire coming through the walls behind the altar? Did she enter the church hours before the fire after being brutalized, did she pray with the Baptist hymnal to seek some spiritual relief, then fall asleep under the pew and doze to her death? Smoke inhalation—the cause of death—would have prevented Amanda from waking up. Ever.

"Would she have been in a lot of pain from the broken jaw?"

Jackie purses her lips. "Tough to say. Boxers have been known to get their jaw busted in the first round and finish twelve rounds of solid shots right on the bone. Other people break a nail and run to the emergency room. She certainly would have known her jaw was broken. But if she'd been raped as well, the girl had plenty on her mind. She might have just wanted to bear the pain until morning or until she could calm down. Who knows what goes through a seventeen-year-old girl's head after a shitty thing like that? Me? I might have been glad just to be alive after a rape. Then I would have turned pissed."

Jackie's musing ignites another train of thought for Nat. Amanda Talley was wandering on foot, according to her father, so she could easily have been victimized by someone who saw her and picked her up. Afterward, she felt defiled as Jackie implies she might, and relieved to have survived the ordeal. She wandered in pain to the Victory Baptist Church, a new religion and community that had recently intrigued her. She went inside on her own, she prayed, she fell asleep. The church burned—whether by Elijah or another—and she was inside, unknown to the arsonist.

All good theories, Nat thinks. None of them backed by proof. None of them rules out Elijah. Who is the church burner if not Elijah? Whom did she drink with, fight with, have sex with? Amanda had no boyfriends in Good Hope; it's a small town, plenty of people would have noticed if she'd even been on a date. Fentress's tale of violence and revenge is just as good as Nat's assumptions. Better. The prosecutor has some hard facts on his side. He has a damaging statement by Elijah on television. He has a county willing to believe. Nat has nothing, no alibi, no forensics, no witnesses, nothing but conjecture.

Conjecture will not beat Fentress and will not save Elijah's life.

Nat stands. "Thanks for the time, Jackie."

She rises. They shake hands. The woman's grip is firmer than Nat's; his mind was elsewhere. Quickly he adjusts and squeezes harder. "I hope I was a help," she says.

Nat nods.

"This is your first time on the defense," she says. "How's it feel?"

"Good. Troubling. But good."

"Don't let it suck you in, Nat. You won't do your client any good if you're too involved. I don't get up on the table with my clients. I stay on my feet. Always."

"I try to remember that. It was easier as a prosecutor."

He walks away. Her voice turns him.

"Find a place of peace, Nat Deeds. If I can do it down here," Jackie lifts a finger, "you can do it up there."

Nat smiles. When he rotates away from Jackie Kline, he drops the smile. He crosses the gray, never-rolling river, back to the troubling living.

# THREE

## 1

On Tuesday afternoon, Ed Fentress made his show of probable cause in front of Judge Baron. With no fanfare Baron found sufficient cause to certify the case up to the circuit court of Judge Imelda Hawk.

Now, on Wednesday morning, Nat phones Judge Hawk to request an *in camera* hearing. He wants to argue a change of venue for Elijah's capital murder trial and, pending that, a relocation for Elijah to a different jail in the state. The judge's clerk calls back a half hour later. The hearing is set for three o'clock that afternoon, this is the best Mr. Fentress can do. Then Nat calls Deputy Monroe Skelton, asking to see him after the hearing.

Nat spends his morning drawing up the orders should the trial judge be persuaded to agree. He deals with several phone calls regarding his few civil cases. He changes his phone message to say he will be back in the office tomorrow and heads for Good Hope.

In the car driving east, Nat looks out at the drooping world. He cannot remember the last rain; clearly the plants and trees withering beside the road, the crops listing in the fields drunk on dryness, cannot recall water either. The sun is mashing down, impassioned day after day for almost a month now.

Nat thinks of Jackie's admonition to him yesterday. Find a place of peace. Where is that, he wonders, under this sun? Nat has to find that place but he senses how hard this is going to be for him. On its own, Elijah's case has become wrapped up in so much more. At a very deep level, without intending it to be so, Nat identifies his defense of the accused man with his own acquittal in his hometown. Somehow Elijah also invokes Maeve, and Nat's quandary about justice. The case has become the pole of an unlikely circle, as though odd bits of Nat's past have been magnetized by it and drawn in: Tom Derby, George Talley, Mrs. Epps, Fentress, the centuries-old ways of Pamunkey County. Nat has even confronted the lessons of his childhood, how his mother and father with their lectures and icons raised him to be their image of a good man, and to point his finger at good or evil and be sure.

Where is that place of peace? It is elusive, not there for the asking. Nat thinks maybe he found it once, as recently as eight months ago, when his circle was Maeve, his home, and his job. Maybe. But under this wilting sun, on this road running back to the town where today he does not belong, he questions this belief: Did he truly have peace there, or did he merely have silence? These two are not the same, though they can be mistaken for each other. He wonders, Did Maeve quietly endure him for their years of marriage? Was that peace? What could it have been for her? He knows she tried to be warmed in his light but did he shine it on her from too great a distance, was he no more for his wife than a cold moonglow? Was it peace that he had in his community, or was it remoteness? And his job. It consumed him, like another marriage. Was this because his work was important and he was good at it, or was the prosecutor's office simply the home where he was most comfortable?

Nat ponders until he crosses the Mattaponi bridge and the egg smell intrudes on his reverie. The recovery boiler at the paper mill waves a steamy salute. A beeping lumber truck blocks the road for a minute, backing up its load. Nat looks at a vegetable stand, a crab restaurant, the little grocery store, the gate to the mill, the river in his rearview mirror, and asks them all and more beyond them if familiarity is peace. Or is it just the muting of questions, a hand pressed over the mouth of your life?

When the traffic clears Nat drives through town. The heat seems hostile out in the pastures where horseflies and greenheads worry the livestock. Even cows have enough sense to group and lie down in the shade. The dirt is so dry there are no tractor ruts in the farm roads cut between the big squares of crops, the lanes are all ground flat and dusty orange. The green is turning brown, blade and leaf, and the little hills are taking on the semblance of dunes.

Coming around the bend approaching the Victory Baptist Church, Nat sees a low cloud hover above the trees, as though the church were burning again. Driving closer, he sees the haze is dust and ash thrown into the air by a pair of scampering bulldozers. Nat parks on the shoulder across from the church and gets out. The 'dozers spit inky diesel fumes and bellow like advancing bulls. Nat takes off his coat and tie. He watches them gouge chunks from the pile of seared timbers and carry them to two dumptrucks waiting in the gravel lot. Giant ebony ribs stick out of the trucks' beds like dinosaur bones to be carted away.

Five days after dying in flame, the Victory Baptist Church is to be born again. A twinge in Nat's chest flags some unfairness; Amanda Talley will not be rebuilt.

Nat walks into the brush across the street from the loud machines. He finds the place Elijah sat the night of the fire; it is easy to spot, the grass has been trampled by many feet, a scrap of yellow tape from the police cordon hangs from a sapling. Nat sits. He is fifteen feet back from the road with a clear view of the church site, which is perhaps another hundred feet away across the road. Watching the heavy machines do their work, Nat feels the prick of unfairness grow inside him. But it is not for Amanda Talley. Even with the rising white spire and the colonnaded portico gone, with the breath and growl of tractors ambling under the heat, Nat begins to sense the outer reaches of what Elijah Waddell must have felt crouching here in the weeds and scrub in the deep heart of that tragic night. My daughter, Nat thinks, dug out of their ground. My child's casket moved to another grave, shamed. My color spat on. My wife humiliated. Nat thinks, This is a powerful place to sit.

After a while the tractors stop. The dumptrucks are full and pull away. The 'dozer operators climb down from their great yellow steeds. One moves to sit under a tree. The other stands his ground to speak with Tom Derby, who has walked up the road.

Nat stays in the bushes for a minute observing. Derby is ebullient, slapping the driver on the back. He hands him a Thermos, the man pours a drink from it. Derby waves at the other fellow. Nat comes across the street.

"Hey," Derby calls to him, turning from the machine driver, "what do you think?"

Nat walks up, extending his hand for a shake.

"Tom. Looks like you'll be ready to put her back up pretty soon."

Derby hands the Thermos to the driver, who nods to Nat and ferries the water to his compatriot resting in the shade.

Derby trills, "What can I say? The mill came through. I called the parent company up in Baltimore on Friday. I told them most of my congregation worked at the mill or was retired from it. They put me in touch with their community affairs officer and he said the company would donate twenty thousand dollars on the spot to get the rebuilding fund under way. They say we might get more as we go along. The church members themselves were so shocked they've put up a couple thousand already. One of them is donating the bulldozers and the trucks. The Virginia Council of Churches put in an application for us for state and federal funds. The governor himself called me yesterday and promised help. Nat," Derby rattles his head as though seeing something marvelous for the first time, "I hate to say it like this but it's turning into a doggone miracle."

Nat nods. "The governor." He tries to make himself sound impressed for Derby but thinks instead, Here is another politician turning this calamity into votes.

"It's something," Derby says, "the way this community has pulled together."

Nat struggles to restrain his skepticism, to keep his own counsel after sitting where Elijah sat the night of the burning, then seeing this joy in the church pastor, his old friend. He thinks, Careful, Tom. That's a double-edged sword. Anytime people think and act alike so quickly, they can turn against you just as fast as they will turn with you. Ask Elijah. Ask me.

Derby remains handsomely blithe. He is happy, made gabby by the tractors, the disappearing ruin, and the prospects of enough money to start over. He points at the tired lawn where one of the machines sits quiet.

"We held church on the grass Sunday. We set up tents. I told everyone to come in shorts and T-shirts. After services, the young folks and I crawled through the rubble. We pulled out everything we could save. We're going to reuse the old baptistry, it was just a big lead tub. We'll put the copper cross back on the new spire. We're going to build the new church to look just like the original, that's what the congregation wants, right down to the sparking rail in the middle of the pews and the chorus loft. We'll call it the Second Victory Baptist. These folks around here aren't so hot on change. I figure we'll set up a small showcase in the new building with some of the singed hymnals and such from the fire. Sort of a memorial to the old building."

Suddenly Derby's face alters. There is an obstacle to his enthusiasm. Nat does not say it but he sees that Derby has stumbled over it, the word *memorial* has made him—like Nat—think of them; the two dead girls, Amanda and Nora Carol, and all that is terrible which has spun off from them. Derby shifts his merry tone.

"I've been carrying something for you, Nat. Figured I'd bump into you. Here." Derby fishes in his rear pocket for his wallet. He pulls from it a check, which he hands to Nat. It is written for one thousand dollars to Nathaniel Deeds and signed by Rev. Thomas Derby.

Nat closes the check along its fold.

"What's this for?"

"You're going to have expenses to defend Elijah. You're just an appointed lawyer on this case, Nat. You don't have the funds to defend him like the county does to prosecute. So here. This ought to help level the playing field some."

"Tom."

"Take it."

"Who's this from?"

"I'd like to lie and say it's from the church members but it's not, it's from me personal. When this rape thing came about, a lot of folks that had been willing to take his side kind of clammed up. I'm not making it an issue with these people. They're confused between blaming themselves and Elijah. So I've just decided to focus them on rebuilding the Victory Baptist. But that doesn't mean we don't owe him for what was done. So please take this from me, Nat. I can't keep it."

Nat pushes the check into Derby's shirt pocket. The pastor stands still for it but Nat believes nonetheless the offer was sincere.

"That's not the kind of help Elijah's going to need."

Derby pauses, considering. "What can I do?"

"Visit his wife, make sure she's okay."

"I'll do it."

"And you can try to help me figure out a few things."

"Shoot."

"First, do you remember the day Amanda Talley came to your church?"

"Sort of."

"Did she say anything in particular you remember? Did she show any interest in coming back another Sunday?"

"I don't recall. She just thanked me for a nice morning in church and went on her way."

"Alone."

"Yes."

"Was she on foot?"

"I recollect she was."

"All right. Ask your congregation if anyone knew her well at all. Did she talk to anybody the day she came to church? Who'd she sit with? Ask around, Tom."

"All right."

"Also, ask did anyone see Amanda the night of the fire. Anywhere around town. Walking, riding in a car, sitting someplace. What time they saw her. She ended up in your church. Somebody might have brought her out here hitchhiking, somebody might have seen her go in. I need to know. Anything, Tom."

"I'll take care of it. You know, there was a deputy came by yesterday afternoon. He asked me a lot of the same questions."

"Monroe Skelton? Big black guy?"

"That's him."

Nat thinks, Monroe is probably running into dead ends as well, or he's turning up even more circumstantial evidence to implicate Elijah.

Derby puts his hand on Nat's shoulder. He says, "Something will turn up."

"I hope so."

Derby squeezes Nat's collarbone. "You okay? It doesn't sound like this is going too well."

Nat rubs his forehead. Sweat slicks his fingers.

"I'll be honest. There isn't much to go on. In fact, I've got nothing to defend Elijah with but questions. Not one solid fact. Just blank spaces and doubts."

Derby takes his hand from Nat's shoulder. "I understand."

Nat reads on his old friend's face that he does indeed understand.

Derby says, "But you do believe he's innocent."

"Yes. I do."

"You know, in my line of work we call that faith. It's believing, with nothing to hold on to but questions. Throughout history, people have done remarkable things armed with only questions and faith."

Derby releases over Nat a knowing and remarkable smile.

A fresh, empty dumptruck rumbles up the road and into the gravel lot. The bulldozer drivers stir. Derby casts his eyes over the resurrection of the Victory Baptist, all this activity around him.

He brings his eyes back to Nat to say, "I'm trusting you will too."

## 2

The meeting in Judge Hawk's chamber takes less than five minutes.

She sits like her name, with the attention of a raptor. Her eyes do not blink except in long, slow cascades, then her lids pop up again. Imelda Hawk is a member of the Mattaponi Indian tribe, whose ancestors hunted along the green river from time immemorial, granting the sustaining waters the greatest tribute, taking its name for their own. She is slight and short, taut, with dark hair and freckled skin; it's easy to imagine her in flight with coal-colored feathers. She is married to a big fellow who runs the local granary, but she has kept her native name. Everything about Judge Hawk is sharp, from her wits and her nose to her tongue.

As soon as Nat and Fentress are seated, Hawk asks, "I have spoken with Judge Baron, gentlemen, about your deportment. Now that the preliminary hearing is over and jurisdiction for this case lies in my court, I will assume you've gotten all your chicanery out of your systems."

Nat readies an answer quickly; he wants to speak before Fentress can make some excuse or ingratiating guarantee. But the prosecutor says nothing. He seems confident this morning. Nat holds himself in check and nods with Fentress under the Hawk's glare.

The Hawk nods at Nat. "Go ahead, counselor."

Nat presents first his motion for a change of venue. He cites as his principal reason an intense and biased press coverage that has served essentially to convict Elijah in advance of his trial. Second, Nat claims the crime victim is the daughter of a well-known and powerful local figure; it will be impossible to impanel a jury that has not had some contact with Sheriff George Talley.

The Hawk listens. Nat reaches to his briefcase, saying, "Judge, I've drawn the order for you to look at."

She holds up a stopping hand. She addresses Fentress. "You got something to say?"

Fentress extends his lower lip. "No, judge. I think you're about to say it for me."

Judge Hawk hesitates. Nat can see she does not like this smugness, but Ed Fentress was handed to her and the other judges in Pamunkey County by the electorate ten years ago and again every election since. She turns to Nat.

"I'm going to deny your motion for a change of venue. I think the people of this county can hear any case and do it fairly. I'm not going to tell them they're stupid or that they're too angry or influenced by the media to make a clearheaded decision. That church was burned in their county. That girl was one of their own. Elijah Waddell is one of their own too. This is a Pamunkey County matter and I believe the folks here are up to it."

"Judge."

"That's the way I'm holding, Nat. Unless you can tell me something I haven't already heard to change my mind, that's the way it is for now. That can change, but not today. Anything else?"

Nat regroups. He knows when the Hawk says, Move on, you don't backtrack.

"I want Elijah moved out of Rappahannock."

Again the judge is decisive. "No. If I allow that, then I send the exact signal to the county and your inevitable jury that you don't want, Nat. It'll be one more prejudicial item in the papers and on TV. Folks'll figure something is awfully suspicious about Elijah or Talley or both, so much so that the court had to step in and keep them apart. No, that'll cloud issues even further." She turns from Nat to Fentress. "Ed, you tell George Talley for me I'm sorry about his girl but I will gut him like a perch if I hear him going anywhere near Elijah Waddell. You got me?"

"Yes, ma'am."

"Anything else, gentlemen?"

"No, judge."

"Then good afternoon."

Nat and Fentress stand to leave the judge's chamber. Before they are out the door, she adds, "Listen, the two of you. Some people of this county have made a few bad judgments in the past week. But these are all basically good and God-fearing people. They're not the bigots the newspapers say they are and they're not fools. We are going to trust them and the rest of the county folks right up to the last possible moment until we cannot. And you two are going to lead the band on that, you understand? We are not going to add fuel to any of the fires burning out there, racial or otherwise. Now, good day."

In the hall Fentress says, "Told you." Nat wants to slam him against the wall. Fentress doesn't notice this. He asks Nat if he wants to get a cup of coffee and Nat realizes a body slam would be wasted on Ed Fentress, the man would endure it, then fix his hair.

"No, thanks." Nat speeds his walk to pull away. He clomps down the steps, wondering when something in Elijah's case will go his way.

Outside, the heat is like stepping into a hedge of prickles. No matter how long you live in the South, you don't get used to this, moving between air conditioning and swelter. Nat walks under the canopy between the courthouse and the sheriff's office.

He finds Monroe at his desk.

"Money. You ready?"

Monroe scrunches his face. "I called him. He's at home."

"Good. Let's go over there."

Monroe shakes his head. "He doesn't want to see you."

"You told him we were coming?"

"No, but it's his day off. He's not gonna want to be bothered."

"That's perfect. He won't be in uniform."

"The man's always in uniform, Nat. He doesn't have to be wearing it."

"Come on."

"I told you I'd talk to him. I didn't say it would be today and I didn't say I'd be standing next to you when I did it."

"But I want to talk to him today."

"Go ahead. Take your chances."

"I need you there."

"I know you do. The man'll see red if he catches you coming up his drive. You're the lawyer for the defense. Why should I go with you? I can pick my own time."

Nat steps closer to Monroe's chair. "Because while you pick your own time my client spends another shitty day in jail. And because somewhere in our past I'm sure I did you a favor. You owe me."

Monroe feigns confusion. "I don't owe you this much."

Nat grabs the large man by the shoulder of his jersey. "Up."

They ride to George Talley's house in Monroe's patrol car. On the way the two do not talk about how they will handle George Talley in his own den. Each man has a separate relationship with Talley, formed over many years. Likewise they have separate concerns. Also they do not speak of their suspicions in the Waddell case. Nat knows Monroe has not closed the book on Elijah. The deputy is obviously conducting his own probe, trying to fill in the blanks as he sees them. Nat does not mention what he learned from Jackie Kline about Talley's interference with the postmortem exam. Monroe does not speak of why he agreed to come along to question his boss. But there is something both men want to find out from Sheriff Talley. Nat wonders if it will prove to be the same thing.

The sheriff lives on a quiet street in a new development. His house is one of several brick ranchers. The trees here are not yet mature so there is little shade.

Talley answers his doorbell. He is barefoot, in shorts and a white T-shirt. He says, "Well, well. It's the Mod Squad." There is nothing hostile in the sheriff's mien. He seems calm, tired. He says, "Come on in."

Nat and Monroe follow Talley through the kitchen, where he grabs a beer and offers the two visitors the same. They decline. Talley leads them onto his porch, which is walled by glass to make a Florida room. All three settle into wicker rockers.

"I don't think you've been over here," Talley says to Nat, motioning to his brick house. "I been here three years now. I was one of the first to buy into this development." It sounds friendly enough, a brag on a good purchase. But it is a rebuke, a hint that Nat is not considered a friend—four years and Nat has not ever visited—in this home on this day.

"It's nice."

Talley points the neck of his beer bottle at Monroe. "You didn't need to bring the muscle, though." He smiles at his deputy. This is a joke; George Talley is the muscle and he knows it. Nat thinks this is why the storm that Monroe predicted from the man has not come. Talley is confident.

"George, I didn't get a chance at the funeral to tell you how sorry I am. You know that."

"I do. I saw you up on the hill. Like some poet up there."

Nat thinks of what happened when he came down from that hill, the recoiling of his town, the encounter with Maeve. He pushes them all away for now.

"I've got to ask you a couple questions. It'll only take a few minutes."

Talley sips the beer. He paces himself.

"This isn't a deposition."

"No."

"Then what is it?"

"I'm just trying to piece some things together about what happened that night. That's all."

"Nat. Hold up." Talley's face pulls in, his eyes narrow. Here it comes, Nat thinks. But, oddly, the sheriff's voice does not mirror the ire in his eyes.

Talley tilts the beer bottle at Nat. He says, "Let me tell you straight, because I know you respect that. I'm being a good guy letting you in my house at all. In case you forgot, and I'm thinking you haven't, you are defending the son of a bitch who raped and killed my only child. I don't hold that against you because I know Baron brought you in on it. But don't think you can interrogate me in my own home three days after burying my daughter. All right? And Money, what the hell are you doing?"

Nat glances at Monroe. The deputy's brows are knitted. He stares at his superior. Talley's controlled tone pulled no reaction from Nat or Monroe. So he stands. He sets his beer on the straw side table.

"Come on, Nat. Walk with me over here. I want to show you her room. Where she slept just a few days ago. Where Amanda kept her clothes in her dresser. She had a scrapbook too. You want to go through them?"

"George."

"I'll tell you what. You go back and you tell Elijah Waddell I will see him fry. I will personally pull the goddamn switch." Talley glowers with this statement. The veins in his neck have swollen. "Now I'll show you boys out."

Nat stays in his seat. He leaves his voice mild. "George, it doesn't have to be like this. But you need to know I can get a subpoena to ask you these questions under oath. I just thought it best to keep things private at first."

Talley looks down. "A subpoena."

"George, come on."

"Get it."

Monroe speaks. "George."

Talley barks, "Stay out of this."

Monroe lays his elbows on his knees. He fills the rocker.

"It's not just Nat asking," he says. Talley and the big deputy lock eyes. Monroe says, "It's me too."

Talley cocks his head. "And who are you?"

"I'm the investigating officer in a murder case in my county. Now please sit down and talk to us or we'll be back this afternoon. And then we'll talk on the record."

George Talley nods to himself. He studies the two men in his brick house come to examine him, one his employee, the other the lawyer for the enemy. The sheriff sits and takes up his beer. He rocks back and crosses his bare legs.

"This is over when I say it's over. Understand? Now who's asking?"

Nat draws a breath to begin. But Monroe's voice comes first. Nat glances at the deputy. The man has flipped open a small pocket notebook. He holds a pencil.

"You've said Amanda left here on foot a little before eight o'clock Thursday night."

"I have said that. Yes."

"Did she say where she was going?"

"No. It was after dinner. She just wanted to go out for a walk."

"Did she have anything to drink at dinner?"

"What do you mean, alcohol?"

"Yes. Did you serve her a beer? Glass of wine?"

"No. I did not give my little girl alcohol. Never."

"What did you talk about that night? At dinner, before she left."

"Nothing. The usual."

"Usual what, George?"

"Father and daughter. You got a boy, Monroe. You know. It doesn't have to be about anything particular."

"No, it doesn't." Monroe pauses to add something on his note-pad. In the gap, Nat wants to step in but instead contains himself to let Monroe carry on. The deputy seems to have come out of the gate on the right track.

"Was there any tension between you and Amanda recently? Arguments over anything?"

"No."

"Well, that's good. But like you said, George, I raised a boy. A good boy, but when he was Amanda's age there wasn't a day went by we didn't have something to butt heads over. Him and Rey Ann, too. So what was it, George? There was something. She spent a lot of time walking around the county by herself. She left here Thursday night after dinner on foot. Did you two have any words?"

"What are you asking, Monroe? I want to know what you're asking." Talley uncrosses his legs. The wicker rocker creaks.

"Nothing, George. You say you two had no reason to argue. I'm just being sure. That's all."

Talley holds his tense posture. His eyes quickly shift to Nat, as if to say, You get him off my back. But Nat keeps his face immobile.

Monroe continues. "Did you know your daughter attended a service at the Victory Baptist Church about four weeks ago?"

Nat watches Talley. He can't be sure but the sheriff seems to flinch.

"No. No I didn't."

"George, she was seen by lots of folks there. She spoke with the preacher. You know Deputy Benson goes to the Victory Baptist. He didn't mention he saw her? No one said anything? It was a little ir-regular for her to be there."

Talley pauses now. His eyes burrow into Monroe. The sheriff appears to assess the danger of the man posing the question and determines he need not fear him.

"I guess, yeah, Amanda spoke to me about it. I didn't put much stock in it."

"Why not?"

"Because, Money, she's Catholic." George Talley stops. This is an honest, grieving father's mistake. He lowers his eyes. After a moment the sheriff corrects himself. "She was Catholic."

Monroe grants Talley a few seconds before proceeding. He scribbles in his notebook. Then he says, "But this wasn't a bone of contention between the two of you."

"We talked about it."

"All right. Now, how often do you attend St. Bede's?"

"Every Sunday."

"And sometimes during the week?"

"You know I do, Monroe. You know my schedule as well as I know yours."

"That's true, George. We been together a long time."

"We have."

"How often did Amanda go with you to St. Bede's?"

Talley blinks. Monroe waits. Then he says, "George, I can ask over at the church."

Talley takes his time.

He says, "She hasn't gone with me in two years."

Monroe does not ask in words, Why not? but simply lifts his chin to Talley. Nat is amazed. He has long underestimated Monroe Skelton. Perhaps everyone has.

Talley answers. "I don't know why she stopped going."

"But you wanted her to go to services with you."

"Any father would."

Monroe does not respond.

"The girl had a mind of her own," Talley says. "Anyone who knew her will tell you that." Nat notes the sheriff's answers are growing defensive and waspish. He senses the nearing end of Talley's cooperation. If Monroe is going to go for it, it better be soon. And he does.

"It is possible Amanda was thinking of switching from Catholic, maybe becoming a Baptist?"

George Talley snaps, "No."

"But she hadn't attended church with you in two years. And last month she went on her own, on foot, the three miles out to the Victory Baptist. She went up to Pastor Derby and told him she enjoyed the service. Then she told you about it. So it must have meant something to her."

Nat recalls the hymnal found under the girl's hand. The night of the fire she walked again to the Victory Baptist on her own, he's sure of it. She went to read. To think, pray, recover. But this time she went late at night when no one, not her father or the thousands of people he knows across Pamunkey County, could spy her and tell him.

Nat stitches bits together in his head. A month ago Amanda Talley attended the Baptist church against her Catholic father's wishes. Four weeks later, on a night when the girl walks to the country church, after a physical fight, after a few drinks, after sex, she opens the unlocked church doors before midnight, when Elijah started his vigil. She sits down to read, maybe lies down under a pew to sleep, refusing to go home. And on this same gnarled night the Victory Baptist burns.

Monroe does not point a finger or even pronounce the accusation, but it is there, hovering over Sheriff Talley like a sword: He and his daughter argued the night of the fire.

Talley also knows what has gone unsaid by the two inquisitors in his fresh brick home. He too is a lawman, himself a canny investigator. Nat observes on the sheriff's reddening face that the man has had enough. It's time to leave.

Monroe spots this too. The deputy turns to Nat. "Anything you want to ask?"

Nat thinks, Thanks, Money. You hack him off then turn him over to me when he's ready to explode.

"No. I think we're done. George, thank you."

Nat and Monroe stand. Talley does not rise to see them to the door. He sits with bowed head, swirling the beer bottle in his grip in tight circles. His eyes bore down into the brown bottle throat, as though into a tiny wishing well that he is trying to stir up to work for him. Nat hears the sheriff's breath come hard through his nose. The back of his neck is crimson. The man is biting his tongue.

Monroe says, "George."

Talley replies without looking up, "Git. Right now. The both of you."

Nat and Monroe do not walk into the house but take their leave through the Florida room's glass door. Talley rocks behind them.

In the squad car, Monroe drives slowly, intently. He is focusing on something. Nat asks the big deputy, "You going to be all right with this?"

"With what? George?"

"Yes. After this little session we just had."

Monroe blows under his mustache. "Aw, he's not gonna mess with me. He'll talk some shit maybe but I get George Talley too many votes from the black folks. Job security is one of the advantages of a small county."

Nat asks, "You changed your mind yet about Elijah?"

Monroe issues a nickering flap through his lips, like a horse.

He says, "Still working on it."

Monroe keeps his gaze straight ahead, measuring evidence, and says, "But the girl in the fire. It's hard to see your boy as a rapist and a killer. Though he still might have burned that church."

Nat is stirred by this small vote of confidence. It's a relief to have another voice, especially the investigating officer's, speak of seeing cracks in the town's belief of Elijah's guilt of capital murder.

But there remains a mound of proof and circumstance bearing down on Elijah that even this deputy's support will not remove. The facts and presumptions against Elijah that are already in Fentress's possession line up in Nat's mind and file past. Though it is not a long column Nat is afraid—based on his lengthy experiences as a prosecutor and with Ed Fentress—that it may be long enough.

"That's good to hear, Money. But there's a lot of evidence pointing the other way."

Monroe nods.

He says, "Yep. But not all of it."

The deputy leans past Nat to the glove box. Opening it, he pulls out a plastic sandwich bag. Sealed inside is a silvered square. Aligned in five numbered rows on the square's face are tiny red orbs under a plastic sheath. About half of them have been pushed out.

Birth control pills.

Nat's heart leaps. He says, "Amanda Talley."

"You got it."

"Where?"

"George's desk."

Nat gapes at Monroe.

"You went into the sheriff's desk and took these?"

"Uh-huh."

"Does he know?"

"Nope. I guess if he looks for 'em he'll wonder. He'll think he threw them out or something." Monroe directs Nat's eyes to the packet. "Count 'em. The directions say you start on the first Sunday after a period. If you begin with a Sunday, then the last one was taken on a Thursday."

"The fire was early Friday morning."

"George took these from her."

Nat looks at the pills. Possibilities form fast in his head. "They had an argument at dinner. Somehow he caught her with these. George is Catholic. He blew up when he found out she was having sex and using birth control."

Nat rattles the Baggie. "Money, you know what this means."

Monroe says, "Amanda might have had a boyfriend. And if so, he was a secret boyfriend, too, nobody's stepped forward so far. I think I'm gonna spend a little time tracking this down."

Nat tosses the plastic bag up and catches it, a small celebration. He knows this evidence is only circumstantial, no heavier than the packet of pills itself. But it is the first real token that argues even slightly in Elijah's defense.

"Even if whoever he is didn't have anything to do with the fire, he might be able to fill in some gaps. He's got to know more than we know, Money. And if we have a boyfriend, the rape charge gets a lot tougher to prove."

"If he's out there, I'll find him."

Nat says, "Don't show these to Fentress. Don't show these to anybody. If Talley finds out, he might destroy other evidence. You keep them, all right?"

Monroe leans again to close the glove compartment. "No, you keep them. If I have to, I'll testify later where they came from."

Nat is incredulous. "They came from George's desk."

"That's what I said."

"When did you take these?"

"This morning. Nobody saw me."

"Jesus. What made you look in there?"

"I got to thinking about last Friday, the morning after the fire. George came into the office just when I was getting off the midnight shift. He was in a badass mood. He woke up that morning at home and Amanda was gone, she hadn't come in all night. He went roaring around the office about eight o'clock. Sent two cars out to find her. Tried to send me but I told him I was off duty. I was leaving and I walked by his office. I saw him open his desk drawer and slam something inside it."

Nat recalls the greeting he received from George Talley on that Friday afternoon. Talley had gotten himself back in hand, he was in friendly attack mode. George stopped Nat at the sheriff's office door, squeezed Nat's hand like a nutcracker, flattered him, then turned him away. Nat thinks also of Talley's intrusive behavior with Jackie Kline.

Monroe says, "George is right. I've known him a long time. He's been different ever since the funeral, just like he was back there a few minutes ago in his house. He didn't blow up when he saw us, he was cool, right up to the end. He's hiding something. And he was lying to us, Nat. Him and that girl fought like cats and dogs."

"But you can't go into the man's desk without a warrant."

"Bullshit. I don't need a warrant to go into my boss's desk. I needed an ink pen. Law says any evidence I find in plain view during a lawful search is admissible."

The deputy grins at the road. He is pleased with himself.

"I was lawfully searching for an ink pen."

## 3

That night in his apartment Nat pours a scotch over ice. Drink in hand, he sits on the rental sofa in front of the rented television. The late evening news is on. Central air conditioning encases him in a false autumn. The glass chills his palm. He does not drink, nor does he listen to the reports on the TV.

It was a long day. Returning from Good Hope after six o'clock, he spent another four hours in his office doing the work he should be spending regular billable hours on. It is eleven o'clock now. He will not drink the scotch. He poured it only to pretend normalcy; a scotch in your hand can connote satisfaction. Nat knows it is an artifice and sets the glass on the coffee table.

He does the same with the television, cuts it off, the thing was turned on simply as chatter, like the drink, to convince him he is grounded, at home. Nat pulls his feet up on the sofa and lays back his head. He gazes at the chintzy white apartment ceiling, finished in tiny spattered stalactites of plaster, insinuating the roof of a cave in miniature. But the sofa is long enough for him to stretch out. He closes his eyes.

He knows what he has to do in the morning.

# FOUR

**N**at enters Judge Hawk's chamber a few minutes after noon, the appointed time for the hearing he has requested. He arrives late on purpose. The Hawk, like all judges, expects punctuality, but Nat intends to encounter Fentress and George Talley not in the courthouse hallways or stairwell, only in front of the judge. But when he steps into the anteroom leading to the judge's office, there, pacing like a jungle cat in front of the secretary's desk, is the sheriff. The Hawk's secretary is a woman in her sixties. She ignores Talley for her typing.

Nat brakes in the doorway. Talley squares to face him. Nat steps forward, his arms at his sides. In his left hand hangs his briefcase. If Talley were to take a swing at him, Nat could not defend. Talley moves directly into Nat's path. Nat stops. His tie is an inch from the buttons on the sheriff's shirt. The secretary quits tapping and sits still as a figurine.

Nat says, "George, I have a hearing inside. Please."

Talley is so close Nat watches the man's nostrils flare. Talley is three inches taller, at least fifty pounds heavier. The man's mouth is turned down like a scimitar.

Part whisper, part curse, Talley says, "I swear to God." It is not a statement of surprise or dismay. It is the preamble to some fearsome oath.

Nat nods. He quietly says into the man's hooded eyes, "I understand, George." Nat sidesteps the sheriff, who holds his ground like a tree trunk. He says, "Excuse me."

Nat reaches for the doorknob to the Hawk's office. The brass knob is slick in his hand, his palm has gone sweaty. He moves inside the office and closes the door, feeling like he has just escaped a tiger cage. Behind him, he hears the Hawk's old secretary say, "Sheriff, sit down please."

Fentress does not turn to acknowledge Nat's entrance. The prosecutor sits with his legs crossed, his hands in his lap. Judge Hawk eyes the empty chair where Nat should have been three minutes ago.

"Sorry I'm late, judge."

"Sit, Nat. Let's get on with this."

Nat unsnaps his briefcase. Fentress moves his hands from his lap to the arms of his chair and says, "Your Honor."

Nat's voice jumps over him. "Ed, do you mind? Give me a moment."

Fentress, still without looking at Nat, laces his fingers.

"Of course, counselor."

Nat takes out the order he drafted this morning. He closes his briefcase. He wants to be the first to speak.

"Judge, thank you for the hearing on such short notice."

"Don't thank me," she says. "I agree with you that so long as we move fast, we can stay ahead of the news reports. I'll make time for you on this case, Nat, and you too, Ed. Don't abuse it, you understand?"

Both lawyers mutter, "Yes, ma'am."

Judge Hawk looks between their chairs at her door, on the other side of which Talley likely continues to pace and the secretary glares at his interruption of her work. With a long blink, the judge brings her head around to Nat.

"Go ahead. And let's be quick, before the sheriff tears up my waiting room."

Nat clears his throat. He laces his own fingers in his lap, then notices he is copying Fentress. He drops his hands onto his knees.

"Your Honor. I'm making a motion to exhume the body of Amanda Talley."

Now Fentress's head whirls around. "Why?"

The Hawk lifts a sharp finger. "Ed. Don't make me say this again. This is a hearing and I'll conduct it."

She returns to Nat. "Why?"

"Your Honor, I've got several reasons. First, and since Ed knows this I don't mind saying it in front of him: So far there hasn't been much evidence to support my client's claim of innocence. No witnesses have come forward. The forensic evidence was all but destroyed in the fire. The state's case is mostly circumstantial and I need to be able to rebut it. Assuming there will be no witnesses, the girl's body is the only piece of physical evidence I believe might still yield more clues. Obviously, I need to exhume it to pursue that."

The Hawk says, "A full autopsy was done, wasn't it?"

Impatiently, Fentress interjects, "Yes."

The judge lets this slide. "Who did the postmortem?"

Nat answers, "Assistant Chief Medical Examiner Jackie Kline."

"She's competent. I've heard you say so a number of times in court, Nat. What's the problem? Why should I allow you to do something as potentially disruptive as exhume the sheriff's daughter if the autopsy was done properly? I need a compelling reason before I'm going to allow that."

"The girl had a broken jaw."

"What about it?"

"Your Honor, the M.E.'s report clearly indicates that on the night of her death, Amanda Talley had sex. She had a few drinks earlier in the evening. And she suffered a broken jaw. Dr. Kline's belief is that the jaw was broken before the fire, quite possibly by a right-handed punch. Now, without witnesses, the semen and the alcohol are dead ends and all Mr. Fentress and I can do is make guesses about them. But someone or something hit this poor girl in the face. It's assumed by the prosecutor and most of Pamunkey County by now that Elijah Waddell did that with his right fist. I believe that if I can reexamine her jaw, we may discover any number of things. Perhaps she wasn't struck by a fist at all but by something else, like a bottle or a two-by-four. There may be splinters left in her flesh. She might have tripped in the dark walking along the road. Anything like that will mitigate the prosecution's simple presumption that Elijah punched her and raped her. The more details we can uncover about Amanda Talley's final hours, the greater will be the state's burden to connect them to my client. Maybe Amanda encountered someone other than Elijah that night who meant her harm. Maybe someone else drank with her and had sex with her. Maybe someone else burned the church, like my client claims."

The Hawk engages in another long, contemplative blink. Her lids fling open with her query. "And how is exhuming the body going to further that, Nat? You already have sufficient x-rays of the broken jaw, I assume?"

"No, Your Honor. There are no x-rays at all of the girl's jaw."

Fentress shifts his posture at this, to glance at Nat. Perhaps the prosecutor didn't pick up on that omission in the report. Or is he reacting to the fact that Nat did?

The Hawk taps a finger against her lips. Nat lets her consider in silence.

She says, "That's curious. Do you know why?"

Ed Fentress says, "Judge, it's simple. The M.E.'s job is to ascertain only the cause of death. Just like Nat says, Jackie Kline determined that Amanda Talley's broken jaw was suffered before the fire. There was no need for her to x-ray the jaw if it didn't contribute to the girl's death."

Nat is struck by Fentress's answer. These are the exact words Jackie claims George Talley used to convince her to speed past the girl's busted jaw.

Nat almost bursts out with this information to the judge, right in front of Fentress, with Talley just outside the door. Nat stops himself. It's better, he thinks, to know some things they don't know you know.

"Your Honor," Nat says, "my client has to be tried in a county that has obviously been predisposed against him by publicity and the notoriety of George Talley. It may as well be a crucifixion. Also, he has to be jailed under the auspices of the father of the girl he is accused of murdering. I ask you to allow this motion for exhumation, Your Honor, to balance the scales. Elijah Waddell is entitled to every opportunity to prove his innocence, judge, even to those measures which may prove to be painful. Don't deny him that."

The Hawk mulls this over. She says, "Ed?"

Fentress responds dryly. "That's a very impassioned speech, Nat. Part Bible, part Constitution. But I don't think this court or my office is engaged in denying your client anything he's entitled to. You want to talk about evening the scales, how about this."

Fentress holds up his two immaculate hands, as though they are the plates of a balance. He elevates one hand.

"Over here, we've got your vague presumption that maybe something exculpatory will come out of your x-raying the girl's jaw. You've expressed nothing to back that up but a gut feeling. Your client is not in jail for hitting Amanda Talley, he's in for rape and murder and arson. The broken jaw plays no role in those charges, just like it played no role in her death. At best, it's a wild-goose chase."

The prosecutor lowers the hand, now presumably empty of the mud he has slung on Nat's motion. He lifts the other, corresponding hand.

"Now, over here we've got the exhumation of a recently buried girl, an emotional act which will traumatize this entire county, not to mention her grieving father, who is a loyal and long-standing public servant. Just the request of such a thing has sent Sheriff Talley into a state, as I'm sure you witnessed on your way in. Now, Nat, you and I have been given instructions by both Judge Baron and the—" the prosecutor catches himself with a wry, apologetic grin at the district court judge; he continues, "by Judge Hawk here to do everything we can to keep this case from becoming an incendiary bomb in our county. I don't see how digging up Amanda Talley is consistent with that instruction."

He lowers his hands. He says to the Hawk, "Frankly, Your Honor, this motion looks vindictive to me."

Nat explodes. "What?"

"Gentlemen!" Judge Hawk slaps her desk.

Nat shoots Fentress a look that the prosecutor does not turn to see. The man has leveled a charge of unethical conduct at Nat and has done it unruffled. Nat's instinct is to haul George Talley into the room, get Jackie Kline on the speakerphone, and grill Fentress and his pal the sheriff about what they both know regarding this un-x-rayed broken jaw and their suspiciously tandem rationales. Instead, he buries his doubts deeper, as ammunition he will use only when the boys think he is all shot out.

The Hawk directs Fentress, "Explain yourself."

"Your Honor, the defense hasn't got a leg to stand on in this case. He said so himself two minutes ago. This motion is just Nat's way of pressuring the commonwealth for a deal. If I agree to drop the capital charge down to second-degree murder, you watch how fast he changes his mind about putting everybody through an exhumation. Certainly I can appreciate my colleague's zealous efforts to save his client's life, but this is more than inappropriate—it's an ugly attempt to haggle."

Through these words Nat imagines himself manning his Confederate trench deep in the pine woods outside town, fending off a bluecoat attack. Each of Fentress's words is a cannon shot whizzing past his ducking head. He clamps his teeth, grips the arms of his chair grimly like a musket stock, and waits for Fentress to tire in his firing. When the prosecutor has finished, Nat checks himself for wounds and finds none, he has hunkered and weathered it, kept his head down and his mouth shut.

The Hawk engages her eyelids again, lowering them slowly, almost as though she is calling an intermission. It is a tense interval around her broad desk, a resting battlefield, until she draws up her lids. Nat sees she has moved behind their cover to aim at him.

She asks, "You calm enough to give me a response?"

"Yes, ma'am."

"Go ahead."

Nat begins to marshal his reply. But there are too many words competing to be heard. He cannot pick and choose among them for only the ones he wants, they charge too fast, they will swamp his struggle. So he decides again to wait and says only, "Judge, I request that you sign the order." Nat lays the papers on the Hawk's desk.

"That's all?"

"Yes, ma'am. I don't figure I have to defend my record as an attorney in front of you, judge. You know me. For that matter, so does Ed Fentress. I'm not going to take his remarks too seriously, and I'm assuming you're not either. And I don't see the need to rephrase my position on the exhumation. I've stated my reasons."

The Hawk nods. "I appreciate your brevity and your control, counselor." The judge pushes a button on her telephone. "Karen, please ask the sheriff to join us."

In a second the door is pushed open. George Talley surges in. He is pulsing.

The judge says, "Grab that chair and sit down, sheriff."

"No, thank you, judge. I'd rather stand."

"And I'd rather you sit."

Fentress says over his shoulder, "George."

The sheriff strides to another leather chair against the wall. He folds into it, looking ready to spring out of it too.

The two elected officials keep their profiles turned in stony fashion to Nat as though he is not in the room. Little Judge Hawk skirts her eyes between the two camps. She has conducted this hearing that way, with the silence of an Indian, moving from Nat to Fentress and now Talley without needless sound or motion, using only her eyes and a few firm confident words placed like the flawless footfalls of a native woodsman.

"Sheriff," she says, "as next of kin you have the right to speak on the defense's motion to exhume the body of your daughter. I left you waiting until now because I wanted the two lawyers here to present their arguments to me and not to you. I apologize but I felt that necessary. This is a charged issue for all of us, most of all for you. You understand?"

"Yes, ma'am."

"Do you have any questions about this proceeding before you start?"

"Just one. Have you already got your mind made up?"

The Hawk considers. "That's a fair question, sheriff. No, I do not."

"All right, then. I'm against it. There's nothing more sacred than a grave, Your Honor. My poor Amanda died the most horrible death you can imagine. She was raped and she was burned. That was a torment for her and it'll be one for me 'til I die. But at least with her in her grave and at rest, with the Lord's blessing already laid on her, she and I can start on the road to some peace, her in Heaven and me here on Earth. You pull her out of the ground so's Nat here can go poking for something that's not there, then both Amanda and me will have our peace, such as it is, just torn in pieces all over again."

Talley stops. He takes a breath. "There," he says, grinding his jaw, "I'm against it."

The Hawk steals a glance at Nat. Her face betrays nothing. She slips back to George Talley.

"Sheriff, you talk about peace. I appreciate that. And I wish it for you, along with my sincere regrets for this tragedy. Now let me ask you a question. Do you think you can find any lasting peace until you've caught and punished the person or persons responsible for what happened to your daughter?"

Talley's face grows even stonier. "No, ma'am."

"Right now," the judge asks, "do you think you've got the right man in your jail?"

"Elijah Waddell. Yes, judge, he's the one."

"Are you absolutely sure?"

"Yes."

Fentress quickly shifts in his seat to lay a hand on Talley's forearm. The prosecutor says, "Judge, what the sheriff means is . . ."

The Hawk never pulls her eyes off Talley. "Quiet, Ed."

Fentress withdraws, stung.

She says, "Sheriff. What I'm asking you is: Are you certain that Elijah Waddell is guilty? Is having him in custody the first step for you on your road to peace?"

Talley is not stupid. Nat can tell that the sheriff spots some trap the judge is laying for him, some information she is quizzing for beyond the question. But he charges ahead because that is George

Talley, the athlete, the small-town politician, the bully, and the grieving, wrathful father with something to hide.

"Yes, judge."

"All right, sheriff. Thank you for your candor. You may go."

Talley stands. "What are you going to do?"

"I'm going to ask you again to go, sheriff. If you please."

George Talley now looks at Nat and there again is the threat. But
there is something more, something already done.

When Talley has left, Judge Hawk reaches to Nat. "Let me see the
order."

Like a brace of quail Fentress's hands fly up with his words.
"Judge, I ask you again to consider the impact of this motion. Not
just on George Talley but on the whole community."

The Hawk's eyes absorb the writing on the two pages. She takes
up an ink pen. She lays one sheet flat, poising the pen's point above
it. She looks up.

"Ed, I'm going to forget everything you said in here today. In several instances your tone to me was improper. Your accusation of defense counsel was nothing for you to be proud of either. But I'm
going to say something right now I want you to remember. There is
only one time in the United States of America when it's appropriate
to say that a man is absolutely guilty and that is after due process in a
court of law. Judging by what I just heard from your sheriff and what
has fallen from your own lips, we may just as well just skip the trial
for Elijah Waddell. Until his counsel tells me that's what he wants, I
am proceeding to trial under the presumption that this man is *innocent.* Keep this in mind: You and George Talley will do your jobs a
sight better for this community if you keep a little doubt handy yourselves." The judge switches her gaze fast to Nat, barely a moment
travels with her. "You conduct this exhumation with alacrity and dis-
cretion."

"Tomorrow morning, judge. I've already spoken with Jackie Kline,
she's made time in her schedule to get on this as soon as the body arrives. I'll make the rest of the arrangements with St. Bede's as soon
as we're done here."

"All right. Now, gentlemen, the moment I hand this order to the clerk the press is going to be on it like white on rice. I don't want to read or hear anywhere that either of you is using this as a pulpit to further your case."

Both men nod. Nat says, "Judge, you could seal the order."

"No. This is a public case. The people of this county are going to see justice work. That includes Elijah Waddell and George Talley. That's our job and we're going to do it." Keeping to her custom when she completes a thought or a command, the Hawk asks, "You understand?"

The prosecutor and the defender answer while the judge's pen scratches her signature.


## 2


There are clouds. They are not the large mansions of mist which might foretell a shift in the weather but merely small, scudding voyagers come fleeting one by one above the cemetery this backward morning, when the living have come to take the dead to judgment.

Nat detects no rain in these clouds though he thinks there ought to be after so long a spell of dry hot days. Likewise he sees no tears in the faces of the rabble around Amanda Talley, though he thinks there ought to be. These are not eyes that cry. They are glass camera eyes and jaded reporters' eyes, which have seen worse than this. Old Omohundro's eyes which observe only his jabbing shovel blade and the dirt pileup. Some strangers jaunting their dogs along the cemetery have stopped to watch. A dozen young men and women who Nat ventures want to be holding signs, making a fuss, shouting old Omohundro away from Amanda's grave, though it is too early for all that noise so they stare with indignation on behalf of unwitting Christianity and their own ignorant youth. Another dozen are older folks, locals who spotted the chance to be close to something that is in the news, so came out this morning to the cemetery with breakfast bags from McDonald's. And George Talley, standing aloof and hard as a headstone.

The priest of St. Bede's talks quietly with Monroe. These two supervise the exhumation. Nat waits beside the long hearse that will return Amanda to Jackie Kline's silver table. Old Omohundro rams his shovel into the clay pile like a spear into a beast and he is finished digging. The casket is lifted by ropes and hooks and set on the grass, then wiped down by Omohundro and the priest. The cleaned coffin shows no trace of having been underground for five days, it still gleams of polished brass and waxed wood. It is a strange and re-versed moment, the fancy box resting alone, the stern father standing alone too, for when this coffin was last seen, it and George Talley were surrounded by much weeping and speech and a colorful throng of pastels dotted with black under a hot, clear sky. Now there is only the clicking of cameras like locusts, a handful of whispers and anger, napkins, cold curiosity, tethered dogs, and clouds. This all feels up-side down, like a retreat from honor. Nat thinks Talley was right; peace has been delayed.

Talley does not take a step or unfold his arms. Monroe shakes the hand of the priest, then walks beside the four funeral-home employ-ees hefting the coffin to the hearse. Newspaper photographers flank the procession. Nat slips back to his own car to stay out of their fo-cus. This morning's Richmond newspaper trumpeted a second-page headline: GIRL'S BODY EXHUMED TODAY IN FIRE MURDER CASE. The story contained no quotes from Nat or Fentress, both referred to as "unavailable for comment." Talley was quoted as saying only, "We'll see." Last night on the late TV news in Richmond, three stations mentioned this morning's exhumation in the mill town of Good Hope. Scanning the channels, Nat watched interviews with two lo-cals: First, Pastor Thomas Derby stated that his congregation was fo-cused on fathoming and forgiveness. Derby told the interviewer he was certain there was a good reason for bringing up the body of the poor girl and folks should try to understand the legal process and not react. Second, Sheriff George Talley sucked in his cheeks at the question of what he thought of this procedure. He said to the cam-era, just as he'd said to the newspaper, "We'll see."

Nat did not need to drive in to Good Hope this morning. Monroe is on top of things. Nat could have waited for the call from Jackie Kline that the hearse had arrived at the medical examiner's offices. But he wanted to see firsthand what effect, what ripples, the first wave of news of the exhumation was having here. So far, people are just watching and talking. That's good, Nat thinks, let them talk. A barking dog does not bite.

The casket is loaded into the hearse. Nat follows the black Cadillac and Monroe's cruiser through town, across the river bridge, and onto the interstate. The sun has loft now. The clouds disperse once the casket is on its way. Another fierce day. Nat wonders if the clay at the bottom of Amanda's hole is cool to the touch. Perhaps she would have preferred to stay in her shy dark, but the girl deserves truth, no matter what that turns out to be. She needs to make this trip. Others are using Amanda to protect themselves, to tuck away some secrets into her grave with her. This is not kind to her. What could be worse for your soul than to have lies and the needless hurting of the innocent trail your life just as you're trying to let go of it? Won't such weight make her sleep restless? Yes, Nat thinks again, Talley was right. This is all about peace.

At the medical examiner's office in Richmond, Nat and Monroe get into a sort of lockstep with the men bearing Amanda. They follow the men up onto the loading dock platform where they set her down and ring a buzzer for entrance. The casket is dissonantly festive and bright against the cement pilings and metal doors. The box shows its discomfort at being above ground.

Jackie Kline comes to the door. The men carrying Amanda file past, they know where to take her.

Jackie says good morning to Monroe and Nat. Monroe nods and follows the casket. He will watch Amanda's unloading and the x-rays. Jackie asks Nat if he'd like to come too.

"No."

"This is my fault," she says, touching Nat's wrist. "I shouldn't have let Talley push me."

Jackie can do this, Nat thinks, she can admit fault and smile. There is no shame. While we live, we err. She accepts it. The dead taught her this.

"It's okay. Just find me something."

"If it's there, Nat, I'll bring it back alive."

She deposits him on a sofa outside her lab. The funeral-home men walk past him to go out on the dock and smoke. Empty-handed, they become just big, suited boys, talkative and animated.

Nat imagines the worst, the crackling of blackened Amanda when she is lifted out of her box and onto the table, the reek. Nat marvels at the big African-American deputy and the cherubic Jewish doctor, while he sits at a distance. Is that what those two know, that reality is never as bad as what we invent? Nat is tempted to pinch his nose and walk through the door to the lab, to be counted beside these two people he admires. To face Amanda personally and promise her something. But he doesn't move. He smells smoke and hears the banter of the four hearse men.

Thirty minutes later, Jackie comes out of the lab. Under her nose is a dab of unguent, scented menthol to chase the stench of decay. Bits of cornstarch lighten her hands from rubber gloves. She carries a rumbling x-ray sheet. Nat stands.

"Come outside with me," she says. "I've got something to show you."

Walking down the hall, Nat asks, "Is it my lucky day?"

"If you're clever," she says. "And you are clever, Nat."

Out on the dock, Jackie tells the four men that the body is ready to be returned to the cemetery. They stub their talk and cigarettes. They rise to their task, grim and quiet again, they are professional bearers of the dead. Jackie hands the x-ray to Nat. He holds it over his head to view it with bright Heaven as backdrop.

Amanda is turned on her left shoulder, her skull is in silvery profile. Nat sees the break before Jackie points it out. He sets his fingertip to the smooth sheet.

"Right there," he says, indicating a cottony place on the ghost jawbone. "That's the broken spot, right?"

"Wrong." Jackie's finger displaces Nat's against the film. "The break is right here." She traces a vertical white line in the jaw no thicker than a thread.

"Then what's this area?"

"That," the assistant chief medical examiner says, "is your lucky day. That is an old break."

Nat is stunned.

Someone else had hit Amanda Talley in virtually the identical place on her jaw.

"How old's the first injury?"

Again Jackie Kline highlights the x-ray with her moving finger.

"See this dense area here? When a bone breaks, it heals harder than the original, like a calcium callus. This ridge on the cortex, the outside of the bone, is pretty well built up. It healed normally. It held under this latest impact but the jawbone snapped right next to it."

"How old?"

"Hard to tell. My guess is three to four years. Maybe less, but no more. If it was in fact a punch, you can't hit a girl younger than fourteen this hard without breaking a lot more than jaw. You'll take out teeth and maybe part of the cheek, depending on the size of the fist and the force of the blow."

Nat waggles the x-ray. "Can I keep this?"

"I shot a few. Keep it."

"Do me another favor?"

"What?"

"Take until tomorrow to write this up. I want a little lead time on Fentress."

She smiles. "He'll be lucky to get it before next week."

Nat leans and kisses her on the forehead. "You're a lifesaver."

Jackie Kline laughs because, of course, she is not. She walks to the loading-bay door to go back inside. The door is held open for her by Monroe. He thanks her, then steps out into the building. Under Monroe's nostrils his mustache glistens from salve.

The deputy says, "It's speculation, Nat."

"I know," he answers, "I know."

Nat holds up the x-ray again. The image there is light where it should be dark and vice versa. Perfect, he thinks. It has been a day of vice versa.

He says, "Someone hit Amanda four years ago. Money, you know it wasn't Elijah Waddell. And someone hit her the night of the fire. I'm betting that wasn't Elijah either."

3

Of course it was George Talley who punched her. Everything Nat knows about the man confirms this. Nat is sure Monroe agrees, though the deputy took his leave from the medical examiner's office this morning without saying it.

"Look," Nat said to him on the dock, "George and Fentress and the judge are all going to want to know what's on this x-ray. Can you give me a break? Just today. One day."

Monroe donned his stiff felt hat. "You don't ask an officer of the law for a break, counselor. It's illegal."

The big man ran finger and thumb along the brim of the hat, settling it. "Right now I'm going to handle a little more business in Richmond. Then I'll head back late in the afternoon. Probably go straight home. I'm going to take my wife out to dinner in Newport News. I expect I'll be hard to reach, I don't answer the phone or my beeper when I'm with Rey, she'll kill me. Tomorrow morning, at breakfast, I report in. That's not a break. That's my schedule."

So now it is three o'clock. Nat has the birth control pills and the x-ray on his desk. His answering machine announces his absence to many callers, most of them clients getting lousy service from their lawyer this past week. Two of the calls are from Ed Fentress.

Of course it was George Talley. He and Amanda argued at dinner. Over what? She very likely had a boyfriend. She'd had a few drinks with someone earlier that evening, probably slept with him too. She may have come home directly from his bed. George may have smelled the alcohol on her. He may have seen the sex on her. Either way, he challenged her. With the drinks still hale in her blood, her lover's arms still fresh around her shoulders, Amanda picked up the gauntlet. She fought back, and the confrontation unleashed something in her long held in check. She summoned the gumption and told George where she'd been and what she'd been doing. But not with whom, she would have kept that secret. At last Amanda was breaking free of the constraints of her father, finally standing on her own, an independent young woman with her own maturing life taking place right under his nose. The sheriff grew angry. He tore her purse from her or tussled with her and dug into her pockets or went into her room to roust through her dresser, somehow he found the pills, she may have thrown them at him. He shook them in her face and lectured her on the tenets of Catholicism, which he thought he'd raised her to believe and obey. Amanda rejected those canons, good for others, not for her. She told him in fact she'd been thinking about joining the Baptist church. In this way the girl rejected her father. And her father made a fist of his powerful hand and floored her.

She ran out the door into the summer dusk. Her jaw was broken and painful. Her spirit was aching too but perhaps for the first time it was soaring.

She stayed out of sight, ashamed, her jaw swollen and bruised. That's why no one saw her that night. She walked three miles to the Victory Baptist Church. She went inside and sat down to read and pray. After a while she fell asleep beneath the pew, her head propped on her arm to ease her sore jaw, her hand on the hymnal she'd been reading. She wouldn't go home. Maybe in the morning she would call her mother to come get her. Maybe she would ask her boyfriend to drive her back to Maryland. But that night, she had to hide from her father's savage anger. Meanwhile, Elijah, wandering the county in his own lonely misery—staying out of sight too—arrived across the street at midnight. He crouched in the woods, shattered and wrathful. He drank a six-pack. An hour and a half later, someone ran up through the dark, torched the church, and ran off. Elijah watched. Or Elijah himself crossed the road and burned it and did not run off. Either way, the arsonist did not know the girl was inside. But the fire knew she was there. And Amanda died.

When Talley found out, he lost whatever control he had left. He attacked Elijah in the jail, then went to see his old ally Ed Fentress. George was in distress. He told Ed about the argument with his daughter the night before, at dinner. He told him she ran off and never came back. She must have encountered Elijah Waddell in the night. He raped her and burned her in the church. Fentress was sympathetic, sad for his old friend, and secretly thinking: capital murder. Then Talley told Ed the bad news. Before Amanda ran out the door for the last time, at the end of their argument, he'd hit her in the jaw. Hard. Fentress listened. Talley admitted he'd hit the girl another time, too, four years ago. He was afraid something might show up at the autopsy. It could ruin his career if it got out, even a rumor of that kind of thing. The prosecutor calmed Talley down. He probably gave Talley a lecture about the man's anger, told him to get it under control, never do this sort of thing again. But for now, they could handle it. Together. Buddies. Elected on the same ticket, linked at the ballot box. Fentress told George to go to the medical examiner's office on Saturday morning to identify Amanda's body. He coached George on what to say to spur Dr. Jackie Kline to skip over the x-rays of the girl's jaw. Tell her to hurry up. The jaw had nothing to do with the cause of death. Don't waste time. You want to bury her on Sunday after church. Insist. Don't leave until she's done with the x-rays.

Speculation. Just like Monroe said. A connect-the-dots picture where the dots are yards apart. It's a good theory. The pieces, the characters, all fit together. But where is the proof, so that the theory not only fits but holds together in court? Fentress has a hypothesis also, one that he's confident will sway a jury to sentence Elijah to death. The prosecutor has evidence for his circumstances. Nat has speculation.

Nat's phone rings again. He monitors the message. It's from another reporter. He ignores it.

Proof, he thinks. If the sheriff broke his daughter's jaw four years ago, he must have taken her to a doctor. Jackie Kline said the x-rays show the old break had healed normally. That could mean the jaw was set, maybe wired shut.

Nat is pierced by a sad cut in his gut. The sheriff's young daughter, fourteen years old at the time and so vulnerable and needy, may have spent months in Good Hope with her jaw bound closed, walking the river, head down on the sidewalks, and neither Nat nor anyone else noticed. Though she was surrounded by people, she was close enough to no one to speak of it, and if she did give it voice, she probably made up some cover story. Such a load for a child to carry, to be beaten by her father, then forced to conceal it from everyone, even her mother, to shield him. To have to find a way to forgive him and live with him. To learn so young of the violence of love. To be alone with this. That is terribly sad, Nat thinks. Woe for all of us who are so blind we did not see Amanda Talley.

George, you son of a bitch.

Nat composes his thoughts, away from outrage and self-disappointment; they will only mire him. Reason.

Okay, George, he thinks, exhaling. You left me a trail. Somewhere.

In his mind, Nat sees the large father strike the young daughter. He sees the anger dissipate when the girl hits the floor. Nat hears the sheriff's cloying apology. Sees him working his sore fist.

He lifts his child. Sorry. I'm sorry.

Talley sees her jaw is busted. He takes her to his squad car, to the doctor.

And, Nat thinks, if you took her to a doctor, there's a record.

An emergency room.

You would have gone to a big hospital in Richmond or Norfolk, not wanting to risk the information leaking to the voters in your own county. Domestic-abuse charges would end your run as sheriff.

Nat considers the daunting task of subpoenaing every hospital within fifty miles of Good Hope for their emergency-room records dating back four years.

Then he recalls that every instance of suspected child abuse must be reported to the police by the admitting staff in all hospitals in Virginia. George wouldn't have taken Amanda to a hospital out of town. No. He would have stayed right here in Pamunkey County, where as sheriff he wields influence, where he would have the best chance of stemming the damage and disguising the record. Where he is the law.

Nat looks at his watch. It's four o'clock. His phone rings. An insistent voice leaves a message. Again it is Ed Fentress.

Nat gathers the birth control pills and the x-ray, those paltry bits that argue for Elijah's innocence. With them in hand and an idea in his teeth, he drives back to Good Hope.

# FIVE

1

At times the world, so bright and wide, becomes a tunnel. Nat thinks this. It is something to relish, this narrowing. It is empowering to have so defined a course, so tight a focus, like a wounded tiger, like spawning, like marking a target with crosshairs.

Nat sits in his car in front of his house, waiting for Maeve. It is after five o'clock and it is hot. Cars roll past on their way home from work or to the mill for the evening shift. He knows they recognize his car, they see him inside it. He is parked beside the curb at the edge of his own lawn, on his street where he has not been in eight months. Everyone knows. They and their gossip and mixed opinions are outside the tunnel. Nat waits inside for Maeve.

It was easier in his office to conceive that he needed her help than it is to come here and ask for it. Worst is the waiting. Nat tries to keep himself in the bore of the tunnel and he does, the world goes by murmuring or not, he doesn't care. But the tunnel is not completely dark, and this is a problem. It is paved with glowing bricks, each one a separate memory. The memories emanate from those mundane items that are within fifty feet of where he sits sweating. The garden hose, the lamppost, the sidewalk, and the gliding silence of her soft nurse's shoes on it, the secrets of the backyard. Nat fights with these and more inanimate objects he has not touched since Christmas. It's like a scene from a cartoon movie, the common things have mobilized and come at him, some crying that they miss him, some irked at his absence, a few ambivalent for they like Maeve better, a battalion in his imagination. He closes his eyes and this does the trick, the tunnel closes down and is secure for him. But he has to leave his eyes open. He wants to spot Maeve coming up the sidewalk from her bus stop the moment she spots him. So he pictures the seasons that have come and gone in the yard since Christmas without him, the front door of the house opens and closes a thousand times in a row and not once for his passage, the lights in the living room are switched off every night with the twists of one wrist, and the lamp in the upstairs bedroom burns until she quits reading and goes to sleep.

This is the tunnel where Nat waits for Maeve. He thinks he would still sweat in here if it were the dead of winter.

Until there is the bus. She does not move forward on the sidewalk. She instantly stops at the sight of his car in front of the house. She is all in white, in her nurse's garb. This is the opposite of the mourning black she wore at the funeral; Nat thinks of a film negative. He is again aware of the topsy-turvy, backward nature of the day. He gets out of the car. She stands her ground two hundred feet up the street, beneath a giant elm. She is like a little figure dabbed into a painting for perspective, so much of the artist's effort is put into the tree and street, and for her just two gentle strokes, one of white and a smaller, black stroke for the corona of her hair.

Nat wants to step forward but it doesn't make sense to go to her and then come all the way back to the house. He catches himself at this, his habit, his defense, of allotting right and wrong, sense and nonsense. He swallows and moves toward her.

Maeve does not correspond. Something about the white, Nat thinks, closing the distance to her. She is clothed in the color of innocence, it seems to entitle her. And maybe it does. He walked out on her at Christmas. She tells him now with her inertness and whiteness and coolness in this heat that he must walk back to her. And so, wondering what expression is on his face while he does it, he walks.

He reaches her. "Hi," he says.

"Hi."

Nat thinks this is comforting, this simple beginning. Even with so much towering around them and looming between them, there is Hi.

This is the first sound of his wife's voice he has heard not from his answering machine but from her mouth, since snow.

They stand addressing each other, four feet apart. There is an element of a showdown in their stance. This is unintentional but Nat senses it. He turns to face the house, where she faces, implying that she move up beside his shoulder and they walk together up the sidewalk. She steps and they are side by side. She swings her arms. Her gum-soled white shoes make no sound, her white dress kicks with her strides. Nat is all rigid and dark in his lawyer suit and hard shoes. He wants to swing his arms too but that is not his gait. When they used to hold hands his arm would swing linked to hers. He laments that he cannot do this now. He thinks suddenly he has let too many steps go by without talk.

"How are you?"

"I'm fine, Nat."

"You look great."

"Thank you."

He could go on. There is more tense protocol to observe, equations, simple questions for them both to ask, begetting answers, biding time. But Nat stops walking. Maeve halts too. He turns full front to her.

"Okay."

She pauses and nods. She says, "Okay."

And with this they have agreed to suspend the manners, perhaps to return later. That will be determined. Right now, he says, "I need your help."

It is a naked truth. Maeve says, "Come in the house," to move the nakedness inside.

Nat follows her. He climbs his steps, touches his railing, enters his house. He makes himself stop viewing things this way. It is warped and self-indulgent. It could go on and on. He needs a sharper focus.

They sit primly on the sofa. Both have their knees closed, their hands in their laps. Nat in his suit feels like he is selling insurance.

"You're not comfortable," she says. "Coming to me is hard for you."

"Yes."

"Take your coat off. It'll make you feel a little more like you're at home."

Maeve stands. She puts out her hands for his jacket. Nat peels it off and hands it up to her. His shirt is wrinkled from the wait and perspiration. He is self-conscious.

She hangs the coat in the closet. She continues to the kitchen and collects lemonade from the refrigerator, ice and glasses. Nat watches her motions. She has the sure hands of the caregiver. She is smart to walk off some distance but stay in sight, to keep silence at bay for a few moments not with words but with pleasant house sounds. Nat eases his damp back against the sofa cushions.

Maeve returns with the lemonade. When she sits, she too takes a different posture, more relaxed and skewed. She sips and waits.

He says, "It's about the case."

"I figured."

He brings the drink to his lips and takes a gulp. "The lemonade's good."

She sips.

"Nat?"

"Yes?"

"Ask me. You need something from me and it doesn't have any-thing to do with our marriage. So you're not coming to me as my husband. You've come as a lawyer. Don't get mad but I'm used to you in this role. It's okay. Just ask me."

Something about the white she wears, the cold glass she's put in his hand, the mildness of her voice, her casual posture. She seems right to rebuke him. It was easy for her to say and, oddly, for him to hear. Nat did not expect it, or for his denunciation to feel deserved. He never considered that Maeve might be angry with him, the man whom she wounded. It is another reversal on this day. There are forces at work. Nat gives in.

He sets his lemonade on the coffee table. Their coffee table.

"Elijah Waddell did not rape that girl."

"You're his lawyer. I expect you to say that."

"Not if it wasn't true. He didn't do it."

"How do you know?"

"I can't tell you. Don't take that wrong, but right now I just have to play some cards close to the vest. But a little at a time I'm finding out some things that point away from Elijah and at somebody else."

"I won't ask who."

"I don't know who. Just someone else."

"Did Elijah burn the church?"

"He says no. It's going to be tough to get him off the arson charge. There's too much against him right now. First I've got to make sure he stays off death row."

Maeve sets her lemonade glass beside his. She rubs her palms on her skirt.

She says, "Before I agree to help you, you have to tell me something."

"All right."

"I want to know that you're sure about what you're doing. I don't want to help you get somebody off, Nat. I was a prosecutor's wife for eight years. I believe what I learned from you, that criminals should be punished. That they shouldn't walk away on a technicality. That the ideas of guilt and innocence matter as much as the rules you use to prove them. So tell me this is not just some of Nat Deeds' zeal at doing his job, trying to win and prove how good a lawyer you are. We all know how good you are. Tell me instead that your client is accused of something you are positive he didn't do and you are the only one standing between him and injustice. I used to know you, Nat. Justice mattered to you more than anything in the world. Tell me that's still the case and I'll help."

"It's still the case."

"Good. Now here's what I want from you in return."

"What."

"The same. Justice."

## 2

When they were first married, Nat used to play a game with her beauty. He would look away from her, gaze at something else for a few moments, then look back and enjoy the rush of seeing her again. It was like clearing your palate before a fine wine, or departing a favorite place in the world, knowing you would come back soon. And sometimes he would drive her to the market and stay behind in the car, telling her he wanted to rest or read while she shopped. But when she came out of the store wheeling a cart he was watching, pretending he did not know this comely dark-haired woman. He watched her advance to his car, unbidden, magically, and get in beside him, thrilling him. It was fun. It was love.

There is a risk to loving a beautiful woman. You must be careful to love all of her, even though the surface of her is so arresting. You must let her into you, and not be so unrelenting to enter her. She has words for her perfect mouth, she has destinations for her shapely legs. She has a life that is not beautiful but plain, like yours. You must push past the beauty that draws you, you must embrace the true woman behind it, or you risk believing a fiction, that you love her. And you do not.

Right now on the sofa her knees are inches from his. She has turned to face him and waits to hear what help he needs. Nat looks at his wife's knees. But this is not the same Maeve, not the pliable woman of his mind and his old marriage who existed around him and lay beneath him. This is someone with steady hands and firm eyes that claim, Trust me, and I will help you. Or don't trust me and you can get up and walk away again.

He says, "George's daughter."

She supplies the name quickly. "Amanda."

"Did you know her?"

"I know she was lonely. Sweet. She was trapped here in Good Hope, I think."

And, Nat thinks, she died on the night of her liberation.

Maeve says, "She walked a lot. She liked our street. The old houses, porches, the big trees. We never spoke. But you could tell."

Nat envisions another scene, the meandering child skimming along the sidewalk, the quiet beautiful nurse on the front porch, the two meeting glances. Had they spoken they might have helped each other. Maeve can only help her now.

He says, "When she was found after the fire, she had a broken jaw. The medical examiner didn't take any x-rays of Amanda's head."

"Why not?"

"I can't say right now. But the circumstances look a little suspect."

"So you had her exhumed."

With this statement, Maeve tells Nat that she has followed him in this case through the media.

"I got the x-rays back this morning. Maeve, the M.E. thinks her jaw was broken by a right-handed punch the night of the fire. The x-rays show the same thing might have happened to Amanda a couple of years ago."

"Somebody hit her? When she was a kid?" Maeve the nurse reacts to this, she is always incredulous in the face of violence against children.

Nat brings a finger to his own jawline to illustrate. "Broke her jaw. In the same place. When maybe she was as young as thirteen or fourteen. I think it's possible the same person who hit her then might have hit her the night of the fire."

Maeve opens her lips. They make a smacking sound.

Nat supplies the answer. "George."

Her lips stay in a surprised oval. Nat continues. "I've got a theory. And I've got a few things that indicate I'm headed in the right direction. Listen and tell me what you think."

Nat lays out the emerging story of Amanda's final night. Rendering it to Maeve, the dots don't seem so difficult to connect. He does not divulge Monroe's pilferage of the birth control pills or the sheriff's bizarre interference with Jackie Kline's autopsy. But there comes from Nat a new flow to the tale. Maeve nods intelligently, believingly. In her demeanor he reads also an honest shock that it is Sheriff George Talley her husband is after. A lot of people, Nat thinks, are going to feel that way.

"It's a shred," he concludes. "But if I can show that Talley hit his daughter four years ago, then I can at least go in front of a jury and point to an acceptable alternative to Elijah's hitting her the night of the fire. Reasonable doubt, that's all I need to establish. Right now there's nothing but circumstantial evidence linking Elijah to Amanda. If I can cast some doubt on the broken jaw, I can lessen one of the crucial links to the rape charge. If I can do that, then there's no capital murder."

"George will never admit he hit her that night. Or ever."

"He doesn't have to."

She says, "You fight dirty."

"I fight, Maeve."

She reaches for her lemonade. She sips, bringing to a close some portion of their meeting. The plea portion.

She says, "You need the hospital records from the first broken jaw."

"Yes. My guess is he took her to Pamunkey General. George would have stayed local with this."

She considers this. She agrees.

"Just get a subpoena. You don't need me."

"I have reasons for wanting to keep things quiet."

"Can you tell me what they are?"

"Sleeping dogs."

"Let them lie."

"That's right. There's already been one attempt to hide evidence. I don't want any more. I don't want Fentress or Talley to see me coming. Not yet."

She sets down the lemonade. Another passage of their meeting is done.

She asks, "When?"

Nat takes up his cold glass. He drains the lemonade with a high tilt. The ice cubes rattle. He sets down the glass with a flourish.

"Now," he says.

3

Pamunkey General is a fifty-bed facility built in the mid-1960s. It is the only hospital in the county, serving all twelve thousand residents. Because the county is mostly rural and so spread out, the hospital is underutilized. In the last few years, noises were made by the board to close down the hospital as unprofitable. When that news broke, money quickly poured in from the rich people who keep big summer homes on the river and farther up on the Chesapeake Bay. These folks, mostly from Richmond, want the hospital nearby and ready for them and their families and so have begun to endow it. Pamunkey General is not flashy or up-to-date but it is steadfast and kind, which makes it very much like the people of the county it serves.

Maeve has not changed out of her nurse whites. Nat is wrinkled, his tie is loosened. He follows her past the hiss of the automatic sliding doors. Once inside the air conditioning, he pulls up his tie and buttons his collar. Maeve greets the elderly volunteer sitting behind the registration desk. The woman adds to the air of stability of the hospital; she or another like her has been in this seat behind the registration desk since the hospital opened, one day they will tear the building down around her. Maeve told Nat in the car to say nothing to anyone, just get in her wake and stay there until they have what they are looking for. Nat nods to the old volunteer, then slips behind Maeve through the door marked RECORDS.

The room is not much larger than Elijah's cell. It's painted the same institutional green. One wall is given over to shelves of manila file folders, stacked from floor to ceiling. They resemble bunches of drying tobacco and give the room a musty, papery aroma. Against the opposite wall is a desk. On the desktop are arrayed eight long, gray metal cases, the kind library cards are kept in. Each case is labeled with three or four letters of the alphabet. Maeve sits and lifts the lid of one, like opening the mouth of a gray alligator. This box is designated S-T-U. Nat guesses there are more than a thousand three-by-five cards inside.

He makes an amazed chuckle. "No computers? Isn't there a computer?"

"Computers crash. Note cards don't." Maeve runs the fingers of both hands across the tops of the cards. Nat watches. He thinks this is arcane, no computers, but some other part of him likes it, hinting of old-timey health care, house calls and aspirin, and he misses living in this small town. His skin crawls a bit with fear they will be caught in the records room. He's been instructed to maintain silence if someone walks in while they are searching. Maeve will handle it.

"What'll you say?" he asked her in the car.

"I'll tell them to get out."

Nat uttered the Judge Baron "uh-huh" and let it go at that.

Maeve's fingers halt, holding apart a divide in the cards.

She says, "Here we go." She separates the card from the case.

Nat gazes over her shoulder. The card is handwritten in ink. Across the top is Amanda Talley's name. Beside her name is the number 31054. Beneath this, down the left margin of the card, are dates, one each written on five separate lines. Beside each date is another number. The first two digits of these numbers clearly correspond to years; the first entry is 92-2003. All the entries are scribed in different handwritings and ink shades.

Maeve says, "Every time somebody comes into the hospital for the first time, they're given a master number." She lays her finger beneath the 31054. "This is like your name here in the hospital. It's attached to every visit and procedure when you come in." She pats a fingertip on the column below Amanda's name. "These are the dates of each visit. Next to the date is the number of the registration form that follows you while you're here. When you register at the desk, or even if you come in through the emergency room, the person at the registration desk pulls a numbered sheet off a pad. These forms are numbered in order, just like a checkbook. At the beginning of each year, the numbers go back to zero. The number of that sheet gets written right here on these three-by-fives as soon as it's pulled off the pad and handed to the attending nurse." Again Maeve taps on the card. Then she lifts her finger as though to pinpoint Nat's attention. "That's the form we're looking for."

Maeve slides her thumbnail down the five entries on Amanda's card. She stops below the fourth one, dated July 2, 1998. Below this, the final entry is for August 11, 1999.

"You said the first broken jaw was as long as four years ago. It might be one of these two." She holds the card up for Nat to see closely, indicating the last two dates, July '98 and August '99. "Let's find her master file."

Maeve stands from the chair. She wastes no time. Her hands dig into the wall of yellow sheaves. Nat catches himself doing nothing but admiring her. In his years married to this woman he never once came to this hospital to see her work, to discover her competence. She finds Amanda's master file before he can comprehend the difficulty of the task, there are thousands of files here, dating back almost forty years. She frees the folder from its brethren and slaps it on the desk. Pulling out the chair, she mutters, "Let's see what we've got."

Maeve quickly sits and hurries with the folder. Nat thinks this is not out of concern for being caught, like his own edgy nerves. She is energized by the investigation. She is breaking a major hospital rule of ethics by letting Nat view private medical records without a court order. She seems to have taken something personally, but not on behalf of Nat or Elijah. She appears very eager either to absolve George Talley or to nail him.

Why does Maeve care about the sheriff? What is he to her?

Nat understands.

"It was him," he says.

Maeve's fingers stop on the lines and scribbles. Her head stays turned from him.

"George," Nat says. "You slept with George Talley."

He stares at the dark crown of her head, miraculous that he sees it bob slowly up and down. Yes.

She says, "I thought you didn't want to know."

"I didn't."

"What now?"

The back of her head stills. He sees George Talley's strong, veined hand cradling it, laying it on a pillow.

"Why?"

"Why George," she asks, "or why?"

He pauses, confused by the distinction, dismayed that there might even be one.

"Why?" he asks; then, because he cannot stop himself: "Why George?"

His wife pivots. There are no tears in her eyes, no quiver on the perfect mouth. She stands from the chair all in white and that is angelic. Nat wants to cry out, No, stop! He wants to thwart this boldness, explain to her he has scripted this moment over and over in his head since they've been apart, this episode where it all comes out in the open, and every time she is crying and contrite, she is not trimmed in white but in penitent browns and blacks. But his wife is not sorry, not at all sorry, and Nat has forgotten his lines.

She asks, "You want this right now too?"

"Yes."

Maeve holds out an arm, as if to receive a shot. The skin on the inside of her arm is white, her dress is white, the snow of Christmas was white, the clouds above Amanda Talley were white. Nat thinks again there is something about the white Maeve wears: Yes, it is the color of surrender.

"Feel that," she says. Nat will not play. She insists. "Touch me."

He lays his palm on her forearm. White. Cool.

She shoves his hand out of the way. She pinches herself hard. The white engorges with red and warmth.

"Flesh and blood. That's all. Just me. Not an ideal. Not someone out of a fairy tale. Just me."

She lowers her arm. It rises immediately with the other in a sharp gesture.

"You want to know what I was to George Talley? I was nothing. *Nothing*. I wasn't some woman he'd wanted his whole life or something he'd built up in his head or a dream girl. I was a cheap prize, a kewpie doll. I wasn't even a nurse or Nat Deeds' wife. I was a fuck."

Nat jerks at the word. It has hard consonants, edges, like teeth.

She continues. "Nat, you need to know. George Talley was never your friend. He's been after me for years. He just wanted to get me in bed. That's all. I don't even know why, maybe to get at you for something, maybe he's just horny in a small town. It never mattered to me. I ignored him. But you know what? Finally? After years of being nice to him in public and telling him to leave me alone in private. After months of wondering where you had gone to in our marriage, you were close and far away all at the same time and that was terrible. From where I stood it looked like your job meant as much to you as I ever could. Your image of yourself as a brave and good public servant, your image of us as the perfect couple, it all started to mean more to you than the real flesh-and-blood us, Nat, the real you and me, our real marriage. Anyway, finally, after one more long, cold, alone day, I let him do it. I slept with him. He treated me like an object and I treated him like one and for once, for just that one evening, Nat, it felt good. With George there was no pressure to be something more than I am. I just had to lie there and do it."

"Do you love him?"

"For God's sake!" Maeve poises a vexed hand to slap at his chest, then lowers it in frustration. "How can you ask me that stupid question? Are you listening? I love you. You. But you pile so much on me with your . . . your unrealistic expectations and your romantic crap all the time about who you are and who I am and what we represent, it's like living in a Norman Rockwell painting. You thought so much of me that in the end you didn't think of me at all."

Maeve laughs. She throws up her hands at Nat as though he has achieved something of note.

"It was like you were in love with another woman. Jesus, Nat. Day after day, you only saw what you wanted. Not what you had."

His wife lowers her white arms. Her voice is resigned, calmed by truth.

"Me. Just me. And I felt taken for granted. I was overlooked and unappreciated. I couldn't leave you. But I needed to break the mold."

Nat is besieged. Images of his wife and Talley assault him as though they are not two but a writhing thousand. Her words *fuck* and *cheap* and *lie there* missile past him, driving his head down. He fights to ward off the visions and sounds; he forces himself to look at her through a battle mist in his eyes of emotional weaponry and remembered snow. He falters. He finds he has nothing to shoot back with anymore, no banner, no drummer, no reserves. He is vanquished.

He says, "You broke my heart."

Maeve cocks her head. She gently says, "Oh, Nat. It needed to be broken."

She reaches for her husband's hand. He watches her come, an advance on his position, he lets her flesh and blood cross and take his battlements. She gathers in his hand.

She says, "I love you. And I love all your crap. I know I broke your heart. I was weak. I admit it. I was needy. But so are you. All this nonsense about what's black and white and right and wrong, all the lines you draw, it's just armor you wear. It looks like strength but it's not. You're as feeble and human as I am, Nat Deeds. Our whole time together you hid in your work and your old-fangled notions of what a man ought to be, and a woman and a marriage. And for a long time I bought into that. I hid inside you. I think it's time we both stopped hiding. So, I'll step out in the open first. I miss you. I love you. Please forgive me for hurting you. You drive me crazy and you'll have to quit that."

She lets go of his hand. She says, "There. Now please take me back."

Nat's hand hangs in the air where she left it. He says nothing.

"Nat?"

"What."

"Can you do it? Forgive me? Change for me? Can you meet me halfway?"

Nat sees the white of Christmas snow and her nurse's dress and the fog of warfare, it all dissolves into his desire for surrender, becomes a willing white flag. He wants the hostilities to end, he wants his service to be finished. More, he wants to walk away from his outpost, across the shelled and pocked ground of the past eight months, to her. These are the things he wants, but he cannot hoist that white flag so quickly. In every action, even when the battle is over, some still want to fight.

"Halfway," Nat says. He smiles. "Seems like a long way."

Maeve raises her arms. Nat resists his final yielding. She doesn't wait for him to step into her embrace but brings it to him, signaling that she will go further than halfway if she must, if Nat cannot. She holds him tightly. She kisses his neck and simply holds him more.

Then she whispers into his ear, "All right. Tell me the truth. Can you get past George Talley?"

Nat speaks out into the records room. "No."

Her hair floats against his cheek. Softly she nods. "I didn't think so."

Maeve pulls her chest from his, releasing his arms. She turns her eyes to the table, to the files.

"Well," she says, sitting, her voice resigned, "if you can't forgive him, let's see if we can nail his ass instead. That ought to make you feel better."

Nat laughs. He's never heard her curse like this. He lays a hand on her nape. She wears white; he recalls a long, sequined gown. He wants to marry her all over again, start everything fresh. He will be glad once he's been captured at last. His has been a lonely vigil.

Bending over her shoulder to see into the open file, Nat hopes for one more turnaround, one big one for Sheriff George Talley and for Amanda.

Maeve flips pages in the folder until she comes to the chart for July 1998. She drags her finger down it. The page is divided into three sections. The first portion contains the patient's personal information—name, address, and other necessaries. The middle is filled in by the attending nurse who first sees the patient. The bottom part belongs to the doctor who writes his diagnosis, plus any prescriptions, treatment, and recommendations. Nat follows Maeve's fast-moving finger. There is Amanda's name at the top of the form. Maeve floats past these lines to the middle. Before Nat can read more than a few words she lifts the page at the bottom and turns it over.

"No," she says, already beginning her scrutiny of the last page, the one for August 1999. "That was for some glass she stepped on by the river. Five stitches in the right foot and out the door."

"Who was the doctor?"

"Jorgensen." The family practitioner, the local M.E., who looked away from Nat last week at Amanda's funeral.

Maeve slides her gaze down the page. Nat peers closer, feeling inadequate against the speed with which his wife scans the file.

Again his eyes cannot keep up the pace of her diving finger. He capitulates and stands straight, easing his back.

He lays his hand over the top of her head. He leaves it there as a sort of cap in the seconds while she reads. He looks at the backs of his fingers and wrist. Not a powerful hand, he thinks, not an athlete's mitt. Not a hero's hand. My hand. And like any hand, I hold everything in it. Wisdom and ignorance, battle and peace, good and evil. It's a man's hand. Fragile. Common. Flesh and blood.

She says, "Here we are."

"What?"

"Here's your broken jaw."

Nat feels a thrill. He was right. Talley brought Amanda to Pamunkey General.

Maeve's finger beats a quick tattoo over a scribbled entry. She flows past it, over more writing Nat cannot decipher quickly but he tries because the hunt is joined. Maeve works her finger far ahead of him. She tumbles down to the doctor's notations, touches them softly like touching braille, then raps the table with her knuckles.

"Damn. Her bike."

Nat stops reading. Maeve lifts her eyes to him. The light does not explode in their darkness but plunges into them to cluster in constellations.

"It says she fell off her bike and broke her jaw."

A plug has been pulled in Nat's chest, his thrill leaks out.

"Nothing about a punch?"

"Not a word."

Nat grits his teeth. He takes a deep breath and lets it go miserly through his lips, giving voice to the leak that is deflating him.

"Who was the doctor? Jorgensen again?"

"Yes."

"Can I take a look?"

Maeve stands to switch places with Nat. He takes the chair, she moves behind him. He notes that she does not reprimand him for his desire to look more closely at the file, she does not act superseded. She might have, because that is what he is doing. But she is being cooperative and forgiving.

Maeve sets her hand atop Nat's head in a fond reenactment. She leaves it there. It is not a distraction. Nat smiles and reads.

His eyes adjust slowly to the slapdash handwriting. The emergency-room nurse, Hilda Bradford, noted the girl's badly bruised left jaw, plus a small cut at the point of impact. The jaw was loose and clearly broken. She states that the father of the patient, George Talley, described the cause of the accident as the child falling from her bike after riding over a root growing through a sidewalk. The sheriff claims his daughter landed hard, smacking her face on the edge of the street's concrete curb. Jorgensen confirmed the nurse's observations. The doctor took some x-rays, set the jawbone by wiring the child's mouth shut, then prescribed a painkiller.

This is wrong, Nat thinks. His instincts rage, Something is wrong. George hit her.

"Dead end," says Maeve. Her hand kneads his head in sympathy. "Just a bike."

Nat makes no response. He glares more at the scrawled page, as though the lines and scratches will rearrange themselves for him into something he can use as incriminating evidence and—he is honest with himself—some measure of vengeance. That would be justice, for that to happen. He stares, and justice does not emerge. He tries to coax it out of the garbled details on the page, wants them to crawl like hornets over a hive into some more purposeful shape for him. Nat knows through experience that crooks and sons of bitches always leave their spoor. Where is it? Nothing. In his mind's ear he hears Maeve say it again. To George Talley she was nothing. Nothing. And that is what the man has left behind.

Then Maeve sees it. Nat would not have caught it. Not ever.

She mutters, "The number."

"What number?"

She says, "Move."

He is slow, still dejected at his failure to find something in this file, and a little confused.

"Why?"

"Look at the form." She yanks her hand from the top of his head so fast she musses his hair. Her finger stabs past his ear down to the upper right corner of the page. She taps the digits there.

"Look. The number."

"It's 99-2309. What about it? You said the forms are sequential, like a checkbook."

"They are. And just like a checkbook, if there's one missing it has to be accounted for."

"Okay, but there's no form missing. It's right here."

She tugs at the chair back. "Move!"

Nat rises. She fills in behind him, rapid as a relay racer. She flings up the lid to the long gray S-T-U master card file. She digs again through the index cards with dexterity, her fingers urgent. Nat holds his breath. What is she looking for?

In seconds Maeve exposes the right master card. Amanda's name is written across the top. There is the row of five entries. She snatches the white card out of the casing, like pulling the alligator's tooth. She holds it high, triumphant.

"Read the number on the form for Amanda's last visit."

Nat's heart squeezes. Adrenaline pricks his torso.

He says, "It's 99-2308."

Maeve rotates the card, front to back. "There's no record of 2308 being voided out. It was filled in, Nat. Then for some reason it was replaced by 2309."

Maeve stands. The stars are bursting now in her huge night eyes. Maybe that is what radiates inside Nat's chest, the twinkles, the far mysteries.

She wraps her arms around his neck. She puts her face so close to his that her eyes and smile go fuzzy. Nat draws his head back to bring her in focus. He sees that Maeve's smile is melancholy.

She holds the card out for him. "See the name of the admitting nurse?"

"Yeah. Hilda Bradford."

Maeve sighs.

"Hilda won't be glad to see us."

## 4

Maeve gathers the index card and Amanda Talley's file. Nat doesn't ask if this is allowed. In her other hand she cups Nat's elbow. She guides him out of the records room and farther into the hospital.

He asks, "Why don't we go straight to Jorgensen?" Nat tries to mute the pleasant tug in his chest at evening the score for the doctor's snub.

"No," his wife says. "That's the wrong approach."

"Why?"

"Trust me, Nat. We won't get anything out of Jorgensen. He's a doctor."

Nat suppresses a feisty, competitive urge. Calmly, he says, "And I'm a lawyer."

People pass by. Maeve stays quiet until the others are gone down the hall. Nat tries to say more but she raises a hushing finger to him. She leads him along the hall, then halts at a glass door opening out to a bricked courtyard. She steps into the heat, holding the door for him to follow, and he does, across hot bricks to a circle of shade beneath a tall crepe myrtle. It is six o'clock. Surrounded by high walls and windows that beam collected heat, the courtyard is like an oven. The day in this contained space has a fatigued and overcooked feel. Nat thinks Nature has made some point; Enough, he urges, let it rain. The egg stink from the plant has mounted the hospital walls to tumble into the courtyard. On the other side of town, mill workers tramp to a new shift. The river steams, tugboats blow the arrival of a chip barge.

Maeve sits on a bench beneath the tree. Nat joins her. The leaves of the low branches are still. The bricks hum in the temperature. No one else is outside with them.

She says, "If Jorgensen tampered with that form, he's not going to admit it. Never. That's a huge no-no in medicine. There's a rigid protocol for forms. Our records are the patient's history, they're all we've got. A doctor could lose his license for altering a written chart. If Jorgensen did something like that, he was under a lot of pressure to do it."

Nat says, "Probably from Talley."

Maeve nods.

He asks, "But what about Hilda? Why would she get involved in something like that?"

"Hilda Bradford had an affair with Charles Jorgensen."

Nat's eyes widen.

"You're sure?"

Maeve flattens her face into a look that says, It's a small hospital, a small town.

He asks, "How long?"

"Years."

"Was it going on in ninety-nine?"

"Yes."

"Is it over?"

"Yes. He ended it."

Nat shakes his head. He's known the doctor for a long time. He says, "Jorgensen and a nurse. That's . . . that's hard to believe."

Maeve gazes deep into his eyes. "Why?"

Nat does not speak his reply. Because I am naive, he thinks. He averts his eyes from hers. He does not want to look at his wife with the direction of his thoughts. Where has he been all this time? Here, in Good Hope. Growing up. Then he was married, working, living here. He was not isolated, he was always a part of the community. How could he not recognize that these things went on all around him? How can he sit here right now and still be so shocked and disappointed at Talley, at Hilda Bradford and Dr. Jorgensen, at the deacons of Victory Baptist, at Tom Derby the alcoholic, at Maeve? Nat calculates. He knows the answer and is embarrassed, like a child caught badly playing an adult game. He has been hiding, just as Maeve said. He never relinquished his need for the musty romantic codes inherited from his parents, invented out of history, absorbed from movie screens. He was small as a boy and sometimes picked on, so he fought back on his imaginary battlefield in the woods, defending his pretend creed (the creed of men) against shadows. As an adult, he found a real battlefield and genuine esteem on it. The courtroom. He prosecuted crimes. He steeped himself in law and justice, he put on blinders, so that he did not notice the prevalence of smaller crimes all around him, the daily atrocities in Good Hope, committed in offices and bedrooms and around dining room tables, behind backs and beneath masks of flesh. Infidelities, bigotry, lies, backstabbing, private savagery. The nasty, the petty, the unheroic. He walled himself away from these things, refused to see them in his parents, his friends, and his wife. He lived like this, a full-grown man still playing a boy's pretend game, defending a boy's fort of virtue. Then Maeve slept with another man and Nat's walls did not crumble, they grew stronger around him. They separated him fully at last. They drove him away from home. And until today, this day when everything is reversed, he could not get free. Now Nat takes a look at his walls from outside them, the side Maeve and others have seen. They are ramparts of cowardice and willful blindness. Obstinate pride. He thinks, I am naive. I am ashamed to have believed and acted as though I stood apart from the world. All this time they saw me and laughed behind their hands at me. I am pretentious. I am a buffoon.

Nat does not speak yet. Instead, in contrition and humility he lifts her hand to his lips. He kisses the skin white as linen.

"I'm sorry I ran out on you. I was in my own little world."

She slips her hand from his to grace fingertips against his cheek.

Maeve is kind. She says, "Not such a little world. It had very big notions in it."

He shakes his head. He closes his eyes and sees it, the strictures.

"No, it was tiny. It was made out of just one man."

He lifts his lids and there she is, touching him. He gazes along the span of her arm reaching to his face, connecting him, inviting him to cross.

"I want to live out here with you," he says. "I don't know how it's going to work out, but I'll try. You know me, Maeve, I'll try hard."

Her hand slides past his cheek, behind his head. She pulls him

into a kiss, even with the many windows and the hallway door peering over the courtyard. Overhead, the still canopy of the tree, for a
moment, makes for them a green night.

She pulls only a breath away from the kiss. She says, "We'll try
hard." The saying of the words brushes his lips.

When they step out of the shade to cross the courtyard, they do
not hold hands. For now, they have done what they can for their marriage. It's time again for Amanda and Elijah. But for Nat, following
his wife, the glowing hot bricks and the rotten mill smell seem to belong to yet another receding world. His head swims.

When they reach the emergency room it is quiet. Nat is glad they
don't have to track down the nurse. She is there, at a desk behind a
glass partition. Nat senses momentum.

He holds his ground and watches Maeve cross the room to speak
with Hilda Bradford. On the desk Maeve lays out Amanda's card and
master file, flipping to the last stapled page. The older nurse's face
and body language appear unwilling, conflicted. Nat expects this.
Out of the blue, Maeve Deeds has unearthed an episode that Hilda
no doubt thought was long over. Along with it Maeve has reopened a
painful chapter in Hilda's life. A failed affair, one that lasted long
enough for the lonely nurse to fall in love, to hope. Should she continue to safeguard the married man who jilted her? A doctor who can
fire her? Should she get involved in a tussle with the powerful Sheriff
Talley?

Maeve looks at Nat through the glass partition. This is his signal
to enter. He navigates the chrome tables and banks of lights. His
shoes are not silent.

"Hilda," says Maeve to the seated nurse, "this is my husband, Nat."

Nurse Hilda Bradford is a woman alone. Nat's keen sad eye measures her makeup, her darkened hair, painted nails, the banked fire
inside her. She gambled and lost in her forties and now early fifties.
Hilda Bradford clearly does not like attractive Maeve Deeds and now
spreads that dislike to her husband, the lawyer who marches out of
the heat of Good Hope into her ER to ask her to choose a side. She
chose once, Nat thinks, and it went wrong.

"Miss Bradford, thank you for talking to me."

She eyes him with a cocked head.

"Don't thank me, Mr. Deeds. I'm not talking yet." Her twang is southeast Virginia. Nat thinks, She was born here. She's always been here.

"Even so," he mildly says, "I have to ask you a very important question. It could help save a man's life." Nat pauses to look about the emergency room. This is his jury drama routine. "I know that will matter to you. That's what you do."

She nods, nibbling at the compliment through her distaste and reluctance.

Nat continues. "I'm sure you're aware I'm Elijah Waddell's attorney. It's my belief that he's innocent."

"Of course it is."

"You can help me prove that, Miss Bradford."

She is obstinate. "He burnt that church."

"So the newspapers say."

"That poor girl was inside it. Why should I help you say he didn't do it?"

"Then you needn't help me. Just tell me the truth. If that's a help to me or not, your conscience is clear, you've got nothing to do with it. That's fair, isn't it?"

"Fair for you maybe. But you're asking me to go against people I respect. People I work with. What's fair for them, Mr. Deeds?" She refers to Charles Jorgensen. Nat observes that she does not relish revealing the man's secrets, as perhaps a rejected lover otherwise might. Hilda Bradford still carries a torch for the doctor.

He says, "You'll be going against them with the truth, Hilda. But upholding a lie? A lie goes against a lot more than just a few people. You know that."

Nat waits. The woman's lips tuck in. Nat glances up to Maeve quickly, to warn her what he will say next.

"I know you've been lied to by someone." Hilda Bradford tenses. She whips her head around to Maeve, the obvious source of this information. Nat keeps the pressure of his voice on her to gaff her head back to him, to hold her in the chair, under his influence. "Look at the damage it's done in your own life. Where's the honor in covering a lie, Hilda? Where's the good in watching selfish people get away with something while the blameless, the trusting, the children pay for it? You know better than me. You tell me the answer to that and I won't ask you any more questions."

Hilda Bradford breaks her eyes from Nat's. She looks past him into the open air, where she sees images. She blinks back tears. What invisible memories does she see? Whatever they are, they make her softly say, "Why does everybody want to tear him down. He's a good man. A good doctor."

Maeve lays her hand on Hilda Bradford's shoulder. Nat says, "I know he is."

"George Talley. You. His wife." Her mouth twists. "You know she doesn't love him."

Nat and Maeve keep silent. Nurse Hilda Bradford's injury is the hardest kind to heal and the longest to knit. It always, always scars.

She releases a deep breath. It is a sigh of farewell to those scenes flitting past her.

Nat wants to pity her. But he can't. He bears down. He leans close, resting his hands on the arms of her chair.

He says, "Hilda, I don't have to tear him down. I came here to talk with you off the record. Quietly. All I want is for you to tell me about the night Sheriff Talley brought his daughter in with a broken jaw three years ago. Tell me right here and now and I promise I'll do everything I can to make sure the fewest number of people know about any of this. Believe me, I don't have any interest in making trouble for you. Charles won't ever know you told me. But if I have to come back with a subpoena and make you answer me under oath and on the public record, Hilda, I swear I will. And I'll do the same to Charles and Talley and anybody else who can help me prove Elijah Waddell is innocent. So."

Nat reaches to the nurse's desk. He straightens Amanda's three-by-five card and the open folder on the table. He points first to the last line on the master index card, dated August 11, 1999, which corresponds to form 99-2308. Next he indicates the form itself in the folder. Number 2309.

"What happened to 2308?"

Hilda Bradford again gazes off. There is a new image there. A tired, resolved visage settles on her face. She lowers her eyes to the form.

"I remember it was late in the afternoon," the nurse slowly says. "George Talley brought his daughter to the ER in his squad car. He came rushing in past everyone, making a fuss that his daughter needed to be looked at. I walked over. I told him to go on up front to the registration desk and sign her in there and I'd have a look at her while he was doing that. He refused, like I had no place telling him what to do. Said he was staying right there by her. I remember she had a badly bruised jaw on the left side. It hurt her a lot. It was loose in my hand, so I figured it was definitely broken. Talley was going to stay right there no matter what I said so I just went ahead. I asked her.

" 'Honey, how'd this happen?'

"Talley spoke right up. 'She fell off her bike. A root was sticking up out of the sidewalk down the street from our house. She didn't see it and fell off. She landed on the curb, on her face.'

"Without bringing attention to it I looked the girl up and down. She was just wearing a T-shirt and shorts. She had no barks on her shins or knees. Her elbows weren't scraped, her palms were clear. There was no indication whatsoever she tried to break a fall like that. He was telling me she just keeled over and landed on her face. I asked her.

" 'Honey, is that so? You fell off your bike?'

"She couldn't have been more than thirteen or fourteen at the time. I remember thinking she was going to grow up a pretty little thing. If that George Talley let her grow up at all.

"She said, 'Yes, ma'am.' And she looked behind her, kind of in a cringe, at her father. She trembled. Well, when she did that I knew he'd hit her.

"I told them to wait right there. I went up front to registration and got the form myself."

Nat says, "Form number 2308."

"Yes. I took it back and sat down with George Talley and I swear it was like sitting down with the devil, that man just seethed at me, at every question I asked."

"What questions?"

"If he'd seen her fall. Where on the street did it happen. What time. Just anything I could think of to maybe trip him up, kind of innocently. But he had it all thought out. And he had that girl too frightened to make a peep. He was ready for me. The devil came prepared."

Maeve has moved beside Nat. She asks the next question.

"You wrote that down? That George Talley hit her?"

"What I wrote down was that the story of his little girl falling off her bicycle was inconsistent with the injuries I observed. The only way she could have fallen off her bike and sustained only a jaw injury was if she'd had her hands tied behind her, and I very much doubt she did."

"So someone reading your report could have concluded George had hit her instead."

"That was my intention in the way I filled in the chart, yes."

"And Dr. Jorgensen was attending the ER. He looked at Amanda next."

"Yes. I handed the girl over. I gave him her form. Then I went about my business, figuring we'd call Child Protective Services after they left."

Maeve kneels. She rests her hands on Hilda Bradford's knees, to reassure the woman, to coax more from her. In his mind Nat sees Hilda, three years ago, talking gently like this with Amanda, trying to get at the truth.

Maeve asks, "Charles was alone with Talley?"

"Yes."

"After examining the girl and talking with Talley, Charles came back to you. About the form."

"He had another form in his hand."

"Number 2309."

"Yes."

"What did he say happened to 2308?"

"He said he'd spilled coffee on it. Said he went up front to registration and got another one."

"There's no mention on Amanda's card of registration's voiding out the first form."

Hilda gives a rueful smile. "He just snuck it out. You know that. The doctors in this hospital don't know anything about our filing system. Charles had no idea of a master index-card file. They're not the ones who go get the records. We are. He just figured he'd get a fresh form and start over and no one'd be the wiser."

Nat leans in again. "What do you mean, start over?"

"When he came to me with the new form, he'd already filled his portion in." Hilda lifts the manila folder from her desk. She runs her finger under Charles Jorgensen's entry on form 2309. "Right here. Bicycle accident. Broken jaw. He made it real simple and clean."

Nat has taken over again from Maeve. His wife pulls back.

"Charles told you to fill your section in again. With the bike story."

"He told me I was not qualified to make such a judgment on Sheriff George Talley that the man had struck his daughter. He said I was not a psychiatrist or a mind reader and should stick to being a nurse. Said the man would never do such a thing and that I was obviously mistaken. He shoved that second form in front of me, handed me a pen, and said to write what Amanda Talley had told me happened, that she fell off her bike on a root near their house." Hilda moves her finger, shaking now, beneath her own writing. She reads for Nat the first sentence of her report. "Trauma to jaw induced by fall from bicycle."

Hilda brings her hands back into her lap. She sits as though on a witness stand, gathered, fearful, cathartic.

She says, "It's all right there. I wrote it down just like George Talley said. Word for word. Damn his eyes."

Hilda dabs at her own eyes.

Nat backs off a step. Hilda speaks what is on Nat's mind.

"You know this. Talley's like old J. Edgar Hoover. He's got something on everybody in this county. You make a wrong step around here and he'll know it. He'll hang on to it like gold, and he'll make sure you know it too. Then he'll spend it when he sees fit. He had something on Charles. Something. And he sprung it on Charles that day when he broke his own daughter's jaw. He's a devil, that one."

Nat has no more questions for Hilda Bradford. Nor does he have anything to ask Charles Jorgensen. She's right. Talley held sway somehow over the doctor. It doesn't matter what it was; it could have been anything, speeding tickets, drunk driving, maybe even the doctor's affair with Hilda. Whatever it was, it's long gone and was never made part of the official record. It stayed in George Talley's hip pocket. That's where it will remain. George will deny it. Charles will deny it. And that will be the end of it.

Three years ago, there were no roots sticking out of the sidewalk along George Talley's street, or even last week when Nat went to see the man at his home. Three years ago, when Amanda was supposedly felled from her bike and busted her jaw, the neighborhood was brand new. The trees for a mile in every direction of George's house were little more than saplings. This is another velvety lie. Like the others, Talley will find a way to deflect it. No need to follow it further.

So Nat has finished here. He will not ask the softly crying nurse why she didn't report Talley's abuse of Amanda, why she didn't plead with Charles Jorgensen not to change the form. Nat will not make Hilda Bradford admit out loud she was protecting Charles, that she loved Charles. What we will do in the name of love is the equal of what we will suffer in its name.

He will not ask her to testify in a trial. There will be no trial.

"Thank you, Hilda. You've been a great help." He smiles down at her. "I hope that's okay."

The nurse closes the manila folder on the desk, puts the index card on top of it, and pushes it away from her. She wants the distance to begin now.

Maeve takes the documents in hand. She says, "Thank you, Hilda. I'm sorry if we've upset you."

Hilda will not lift her eyes.

Maeve makes for the edge of the partition. Nat stays behind for a moment.

"Hilda. I'll keep my word. I won't use anything you've told me unless I absolutely have to. I don't think I'll need it. But I had to be sure. I am now. Thank you. Goodbye."

Nat and Maeve do not speak walking the hall toward the registration desk. She asks him to wait in the reception area while she replaces the file and card.

When she comes out of the records room, she walks up close.

"Nat."

"What."

"This is a little tough for me to ask."

"Okay. What."

"Will you have dinner with me?"

"No. Thank you. But I have to go home."

"Do you have to?"

"No. But I ought to. Having dinner with you tonight is not us meeting halfway. It's about three-quarters, and it's your way, not mine. I'm going to need some time with this. Much as I want it to go right, I know it can't go fast."

Maeve keeps silent. She seems aware that he is right.

She kisses his cheek. "Tomorrow. We'll talk."

She turns on her crepe soles, making no sound but the swish of her white dress and she walks, wafts away, like clouds.

Nat thinks, It's over. The day of reversals.

But it is not, because out in the hospital parking lot, Monroe Skelton leans against Nat's car, waiting for him.

"Money, what are you doing here?"

It's a reflexive thing to say. Nat knows the deputy would come to find him and wait like this only if there was something important about Elijah.

Monroe makes his face blank. The news will not be good, Nat thinks, not good for someone.

"How'd you find me?"

"Good police work." Monroe shrugs. "I saw your car."

"So what have you got?"

There is no one else in the parking lot. Even so, Monroe looks around to assure privacy. He steps close to Nat, the difference in the two men's size is night and day, the same as the difference in their color. Nat cannot take on the blandness and control of Monroe's presentation. He's too drained by his day, the revelations of Maeve, and the weight of Elijah's case. Whatever Monroe has brought him might take Nat off his feet. He says, "Wait."

He takes Monroe's place against the sun-hot car hood. Monroe folds his arms over his chest. The big deputy speaks now without cue.

"I contacted Talley's ex up in Maryland. Asked her if she knew her daughter was taking birth control pills. She said she didn't, but she didn't seem surprised. Sounds to me like Amanda wasn't getting much parenting from either direction."

"No," Nat says.

"This afternoon I drove out to the pharmacy listed on Amanda's pills. It's in Hampton. The pharmacist looked up the prescription and the transaction."

Nat only asks, "And?"

"The scrip number was from a doctor down there, also in Hampton."

It's clear Amanda was keeping her sex life a secret from her parents. Not unusual for a teenager.

Who drove the girl to the doctor's office in Hampton?

"The transaction?"

Nat guesses what Monroe will say next. He guesses correctly. It is a relief and a tragedy, and the revelation makes him glad he is leaning against the hood.

"It was paid for by Tom Derby's credit card."

5

Nat searches for Tom Derby. He makes phone calls to Derby's house, to Mrs. Epps's, he drives to the dusty building site of the new Victory Baptist, leaving messages at every place. No one knows where the preacher is. There is nothing for Nat to do this late in the afternoon but head back to Richmond through the shimmering heat.

Over the forty-minute drive, Nat's heart sinks. Why did Derby take Amanda to Hampton and pay for her birth control pills? Is Tom the missing boyfriend? Or was it just an act of adult compassion, doing something for the girl she could not have gotten her stern father to do? In either case, Derby has been hiding something vital to Elijah's defense. He's concealed his relationship with Amanda Talley, he's lied directly to Nat about it. After more than twenty years, Derby is still hiding. The one question—What has Tom done?—spins in Nat's head and the hot road goes by mostly unnoticed.

When Nat enters his apartment, his phone is ringing. It's Derby.

"Nat, I'm glad I caught you. You've been leaving messages all over. What's up?"

Nat sets down his briefcase but remains on his feet.

"I found out something today I don't like."

Derby snickers. "Just one thing? You had a good day, then."

Nat makes no reply.

"Was it about Elijah?"

"About you."

For moments, nothing returns from the phone but the sound of one long breath.

"Go ahead."

"You paid for Amanda Talley's birth control pills in Hampton."

Derby waits. Nat is about to repeat the charge when Derby answers it.

"Yes. I did."

"Why did you buy her pills, Tom?"

No reply. Nat prods.

"Were you her boyfriend?"

Again, Derby does not answer. Nat pushes his point as though there is a jury watching.

"Listen to me. There's an innocent man in jail right now who needs you to answer me with the truth. Were you having sex with Amanda Talley?"

Derby's exhale fills the receiver in Nat's hand.

"Yes."

"The night of the fire?"

"Yes."

"Did you drink with her that night?"

"Yes."

"Dammit, Tom!" Nat can't stop himself. "Dammit, why didn't you say something?"

"That's a stupid question."

Nat is taken aback, not supposing Derby would be offended by these questions. He expects shame. In the silent seconds that follow, Nat hardens toward his friend.

Derby says, "I'm sorry, that was uncalled for. It's just I don't like being reminded of what a coward and a bastard I am."

This mollifies Nat. "I understand. But why didn't you tell me?"

"Why didn't I just stay away from the girl in the first place. Nat, the man who had sex with Amanda is the same man who couldn't come forward after she was gone. What'd you expect?"

Derby's right. Nat expects too much, always too much. This is what Maeve has asked him to stop.

"What are you going to do?"

"I'm going to go see Fentress in the morning."

"Will this get Elijah out of jail?"

"No, Tom. This'll go a long way towards casting reasonable doubt on the rape charge. But there's still nothing pointing away from Elijah on the arson. The girl was in the church when it burned. It's still a homicide."

"Nat."

"Yeah."

"They're going to throw me out of the church."

"They will," Nat says. "Yes, they will."

"What can you do for me?"

"I don't know that I can sit on this, Tom." Nat licks his lips, then speaks what's on his mind. "I don't know that I should."

"All right. Give me as much time as you can."

"I've got some more things to ask you."

"Can it wait 'til tomorrow?"

It can, but Nat wants to know everything now. Before he can say more, Derby tells him, "I'll talk to you tomorrow, okay? Just give me a day to figure this out."

"All right. For you."

"Thanks, Nat."

Before he hangs up, Derby says, "Elijah has himself one hell of a lawyer."

Nat stands with the receiver in his hand for several seconds, listening to dial tone. He is not prepared to spend the night with his unanswered questions. He sets the phone in the cradle to silence the little wailing.

Nat folds into a chair before the window and watches the reluctant sun go down.

# Six

## 1

Nat sips Styrofoam-cup coffee. He sits in his car in the courthouse parking lot. His windows are down, his elbow is on the sill. He feels like a cop on a morning stakeout. It's eight o'clock. The steam whistle at the mill blows shift change, an archaic touch from the 1920s. No one in the town has ever asked the mill to stop blowing that whistle. It is holy here, a call to service, to lifeblood.

Nat loves the curtain-raising hour here in Good Hope. The heat is at bay. The sunlight is rosy and sharp, cutting long shadows behind the parking meters and stop signs. Seagulls dive for minnows in the river shallows or, failing that, swoop around town checking out last night's garbage behind the restaurants. Engines grumble, dogs are walked. Things wake up together here in Good Hope, as though they all slept in the same room, like siblings.

He is stalking Ed Fentress. Yesterday there was no time to get an appointment for this morning. So Nat drove in early and waits in the parking lot. He wants to be in front of the prosecutor first thing. In his briefcase are Amanda's birth control pills and the x-ray of the girl's twice-broken jaw. In his head are items out of turn: forms 2308 and 2309; an image of the Baptist hymnal beneath Amanda's one spared hand; sad Hilda Bradford; the remembrance of Dr. Jorgensen at the funeral mumbling to his wife who does not love him before both turned away from Nat; a fresh, flat sidewalk stretching for miles, nothing to unseat a summer girl riding her bike, a white shining lie. There are visions of George Talley's big crashing fist, and George Talley's illicit caresses on Maeve's naked body. There are Amanda and Derby in his church car driving to Hampton. There is Maeve's kiss in the courtyard, wonderful, not yet large enough to cover the stain, but the memory and the promise of Maeve are; and Nat's intentions for Talley are too.

At eight-thirty Fentress pulls into his spot across the lot. He does not notice Nat's car and proceeds up the steps into the courthouse. Nat rolls up his window. He opens his briefcase and removes a thin envelope. He closes the case and leaves it on the seat. He hopes he will not need the rest of its contents this morning.

He is one minute behind Fentress up the three flights of stairs. He finds the prosecutor alone in the office, the secretary doesn't come until nine. Nat approaches. Fentress makes coffee, his coat is off, in suspenders and starched sleeves.

Fentress does not look up. Jovially he says, "Hey, it's the early bird. Come to get a worm?" He did see Nat in the lot. Nat thinks he hates Fentress's cool.

Nat walks past him. "In your office, Ed."

Fentress keeps his head to his task. His voice grins. "Want some coffee to wash down that worm?"

Nat sits facing the prosecutor's empty chair and neat desk. Looking out the window, the mill's boiler plume and some darting seagulls help him wait while Fentress mixes his cream and sugar. The prosecutor ambles in. He sits as though in front of a conference of thousands, proper and orchestrated. His manner is detached but somehow still intimate. The man is always in public.

He says, "I don't have much time this morning, so if you don't mind." With this Fentress stirs one finger in the air as though in his coffee. "What can I do for you, counselor?"

In a voice curt as a telegraph, Nat says, "The night of the fire. George Talley punched his daughter in the face. He broke her jaw.

The next afternoon when she was found dead, he went to you and told you. You knew about it."

Fentress brings his coffee mug to his lips. The porcelain is splashed with the logo of some law enforcement society.

"I knew no such thing." He swallows. "That's dangerous conjecture, Nat."

"Dangerous for me?"

"That's right."

"Ed."

"What."

"Put the goddam coffee down and listen to what I have to say. Because I'm going to say it once to you. After that, if I have to, I'm going to say it to Judge Hawk. And I'm going to lay out for her all the evidence I'm not showing you."

Fentress dares Nat. He takes another gulp.

He says, "Fuck you, Nat."

Then Fentress lowers the mug. He lays his cuff links on his desk. "All right."

Nat brings up a finger. He points it out the window, down at the sheriff's office building. He thinks the rotten-egg smell in this town isn't the mill so much as it is these two, Talley and Ed Fentress.

"Three years ago George Talley smacked his fourteen-year-old daughter so hard it cracked her jaw. I have witnesses. I have evidence. Then the night of the fire they argued at dinner. Amanda came home probably smelling of alcohol. George got into an argument with her and she told him off, once and for all. She told him she had a boyfriend. She'd been having sex. On that point I have evidence. And I have a witness."

"You got the boyfriend?"

"I got him."

"Who is it?"

Nat has made up his mind to do as Derby asked and protect his name as long as he can. Monroe will continue the investigation of the girl's death, so Nat will not long be able to keep Derby out of it. But for today, let Ed Fentress do his own detective work.

"Not important for now. But I have him and he'll testify if he has to. George told his daughter what she was doing was offensive to the Catholic Church. Amanda answered him she was considering becoming a Baptist. George blew a gasket at that one and punched her. When he did, he broke her jaw for the second time, half an inch from the spot where he broke it four years before. She ran out of the house. She went to the Victory Baptist Church to be alone and sort things out. She fell asleep. While she was inside someone burned the church."

Fentress snorts. "Someone, my ass."

"Shut up, Ed. In fact, fuck you, Ed. Someone burned the church, not knowing the girl was in there. The next day, after her body was found, Talley came to you for advice. He told you he'd belted Amanda the night before and was afraid it would come out at the autopsy. The M.E. sees the old injury when she x-rays Amanda's jaw, questions it, an investigation follows, a cover-up is discovered, and George is screwed. So he came to you and asked how he could stop that. You told him how. He hit her. You knew."

"You're on dangerous ground."

"You knew! Elijah didn't hit that girl! He didn't rape her, he never laid eyes on her in his life. You hindered an investigation. You withheld information."

"That's enough, Nat." Fentress eyes him. "You've got nothing there but speculation. Leaps of logic and wild-ass theories. So you got the boyfriend. Big fucking deal. That doesn't prove she wasn't raped after she left him. It doesn't prove or disprove anything. You've got nothing but conjecture, across the board. You don't have me and you don't have George."

Nat doesn't move. He issues his words from a pacific frame.

"What I do have is an appointment with the Hawk this afternoon. I intend to show her a lot that I'm not willing to share with you right now, considering who your allies are and what you've got to hide. Now, if I'm wrong, or if you think I'm bluffing, you've got nothing to worry about, Ed. Come to my meeting with the judge. But if I'm right, you'd better ask me right now what it is I want."

Fentress squints as though he is looking into a spotlight.

He says, "Okay. For the sake of argument. Bottom line, what do you want?"

"You give up the capital. You give Elijah second-degree murder with suspended time."

The prosecutor plays with the coffee mug. He spins it around twice before he answers. Outside, gulls gambol behind his head in the mounting morning.

"You're out of your mind."

"Are you saying you're going ahead with capital?"

"That's right. And I'm going to win it."

Nat stands. He shrugs his suit coat into place. He anticipated this first line of resistance, this denial. He says the lines he prepared.

"You might."

The prosecutor's face stays stony, careless.

Fentress says, "I will."

Nat plants his feet. "Let me tell you something, Ed. I think you're right. You just might get a conviction. To be honest, I like your case against Elijah. I've got zip for evidence to dispute the arson charge and you know it. Elijah was there, he had motive, opportunity, he was drunk, he's made incriminating statements, he beat up that dealer in Norfolk. He's black, he's got a white wife. You've got a well-known, innocent white victim, a teenage girl, daughter of a local hero. It all adds up. It's nice stuff. The county folks might buy it, because you'll do a good job selling it to them. I'm not going to put on a real big defense, mainly because as I said I don't have much to put on. Mostly just what you said, speculation."

"What's your point?"

"Just to let you know what I will do. I'm coming after you and George Talley. I'm going to smear blood and ashes all over the two of you. Even though I may not have enough for Elijah, I've got a boat-load to point a finger at the two of you. When I'm done in that court-room and in front of the press you're both going to be staring down an obstruction-of-justice charge. I'm going to prove that you protected your precious buddy the sheriff and tampered with evidence to keep him clean. George is going to look like the violent out-of-control bastard he is. And you're going to look like a dirty little local politician who got in over his head. After this trial you'll have to vote for each other in the next election to keep from getting skunked. I give you my word on that."

Fentress fingers the mug. The coffee has stopped steaming.

Nat says, "You might not crack. But I guarantee you, with what I've got on Talley I can break him wide open. He'll hand you over, Ed, and save some of his own worthless hide. I'll take that trade. But you won't like it."

Nat pivots away. He takes one step to the door.

"First degree. That's the best I can do."

Nat turns. "No. If Elijah burned that church there was no premeditation to commit murder. You've got no evidence to connect him to the girl. There was no rape, no assault. Second degree. And time suspended."

"How much time off?"

"He serves five, tops."

Nat reaches into his coat pocket. He tosses the envelope onto the prosecutor's desk.

"There's a letter for the plea agreement. Sign it. You write up the order for the judge. I'll go see Elijah."

Fentress undoes the envelope. "What's your hurry?"

"I want this over and done with for a lot of reasons. First, once this hits the press, the person who actually did the burning will probably think he's in the clear. He'll make a mistake, he'll do it again, something. This might flush him out in the open. The rest of my reasons are none of your business."

Fentress reads the contents of the letter. He says, "When the folks around here see this, they're going to be pissed. He goes from capital murder to five years in jail. I don't know."

"That's your problem."

Fentress clucks his tongue at the paper. "Nat, old buddy, you're taking a big one away from me."

Nat is disgusted. "Just sign the damn thing and let me get out of here."

He watches Fentress scribble his name at the bottom of the letter. The man spins the page across the desk when he is done.

Fentress leans back in his chair.

"So who's the boyfriend?"

Nat makes no reply. The prosecutor sits mute and staring while Nat tucks the agreement into his coat. Then he says, "Jesus, why do you have to take all this so personally? Coming after me. What the hell is that?"

Nat does not answer this either. Instead, feeling the signed agreement in his pocket firm against his chest, he says, "There's something else."

"What? You didn't get what you came in here for?"

"Not yet."

Fentress leans back in his red leather wingback chair. He opens his hands, like throwing open a strongbox to Nat, Take what you want.

Nat says, "I want the worm."

## 2

Children play on the browning grass. Women swap sandwiches and sodas and mind each other's kids while trips are made to the rest room or back to the cars for fresh diapers. They all know each other. Their men are inside. They come here weekly for scheduled visits. Some have come for several years. Their children grow up on this grass, or in winter, hunkered inside in the green waiting room kicking their legs, getting shushed, waiting for a guard to call their mamas' names to go past the heavy door, inside. They see their daddies behind glass, they listen to sweetnesses or stern counsel over warm, dirty phone receivers. It is the extended family of the imprisoned. Some of the women recognize Nat, they say, " 'Morning, Mr. Deeds," holding no grudges for his efforts to put their men away. A child stops him on the steps, her hair in cornrows and beaded, she is a beautiful child. She lifts two empty hands to him and says, "Here yo' present." Her voice is that bow tied around the gift of life, childhood, the box not fully opened, the gift inside still to be revealed. The child is oblivious to the fact that this is a prison; this is just a long game of hide-and-seek where Daddy hides inside. Nat leans down to take the pantomimed offering.

He says, "Thank you." He pretends to tuck a box under his arm. A mother smiles. The child turns away to another child, a fat baby, and says, "And here yo' present."

The guard knows Nat too. He is an impossibly burly man. He gives a thumbs-up in the door window, his thumb is the size of a steel rivet. The lock buzzes and Nat hauls on the handle. The door weighs a lot.

He asks through the bulletproof glass at the barricaded kiosk inside for Elijah Waddell to be brought to an interview room. The guard says he'll have him put in number three. Nat waits at a door of bars for his escort guard. Echoes, sad and burdensome, flow past him from unseen halls. They are echoes with sharp edges, pared of every soft sound, they are clangs and tinny shouts, like stripped cars, dead down to the essentials of noise.

Nat is taken to the same cinder-block room where he first met Elijah a week ago. So much has happened since then; he has a flash of nostalgia for this room. Then he thinks that all those events and changes and reversals have happened in his own life. Nothing has happened for Elijah in the week past, nothing but drone days and nights, an increasing jeopardy. Worry and fear.

Five minutes pass. Then the door creaks open and the clatter of the hinges and locks dice through the room. Elijah is deposited inside by another of the prison's meaty arms. The door shuts. Elijah appears to need watering. He is wilting. His muscles seem tighter, the veins in his arms and neck distend as though rushing about his insides to distribute the last remaining bits of sustenance. He is bent, a parched reed. Nat stands.

The chairs screech. Elijah sits, Nat too.

Elijah says, "What've you got for me?" No greeting, no formality.

Nat reaches into his coat pocket. He spreads the signed letter on the table.

"A deal."

Elijah does not pull his eyes from Nat. He does pull the paper to him.

"What deal? What'd you do?"

"Elijah. Understand something. You're facing the death penalty. Rape and murder. My first priority is to derail that and keep you alive."

Elijah lowers his head. He rubs the space between his eyes. "You know, when I hear you say those words, I can't believe them. Rape and murder. Death penalty. I just can't. What the hell happened?"

"I don't know."

Elijah does not blink, his eyes are busy with nothing but Nat.

"You're my lawyer. You're supposed to know."

Nat is honest. "I'm trying to find out."

"So in the meantime you got me a deal."

"It's right here." Nat indicates the letter.

With one finger Elijah rotates the page. He reads quickly. Nat watches the dark finger trace while lines form in Elijah's brow.

Elijah looks up. "Second-degree murder."

"A killing in the commission of a felony without premeditation. The girl died as a result of the church burning. We can't change that fact and we can't change the law. You won't get manslaughter or any lesser charge, Elijah. This is it. Second-degree removes the rape charge, but it still makes you responsible for the girl's death."

"Even though I didn't do it."

Nat repeats. "Even though you didn't do it."

"And what if I don't take your deal?"

"We'll go up against Ed Fentress on capital murder. He'll insist on a jury trial."

"And?"

"I honestly don't think we can expect an acquittal. The best-case scenario would be second-degree murder, which is what I've got for you right now. But we'd have to be successful at the trial in severing any link between you and Amanda Talley, which I give us a fifty–fifty chance of doing. Fentress will claim a random encounter the night of the fire, and that's as hard to prove as it is to disprove. They've got no witnesses, we've got no alibi. And even if we get second-degree from a jury, you won't do better than five years. I doubt a jury'd be that generous. You know the worst case. Death row. Don't underestimate Fentress and Talley. They want you bad, for their own reasons. They have a decent case against you."

"What'd I ever do to Fentress?"

"You didn't do anything to him. You did something for him. You gave him a chance to get his name on television."

Elijah licks his lips slowly. He shakes his head. "Shit."

"I don't want to take them on, Elijah. I've got nothing, I swear to God, nothing to put on in your defense for the arson. They've got a strong circumstantial case. In front of a local jury it's probably enough. Until something turns up, unless the person who burnt the church comes forward, this deal is all we're going to see. I say take it. Then we'll search like hell to find the real arsonist."

"Who's searching?"

"The deputy who arrested you. Monroe Skelton. I think he's on our side. He's good. And he's honest. He's on it, Elijah, that's all I can tell you."

"You think he'll find the one who did it?"

Nat considers the odds and shakes his head. "No. Not unless the guy burns something else and gets caught. No, Elijah, I don't. But we'll see. We'll just have to wait it out."

Elijah mulls this over.

He says, "We'll wait, huh."

"Yes."

"Where you gonna wait, Nat? In your living room? On vacation?"

Nat watches Elijah. It's obvious the man wants to rise and smash the table, punch holes in the thick concrete walls, repel anything and everyone who would stop him, and walk free home to his wife and dog and cornfield. Elijah Waddell wants to go home; that is the juice which has stopped flowing to him, the lack of it is what withers him.

Elijah wrestles with the dark angel of his predicament. Nat continues to watch. The man blinks.

Nat says, "Elijah." That is all he can say.

Elijah says, "You know they weren't going to let me and Clare alone. From the moment Nora Carol was born. From when I married

Clare. Maybe from when I was born a black man. They don't admit it out loud. They don't say it to each other. You don't read it in the paper anymore like you used to or see it on signs over the bathrooms. They don't call us colored or nigger anymore and they think that's it, they've put an end to it. They've forgiven us and accepted us, like black folks are something to be forgiven and accepted. They think they've done their jobs and now they're all right because they don't hate us anymore. But all they've done is turn their hate into fear. They're still scared shitless of me. I walk in their world. I walk right beside them in the front door and I don't hang my head. I took one of their jobs. I took one of their women. I took one of their babies and I made it half me. So they're gonna cage me. They're gonna fight me down 'til I bend my neck. Until I give it all back. See, because it was never mine to take, it was theirs, always from the start. And if I won't hang my own head they'll weigh it down for me until I do. If I don't hand everything over they'll rip it out of my arms. They got to beat me, Nat. That's the way it's set up, even if some of them wish it wasn't so. And they got to beat you too. They're gonna win. They got to win. Or it all falls apart."

Nat makes a great show of shaking his head. "No," he says, "no. As long as you stay alive we stop them from winning. Keeping you alive keeps us fighting."

Elijah says, "Alive isn't much. Alive isn't living."

Nat puts a hand on Elijah's fist. He says, "Please."

Elijah studies Nat's hand on his. Their flesh is shaded as differently as color allows. Elijah releases a sad chuckle.

"What's funny, you know, about all this, is really, I didn't do it."

Elijah pulls away. He lays a reluctant finger on the letter.

He says, "So it's second-degree murder that'll keep me alive. A twenty-year sentence. That's a hell of a thing."

Nat quickly lays out the facts. "The judge has to abide by sentencing guidelines. That means she's got to impose at least twenty. But Fentress has agreed to have the judge suspend fifteen of it."

"How much time will I serve?"

"No way of knowing what Judge Hawk will do. She's not bound to this agreement between me and Fentress. She can cut the time as much as she sees fit. With the rape charge dropped, our chances are a lot better. I'll fight like hell for you. She might let you off easier. Or she might nail you with the whole twenty. But whatever she says, you'll have to serve at least eighty-five percent of your sentence. There's no parole in Virginia until that portion of the time is done. So the least you'll do is four years and three months."

Elijah lowers his eyes. He mutters, "Four years, three months."

Nat lifts the letter from the table. He slides it into his jacket pocket.

"Elijah, listen to me. Don't fight this. I know it's not fair and it's not right. And I promise you I will not take my teeth out of this thing until you're back home with Clare. Something will come up. Take the offer. Let's see what the judge says."

Elijah stops looking into Nat's face and lowers his eyes to the bare tabletop. Elijah knows that Nat wants to give to him, to dribble hope over him, anoint him with it, but Elijah is right to look away. There is no hope in Nat's eyes, no relief, nothing beyond the unjust, life-stealing deal written on the folded paper in his pocket.

Nat takes Elijah's silence as his own, like a cushion, and sits with it for two, three minutes. Nat waits, thinking that when his visit is over, he does indeed get to go home; and this man, who should have the right to do the same, to embrace the woman and the life he loves, will not.

With the backs of his knees Elijah pushes away his chair. The screech is so loud the guard outside the door interprets the meeting is over. The door opens to more grates and rasps. No one comes in, just the door swinging open, an ominous, futuristic prison scene. Nat keeps his seat.

Nat asks, "What about Clare?"

"Leave her out of it."

"She's your wife."

"You're my lawyer."

Nat has no more words. Now it is his eyes that drop to the table.

When Elijah turns from him, Nat raises his gaze to see the man in tired orange trudge toward the open door.

"Take it," Elijah says into the room.

3

Nat and Fentress sit across from each other in Judge Imelda Hawk's anteroom. The prosecutor is poised with legs crossed. His socks are stretchy and gossamer over his ankles, his shoes have a sheen. One shoe bobs as though there is a song in the man's head. He gazes at Nat without expression beyond an unflappable smile, like he is window-shopping.

The Hawk's elderly secretary taps on her computer keyboard. The judge has left them waiting out here for five minutes and Nat is edgy. He doesn't know where to rest his eyes, he doesn't want to stare back at Fentress. His hands are laced in his lap; he taps his thumbs together until he realizes he has been drawn into fidgeting. He is upset with himself for being disconcerted like this just sitting across from the man. Fentress starts to drum his fingers on the upholstery. Nat hears the man humming.

Nat snaps, "For God's sake, sit still."

The secretary's head whips up. Fentress clucks his tongue. "Touchy, touchy." The prosecutor quiets his voice and his fingers but his veiled ankle continues to throb. His smile widens. Fentress adds, "What have you got to be nervous about? You're the man today."

Now Nat has something to say: Because I don't like sending an innocent man to jail. And I don't like keeping guilty ones out, Ed.

But the old secretary receives a beep and a muted voice and answers, "Yes, ma'am." She points at the judge's door. "You can go in now." She adds, "Gentlemen," chastening them both.

The Hawk sits behind her desk, spectacles up. Her black robe hangs on a coat tree beside her, flanked on the opposite side by an American flag. Her desk is clear save for one white sheet, the plea agreement written up and sent to her by Ed Fentress.

She lays her glasses on the desk with an impatient clack while Nat and Fentress take their seats beside each other. She shifts her eyes between the paper and the two of them, up, down, left, and right. The judge's Indian face crinkles in thought while her eyes move, her high cheekbones carve crow's wings beside her sockets.

She addresses Nat.

"So you found something after the exhumation."

"Yes, judge."

"Something good, it seems." Her eyes flit like shot arrows to Fentress. "Apparently something very good, yes, Ed?"

"Yes, ma'am."

"Good enough to make your office back off capital murder all the way down to second degree?"

"Yes, ma'am."

"I have to tell you. It doesn't make the prosecutor's office look very sharp."

Fentress remains chirpy. "No, ma'am. Win some, lose some."

The Hawk does not answer. She waits. In the silence the three of them cast quick glances at each other, Ed to the Hawk to Nat. Fentress is the only one who, after a few moments of this, snickers at the tension.

The judge says, "That's enough. Someone want to tell me what was such a blockbuster piece of evidence that a man accused of capital murder a week ago is being brought before me now to serve less than five years in jail? Either one of you, I don't care. But somebody say something before I toss the two of you and this plea agreement out of my office."

Nat turns his head to Fentress. The man keeps his face in profile, but Nat knows the prosecutor is aware of his look. This is the bargain they've struck. Ed Fentress does the talking. Nat stays quiet as long as the script gets followed.

Fentress says, "Judge, a disturbing thing occurred in my office this morning. Sheriff George Talley came to me and admitted that three years ago, during an argument with his then fourteen-year-old daughter, Amanda, he struck her with his fist, using enough force to break her jaw. At the time he kept this quiet, for obvious reasons. The daughter also cooperated and said nothing about the incident. But after the exhumation yesterday, George thought the x-rays of the girl's jaw might uncover the old injury. So he came and told me what he'd done three years ago, I guess figuring that would bring it out in the open and he might be able to say he was sorry, hoping that would be the end of it. But I became suspicious. After all, the x-rays showed that his daughter's jaw was busted three years ago in almost the exact spot it got broken the night of the fire. I asked the sheriff about this. George was initially evasive but I called upon his honor and my long-standing support of him as a friend and fellow law-enforcement officer. I informed him, in no uncertain terms, that my office would not tolerate any interference or the concealing of evidence by anyone, not even him. I also told him I was going to initiate an investigation immediately if he didn't come clean. So then George told me that, in fact, he had argued again with Amanda the night of the fire, and again he hit her pretty good. Same fist, same place on the jaw as three years ago. As soon as he left my office I called Nat. We discussed the ramifications of this revelation. Obviously, if George admits hitting Amanda Talley the night of her death, the commonwealth's case for rape against Waddell is severely hampered. Without the broken jaw, there's no evidence of force. So Nat offered to drive on down to Good Hope to work out this agreement. As you can imagine, he was pleased to make the drive."

Fentress pauses. The Hawk sucks her cheeks. Nat tastes medicine, the treacly gag of Fentress's words going down.

Nat speaks. "Ed and I have decided that it'd be best for all sides to drop the charges down to second degree. There's no evidence of premeditation in the killing, absolutely nothing to link Elijah to Amanda Talley the night of the fire. But there's also not much evidence to clear him of the arson. The girl did die in the fire. This is our best shot."

The Hawk slides on her glasses. She leaves her hand against her temple.

"George Talley hit her."

Fentress says again, "Yes, ma'am."

"And you want me to suspend fifteen years of Elijah Waddell's sentence."

Nat addresses this. "Judge, even though Elijah accepts this plea, he maintains his innocence of the arson. We're confident that sooner or later he'll be proven innocent of all charges. But the reality of his situation says he takes this deal."

This argument—known as an Alford plea—barely grazes the Hawk. To the judge, this is just another defendant swearing he didn't do it while agreeing to a guilty charge for the lesser penalty it brings. It happens a lot.

Nat continues. "And even if Elijah did burn that church, he was in an immense amount of personal pain. You know what the deacons of the Victory Baptist did to him and his wife."

"Yes I do."

"Then, judge, I think you, more than most, can understand how angry that could make a person."

Nat has taken a chance with this. Judge Hawk's red Mattaponi face, eyes black as an eclipse, go stock-still. Nat imagines this ancient face peering to the sky, the face of hunters and worshipers and judges of the earth. He appeals to that red and different face, realizing even while he thinks this that it's just another racial stereotype. The Hawk squints at him; Nat sees she does not like his oblique reference to her blood origins but she accepts it as a relevant point. She nods, and the nod says, Don't do that again.

She turns to Ed. "Are you prepared to answer for this plea arrangement? The public is going to want to know why you've backed up so far."

Fentress puckers his lips. "Judge, I never have a problem supporting the right thing to do. This is the right thing. Folks'll just have to see it that way or they won't."

She says, "All right. I'll leave it to you. We'll bring Mr. Waddell back into court this afternoon at two o'clock for sentencing and be done with it. Nat, that all right?"

"Yes, ma'am."

"One more thing. I want you to keep George Talley out of it."

Nat objects. "Judge!"

"Nat, quiet down."

"Judge, I have to insist that George Talley be investigated. It's entirely possible he burned that Baptist church himself to prevent his daughter from joining it. I have witnesses and evidence to indicate that. Talley is a devout Catholic. His daughter rejected his religion. It's my guess that's a big part of what they argued about the night of the fire. That's why she went to the Baptist church after he hit her. As far as I'm concerned he's a suspect and a damn likely one."

"Counselor, you will lower your voice and refrain from cursing in my presence. I gather what you're asking. But you curb your tongue, understand?"

Nat feels boiled beside Fentress's cool. "Yes, ma'am."

The Hawk asks, "Ed, the investigating officer on this case is Monroe Skelton, isn't it?"

"Yes, ma'am."

"Tell him I said to check out Nat's concerns without a ripple, without one scent. If I hear anything about it from anyone or I read it in the papers, you and I are going to have a set-to. Also, if any tangible evidence comes to light that George Talley burned that church, I want him charged and brought in front of me so fast his head will spin. Nat?"

He replies through tight lips, "Yes, ma'am."

"George Talley is obviously not a well man. He's got some big problems with anger and honesty, that's been made pretty clear to me. But hauling him in on child abuse charges is not going to bring his girl back or assuage his grief one bit. And I cannot charge him with arson and murder on anything you've brought me this morning—everything you've said is speculation. I will not have Talley keelhauled in the press just to suit your acute sense of justice. This is a small county, and that is no way to treat a man who has up 'til now been an effective and loyal public servant in its behalf. George Talley's not going to have much left so let's leave him that. His daughter's dead, I'm sure he already feels bad enough for that and for what he's done. You want my signature on your plea agreement? Here's what I want from you. Unless our Deputy Skelton turns up evidence that Talley burned that church himself or is involved in some other shenanigans regarding this case, you will shut that self-righteous and risky mouth of yours and allow the sheriff to complete his elected term. Ed, you and he are on the same ballot. How long is that?"

"One more year November, judge."

Nat asks, "Then what?"

The Hawk continues. "I will inform him discreetly in the next few days that he'd better not even think about running again. His days as sheriff in this county are over. I'm willing to let him out to pasture with his name intact, but if he even looks cross-eyed at me I will instruct the prosecutor's office here to bring charges of obstruction and child abuse. That'll help him decide."

Nat hears this and is not satisfied. It is not swift enough, not a nasty enough blow. It lacks spite. It is small-town cronyism. He thinks he can go out to his car, bring back his briefcase, and toss Amanda's birth control pills on the Hawk's clean desk. He can drag Hilda Bradford into court, Charles Jorgensen too. Tom Derby. Monroe. Jackie Kline. Place Talley under oath and go for his throat. He can get subpoenas. Nat thinks he can stand in the middle of this courthouse and shoot off justice and retribution like a lawn sprinkler, get everything and everybody soaking fucking wet with what they deserve.

But compromise is the bed he has made with Ed Fentress and Judge Hawk. And Elijah. And the ghosts of his own parents. And Maeve. Compromise is where he will learn to lie down.

Nat swallows.

"Yes, ma'am."

4

Somebody is tipping off the press.

Nat wades through the lights and lenses and microphones in the corridor outside the circuit court. Stepping through the courtroom doors, the camera lights click off at his back. The microphones are holstered and pads and pens come out. The reporters yelp, gallivanting into the courtroom at his side like coon dogs.

He leaves the pack of them at the bar, they cannot proceed past the swinging wooden gate. He sits at the defense table, naturally now. His briefcase wallops the tabletop. Groomed Fentress is in place. The prosecutor raises the palm of one hand, Hi, neighbor. Nat looks away to the huge county emblem on the wall behind the bench. He wonders, If it fell and rolled on its edge, would it squash Fentress? Judge Hawk makes them wait again. Nat wonders, Who is the news media's source in the courthouse? The courthouse clerk? Fentress himself? The Hawk's curmudgeonly secretary? Whoever it is, the press comes panting whenever the master—a story—beckons.

The bailiff intones the judge's introduction. Everyone stands. The Hawk enters and takes her seat. She is so short her head does not rise above the chair's back. She is framed by the chair, red face, red leather, black robe. Everyone sits. The judge says, "Bring in the defendant."

In handcuffs Elijah is escorted into the courtroom. Before he is brought to the defense table, his cuffs are removed. Nat sees the ugly brand of Talley on this, to bring the man into view in fetters, then unlock him in front of the press and the court and the public. It is a needless and shaming procedure. Nat chews on the revenge against George that is baking too slowly.

Elijah sits beside him, rubbing his wrists. His brow is sweaty, the neck of his orange tunic is wet. Nat thinks the deputies probably made him sit in the transport van out in the heat until the judge called for him. Nat looks at his client, this targeted, unlucky man.

"You okay?" Nat asks with concern.

Elijah says only, "Let's get on with it."

Nat understands. Elijah cannot be grateful.

Nat stands. "Your Honor. The prosecution and I have worked out a plea agreement." Nat holds up the page prepared that afternoon by Fentress. The Hawk motions to the bailiff. The deputy goes to the defense table. He ferries the sheet to the bench.

Judge Hawk reads the agreement as though for the first time. In the gallery, the press rustles.

"Mr. Fentress, you agree to this?"

"Yes, ma'am."

"Mr. Waddell?"

Elijah stands.

"Mr. Waddell, you understand I am not bound by this agreement. This is a plea arrangement that has been arrived at solely between the attorneys in this case. Before you enter your plea today, I want to be sure you're aware that I can hand down any penalty under the law I see fit. Do you understand, sir?"

"Yes." Nat hears the voice from the well that is within Elijah. He sees the face that is the portal of the well, dark and hollow, receiving all that is dropped in, to answer with only a faraway toll.

The Hawk pauses. She looks into Elijah's unlit face, waiting, as though waiting for the sound of the coin she has tossed in to be returned. She seems saddened the well is so deep.

After a moment she asks, "Sir, have you read this document?"

"Yes."

"Do you understand, Mr. Waddell, that you are waiving your right to trial with this agreement?"

"Yes."

"And do you understand that you are waiving your right to an appeal with this agreement?"

"Yes."

"Madam clerk." The judge reaches the page out. From her box below the bench, the old clerk grabs it and makes an entry in her log.

The Hawk knits her fingers and leans on her elbows. The courtroom is silent except for the scribbling of the press in the rows behind Nat. He thinks of scratching dogs.

The Hawk says, "Mr. Waddell. I understand that you have entered an Alford plea. This means you are accepting guilt without admitting to the arson of the Victory Baptist Church or taking responsibility for the death of Amanda Talley. It means you have accepted this plea agreement simply as a way to avoid the charge of capital murder brought against you by Mr. Fentress over there. And you are avoiding a finding or a plea of guilty in case of any civil repercussions. That makes sense. I suppose I and the people of this county will have to live with our questions."

Elijah slowly brings his face to Nat, whose eyes are waiting for him.

With the manner of an automaton, Elijah's gaze swivels back to the judge.

Elijah says, "Yes, ma'am."

The newspeople in the room scurry in their seats. Nat's stomach clenches. He hangs his head while Judge Hawk pronounces sentence.

Nat feels part of something soiled, a system that allows brutal George Talley to preserve his dignity while others, better men and women, stay mum about him, or go to jail. That lets Ed Fentress sit at the prosecution table unblemished and toothy. That robs Clare Waddell of her husband for five years. A system that makes Nat Deeds hang his head.

Judge Hawk says, "Elijah Waddell, I hereby accept your plea of guilty for the crimes of arson and second-degree murder in the death of Amanda Talley. Accordingly, under the laws of the Commonwealth of Virginia, I sentence you to twenty years in the state penitentiary, to begin immediately."

Elijah's eyes bug. He turns to Nat, panicky. Nat touches his arm. "Wait."

The judge continues. "Mr. Waddell, I have reviewed your record in this community. It's as clean as anyone's. I am also aware of the suffering you and your wife have undergone as a result of some misguided and cruel attitudes in this town. I apologize for these people. I cannot change them, much as I wish I could, just like I know you wish you could bring back Amanda Talley. But we can't do what we want most, sir. We can't make this a better world. We can only make ourselves better people in it. We can only lead by example in small ways. In our quiet homes, in our jobs, in our spirits. We can only love the ones whom God sends in our direction. Little babies. Brothers and sisters of all colors, shapes, ages, and abilities. We can only touch what's put in our hands. This community had you in its hands, Mr. Waddell, and our touch was neither gentle nor just. I admit that, for all of us. You have a right to your rage, sir. But neither you nor any man has the right to express it through mayhem. When you do that you become no better than your oppressors. You sacrifice your role as a leader for your people, and you relinquish your place as a good man in your society. Mohandas Gandhi taught us that. Martin Luther King taught us that. Your response to the deacons of the Victory Baptist was wrong, Mr. Waddell. And it went terribly beyond your expectations. So I am sorry for all of us that we have not banished this small-mindedness from our midst. I am sorry for Sheriff

George Talley's loss of a daughter. And I am sorry for you, for what you have endured and what you have done. I hereby suspend fifteen years from your sentence. Bailiff."

The judge stands. The deputy calls out, "All rise." Nat and Elijah are already on their feet. When the others in the courtroom rise, the stamp of shoes on the floorboards gives the seal of finality to the Hawk's sentence. Elijah is guilty of second-degree murder. He is going to jail. Nat has no real plan or hope for Elijah's release or exoneration. All of this crashes in on him.

Judge Imelda Hawk puts her fists into the folds of her robed hips. She speaks to the standing courtroom.

"Ladies and gentlemen of the press. When you report the results of this proceeding, please also report that my findings go beyond Mr. Waddell's guilt but to the complicity of the county of Pamunkey, the Commonwealth of Virginia, and the whole of our American culture. Please also note that although I only have the power to punish Mr. Waddell in this case, if I could, I would surely slap the taste out of the mouths of a lot more folks around here. This is said with the full knowledge that Mr. Gandhi and Mr. King would not approve. Court adjourned."

The Hawk pivots and strides from the bench. The clerk follows into her chambers. The press streams out the courtroom door, pulled by the gravity of the news, the promise of attention.

The deputy swings alongside to collect Elijah. Nat says to him, "Leave the handcuffs, okay? You don't need them. Let him just walk out of here."

The uniformed man shakes his head. "Sorry. Sheriff's orders."

The deputy begins to jangle the cuffs. Elijah submits his wrists. He cannot look up. They have bent Elijah's neck, just like he said they have to.

"Put those damn things away!" It is Ed Fentress, from his prosecutor's table. "You tell the sheriff it was me who said so. You walk that man out of here now, deputy. No cuffs."

Nat nods to Fentress. Elijah simply lowers his arms, it makes no difference to him, bound or unbound he is not free, not innocent. The deputy complies and pockets the fetters. Elijah walks off, past Fentress without looking. The deputy's hand is on his elbow.

Nat stays at the defense table while all flows away from him. Even Fentress disappears without comment. Nat is alone in the courtroom.

Now that the case is over, he feels the greatest weight, as though the hammered copper county emblem has rolled over him. It is the crush of failure. He knows he has done the best possible by Elijah; Baron was right to call in Nat, no other lawyer could have secured a better deal. Nat squared off against Fentress and Talley and buckled their knees. He appealed to Judge Hawk and won her sympathy. He's done his job. Why does he feel bereft?

He does not want to walk out the courtroom door. He does not want to be bayed at anymore by the press. He's afraid of starting over with Maeve. What if after trying, for the first time in their marriage, to be authentic with her, what if after dropping all his old pretensions, he still doesn't measure up? What if he can't let go, can't forgive, can't accept her forgiveness? He doesn't want to walk out of here, to face Elijah's wife. He doesn't want to watch Elijah begin his sentence.

Who burned the church? Who killed the girl?

Where is Nat's place of peace?

He stands. He takes his briefcase in hand. He has sat for the first time at the defense table. Departing from it, he does not know if he will ever sit here again.

Before he can reach the end of the aisle, his name is called from behind. Judge Hawk's old secretary stands in the judge's chamber door.

"Mr. Deeds," she says, giving his name an odd southern inflection, everything she says sounds like a mild, matronly rebuke, "you have a phone message."

"Thank you. From whom?"

"Pastor Tom Derby. You may call him from my desk if you wish."

Nat follows her through the door. She hands him a message sheet. He waits until she leaves him alone before he dials the number. Derby answers.

"Tom, it's Nat."

Derby says, "Hey. Sorry to bother you at court, but I didn't know how else to reach you here in town. I saw on the TV there was another hearing this afternoon about a plea agreement. Is it over?"

"Yes."

"Can I ask how it turned out?"

"The court accepted the plea. Second-degree murder. Elijah'll serve five years in jail."

Derby seems dismayed.

"That's what you said would happen. I guess I figured . . ."

"Figured what, Tom?"

"Figured you'd get him off. You always said Elijah was innocent."

"It's still arson and still a murder. You don't get off with no time on those, Tom. It's better than going to the gas chamber and being innocent."

"But . . ." Derby seems now to grapple with the fact that Elijah is in jail. "But he'll lose his job. He'll be a convicted felon when he gets out. That nonsense about raping that girl, it'll stick to him if he pleads guilty. Folks around here aren't ever going to forget that."

Nat wants to chastise Derby right here. But he holds his tongue and does not say, If you'd spoken up when you should have, there would have been no rape charge.

"It's done, Tom. Are we going to finish our talk now?"

Derby seems not to hear this.

"God knows what this'll do to Clare. How's she going to take it?"

"It's done, Tom. Unless some new evidence comes up, which I don't expect to happen, or the guy who actually burned the church gets caught and admits it, which is also not very likely, this is the end. Five years in prison. And yes, I still believe he's innocent."

"Yes. I . . ." The preacher fumbles for words. His pulpit glibness is missing. "Yes, I guess it is done."

"We need to talk, Tom. Right now. Where are you? I'm coming over."

For moments the phone is silent.

"This has all been hard on you, hasn't it, Nat. No one seems to grasp that. You've put a lot on the line for that man."

"It's my job."

"It's not your job to be ostracized in your own community. You needed to prove Elijah was innocent. You might have been able to come back home then. It would've made it easier for you."

"I don't know what I'm going to do next. I don't want to think about it. Where are you, Tom?"

"I can't talk with you, Nat. Not just yet."

"Tom. You promised me. You'd answer my questions today."

"I will, Nat. I will. I'll answer for everything tonight. I swear."

"I have your word on that."

Derby pauses.

"Yeah. You've got my word."

"All right."

"But first there's something you got to do."

"What."

"Rosy Epps is in the hospital. She's had a heart attack."

"What happened? When?"

"This morning. About two hours ago. She was at home. She managed to dial my number."

"How bad off is she?"

"Bad. I just left her. She's in cardiac intensive care. The doctor told me she must've had a bunch of smaller heart attacks over the past couple years. She either didn't notice or didn't say anything. Anyway, she's had a big one. They're keeping her on medicine to keep her blood pressure up. But her doctor says at this point it's a death watch."

"Tom, I'm sorry. I know she meant a lot to you."

"Yes, she did. She's still conscious. We had a good talk and I told her I'm sure she's on her way to walk with God."

"That's good."

"She asked me a favor. She made me say I'd get you to come see her. Soon as possible."

"She wants to see me? Why?"

"You ask her that yourself, son. She's waiting. Go right now."

"All right. I . . . all right."

Again the line is quiet. Then Derby says his name, "Nat." The man's voice is setting, dusk.

"Yes?"

"You did your best, didn't you. You did."

"I don't know."

"I do. I know you, Nat Deeds. When it comes down to it that's all you give is your best. You've been like that since we were kids. There aren't many of your type of man around. You tend to stick out. And I know the type of man that prosecutor is. He'd have hung Elijah by his thumbs if it would've furthered his own purposes. I've seen those men. Fat and pious, butter doesn't melt on their tongues. I've preached to them. I've failed to reach them. I've watched them go to Hell. But you beat him. You beat all of them."

"No I didn't."

"Yes you did, Nat. Maybe you just don't know it yet."

Nat has no answer for this. He is not in the mood to accept praise, even from sad Tom Derby. He wonders how many men Derby has tried to stop from going to Hell. Perhaps that's what Tom Derby does, stands there himself at the gates of Hell to warn others away.

Nat says, "Let me go now. Mrs. Epps is waiting on me."

"Okay. Hurry on over there."

"We'll talk later. I'll call you at home tonight."

But the line goes dead. Tom Derby is done.

# MRS. EPPS
# & TOM DERBY

# ONE

All the windows are smashed. Slivers of glass lie about the place, glistening like tears on the front porch and on the lawn. Across the clapboards, MURDERER and GUILTY are spray-painted in hurried black letters.

Monroe brakes his cruiser in the dirt road. He waits for the dust plume behind his wheels to settle before he gets out of the car. Looking over the place, he feels an old stir in his chest. It is the warrior in him. He grits his teeth to clamp it down. It's his job to stay calm, to let others flail and react. Monroe does not know if all men have this warrior inside them. But how else can you live in a world that will injure or rob or kill you, a world that doesn't even pause to clean its hands from the dirty work before it seeks out another, or comes back for one more round at you? How else can you be a man if you don't have this stir in your chest to find someone and kick the shit out of him?

He shakes his head at what he sees, this house. He thinks this is rabid, yellow-belly meanness. Gutless and stupid.

He reaches for the door handle. He makes sure he is in check, that his anger is not going to cloud his observations. He is calm, but breathless and a little scared at himself. He gets out of the car. The early evening air is moist out here in the farmland, hot and pregnant.

Kids did this. One of the farmers came up the road on horseback. He saw them and chased them off, then called the sheriff's office. It must have been a sight, him trying to round them up from the saddle. There are tennis-shoe and bicycle-tire and horseshoe tracks all around in the dust. Crushed places in the wall of corn show where the kids lit out into cover, and where the farmer galloped a bit to get a good look at them. When the farmer phoned the dispatcher he said he recognized only one of the kids. The son of the man who owns the local farm-machinery dealership, Mr. Hillenbrandt. His boy Daniel. A good boy. A fine baseball player at the junior high school.

Monroe walks around the house. Every window is broken. MURDER is sprayed on the rear wall, facing the garden. He steps up on the front porch to peer in through a busted pane. He reaches in and parts a curtain with one ginger hand, careful not to slice himself on the sharp edges. Inside, the air conditioner is still running. Rocks lie on the sofa and floor. The TV screen is shattered. Broken glass in long swords and short bits of mosaic litter the carpet.

The kids beat this house like a downed horse, with cruelty. In his mind he hears the glass break, the horse mewling, the kids egging each other on. Monroe supposes Clare Waddell is at the hospital with her grandmother, Mrs. Epps. The poor old lady had a massive heart attack. He heard the ambulance call a few hours ago on the scanner. Not long after that, the dispatcher radioed him about Elijah's guilty plea. Second-degree murder. Then ten minutes ago he got the call to come out here and see this.

Monroe walks back to his cruiser. His boots squinch on the dirt and gravel. Clare Waddell doesn't have enough on her plate right now. Her grandmother, the woman who raised her, is dying. Her husband, possibly an innocent man, is in jail for the next five years. She held her infant daughter alive for ten minutes, to die in her arms. She buried that baby, then watched the child be dug up and moved. And now this attack on her home. Monroe remembers something, a saying, that Jesus never puts more across our shoulders than we can carry. He cannot imagine then how strong Clare Waddell must be. What would be the last straw for such a woman?

He leans on the hot car hood and takes off his stiff felt hat. He hears a dog bark and looks past the house to the wall of corn. From there a small gray pooch yips at him some more, lifting its front pads off the ground with each bark, before it disappears into the stalks.

He wipes a kerchief across his brow. Those kids didn't make up their own minds to do something like this. They heard it first from their parents. Nat negotiated a deal from Fentress to keep Elijah off death row. Within minutes the news services put it out on TV and radio, they've made the case into a big deal so they have to see it through. Then, in response to the reports, the parents said what in front of their children? What did Danny Hillenbrandt hear in his nice big house in Good Hope? Elijah Waddell got off easy. Damn murderer. Guilty is what he is. He ought to get the chair for what he did. Got off easy. Did Mr. Hillenbrandt also say Elijah married a white girl? Did he say Elijah is black and that's why they went easy on him, we've all seen this kind of thing before? God will get Elijah in the end even if today the court didn't? Did he say, Somebody'll pay for this?

That's how it's done. That's how hatred survives, it gets handed down like weak chins and baldness, generation to generation.

Monroe wonders, How much of the force behind the thrown rocks was racist? How much was just plain mistrust? How much was the sick human pleasure of kicking someone when they're down? He thinks, They're all just labels for the same thing. Fear.

He tucks away his damp kerchief. He looks at the house. He's not going to write up a vandalism report on this. Why put one more article in the newspaper about this whole awful affair? Why feed it? Let it starve. Quietly, privately, Danny Hillenbrandt and friends are going to be out here before nightfall sweeping up glass. A few parents in town are going to pay for replacement windows and a new television.

Monroe decides it will be himself who comes out and repaints these walls dusky rose.

## 2

Nat Deeds is nine years old. He is running to a baseball game, carrying his glove. He has made the Little League All Star team as a third baseman. It has rained that morning, the streets sweat heat. It is still cloudy, not the brilliant sunshine he held in his imagination for his first All Star game. But in his trot the uniform rubbing when his knees pass each other is an All Star uniform, white cotton boasting red and blue letters and piping. He has a less-than-average arm from third base, he is small, but he will stop anything hit his way. He makes good contact with the bat. If he plays, he'll bat seventh or eighth. He wants to get to the field early to help the grown-ups rake the infield, grab a shovel and spread dry dirt out of a wheelbarrow around the batter's box. He wants to see the new lime lines when they are first rolled out. He will run some wind sprints by himself in the outfield. He will hold two bats at once and swing them.

Nat cuts across a vacant lot. He runs fast. But he has made a mistake. The field is muddy. He steps in a puddle, pooled in a hole he did not see beneath the weeds. Mud splashes on his white All Star pantaloons, red clay splotches smirch up to his knees. He stops. He feels the wet muck soaking all the way through the cotton to his legs, like he has peed himself. He cries.

Nat walks out of the vacant lot. He has already run more than a mile from home. The ball field is another half-mile away. To run back home, have his mom wash his pants, he will miss the field preparation, maybe even All Star team warm-ups. And he will have to put the pants on damp, his mom does not have an electric dryer, just a Westinghouse wringer. The coaches will wonder where he is. If he is late they will not let him play. But he was all in white before. He was ready, clean. He was going to be there early. He was going to help.

He stands in the street. He does not know which way to turn and run, home or to the field. He looks down at himself. When he dips his head a tear lands on his left Converse sneaker, leaving a little crater in the mud caked there.

"Nathaniel Deeds?" The voice issues from the house straight

across from the vacant lot. He is standing in front of Mrs. Epps's house. She was his teacher last year, in third grade. She is standing on her brick steps with her hands on her hips. She is very pretty.

"Nathaniel, what have you done to yourself? Come over here."

Nat wants to mutter, but Mrs. Epps would not hear him. He says, "I stepped in the mud."

"I can see that. Come over here and let's have a look at you."

He drags his feet over the road to her sidewalk. His right tennis shoe leaves a clay slime trail for the first few steps. Mrs. Epps walks to meet him. She clucks her tongue at the mess he is.

"That is a beautiful uniform," she says. "I didn't know you were an All Star."

"Yes, ma'am."

"Well, I'm not surprised."

Nat keeps his head ducked, tears on a boy's face are heavy, heavy stones.

He says, looking into his glove, "I have to go."

"Go where?"

"I don't know. Home."

"Why? Because you stepped in the mud? Nat, you're going off to play in a baseball game. You're going to get muddy anyway. Just go ahead on to the field. No one will care."

Nat cannot believe that. No one will care. How can that be? Why are the uniforms white, then? He is an All Star. He will stop anything hit his way. You have to care about that.

"Yes, ma'am."

Nat turns, sluggish.

She says at his back, "How long 'til you have to be there?"

He stops. She was his teacher. She knows stuff. She is the most grown-up.

"I don't know. Soon."

She laughs. "Nat Deeds."

"Yes, ma'am."

"Come inside, all right? We'll fix up that uniform. I've got a washer and a brand-new electric drying machine. You give me fifteen, twenty minutes. You'll be a perfect All Star, I promise. Come in."

She walks him around to her backyard, to the kitchen door. He follows her inside and tromps mud on her linoleum. She says nothing about it. She puts a shower towel for him on the kitchen table, then turns her back while he pulls off his pants and socks. She puts him in a kitchen chair of padding and chrome and sets her machines to whirring work, turning dials, hovering over them, getting them to work fast. She makes him talk about baseball and the All Star team. She gets him to tell about Superman and Batman and Flash and Green Lantern. He turns down cake and milk. He keeps the towel pulled high around his underpants.

In twenty-five minutes his pants and socks are bright bleached white. Putting them on—he has never before had his clothes dried by an electric tumble dryer—is like donning the fur of a cat, the cotton is warm and fluffy, only the slightest hint of moistness. Nat is renewed, freshly minted. Mrs. Epps says she will come to watch the game later. She puts him in her car and drives him the last half-mile to the field. The men are just now shoveling about dry dirt from the wheelbarrow. The All Star head coach is pouring a bag of lime into the line machine. No other players are around. Nat leaps from Mrs. Epps's car, forgetting his glove, and skids, turning back for it. She waves, says, Good luck, and drives off.

Nat will not love her. His friend Tom Derby loves her.

3

Nat halts in the hall outside her room. Gauzy sounds flush through the ward; intercom voices no louder than necessary, peeps of phones, rattled trays on chrome carts, rubber soles squeegeeing across the very waxed floor. Nat stands in the wash of muted noise and girds himself before touching her door. Death is inside. The adversary come. He takes this moment seriously, this pause.

He draws a breath and holds it so he will not gasp no matter what he sees. He pushes on the door. Inside, the drapes are drawn. Late sunshine trickles around the edges of the curtains' folds, glimming only the close floor and ceiling. No lamp is on. There is an empty-house feeling, where only the machines are at work. The room resides in a hospital gloaming; green electric fireflies dance on a screen, clicking crickets sing some secrets to a computer somewhere, there is an end in sight.

The room is not empty. She is in the bed with the top half of the mattress slightly elevated. The bed rails are up, like a crib. Nat releases the breath with his words. "Hi, Mrs. Epps." It was a full breath and he sounds sighful. "How are you?"

The question is answered before she parts her lips to him. She is the gray of ash. Her heart has stopped fully feeding her body and her flesh constricts from the hunger. She is shrunken within her skin, it lies on her in old folds and a million ripply wrinkles. Nat is afraid to touch her, she may flake or break like the frail rod of ash that hangs from a burning cigarette.

"Nathaniel Deeds." Mrs. Epps bats her eyes. She seems too weak to smile. His name is mangled in her pronunciation. Her mouth is all gums. Her jaw muscles have contracted so much she cannot get her false teeth in. The choppers are on the bedside table, bizarre and separate. Tubes lead to and from her nostrils and arms, wires emit from her chest, she is a reclining, exhausted marionette.

"Thank you for coming." Her once commanding voice is reduced to an apologetic rasp. She does not extend her hand but levitates it a shaky inch above the sheet. Nat moves forward beside the bed and slides his hand beneath hers. She relaxes into his palm. Her hand is feather light, as though the soul in her has already begun to lift.

"Mrs. Epps. I'm so sorry you're sick."

"Not sick," she says. She wants to say more, to utter what she is, but it is plain so she lets that be.

Nat nods. Her hair is disheveled, brittle, and frosty as the pillowcase.

"Tom Derby told me you were here. I came as soon as I could."

"Were you in court?"

"Yes, ma'am."

"For Elijah?"

"Yes, ma'am."

"Tell me what's happening."

"This afternoon we entered a guilty plea for second-degree murder. The circuit court judge accepted it."

"Will he go to jail?"

"The least he'll serve is five years."

The bones of Mrs. Epps's face—her sockets, the hinge of her jaw, the bone hole where the nose grows—all extrude as though nothing more than a thin plaster of flesh has been dabbed over her frame. It is uncanny that she is alive inside this veneer. Why? he wonders. Let go, Mrs. Epps.

"It's not right," she says. Her eyes are the only things fully living. She's in there, Nat thinks, she's looking out. Her blue eyes dart with speed and acuity, troubled at the news Nat brings. She says again, "Not right."

"Mrs. Epps, it was the only thing we could do for now. It was the best alternative. Believe me. He couldn't go to trial."

"Clare."

"Yes, ma'am. Is she here at the hospital? You want me to go get her?"

"No. Was here. I sent her home right before you came."

"Shouldn't she be with you? She's your family, Mrs. Epps."

"I know. She wanted to stay longer. Talk. But," the woman shakes her head, "enough."

"I understand."

"Nathaniel Deeds?"

"Yes, ma'am."

"You my lawyer?"

"If that's what you need me to do. Yes, ma'am, I'll be your lawyer."

"Put me next to Charley."

"I'm sure he'll be happy to have you near him."

"Not too much talking. Don't let them carry on."

Nat smiles. He puts gentle pressure around her hand. "I'll ask them to keep it down. But it'll be tough. There's a lot of folks going to miss you."

"Pshaw."

"Yes, ma'am."

"Clare."

"Yes, ma'am."

"I figure half to her. Half to the church for rebuilding. Don't have a lot. Check the bank. Sell the house."

"All right."

"You think that's okay?"

"As long as you feel you've taken care of Clare, I'm sure that'll be fine. The church will be glad for the generosity."

"Thomas."

"Yes, ma'am."

No need to tell her, Nat thinks. No need at all.

"He's your friend."

"An old friend. He's always been very fond of you, I know, Mrs. Epps."

She repeats, "Thomas." No shudder in her caved chest presages the tear. She is motionless. Her eyes redden instantly, like time-lapse photography of a blooming rose. She seems to gaze far past Nat. He looks with her, just for the moment, to the pretty days, to the long ago. The salted drop sluices into a furrow of her cheek.

After a moment she says, "Promise me."

"What, Mrs. Epps."

"Promise you'll help Elijah."

"I am. I will."

"You prove it, Nat. You show them."

"If I can, I will."

"That's my request."

Nat says, "Yes, ma'am."

He has not noticed while they spoke but the old woman has tensed herself. Her head and shoulders are raised from the pillow, the tendons in her neck protrude. He lays a touch on her collarbone to ease her back down. He heeds what returns from his hand, the shock of how decrepit her body feels.

"I made a mistake," she says. "I . . . I could have stopped it."

"Don't, Mrs. Epps."

"They listen to me."

"Yes, ma'am, they do."

"What we did. It was . . ."

"You ought to rest, Mrs. Epps."

"It was wrong. Selfish." Her eyes are fixed on Nat, not as if she looks into him but onto him, like a movie screen. Hers are wide, blue pupils set in clear young whites. Nat holds himself very still, feeling images on his skin. He will bear her disgrace for her to look at.

He quietly says, "Yes, ma'am. It was wrong."

She says, "I raised my hand."

She nods, decisive.

"Selfish."

That is final. It is the teacher's judgment on herself. Homework for her next life.

Nat sits longer with Mrs. Epps, though there is no more talk. He leaves when she is asleep, her hand weighty again in his, but it is just the weight of flesh. He slips his palm out of hers and with a final look at the old woman opens the door to the hall and leaves Mrs. Epps behind.

## 4

Thomas Derby awakes and says, "Yes."

It is as though he has gone somewhere during his nap, to a place of peace and dreams the way computers go somewhere instantly to figure something out, then they come back and report yes or no. Life is all binary anyway, yes or no.

Derby says, "Yes, okay," and sits up in bed.

The sun is down. It's after ten o'clock. He has slept more than three hours. He is groggy, but decisive and euphoric.

He sits on the edge of the mattress in stocking feet. He stands woozily. Some of the teeter in his legs is from the long nap, the discombobulation of waking so late in the evening. Also his head roves a bit from the wane of whiskey in his system. He pads to the kitchen. The glass and bottle are where he left them. He is alone, so of course they are still there, sentinels. Only God could have moved them, and God did not.

Thomas Derby pours another, neat. He starts to tilt the glass straight up, to drain it, but stops himself. He parts his lips only a little, not to mouth the whiskey but to kiss it. He allows it to coat his tongue, mop away the nap and the sway in his legs. He lets the whiskey enter him the way the spirit first entered him, with fire and clarity. He thinks of the way the spirit faded in him, like the whiskey, during a nap, a long time dark.

He can no longer drink in the spirit and renew it the way he can the whiskey. That's what has made up his mind at last. He knows for certain the whiskey is stronger than God in him because he comes back to it more often and it answers him always, warms him, and keeps all the promises to him, while God makes Thomas Derby wait and wonder. Derby simply finds the liquor easier to swallow.

He sets the glass on the counter. There is more whiskey left in the bottle, but he leaves it sit. Like life, there can be enough.

Derby walks back to the bedroom. He looks down at his stocking feet, left-right they go, and for a moment he becomes nostalgic for his feet. They are so far away from his head, he is tall, and he wonders if he has been kind enough to them. His head and chest and hips and hands have had all the fun, eaten and laughed and enjoyed what tenderness there was. His feet have done the thankless work, carried him from town to town, failure to failure. In the next moment, because of that thought, he blames his feet for not taking him better places. He grunts a whiskey noise and looks up from them. Whatever, he thinks to his feet. You might be blameless, none of this may be your fault, but you're coming with me nonetheless.

In the bedroom he slides aside the hollow-core closet door. He hoists a pair of blue jeans off a hook and slides them on. The socks over his feet slide cleanly into the denim legs and Derby thinks, Thank you for not resisting, feet, I'm sorry I got upset with you. I'm sorry you got tangled up with a fellow like me.

Before he pulls taut his belt he slips off the white T-shirt in which he slept. He folds the shirt and lays it in the proper dresser drawer. From the same drawer he removes another T-shirt, this one black, with long sleeves. It has been washed recently and is soft. It smells like the fresh air of a better world. He pulls the shirt over his head

and arms and tucks it in. Last, he picks from the closet floor a pair of
black bull-hide boots he bought years ago on a swing through Texas.
He smiles So long to his feet. Because he is in a chair and bent over
to put on the boots, he is close to his feet. He gives their toes a kind
rub as if they were ten tiny heads of children before he shoves the
whole shebang of them into the cloister of the old leather.

Before he leaves the bedroom, he grabs two belts from the closet
hook. With the belts swinging from his fist like dead snakes, dragging
their tails, he walks down the hall to the living room.

His boot heels walking over the pine floor are not sympathetic,
not the way his socks were. The boots make a sound like a drum ca-
dence, something somber and military. Derby pulls himself erect because of it. He droops the belts over the back of a breakfast table
chair.

From a drawer in the kitchen he removes a legal pad and an ink
pen. He does not sit at the Formica table or go into the living room
to sit on the sofa and write on the coffee table. He sets the legal pad
on the kitchen counter. He stands before it. He likes the solidness of
the boots under his soles. He has traveled many a mile good and ill
on these now steady legs. He has preached thousands of sermons
standing like this. He likes being tall, up above the heads. He always
wanted to be even taller, like a mountain, lofty. Mountaintops are
some of God's favorite sites for miracles.

He touches the point of the pen to the paper. He knows that once
he begins and finishes the letter he will be without purpose. It's time
for his last thoughts. What are they?

Derby is sorry. Sorry to learn that his very last thoughts are not of
God. Instead, unavoidably, his mind lays out before him a banquet of
women and drink. A life smorgasbord. He will miss women and
drink. But his appetites are what gave his time meaning, they were
the moments when his light shone brightest. A woman's trilling voice
in orgasm, a woman's tongue seen through the round glass of a tum-
bler, a woman's teeth in a smile of wonderment at Derby's wit. Not
the faces of congregations that would not embrace him, not the people and churches who released him time and again, no, not them,
kindly and good though they might have been, not them for Thomas

Derby but the demons. The demons who never did let loose of him. Thomas Derby owes them for their loyalty. And now, on the precipice, they are loyal again.

Women and whiskey. Derby thinks, I am not a good man. I'm just plain flesh and blood. He wonders if God can even make a good man out of plain flesh and blood. Or must God work with other, sturdier materials for his good men and women? Must he create them out of a searing passion and a singular death, like Jesus Christ? Or colossal faith like Moses and Joan of Arc? Or unthinkable pain like Job? These terrible things transform the flesh into holiness, blood into history. Who can measure up to these standards, who can suffer such transformation? Who would sacrifice like that today to become one of God's good folk? Who goes to Heaven nowadays? Anyone, maybe one or two per generation? Look around. Look at the people who think they've got their ticket punched, who take that title of goodness and bear it as though goodness were a name you can adopt down at the courthouse. Look at what they do—believing that because they simply say they are good and because they congregate with others who say the same about themselves, what they do is therefore good, like their acts are their following sheep. But you cannot name yourself in that fashion. Only the Father names you. No one wanted to be godly more than me, Derby thinks, no one wanted the brand more. But in the end I could not stand to suffer enough, I could not tolerate sufficient sacrifice. In the end all I had to give was what I was given, my flesh and my blood, and they were tainted from the beginning, weakness was planted in my dust. I could not uproot the demons seeded in my flesh. I just could not prune the hankerings in my blood. So I have grown wild, weedy, away from God. And what I want to know is: Who doesn't?

On the pad, Thomas Derby writes:

*I know I do not possess the courage to do this alive. Forgive me for that because I've always been a coward. Before you judge me, ask if you would have had the courage yourself.*

*This is the truth of what happened. I take responsibility for all of it. Blame me and only me.*

*Before the night of the fire at the Victory Baptist Church,*
*Amanda Talley came to see me. She'd been coming to see me like*
*that since the beginning of summer. I picked her up about three*
*o'clock at a spot we decided on and drove out of town. I first met*
*her back in June, when she came for services. She wanted to learn*
*more about the Baptists. She liked our songs and the simplicity of*
*our praise. She liked the old building and cemetery. She thought it*
*was quieter out here on our little country road, where once in a*
*while a bird flies in the open doors of the church while we're*
*praying. Amanda had a grand spirit in her that was held down. I*
*won't say it was by her father or her other church. She was young*
*and searching for answers, the way the young do. But in Amanda it*
*made her quiet, like somebody poring through books in a library.*
*I'll just say she was more lovely and spiritual than any of you*
*learned. More's the pity.*

*On many occasions we talked about the Lord. She'd call and*
*ask to see me and I'd go get her. As so many are, she was troubled*
*about her path toward God. I wanted to help her get on it. It wasn't*
*long before we became intimate. We would drink alcohol together. I*
*told her I cared for her deeply—I ask you to believe that I did. But*
*I was sorry, we had to be a secret. Sweet girl, innocent girl, she was*
*agreeable to that. So we were each other's secret.*

*Late on the afternoon of the fire, I dropped Amanda off. As we*
*had done on other times together, we'd made love and we'd shared*
*some whiskey. Maybe she drank too much, because of what*
*happened afterward with her father when she got home. Anyway,*
*she must have run out of her house to the Victory Baptist. I assume*
*she came to see me. I reckon she came by the parsonage first but I*
*was out in Williamsburg drinking. So she went in the unlocked*
*church and sat down to wait 'til maybe I got home later, or I came*
*in the church the next morning and found her waiting. Either way,*
*she was in the church when I burned it. I didn't know.*

*Why did I burn the Victory Baptist? Why would a pastor burn*
*down his own house of worship?*

*The Victory Baptist was rotten. Its foundation was never solid,*

*not from two hundred years ago. How could they deny peace to
that little mixed-race baby? How could they say to my face that
such an un-Christian thing as racism is an old and valued
tradition? The Victory Baptist needed to be cauterized. That may
sound crazy but it's not. I wasn't crazy when I did it. I believed
then and I do now the Victory Baptist needed to be wounded so
deeply it would have no choice but to heal in a new form.*

*Who else to do such a thing but the pastor?*

*But I needed to stay their pastor if they were going to heal. I
knew this. I was scared to my bones I was going to be sent packing
again. When the deacons voted 13–0 over my objections to exhume
Nora Carol, I realized I'd lost them. They were no longer my flock.
Even poor Rosy Epps, having to turn against her own kin just to
stay in the good graces of her church community, then dying with
that stain unwashed. When Rosy's hand went up that night at the
deacons' meeting, I knew she could no longer protect me. And I
couldn't bear to think of leaving again, this time losing my
hometown. Where can a man go next when his own birthplace closes
its doors to him? How could I lead them? How could they heal?*

*I sat in Williamsburg drinking, pondering all this. I decided on
two things. One, to stop seeing Amanda. I realized my congregation
and I needed each other more than Amanda and I could ever mean
to each other. Second, I figured a church which has just been
burned is not going to be hiring a new pastor too quickly. The crisis
would give me a second chance. So I drove back to Good Hope.
With kerosene and a match I made the crisis.*

*I took the second chance and it worked. I was right.*

*As soon as the flames were out, the young folk of the church
stepped forward. Under pressure from them, the old guard of
deacons has been disbanded. Elections have been called for to bring
new blood and fresh energy to the church. And I'm at the center of
it all. This moment—my last, as it turns out—just over a week after
the fire, I'm needed more than at any other church in my life!
Check the church rebuilding fund. Look at the enthusiasm for
renewal. Please, folks, keep working to bring the Victory Baptist*

*alive again. But this time, imbue it with respect and charity. Make it a wonderful and important place for the next two hundred years. For everyone.*

*I came home that night from Williamsburg. After more alcohol I walked up to the church and burned it down and she was inside. I guess Elijah saw me from across the street but didn't recognize me because I had taken pains to disguise myself. Once the fire was going I ran home. You know the rest.*

*Today, Elijah Waddell pleaded guilty to a crime he did not commit. He has accepted the ruin which is rightfully mine. I cannot allow that. I must undo it. But as I stated at the outset I cannot step forward alive to do this. I plied Amanda with alcohol and talk of God, I pulled her away from her father's faith. I stood pat while an innocent, grieving man was taken from his home and wife. I waited to see if he might be set free and I might get away with all this. No more.*

*I know the sentence you will give me for my sins will be too great and I cannot face it. It's not the jail time. That I could stand. I just cannot tolerate the thought of more life. I cannot carry my tarnished, splintered cross any farther. And I cannot bear the thought of being exiled from my birthplace.*

*Today I do this one good thing. I admit my guilt and I free Elijah Waddell. But I choose to be judged by God, not by man. The justice He will give me will be what I most deserve.*

*I do not know what lies ahead of me, for I intend to die unforgiven and without honor. This is not such an easy thing to do. I guess I'd best get to it.*

*Whoever finds this letter, please be sure that lawyer Nat Deeds gets to see it fast.*

*Sorry doesn't do it, I know. But folks, I'm dreadfully sorry.*

*Thomas Derby*

Derby sets down the pen. The whiskey bottle and glass flank the scribbled pad on the kitchen counter. He thinks to empty the bottle down his throat to ease what he has to do but decides the quarter-full flask should be left alone as some sort of atonement, a final restraint.

He slides the pages into an envelope and licks it shut. He takes the belts off the chair. Carrying them in one hand, the kitchen chair in the other, Derby steps out through the back door. Behind him, inside the house, his phone rings. It's Nat, he thinks. Derby has kept his word. He has answered all Nat's questions.

He sets the chair beneath a fat branch of the old pine tree in the yard of the parsonage. He smells the sweating sap. The night's humidity touches him, it has a physical presence against his skin as though in the darkness under the pine there are souls nearby crowding him. He thinks to the disembodied, to the ineffable, Wait a minute.

Derby stands on the chair to toss one of the belts over the branch. When it has wrapped over, he ties a simple knot around the branch. He figures the thick black leather won't slip. The silver buckle of the belt dangles near his face. He runs the second belt through its own buckle to make a loop, then attaches the holes of this belt to the hanging buckle. The second buckle and belt make a slipknot. He has to go up on tiptoe to slide his head through the noose. His boots rock precariously on the chair.

Derby asks himself if he has regrets. He does. He asks if he is drunk. He is not.

They will find him in the morning, he thinks. At sunup.

He looks down at the dark grass. He's lived on God's earth for forty-three years, and he's ascended no closer to God than the height of a chair.

He lifts his head. The leather under his chin feels like the strap of a big, big hat.

Thomas Derby leaps high. Closer.

Derby falls.

CLARE & ELIJAH

# ONE

1

**N**at has not slept well. It's early when the phone rings, just after six-thirty. The bell nudges him out of a depth, that desperate sleep the body sinks into when there is only an hour of rest left after a pitching night. The sleep slips off him reluctantly, leaving him melancholy.

Monroe apologizes for the time of the call. He tells Nat to sit up and listen. Nat does not move. Monroe says into the phone, I'm not kidding. Nat puts his feet on the carpet.

Monroe says the case has solved itself. And Nat is not going to like it.

At eight o'clock Nat sits in a booth of West Redd's restaurant on Main Street. He recalls the shock of Monroe's report earlier that morning, but one cannot just remember shock, one relives it, so his hands shake holding the suicide letter. Across from him Monroe sips coffee.

This proof of Elijah's innocence is so costly. Nat can barely make himself think of the letter as evidence. Like scalding water poured into cold, he feels both at the same time, opposites at once. Tom, he thinks, Tom. He wonders what he could have done to help his friend, to have stopped this from happening, but he knows at the same moment the answer is nothing, just as Derby says, nothing could have been done by any man, only God, and God did not save Thomas Derby.

Derby was waiting, to see if Nat would get Elijah off. But he didn't know the weight of circumstance against Elijah that would lead to a plea deal and an admission of guilt. He didn't know Rosy Epps would die begging somehow for Elijah to be exonerated. He didn't know children would stone Clare's house. He didn't calculate how frail he would prove in the end.

Tom.

Nat asks the deputy, "Who else has seen this letter?"

"No one. I called you first. Like he asks."

"Thanks, Money." Nat slides the page across the table to Monroe. He must let it go for now, it belongs to the investigation. When he pulls his fingertips from the edge of the yellow legal-pad sheets, he wants instantly to grab them back to him, to fold them and hide them away and beg Monroe to let Elijah Waddell serve this pitiful man's punishment instead. It is a wrong, ugly impulse. Nat shoves the letter quickly at Monroe to skid it away from him.

Tom Derby, suspended in the sharp slant of daybreak. Without honor. Without forgiveness. Found above a kicked-over kitchen chair, the chair on its back as though it fainted from the sight. Monroe got a call at home from the dispatcher, who got a call from Mr. Snead; the custodian discovered the pastor at first light. Monroe drove out there fast. He woke up the funeral-home owner, then called Nat. Monroe put up police tape all around the parsonage and directed traffic on the road to keep everyone moving, no one was allowed to gawk or get out of his car, until Derby could be taken off in the hearse and another deputy could arrive to secure the grounds and the house. Monroe even shooed off Mr. Snead, who felt he should be allowed to stay because he found the body and he's the one responsible for the upkeep of the parsonage property. Monroe asked the little man if he'd like to make that argument on the way to the lockup. Derby is resting at the funeral home. Nat will see to it that Derby is buried here in Good Hope. If the Victory Baptist won't take him, as well they might not, someone will. Nat will not let their hometown turn him away. This is one fear of Tom's that Nat will ease.

Monroe rises with the letter. Nat says, Go ahead, he'll take care of the coffees. Monroe says, Thank you.

Nat says, "I guess now you can put those pills back in Talley's desk."

Monroe laughs a little. Nat is reminded that laughter is here in the world. That is why we shouldn't want to leave. He wants to talk to Maeve. He needs to see her face and remember also that love is here.

Monroe says, "I already told him I took them."

"What'd he do?"

"Said he'd fire me. I said, Go ahead, George. I'll be at my desk. But he's not gonna fire me. Then he'd have to explain why. And I might have some talking of my own to do. So me and George understand each other right now."

The big man turns away for the door. Nat watches his back and jutting rump head out of the restaurant, sees him pull down the brim of his deputy's hat, making his way up the sidewalk to show the suicide note to Talley and Fentress.

Alone, Nat props his elbow on the table. His hand rises to his brow. He shuts his eyes; behind his lids he sees Tom. Tom without anything, without a breeze to move him, with weasly Mr. Snead the one to happen on him, Tom Derby forfeiting everything.

For what?

To save Elijah.

Nat groans audibly into his hand, for Derby may have failed again.

## 2

Outside the courthouse at nine o'clock there is only one reporter, Sam Worth. He's sort of old-fashioned–looking, with a tilted fedora on his head and a rumpled cotton suit, kind of tropical. He has a small ring-bound notebook and a pen in his hands. He waits for Nat on the steps. Nat stops in front of him.

Nat asks, "How do you do this, Sam? It just happened."

"Police scanner. Twenty-four/seven."

Nat begrudgingly admires that.

The reporter says, "I already been out to the church and the funeral home. I already called you at home and your office. Two plus two equals four. I figured you're here." The man tips the end of his pen at Nat. "Bingo."

This is how Thomas Derby will really die, Nat thinks. This man and his ilk. They'll be the ones to choke Derby, not the belts; they will bury him, not old Omohundro. Their words will send him off, not the tender speech from some other man of God, and they will raise a chorus against Derby. He will not be the tortured and isolated man he was. He will be sordid and public.

Nat says, "I've got nothing for you."

Sam Worth writes anyway. What could he write?

He asks, "What did the preacher's suicide have to do with the Waddell case?"

Nat does not turn away. He is incredulous.

"I said I have nothing for you."

"Then why're you here? The only case you handle in Pamunkey County is Elijah Waddell. You're here for a reason, Mr. Deeds." The reporter puts on a winning smile, but it is as worn as his suit. Nat thinks of the man as a pickpocket and walks on. The reporter calls after him, "I'll get the story."

Nat thinks he never will, no one will, no one can fathom the story of Thomas Derby.

Fentress is already in the anteroom of the Hawk's chambers. This time the old secretary waves them in immediately. The two men almost jam shoulders passing through the doorway. Nat lets Fentress slide in first. Quickly they sit. The judge has the yellow pages in her hands.

"This is tragic," she says, not so much to the attorneys but to her own spirits, to let them know she is moved. "This is . . ."

Fentress says, "Judge."

"Quiet."

Nat watches her eyes. She starts at the top of the first page, reading it again.

When she has finished the letter she turns her gaze to Fentress. "All right, Ed." Because this is a hearing, the prosecutor goes first.

Fentress looks scrubbed. Before he begins he jingles his Rolex watch into place with a shake of his wrist.

"Your Honor, as disturbing as this letter is, it's clearly inadmissible hearsay. Now wait, before you jump down my throat, let me admit two things. I agree that this points very strongly away from Elijah Waddell. It all adds up, it makes sense with what we know about George Talley and the facts of the fire itself. And I personally do not want to keep an innocent man in jail any more than Nat or you do. That being said, let me repeat that I object to this writing as a classic piece of hearsay. It's an out-of-court statement made by someone who will not be available to the court for examination. There's neither corroboration nor witnesses."

Nat jumps in. "Your Honor, it's a deathbed confession. There's plenty of case law accepting this sort of evidence."

Fentress says, "Not suicide notes, judge. Oral confessions, yes, because there was always a witness to the statement who could come into court and testify."

"There's no contest that this was written by Thomas Derby. It's obviously his confession. There's no need for a witness."

The prosecutor says, "You can't admit this note, judge. You know you can't." He brings his eyes to Nat for the first time since they sat down this morning. "You know she can't."

Nat engages Fentress's eyes as if he could wrestle them with his own. "It's not right," he says. "You know it's not right. Why the fuck doesn't that matter to you?"

"That's enough," the Hawk says. Her voice is calm, she is not holding Nat at fault for that outburst.

She continues. "Nat, I want to let Elijah Waddell go. I believe Ed does too. But the prosecutor here has a job to do and, to be honest with you, it looks to me like he's doing it. If I agree that this suicide note is admissible and release your client, what do I do if tomorrow the opposite happens, what if someone hangs themself in town and leaves a note that says I can't live with what I saw, I saw Elijah Waddell rape that girl and burn that church. Is that admissible too? It's not, for the same reason this isn't. If I let Elijah out based on this letter, the prosecutor's office will appeal and they'll win. You're a good enough lawyer to know that."

"Judge, Elijah's innocent."

"I suspect he is. And I will unlock his cell the first moment the law says I can. But if I do it today based on this letter I'm doing you and the people of Pamunkey County no favor. The law's the law, Nat. I've got to hold against you. I'm sorry."

Judge Hawk folds her hands on her desk. Nat looks from her to Fentress. The prosecutor and the judge look at Nat the same way, flatly, satisfied without smugness that they have all done their jobs here this morning. But Nat feels things in the air around them, the air like catacombs, Tom Derby and Rosy Epps and Amanda Talley and Elijah's hands wrapped around bars and weeping brave Clare and a lost baby. There is nothing more he can do, nothing he can resurrect, he is not God.

He says, "Judge, I'd like you to seal this letter. There's no reason for it to be put into the record."

The Hawk asks, "Nat, are you Pastor Derby's lawyer?"

"Yes, ma'am. I guess I am."

She says, "All right. I'll keep this quiet at your request. In addition, I'm imposing a gag order on the two of you and the sheriff's office. We don't need another local uprising in the opposite direction screaming how we ought to free Waddell. So let's keep this to ourselves, gentlemen. Ed, you will so inform the sheriff and his staff. I advise you both to take me seriously as always on this. You understand?"

The two men rise in tandem and say, "Yes, ma'am."

Outside in the heat the reporter is gone. Nat adds the missing newsman to the catacombs, there is plenty of room, the wrinkled reporter and his powers and his invisible partners are all part of the swirling, moody air.

Nat will not tell Elijah of the letter, though the gag order does not extend to his client. He wants to see Maeve but she is working at the hospital and he would only interrupt her, he couldn't see her for as long as he needs right now. He does not want to head back to Richmond, to do what? Sit in his office and take calls, dispense advice?

He has only one place to go, like a chess king in check. He drives to the funeral home to say goodbye, and perhaps more; for if God is anywhere listening this morning, He is beside Tom Derby.

# TWO

## 1

**N**at and Maeve make love. Nat brings to the bed a besieged heart. In his old house, he latches himself into the accustomed brand of darkness of their bedroom. Little things like that, long missed by him; the squeak of the frame, the way Maeve tosses her nightshirt on the floor, he knows where the switch is on the lamp, all these are like snaps on a jacket, he buttons himself in. Still, he is furtive and unsure in his approach to her, like a man for whom others are looking in the streets, some sort of fugitive, and she might turn him out. He is too complimentary, too sweet, too relieved to be here. He communicates in his lovemaking that he is glad to be back. He murmurs to her of his gladness. Maeve lies beneath his whispers, she seems sad even in her peaking. Somewhere in the movements and breathing, somehow like a barging knock on the bedroom door Nat thinks of Elijah in his green cell tonight and Clare in her wrecked home tonight, and Maeve's fine skin for a moment becomes for him sandy and rough. He is no more innocent than Elijah, why should he be with his own wife and Elijah denied? This thought spooks his mind to fly off even further from the heaving platform of the woman under him and he thinks of Derby too, why should handsome Derby be so abandoned? And young Nora Carol and Amanda, both so young forever? Why has God been so remote for them all, and for Nat himself? Nat has no answers, and he thinks he may feel what Tom Derby must have felt, alone with the questions. When Maeve is done Nat lifts his chest from hers though they remain attached. She says to him, "I love you." She has clasped her hands above her head, framing her eyes, dark with a wet spectrum in them like oil, her two white armpits are like cups of cream. Her breathing is quick, and through it he quietly says, "I love you too," and no more. Nat understands that a mistake has been made, that forgiveness for either of them is not so easily purchased.

In the morning they dress for the service, Maeve in black, Nat in dark blue. Daylight in the kitchen is better for them than the dimness of last night's bedroom. They slip around each other preparing coffee and eggs, reading the Sunday paper, they move now better than they did in sex and the feel is of a couple. Still they do not talk much.

Nat rolls down his window on the drive to the church. He puts his left elbow on the open sill and uses that hand to steer. The other hand stays in Maeve's. Her fingertips grace the back of his hand in her lap. Her leg under the dress is cool beneath his palm. The air is soft, not so packed with heat and moisture. Nat thinks some fever has broken in the world this morning. There has been loss, but maybe there is an end and the losses will not grow.

There is no trace of the Victory Baptist. Where the church stood is now a broad bare spot of bulldozed clay. The scorched grasstops have been cut away by Mr. Snead. The charred branches of close trees have been snipped and mulched. Cars park everywhere, even in the clay on top of the church site. The dirt is dry and braking cars kick red dust into the air. But the breeze blows away from the cemetery this morning so the gathering mourners are not affected.

Again the funeral colors are gay, speckled with bits of black. A turquoise tent is set up over the grave. Mrs. Epps liked frippery and inside her shining box she approves, Nat thinks. He wishes he and

Maeve were not so dourly dressed, he thinks the others knew her better and so wore their finest and brightest. She was fine and bright herself, and how could Nat forget? He does not even have flowers to give her. Arrangements are heaped under the blue tent, the area around the grave looks like a winner's circle. He feels Maeve's hand in his and feels also his other, empty hand, which could have brought her something, but he has been thinking a lot about himself lately. Perhaps he will stop doing that.

Mr. Omohundro slouches under a tree in his overalls, making no attempt to stay out of sight or be respectful by standing straight and close-by. He has the franchise, Nat thinks, he is Death, his shovel is the final scythe. Nat wants to chase Omohundro away, throw things at him, blame him. The old man inhales a cigarette, the little smoking death thing is as white and thin as his fingers. Nat looks away, figuring Death is everywhere, you can't chase him off.

The turnout is not as large as Amanda Talley's. But there is something happier here for Rosy than there was for the poor girl. The folks milling about greet each other with hugs and arms linked. Nat is acknowledged, no one slides away or avoids his eyes this time. There is some contrition in the older faces, as though Rosy Epps has taught these people one last lesson. The young ones nod and smile at him and Maeve. These young Baptists are the inheritors of this day; the bulldozed church will arise in their image, the greatest of the deacon dowagers has entered her reward, and they can now hire their own new pastor. The path is clear, so they can smile at Nat. He hopes they will beat out a new path, as Tom Derby requested of them.

Derby is very much absent. Nat wonders that there isn't more discomfort and talk about his suicide. What Nat picks up from only a few hushed conversations is that these people are stirred but not shocked. They don't know why he committed suicide but they knew Thomas Derby, they were aware of his alcoholism and fiery mind. They whisper that he was brilliant but unsure. These attributes, they say, killed him. Within Nat's earshot one woman utters, "He was always walking on eggshells about things, you know. I guess the eggshells just up and broke on him."

Derby will be laid to rest this afternoon in a small service at the

Victory Baptist. As executor, Nat made plans to bury him three miles away at the black Zebulon Baptist, where Nora Carol Waddell is. But some of the Victory Baptist members phoned Nat's office to inquire about the resting place of their former pastor, Mr. Snead among them. Nat told them of his decision to lay Derby to rest with the Baptists up the road. He did not say more. He did not want to tell them he didn't trust them enough to lay Tom Derby among them. Why do that to him? Why store up that day in the future when what he did as their pastor becomes known and he is vilified. They will probably dig him up too. But Snead phoned back and said he'd made some calls around to the old deacons and a few of the younger folk coming up in the church. They wanted Derby laid in their cemetery. He was one of theirs. Nat told Snead that at some point some things might come to light about Thomas Derby which might change their view. Snead said he and some others suspect that might be the case, but a community has all kinds in it. Snead said one of his own relatives in the cemetery was a horse thief and had been hanged for it. That didn't mean he still wasn't one of their own. So Thomas Derby is to be buried among his people, not far from Rosy Epps. His last worry, that he would die without honor or forgiveness, has been assuaged. Nat smiles at this for his old and gone friend. He wonders how many here right now for Rosy's funeral will return this afternoon for Derby's. He is certain only of Omohundro. He sees Clare seated under the tent, accepting condolences. Who will come to see Derby off? Two funerals in one day, four in the town in just over a week. Five if you count Nora Carol twice. That's a lot.

When Nat made the arrangements for Derby's burial with Snead, he said he was going to ask the black pastor of the Zebulon Baptist to speak. Snead replied he thought that would be fine, he'd heard the old fellow was quite an orator. Nat was glad. Derby would have been pleased, too.

Nat follows the crowd toward Mrs. Epps's grave. He wants to hear the memorials. He has his own eulogy in mind for Mrs. Epps and it will stay private. But he owes Tom Derby to get close and listen to what folks say about her.

The young pastor presiding is from a Baptist church elsewhere in the county. The man may be just helping out, or he may be auditioning for the job. Perhaps the Victory Baptist is healing very fast. Good, Nat thinks, again thinking for Derby.

Seated in a folding chair beside Mrs. Epps's casket is Clare. She is alone, Mrs. Epps had no remaining family other than her granddaughter. It appears Clare has forgiven her grandmother, at least for today. Nat does not try to catch her eye, she keeps her face turned down to her dark lap. The preacher speaks well under the blue tarp. Nat tugs Maeve's hand to slip closer, to hear the words over the crackle of cloth and insects. When they are ten feet from the speaker, Nat sees the hole dug for Rosy, and twenty yards farther away the one for Derby. Both graves have sharp square corners, plumb red walls. The digger Omohundro is a master. Derby's grave is placed in a row of former Victory Baptist pastors. Derby will forever be counted among them, he will never again be let go. Rosy is to be laid between her daughter, Carol, and her husband, Charley. Her family is only three feet away on either side of her. If they could, their graves are close enough for the soldier who died long ago to reach over and hold his bride's hand while she holds their daughter's. Beside Carol's grave is the bald red plot of baked clay that was for one day the grave of Nora Carol Waddell. Nat wonders, When it is Clare's time, will she choose to be buried here at the Victory Baptist? No, probably not. Her husband is black and her child is not here. Nat hopes—he even says a quick prayer—that before this sad young woman passes on, these ugly human impulses will have been put away and the whole of their family, from Rosy through little Nora Carol, can rest together in this graveyard. Derby spoke of community; perhaps the new Victory Baptist Church will do a better job of living his words.

The young preacher concludes his remarks, promising Rosy Epps will not soon be forgotten here on Earth, not so long as men honor wisdom and loyalty. Nat grants Mrs. Epps these. This past week's events should not undo a lifetime.

The funeral home has rigged an electronic lift to lower Mrs. Epps into Omohundro's geometrically perfect grave. The parson steps aside to let folks walk past and pay their old friend and comrade a parting respect. Many have a single rose to lay across her coffin. Others simply pat the shiny lid and mutter a goodbye. Nat gets into the line, holding on to Maeve. He wishes he had something more for his old teacher than an empty hand. But it is the hand that held hers close to her destination, and Nat carries inside him her last wish, to find a way to free Elijah. Approaching her coffin, he feels answerable to her for this, wishes he could explain to her the legal reasons why Derby's sacrifice did not open Elijah's cell, how he's done his best. Looking around at the mourners, he feels they all have failed their teacher, and led her as well into failure.

Ahead of where Nat and Maeve move in line, Mr. Snead steps up to the casket. He pauses a long time, with one hand flat on the varnished wood. He wipes away a sniffle. The two were long-standing adversaries in the church, theirs was a singular relationship. Between them, tugging in opposite directions, the Victory Baptist surely was kept on a more even keel. Nat watches the old gentleman rub his hand over the coffin in a way he would never have dared touch Rosy herself. Nat smiles at the tenderness. Mr. Snead straightens to move on. Before he does, he reaches into his coat pocket. He pulls out something long and shining.

It is a crucifix on a silver chain.

He lays the cross on top of the casket amid the flowers. The thing sits there, gleaming, a beacon in the center of the soft greens and mournful bloody reds.

A recollection clicks into place in Nat's mind, a night a few days ago. In the dark car, parked in front of his childhood house, around a dwindling bottle. Derby spoke to Nat of community. That silver cross, he said, was a community, its own little church of three. Rosy gave the cross to Derby. Derby gave it to Clare. They were united by it.

Nat squeezes Maeve's hand.

"Stay here. I'll be right back."

He steps out of line, excusing himself past several of the older church members between him and the casket. He catches up with Mr. Snead filtering away from the grave, heading toward a circle of his downcast friends.

"Mr. Snead. Sir, excuse me."

Mr. Snead turns at the voice, seeing it is the lawyer whom only a week ago he was prepared to confront at Amanda Talley's funeral. But since then he has mollified and let Nat bury Pastor Derby in his graveyard. Snead is sheepish, wanting to continue to be well thought of by this youngster coming at him.

"Yessir, Mr. Deeds. Terrible day."

"Yes, it is," Nat agrees. He takes Mr. Snead's elbow and turns him away from the man's old waiting comrades.

"Mr. Snead, I saw you lay a crucifix on Mrs. Epps' casket."

"Yessir."

"Mind if I ask where you got that?"

"No, sir. It was Rosy's, for years, since we were kids. She always had it."

"Where did you come up with it?"

Snead turns half a step to point back at the red clay spot where the old church stood. The earth is smooth, manicured by this man, the site is an open and waiting palm.

"Before they come and took away the remains of the old building, I sifted through the rubble, for artifacts, you know, to put in a case inside the new church. To remember the old one. I found some chalices, some pretty bad burned hymnals, scraps of cloth . . ."

Nat is impatient. "You found that cross."

"Yessir, I did. I knew it was Rosy's right off. It's got them symbols on it for the twelve disciples. She wore it every day, right up until she gave it to Pastor Derby a few months back when he first got here."

"After you found it, did you show it to anyone. The police or Pastor Derby?"

"Yessir. The morning I found it. I took it to Pastor Derby. I asked him how he thought it come to be in the fire and he said he'd taken it off and left it on his desk in the church the night of the fire. He was glad I'd found it for him, said he'd been missing it. It didn't make no nevermind to me and I didn't think no more of it. I gave it back to him."

The man continues, eager to tell everything, to come clean, not knowing the significance of what he says.

"Then the day Rosy passed, you know, the afternoon before the pastor hung himself, he came to me and gave me Rosy's cross back. He said I should bring it here today and give it back to her. So that's what I did. I reckon he knew even then he wasn't going to be around to do it himself."

Nat pats Snead's elbow before he rushes back to the graveside. He has to get in line before the casket is lowered and the dirt begins to fall. Behind him, Mr. Snead whines, "I didn't do nothing wrong, did I?"

The true answer is Yes—all these forlorn events began with Snead and his damn intolerance—but Nat is no longer prosecuting so he calls "No" over his hurrying shoulder. At the grave, the line is almost finished. All the old folks have passed Rosy and shared their piece with her. No one is left except a few younger folks, teenage girls she probably taught in Bible class. Nat settles in behind them, the last one in line.

The silver cross still shows clearly atop the casket. All the flowers and ferns have been set carefully next to it. Nat walks beside Mrs. Epps, alone with her now.

He lifts the crucifix from the curved wood and balls his fist around it, not caring whether people notice or not. He lays his other hand flat on her box, just where he thinks her arm might be. He envisions again taking the old woman's hand in his.

The young preacher leads the crowd into a hymn. Nat stays a moment under the music, then steps away from the casket. Two big men from the funeral home lower Mrs. Epps by their machine into Omohundro's masterpiece.

Nat lifts his eyes to Clare. The girl stares back at him.

## 2

Some people do attend Thomas Derby's funeral. Nat cries to see them and does not hold back. Mr. Quantrill is there and Dottie and Elmo Orange, and some of the younger members of the church whom Derby encouraged to step forward in the Victory Baptist leadership. There are maybe two dozen folks gathered at Tom's graveside. The black preacher is eloquent for them. The man's voice soars, there is vibrato in some of his rising phrases. He speaks of sorrow mostly, "our sorrow at losing Thomas Derby and his at losing us." Derby too gets a hymn. It is a beautiful thing and Nat does not take his hand from Maeve's and does not rub away his tears, he lets them fall and water Derby's bare clay. Leaving the ceremony, he and Maeve walk past the graves of the Epps clan, at the end of which lies the empty grave of Nora Carol. Nat figures she was in this hole for a day so perhaps she can still hear him even though she rests a few miles away in another grave. She was just a baby and he never knew her. He tells her that her father will soon be coming to visit. This he says out loud; Maeve hears him and begins to cry a little. He kisses his wife on the cheek, she goes back to their home. He hasn't told Maeve why the cross is in his pocket. Only after leaving Derby's burial does Nat himself know.

Clare waits for him on her front porch. This is not the hottest part of the day, the sun's rays have begun to slant. Dusk will purple in another two hours; now everything starts the process of sloughing off the day's gathered heat. The ground radiates under Nat's shoes, cicadas grind in the wilting cornfield. Clare sits like an icicle out here, cool, blond, and white on her porch. The dog pants on the steps beside her.

Nat doesn't wait for an invitation to sit. Clare follows him with her eyes while he slouches against the porch pillar opposite her on the steps.

No offer of lemonade or other hospitality issues from Clare. The girl shows nothing on her face, not even sweat from the heat.

He says, "I wonder did you drop it by accident. Or did you throw it in."

The girl doesn't pull her glare from Nat's eyes.

"I figure you threw it in. You're pretty mad at God lately."

Clare blinks. Nat senses she wants to nod. But the girl has chosen silence, and like the heat and drought of Good Hope, she's sticking to it.

"What did you think, Clare? It would never be found? I guess you're right, who could have guessed old Snead would comb through the ashes like he did. Or maybe you figured it would melt. Don't know why it didn't." Nat reaches now into his pocket.

"But here it is."

Nat lifts the crucifix by its chain. Snead cleaned away all the soot from the fire, he polished the silver up good for Rosy. Her name is etched on its back, the disciples' emblems glint across the front. Clare's eyes cut from Nat's to watch it twist.

"You didn't know Elijah would be there that night. You didn't know Amanda Talley would be inside. You didn't know any of this would happen. It's gone terribly wrong, Clare. But now's the time to end it. That's what we're going to do. I want some answers. I'll take yours with me to see the judge, or I'll take the ones in my head, it's your call."

Clare brings her gaze back to Nat when he lowers the chain and gathers it into a fist.

"Does Elijah know?"

"Yes."

"You told him when you went to see him the morning after he was arrested."

"Yes. But he didn't know beforehand I was going to do it. When he left that night I didn't know where he was going. But he went out there to that church thinking the same as me. Difference is, I burned it and he didn't."

"Why'd you do it?"

Clare's answer is as direct as the question.

"To get 'em back."

Nat nods.

"Why didn't you confess? Why'd you let Elijah sit in jail?"

Clare's eyes narrow at the suggestion. Nat hears the reins on her anger.

"Mr. Deeds, for your information, Elijah told me to stay out of it when I went to see him and tell him what I'd done. He wanted me to let him take the blame. Said I'd just had a baby. And he figured it would be a lot easier to prove him innocent than it would me, since he didn't do it. So we took a chance and did it his way."

She fixes a stare at Nat.

"We put a lot of faith in you, Mr. Deeds."

The notion of faith makes Nat squeeze the crucifix. Is this what God has to deal with, this kind of pressure?

"Yes," he says, "you did."

Clare stands. She is dressed in jeans and a T-shirt. Her hair is bound behind her head, the first time Nat has seen it tucked up so.

"I'm ready to go," she says. The dog stands too. "Will Elijah be out in time to come home and take care of Herschel?"

Nat does not rise with her. He keeps his back against the pillar and rubs his thumb over the silver cross. Mr. Snead's polish smooths the stroke.

She asks, "Why did Pastor Derby say he burned the church?"

Nat's response is hearsay. Tom is not here to answer for himself. Even so, Nat is certain he knows. When Snead showed him the crucifix, Derby discovered who burned the Victory Baptist. He had all the puzzle pieces then. He saw where his piece fit, and could not bear it.

"Tom wanted to help, Clare. Simple as that. He figured he owed you and Elijah. He felt he'd failed you the first time you came to him, with Nora Carol. This was his way of trying to make that up to you."

And in a way, he thinks, Derby was trying to help Nat as well. Tom realized how important it was for Nat to exonerate Elijah, and so put an end to his own guilt, and come home.

Clare lifts her eyes to the cornfield. The stalks have been the barricade around her life out here with Elijah. She seems to say goodbye to it, ready to exchange it.

Into the bruising sky, she mutters a quiet, "Thank you, preacher. Sorry it didn't work out."

"Sit down, Clare."

"Why?"

"Sit down."

The girl bends her knees. The dog appears relieved she is not going anywhere.

Nat stands in her stead. The silver cross goes back into his pocket.

"Tom Derby died wanting to do this one good, last thing. He

wanted you and Elijah to stay together. He forgave you for burning his church. And I think he knew somehow I'd be the one to find out. He trusted me with this decision. He trusted me to forgive him in return. I do."

Clare stares at him, disbelieving.

"Tom wanted it this way, Clare, for his own penance, and I'm not going to undo it. You're no threat to the community. You're not going to do anything like this again. And I'll tell you the truth. Even though I can't condone your burning that church, in a sense Derby was right. The Victory Baptist needed to start over. Amanda's death was an accident. It was a terrible thing that got done, Clare. Terrible. But it was an accident."

Nat walks off the steps and heads for his car. Clare makes no move or sound. Nat drives away, leaving ghosts of dust in his wake.

3

The next morning Ed Fentress does not object to the introduction of the crucifix as corroborating evidence. Nat and the prosecutor meet with Judge Hawk before lunch. Fentress says nothing while Nat requests the Hawk to release Elijah Waddell. Nat asks also that the judge keep Derby's suicide note sealed. He argues that the silver cross supersedes the suicide note as evidence and there is nothing to be gained by releasing it into the public record. The Hawk agrees there is misfortune enough afoot. Fentress keeps his counsel. The prosecutor seems as dispassionate about Elijah's innocence as he was about the prospects of Elijah's guilt. The two notions don't seem to matter to him in principle, only as political expedients. When it becomes clear there is no advantage to be had in resisting, Ed Fentress goes limp. He's like an old-style heroine in the movies, getting her way in the end by swooning over the strong hero's arm. But with her concluding statement Judge Hawk disallows Nat's last-ditch effort to conceal Derby's suicide note. The press, Judge Hawk says. They'll sue to see the note as evidence and part of the public record and they'll win. May as well get it over with quickly. Elijah will be released that afternoon.

In the evening, before supper, Monroe collects Elijah at the Rappahannock Regional Jail. Monroe eats his evening meal with Clare and Elijah on their front porch, looking over the cornfield. The amber silks wave with the dropping of dusk, to a sundown breeze rising out of the southwest. Clare goes inside for a sweater. Monroe and Elijah agree to paint the house that weekend. The new glass panes are going to take a week to be cut and delivered.

On the evening of Elijah's freedom, Nat takes Maeve to a restaurant in Good Hope. Afterward he drives back to Richmond alone.

The following morning three newspapers carry the full and completed tale of Elijah and Nora Carol Waddell, Rosalind Epps, George and Amanda Talley, and Thomas Derby. Only three people know the full truth and they will never speak of it. But, between the three, the truth is a community, a little church with its own saint.

## 4

Thursday morning Nat Deeds walks into Ed Fentress's office. The odor of coffee is palpable. Nat pushes through it; the aroma is so thick he imagines behind him there is a wake of coffeeless-smelling air.

Fentress is at his desk. Nat despises suspenders, starch, cuff links. Hair spray. Smugness.

"Ed."

"Nat. Thought you were through here for a while. At least 'til Baron gets another charity case for you to champion. You did a nice job."

"Thank you."

"Sit down. What's on your mind? I'm busy but I can take a minute."

"It won't take a minute."

The prosecutor catches the stiffness of Nat's tone.

Fentress says, "Then I reckon you won't need to sit."

"I'm moving back to Good Hope."

Fentress hooks thumbs under his suspenders. It's a calculated, old-timey move that is an insult to old-timers.

"That'll be great. Things must be working out with Maeve."

Nat tilts his head. He signals Fentress, She's none of your business.

"So. Do you want your old job back, or you going to try it on your own again?"

"Neither."

"I'm not hearing right. You're not giving up the law, are you?"

"No, Ed. You know I'm not."

Fentress nods. He lowers his hands from tugging on his elastics.

"I'm not going to like this, Nat."

"I expect not."

"You're going to run against me."

"I am."

"You think you can pull it off? Really?"

"Me and Monroe. He'll run for sheriff."

"You already talked to him about this?"

"Yes."

"Well, he's a good man. I think I'll be able to work with him. Talley'll be lucky if he gets to serve out his term after yesterday's paper."

"Ed."

"What."

"You won't beat me. Don't run."

Fentress enjoys this. Nat can see the man hasn't thought enough about what Nat is telling him to laugh genuinely, it's just a reflex.

"Would you please tell me what makes you think you can win this fine chair I'm sitting in, a chair I've been sitting in for ten years now? Please? Because in case you haven't noticed I'm pretty well liked in this county, son."

"You're liked the way George Talley's been liked. You're the kind of evil people call necessary. Until they don't have to anymore."

"This is taking longer than a minute, Nat."

"All right. You obstructed justice. You interfered with an investigation of a murder by withholding information about Talley. You abused your public office."

Fentress taps together his fingertips. His eyebrows knit. These and the discarded laugh are his only outward signs of Nat's accusation.

Fentress says, "You'll never prove a word of that is true."

Nat shoots his own cuffs in his coat sleeves. He's going to leave after he says this. He goes up on the balls of his feet for the pivot. He wants his turn to be a slap. No one has slapped this man in a long time.

"Doesn't matter," Nat Deeds says. "Ask me if I can make the voters believe it."

## 5

In the early morning hours it rains. Few in the county are awake to see it. They hear it first, pattering on their roofs or glugging in their downspouts, they get out of bed to watch. The late-shift mill workers do not know, they are inside making paper. Several bleary-eyed nurses and doctors at the hospital see the drops and pause.

The earth is very parched; it will not make mud for the first two hours of the downpour. The ground wants to guzzle but the rain makes puddles on the stubborn dirt of the fields before it soaks in.

The drops bounce high on the streets and on the roofs of tar-paper shacks. In the river a trillion circles all the same size dot dark water.

The mill smokes right up into the rain, defiant and steady, saying in its good man-made way, My cloud was here first. My cloud is always here for these people, and it will be here still at daybreak when yours are gone.

Dogs left outside drip, cats duck under shelter. Worms wriggle up on the sidewalks, disbelieving the rain will last, and they burrow out to gulp their fill before the wet goes away.

The biggest trees ignore the rain. Their roots shoot deep, they are swallowing water from last spring. But the smaller trees are saved.

The rain is not a spasm, not some passion burst from the sky. It is not wrenching or a kind of release. It's just a falling rain, undramatic and inevitable.

Nat is asleep.

The rain covers everything that is not itself covered. And in that aspect, the rain is so much like love.

# THE END